LOVING THE DUKE

West lay back on the bed, naked save for his drawers, and watched her boldly strip off her nightdress before she climbed into bed with him. He looked at his sooty hands, then showed them to her. "I will mark your skin if I touch you with these."

She said nothing, but caught his wrists and brought his hands to her. She allowed his fingertips to graze her skin. The trail of his hands left the faint smudges he'd predicted. Ria raised her solemn gaze to his. "And I will be made beautiful by them," she whispered. "Everywhere you touch me."

He could have told her she was already beautiful, but was not sure she would accept it. He showed her instead, rolling onto his side and pressing her back, then placing his mark on her, first with his hands, then his mouth.

He swept back the hair at her temples, sifting the silky strands with his fingertips. His lips found the soft hollow where her pulse beat so faintly, and he kissed her there. Her skin was warm, flawless. He kissed her forehead, the corner of her eyes. His head dipped, and he caught ʰⁱˢ ᵉᵃʳˡᵒᵇᵉ with his teeth and tugged; then his ˡⁱᵖˢ _____ ᵗ. He flicked it with the tip ᵒᶠ _____ ʳeath hitch.

His smile imprⁱⁿ_____ He nuzzled the curve of _____ flesh. It left a mark that waˢ _____ ᵍerprints, but no less proof of his intimᵃ_____

She moved restlessly ᵃgainst him, urging him without words . . .

Books by Jo Goodman

The Captain's Lady

Crystal Passion

Seaswept Abandon

Velvet Night

Scarlet Lies

Tempting Torment

Midnight Princess

Passion's Sweet Revenge

Sweet Fire

Wild Sweet Ecstasy

Rogue's Mistress

Forever in My Heart

Always in My Dreams

Only in My Arms

My Steadfast Heart

My Reckless Heart

With All My Heart

More Than You Know

More Than You Wished

Let Me Be the One

Everything I Ever Wanted

All I Ever Needed

Beyond a Wicked Kiss

Published by Zebra Books

BEYOND A WICKED KISS

Jo Goodman

ZEBRA BOOKS
KENSINGTON PUBLISHING CORP.
http://www.kensingtonbooks.com

ZEBRA BOOKS are published by

Kensington Publishing Corp.
850 Third Avenue
New York, Ny 10022

All Kensington titles, imprints and distributed lines are available at special quantity discounts for bulk purchases for sales promotion, premiums, fund-raising, educational or institutional use.

Special book excerpts or customized printings can also be created to fit specific needs. For details, write or phone the office of the Kensington Special Sales Manager: Kensington Publishing Corp., 850 Third Avenue, New York, NY 10022. Attn. Special Sales Department. Phone: 1-800-221-2647.

Zebra and the Z logo Reg. U.S. Pat. & TM Off.

First Printing: August 2004
10 9 8 7 6 5 4 3 2 1

Printed in the United States of America

For my thithter Yvonne,
who puts up with me even when
I'm being pithy.

AUTHOR'S NOTE

The Compass Club stories all begin at Hambrick Hall, an exclusive, though entirely fictional, school in London. The four boys who make up the total membership of the club remain fast friends into adulthood. Like all friends, they connect and collide and go their separate ways, coming together again when the need is there.

The adventures of Northam, Southerton, Eastlyn, and Westphal do not happen one after another, but more or less at the same time. (How convenient, uncomplicated, and boring life would be if my friends would put their lives on hold until I get through *my* crisis!) The books are independent of each other, yet you might experience a sense of *déjà vu* as you read certain scenes. That's because there are some events that are played out again, though from a slightly different direction. Sometimes it's North's, sometimes South's, sometimes . . . well, you get the idea.

All the best,
Jo

CHRONOLOGY

The following timeline is offered to help interested readers put the adventures of the Compass in chronological order. To make certain no important plot points are revealed, the timeline is limited primarily to those instances when the club connects and reconnects.

June 1818: North, South, East, and West picnic at the Battenburn Estate.

North makes the acquaintance of Lady Elizabeth Penrose.

East first hears the gossip that he is engaged to Lady Sophia Colley.

July 1818: The Compass Club attends a wedding at the Battenburn Estate.

East wrestles with the consequences of his rumored engagement.

Aug. 1818: The Compass Club is part of the crush at Lord Helmsley's salon.

South asks East to lend him his box at the Drury Lane Theatre.

Sep. 1818: East travels to Tremont Park for business, returns to London for pleasure.

South, East, West, and North disrupt the comedy at the Drury Lane.

South makes amends to the crowd's favorite actress, Miss India Parr.

Oct. 1818: South escorts North's wife to the gala at Lady Calumet's, while East and West keep North company at home.

Nov. 1818: South's journey to Ambermede is aborted, his companion goes on without him.

North, South, and East join West at their club to console him upon learning his father has died and that he is named heir to the Westphal title and fortune.

West is surprised by Miss Ashby upon leaving the club.

Following the services for West's father, the Compass Club retires to West's home, where they individually seek Colonel John Blackwood's counsel.

South, East, and West offer North their help.

Dec. 1818: West visits his estate for the first time and becomes familiar with Miss Weaver's Academy for Young Ladies.

South spends Christmas at Ambermede.

East spends Christmas in Clovelly, puts a period to his engagement.

North is in London, West returns to London at Christmas.

Jan. 1819: The French Ambassador's winter ball is attended by North and East—West is helpful, attending to certain details in the ambassador's library.

West visits South at the cottage at Ambermede before going on to Miss Weaver's Academy.

Feb. 1819: North, East, and West come together to assist South and Miss Parr.

East's business is concluded with the help of his friends.

Mar. 1819: The Compass Club attends a reception in honor of the Colonel.

North, East, and South help West prepare a special reception at The Flower House for the Society of Bishops.

Prologue

He would never belong. It seemed to him that this was one of the truths of his life. He understood that it had been thus since birth, though at birth he had been supremely innocent of the fact. He could not say with certainty when the knowledge had been impressed upon him. There was no moment that he could recall as an epiphany. Rather, he suspected the truth had been trickling into his consciousness as though from an underground spring for all of his twelve years. Moments such as the one he was experiencing now made him realize how very deep the water had become.

Evan Marchman was a spy. Perched comfortably in the lofty branches of a chestnut tree, Evan had a nearly unobstructed view of the countryside. Where his vision was blocked, it required only that he dip his head a fraction to see through a crack in the spread of leaves. To someone on the ground he was virtually invisible. His position in the crown of the tree might only be noticed if he gave himself away. Evan had no intention of doing that. He might be captured.

And tortured. Surely there would be torture.

He didn't like to think of that. What spy did? he wondered. Better that he should fall from the tree and break his neck than be taken by the enemy. Better that he put a period to his own existence by a planned misstep than be hauled away to the duke's dungeons. Thumbscrews. Leg irons. Hot pokers. Whips. The rack.

Evan reined himself in before all the things he didn't like to think about were the only things he *could* think about. Spy work took considerably more discipline of thought than he had yet acquired, he decided. It was still another thing to which he would have to apply himself. His grin faded slowly, the dimple on the left side of his mouth disappearing with it, as he schooled his features and his mind and waited.

He heard them before he saw them. The sound of merriment was lifted on the back of the wind and carried across the wide green pastures and gentle hills. A flock of sheep raised their heads in unison to see what was toward. The grazing cattle were not similarly inclined. They simply began moving to another patch in the quilted landscape.

Evan had glimpses of the progress of the party coming from the distant manor house. At the odd bend in the road, dust eddied above the carriages, and occasionally a pair of riders on splendid mounts from the duke's stable could be seen breaking free and making a dash over a hillock. No single voice could be heard above the others, no part of speech or song came to the treetop for Evan to make out, but he did not think he was imagining the gaiety of the approaching group. Above the sounds he heard on this perimeter of the wood—the cry of the swallows, the sough of the wind in the boughs, the lapping of water at the lake's edge—he heard a veritable symphony of laughter.

He knew he should leave his cradle in the chestnut before the laughter was under his nose. He was not really a spy. It would be an interminable afternoon if he stayed here. There would be nothing to do but watch them, and nothing good could come of it. His mother would be disappointed in him if she knew what he was about. When he'd left the cottage this morning he had told her only that he meant to go fishing. He'd had the foresight to take his tackle with him, but it was simply part of the deception. He knew he had planned to come here even if he might somehow convince her otherwise.

Knowing that he should make his escape was not the same as doing so. He had been thinking of coming to just this spot from the moment he'd heard of the duchess's desire for a picnic entertainment for her guests. The intelligence had come to him by the usual route. The duchess had informed her secretary, who had made arrangements with the first butler, who had told the cook, who had ordered the kitchen staff, who had exchanged long-suffering glances, then set about making it happen. Evan had heard it from one of the scullery lads who, once away from the strictures of the duke's country house, chattered like a magpie. *Daft* was what Johnny Brown pronounced it. Daft.

"Quality," Johnny had said, rolling his eyes. "The tricks they get up to. Imagine choosing to sit in the devilishly tickly grass, sharing a feast with the ants and the rabbits and the hedgehogs. They ain't got the common sense of common folk, that's what it is. Three dining halls and a breakfast room at the manor and Her Grace decides to take her guests to the lake. Not that anyone will fish for their supper. For their entertainment, perhaps, but not for their supper." Johnny had shaken his head wonderingly and spit. "Daft."

Evan wasn't sure he agreed with Johnny, but with no firm opinion of his own to offer, he kept silent. He had not the least objection to picnics and was happy to indulge his mother's penchant for them. They fished for their own supper, though, and cooked the leaf-wrapped trout on a small, three-stone fire. The tender, smoky flavor could not be captured indoors, and there was something about being outside that lightened his mother's mood. One didn't even notice the devilishly tickly grass, let alone mind it.

Perhaps the duchess was not so different from his mother. Perhaps her mood was also lightened by sitting under the clear canopy of a halcyon sky. Calling to mind the beatific smile that came to his mother on those occasions, Evan could not begrudge Her Grace that same singular pleasure.

He could not imagine, however, that the duchess would beam any smile in his direction. If he caught sight of any unguarded moment of joy, it would be because she did not know he was nearby. She would gladly suffer the steady march of a thousand ants upon her person for an entire afternoon before she would suffer a single moment in his presence.

Lest he embarrass her, anger the duke, and shame himself, Evan remained still as stone in the treetop.

The riders on horseback arrived first. There were four men and two women. One of the women was helped down from her mount; the other leapt to the ground unaided. Two of the men led the horses away and tethered them in a shady spot at the edge of the wood. Evan watched them approach but no one looked up, and the horses did not stir unduly. By his reckoning, they had come as close to him as was likely to happen in the course of the afternoon and hadn't had their attention drawn to him. It was going to be all right. He was safe.

The carriages followed in short order and the passengers alighted quickly, expressing unanimous approval of the splendid countryside before them. Evan thought their view was pretty enough, but it paled beside his own. He was the one who could see the breadth of the lake and most of its length. He could make out the subtle contrast of blues and silver in the rippling, reflective surface of the water. He could see beyond the first rise of the land to the field of wildflowers, and he could watch the shifting wave in the grass as the blades bent in the wind. His horizon was some distance from the one they saw on the ground, and his panorama encompassed a vast portion of the Westphal property at Ambermede. The duke's guests had but a small piece of it; Evan had almost the whole.

The guests fanned out along the lake and hillside, choosing spots for their blankets and baskets. The women wore bonnets trimmed with ribbons the color of mint leaves and wild strawberries, and short gowns of matching polka-dotted calico. They looked bright and cheerful and gay, just as if they were meant to be part of this landscape, rather than apart from it. Even the men, with the notable exception of the duke, did not look out of place. In their nankeen breeches, spencer jackets, and loose linen shirts, they looked at their ease for fishing or swimming or just napping. Most of them were already bareheaded, their hats having been the first thing they tossed to the ground once the rugs were spread.

The Duke of Westphal was still wearing his top hat, a beaver-and-silk affair more suited to the crowded social paths of a London park. He wore kid gloves and carried a walking stick in his right hand. His white drill trousers bore no creases from his confines in the carriage, and the points of his collar looked as sharp as tacks. His jacket followed the line of his shoulders and arms closely, defining the shape of his tall, athletic figure as much as containing it. He did not laugh openly, nor smile with ease, yet he appeared in no way discomfited by his surroundings. He was as comfortable embracing his severity as his guests were in their abandon.

Evan watched the duke offer his arm to Her Grace and gingerly lead her to the blanket that had been set out for them. The duchess was delicate to the point of frailty. She had a fine porcelain complexion and features that were very nearly gaunt. The sharp bones of her face stretched her fair skin taut, hollowing out her cheeks and making her eyes appear more deeply set than they were. She was dressed as brightly as any of her female guests, but the apple-green gown did not infuse her with color; rather, it drained the last vestige away.

Evan saw that clearly when she tilted her head back to make some reply to her husband. Her face was raised in his direction, and for a moment it seemed that she must have seen him. Her eyes rested on a point beyond the duke's shoulder, with Evan directly in her line of sight. If she could have but seen through the fan of broad leaves, she would have spied a face as pale as her own, owing to the fact that Evan thought he might be caught out.

He was not. He watched her smile briefly in acknowledgment of the duke's comment before her head turned smoothly away from him again. Evan's heartbeat slowed and recaptured its normal rhythm. He was pleased to discover that he had not moved in the least or given up any small sound of alarm.

Mayhap he did have a talent for spy work.

It had seemed so remote a possibility when his friend South suggested it as to be laughable. Upon reflection, he realized he *had* laughed. So had the others. North. South. East. "Why a spy?" he'd asked Southerton. "Why not a barrister? Or a surgeon? Exploring might suit me as well."

"It's in aid of the rhyme," South had told him simply. *"North. South. East. West. Friends for life we have confessed. All other truths, we'll deny. For we are soldier, sailor, tinker . . ."* He had paused dramatically. "And *barrister?* It doesn't work now, does it, West? You must see that it doesn't work. The rhyme's the thing."

Evan had said he supposed that was all right, then. He would be the spy.

"Jolly good," East had said, happy to have it settled without having to thrash anyone. He'd offered up a scone instead of a handshake.

North had rubbed the slightly crooked bridge of his nose, a gesture not quite as absent as it appeared. Without saying a word, he reminded everyone that Evan had broken that appendage and left his handsome countenance with rather more character than his mother thought was good for him. They all agreed it was just the sort of facer a spy might have to plant someday.

Evan realized that delivering a sharp jab to his enemy's nose would only be necessary if he were caught. It remained outside his current plan. He would not allow that to come to pass. Comfortably cradled as he was in his tree, he was not likely to give himself away or be discovered by happenstance.

Setting his mind to the present, Evan let his gaze slide away from the Duke and Duchess of Westphal and concentrate on the youngest members of the lakeside gathering. Not all of those enjoying Their Graces' hospitality were adults. There were half a dozen children among the guests. The oldest was the heir, Will Fairchild, Lord Tenley, two years Evan's junior. He was organizing the play for all the other children, deciding who should hide and who should seek and where they must go and where they should not. His voice was pitched high, and the cadence was clipped. There was no question that he would be obeyed. Tenley was not so much eliciting cooperation as issuing orders, and each word was carried easily to the very top of the boughs. Evan wanted to plant him a facer.

Whether out of fear or respect, the others fell in line. Except for the youngest among them, Evan did not know their names. The little girl with the shock of hair so blond it was almost white in the sunlight, he had learned quickly was Ria. Within moments of alighting from the carriage, someone was always calling to her. "Ria, come here." "Don't wander, Ria." "Stay away from the horses, Ria." "Ria." "Riiii-aaa." Evan wondered why they didn't tether her. At the very least, she required leading strings.

"Maa-riii-aaa!"

So it was not "Ria" at all, Evan thought, but "Maria." Watching her fairly fly among the guests, sturdy legs churn-

ing over the blankets and into the high grass, always within a
hairsbreadth of taking a spill, no one could be blamed for
rarely using her Christian name. There was scarcely enough
time to call out three syllables when two would do. Someone
caught her—her father, Evan supposed—before she went
towhead over bucket into the duchess's picnic basket.

The duchess was not at all disturbed by the interruption.
Quite the contrary, Evan saw. She helped steady Ria, fluffed
the toddler's halo of bright hair, and spoke to her gently.
Evan expected that, for it was known throughout Ambermede
that the duchess had a particular fondness for children. What
gave Evan pause was that the duke's actions were no less attentive. He actually picked up the child, gave her a little toss
and shake which made her squeal with delight, then permitted her to pummel him for another turn of the same. His
Grace obliged without hesitation.

No one in the village had ever mentioned the Duke of
Westphal giving so much as a tinker's damn for children.
Evan would not have believed an account of His Grace's actions if he had not been witness to them. He hardly knew
how to think about what he had seen, let alone how to feel.

It was easier to push his own uncertain responses to the
back of his mind and concentrate on his wider view of the
party. Tenley had been able to insist that some of the adults
join his spirited game of hide-and-seek, and it wasn't long
before the participants were sprinting toward the available
hiding places. The woods were a natural destination, but no
one chose his chestnut to hide in and no one climbed so high
in any of the nearby trees. The game came to an end in less
than an hour, and Tenley marshaled his troops to play tag,
blindman's buff, and finally, capture the flag. They cooled
themselves off by stripping down to their drawers and shifts—
even the participating adults—and leaping into the lake. The
splashing and dunking and laughing finally was enough to
force a large family of ducks to flee the water for the relative
safety of the verdant hillside.

When the energetic play wound down, there was a retreat

to the blankets. Baskets were thrown open and they shared the bounty. There were platters of roast beef and lamb and chicken, great round loaves of fresh bread, and an abundance of fruit and cheese and wine. There was little movement following this repast. Someone suggested charades, but there was no enthusiasm for it. Even Tenley had stopped insisting that they *do* something and seemed glad to lie stretched on a quilted rug, belly-up in the sunshine. Some of the guests slept, others read, a few played quietly at cards.

As a whole, they were at peace, Evan thought. From his vantage point it was rather more boring than comforting, but he supposed this was also part and parcel of being a spy. There was bound to be boredom, and he would have to learn to manage it. To that end he mentally reviewed all the Greek gods and goddesses and their Roman counterparts, then the royal lineages of the houses of Europe since Charlemagne. When he returned to Hambrick Hall in a few days' time, he would wager South and the others that he could recite the latter in just under one minute. It was sure to impress, and possibly earn him a few farthings.

He was contemplating how he might spend his winnings when a stirring among the duchess's guests caught his attention. To be strictly accurate, it was the stirring of a single guest. Young Ria was up and moving. Evan did not know why no one else seemed to notice. It was true there were more people napping than had been some ten minutes earlier, but there were still those who were engaged in cards and quiet conversation. None of them shifted their attention to call to the girl, and Evan had to believe they had not seen her. Her mother and father—at least, Evan believed he had identified the proper pair—were lying like spoons in a drawer, dappled by the late-afternoon sunshine. The mother's upper arm was set in a curve that had been shaped by her daughter's presence. It remained just so. If Ria took it into her head to return to the blanket and wriggled herself back into place she might never be missed.

Evan did not think that was going to happen. It looked to

him as if Ria was chasing something—a butterfly, perhaps, or bit of duck fluff released to the air when the fowl had hastened to the hillside. Whatever it was, Evan realized the invisible currents of air were lifting it away from where the guests lolled on their blankets and gradually leading the child to the lake. It was no direct avenue she took. The path she made through the grass went to and fro, sometimes circling back for a short distance. Her progress was marked by clumsy pirouettes and several spills, but she was a game one, getting back to her feet each time, determined to capture the elusive thing that was leading her on.

Evan's eyes darted back to the guests. Ria's absence was still unremarked. No one turned to look in her direction. No one raised a hand or spoke sharply to call her back. It did not matter that the child's route to the lake was a circuitous one; it was still leading her directly to more danger than she could properly comprehend.

Evan realized he would have to make himself responsible for her safety. He was the one who saw the peril, and it was incumbent upon him to do something about it. Calling out to the others was out of the question. Precious minutes could be lost while they determined where he was and exclaimed over his hiding place. He would be thoroughly chastised if he were fortunate, boxed soundly if he were not, and it was doubtful they would hear what it was he was trying to tell them. Ria would be at the bottom of the lake by then, her tiny lungs unable to hold enough air to keep her afloat, her sputters and cries unheeded because of the uproar his presence would most certainly cause.

Evan made his descent quickly. His lithe, athletic body was honed for just this sort of challenge. His fingers and feet touched the branches only long enough to feel them under him, and then he was moving on, always downward, always accelerating, taking the last twelve feet in free fall, dropping to grasp a branch by his fingertips, then swinging to the ground. If anyone saw him now, he did not pause to acknowledge it. The force of his drop from the tree caused him to crouch for a moment. Like a runner at the start of a sprint, he pushed himself up just enough to begin his charge for the lakeside. He did not stay in the shaded wood. There was no time to dodge trees and hurdle the underbrush. He ran to the perimeter of the clearing and kept on running across the open field.

There were cries now, all of them at his back. There were people yelling at him to stop, to explain himself. Someone hollered, "Thief!" Evan did not know what had prompted this last, but he ignored every call for his return and set his course for the bright dervish that was about to spin over the bank and into the water.

He launched himself at the child, his lean body stretched taut, no part of it touching the ground for a moment in perfect defiance of gravity. The full-out effort was not enough. His fingertips brushed the child's calico hem but could not grasp it, and the spinning, laughing top that young Ria had become hurtled itself into the drink.

Evan's breath exploded from his lungs as he hit the ground hard. Someone screamed, but he did not mistake that the concern was for him. He turned his head in time to see Ria disappear under the water. Her hair was not so bright as it had been moments earlier and he understood she was going down for the second time. The ground vibrated beneath his cheek as the guests thundered en masse toward him. Before he could think better of it, he followed Ria's example and rolled down the bank into the lake. The water was deeper than he had expected. He had hoped the ground slope would continue at the same angle underwater. It didn't. The earth dropped away in short order and he found himself blindly thrashing about in search of daffodil-yellow calico.

It helped, he decided much later, that she was thrashing about as well. Even though she was no match for his length and breadth, Ria's movements were every bit as energetic and urgent as his own. His arms collided with her short ones, and his fingers locked around her wrists. The water bubbled with their expiring breaths, and Evan's feet churned up silt. He pushed off the bottom and surfaced with Ria clinging to his neck. He blinked hugely, though perhaps a fraction less wide than she did, and tossed his head back to clear the curtain of hair from his eyes.

The men were all gathered at the edge of the water now, precariously balanced on this steepest part of the slope. The women, including the duchess, were standing on the more gentle rise, many of them with their arms outstretched as if they could draw Ria to them by sheer force of their collective will. Evan took them all in in a single glance and wished that he might hand the child off and disappear under the water himself.

It was not easy to do so because Ria's fingers were now tangled in his wet hair. When he tried to put her from him, she held on with those stubby tentacles until he thought she would take his scalp. He could hear the crowd shouting at him but could make out no single order or accusation above Ria's pitiful wailing.

Evan tread water using only his legs, keeping both of his arms securely around the child's shuddering frame, and moved closer to the edge where someone might be able to grasp her. He did not expect to be helped out himself, so it was something of a shock when Ria was finally separated from him, and he was hauled from the lake. The manner of his rescue was none too gentle. While a squalling, squealing Ria was passed by a succession of cradling arms to her mother, Evan was pulled up abruptly by the scruff of his neck and shaken hard.

It happened too fast for him to comprehend what they were about. A dull roar thrummed through his head as the first pair of hands that seized him held him still while a second pair delivered a thundering box to his ears. He might have cried out, he thought, but he could not be sure. He hoped he hadn't. It was too lowering.

He was spun around and pushed forward to face the duke,

stumbling when he was released and almost falling to his knees. He managed to steady himself just in time to take the first blow. Westphal's walking stick whistled through the air before it came down on Evan's shoulder. Evan dropped like a stone and rolled to one side. The second strike caught him squarely on the back, raising an immediate welt beneath his wet linen. He made himself a hedgehog, rolling into a ball, hugging his knees to his chest to protect his face from the blows. His back and buttocks were exposed, and the blows rained down upon him.

They were still shouting at him, but he could not hear what they were saying. Did they think he had *pushed* the little girl into the water? Didn't they know he had *saved* her?

As humiliating as it was, Evan opened his mouth to explain. No one really heard him, of course. He wasn't certain his voice had risen above a whisper, and he was still curled like a hedgehog with his mouth very close to his knees. Pride warred with pain, and pain won. He rose on all fours and tried to crawl off, his only thought now to escape the blows and find some sanctuary where he could lick his wounds.

He collapsed as the stick caught him between the shoulder blades. He could not draw his knees forward this time, but lay sprawled on the bank, his face turned to one side, his eyes closed. A long breath left his body. Pain no longer stung him. It swelled like a wave across his skin, and then it was gone in a rush of heat. He imagined he felt small, stubby fingers tangling in his hair and an oddly familiar weight clinging to him. A cry shrill enough to penetrate the roar in his ears was the last thing he heard. There was no time to wonder if it was his own. He shuddered once and was still.

Evan was alone when he woke. He had not expected it to be otherwise. There was no reason for any of them to linger over him, especially not Their Graces. It would be their desire to put this unfortunate encounter from their memory. Evan doubted anyone would ever speak of it, most particularly the adults, who would not want to be made disagreeable to the duke or his duchess. Tenley might say something.

He was impulsive enough to do so, though he might think twice about risking his father's disapproval. The young heir did not need to worry that he would have to bear the brunt of Westphal's punishing walking stick, however.

The duke saved that sort of retribution for his bastard child.

Evan was carefully stripping off his shirt when the door to his room opened. It had been four days since he'd returned to Hambrick Hall for the start of the next term and a full week since he'd received the caning. He had not been able to hide his injuries from his mother, but until this moment he had been successful in hiding it from the Compass Club.

North, South, and East skidded to a halt just inside the room. Evan might have laughed at their abrupt, comic stop if he had not been so keen to draw his shirt on again. He was grateful when they shut the door quickly.

To their credit, none of them spoke of what they had seen. Evan was grateful for that. He finished tucking the shirt into his trousers. Ignoring the weeping wounds that had made the shirt sticky in the first place, he picked up his jacket. Brendan Hampton, the one they called "North," stepped forward and took the jacket. Making himself useful as Evan's valet, he held it out so that shrugging into it would not be as painful a process for his friend.

"Thank you," Evan said, not quite meeting North's eyes.

Gabriel Whitney, "East" to the others, offered one of the iced cakes he was carrying. "Cakes always help," he said. "These arrived in today's post. Came straightaway to share them. Can't eat them all myself, now, can I?"

Evan was polite enough not to disagree. East's rounded figure was evidence to the contrary. He took a cake and sat down gingerly on the edge of his bed, inviting the others to join him.

Matthew Forrester, the young viscount Southerton, folded his legs under him and dropped to the floor tailor-fashion.

He accepted one of East's iced cakes and bit into it with considerable relish. He spoke around a mouthful of food. "You'll tell us when you're of a mind to, I suppose. And if you're never of a mind to, it doesn't matter. We're still your chums, West."

Evan nodded once. It was quite possibly all that would ever be said on the matter. He didn't doubt they had a very good idea who had raised the welts on his back and backside. It didn't make it less humiliating to him. He still wanted to plant someone a facer.

As if reading his mind, North rubbed the bump on his own nose. "Would you like to take a poke at me again? You look as if you want to take a poke at someone."

East's rounded jaw came up and he pointed to his first and second chin. "You might want to take a crack at one or both of these."

South indicated his left cheek where he had pouched most of his iced cake. It was swollen like a chipmunk's. "Go on. Take a swing. A little punch to help you wash down your cake."

Evan rolled his eyes at South's wordplay. It saved him from having to make another reply. His throat was uncomfortably tight, and speaking would have been a severe trial. Their willingness to accept an injury in order for him to shake off so much ill feeling was a reminder of how they'd become friends in the first place.

They never seemed to mind that he was a bastard half as much as he did.

He spoke finally, swallowing hard, hoping it would seem that the cake was the cause of his difficulty. "I should rather like to flatten one of the bishops."

"Brilliant," South said, wishing he'd thought of it himself.

"Excellent," East offered, brushing crumbs off his chest.

"Top drawer," North said approvingly. "Really, top drawer."

They all rose to their feet and made for the door. Even though the purpose of their club called for them to be "sworn enemies of the Society of Bishops," they had never set out to provoke a fight before. They arrived in the cobbled court-yard of Hambrick Hall wondering how they might begin the thing when one of the bishops whispered, *"Bastard."*

It was surprisingly easy after that.

Chapter One

November 1818

She thought she might have heard their laughter. She had been told that if they were together, she could depend upon hearing it, no matter the circumstances that drew them together. But surely not, she thought, not this evening. Not when the circumstance was death.

"You'll have to move along, miss."

She pretended she hadn't heard. She'd been successful at ignoring the instruction earlier. Perhaps he would conclude she was deaf or daft and make allowances. It was not as if she was making a nuisance of herself to anyone but him. Indeed, there was no one on the sidewalk at this late hour to be the least bothered by her presence.

She supposed he was puffed up by his own importance. He was splendidly turned out in gold-braided livery that must rival even that worn by the king's servants. He stood as a sentinel at the top of the stairs, zealously guarding the entrance to the gentleman's club as if his life depended upon it. Mayhap it did, she considered. If she were to manage somehow to breach his defenses and enter this exclusively male sanctuary of port, cigar smoke, and leather armchairs, he might well be dismissed, turned out without a character, and left to fend for himself and his family by taking up a career as a cutpurse.

It would be her fault if he was forced to crime. She almost found the resources to smile at this odd flight her thoughts had taken. The explanation for the bent of her mind could be found in her deeply weary bones. Her teeth were near to chattering with the damp and cold of the evening. Hugging herself beneath her woolen cloak was no longer effective in warding off the chill, nor was tugging on the hood to keep the runnels of water from spilling into her hair.

Moving along was probably just what she needed to do. As though it were at her own inclination, rather than as a result of his instruction, she began walking slowly. She did not remove her eyes from the windows of the club as she did so, but they were set too high above the sidewalk for her to have a clear view of the interior. Earlier she had watched the club from a vantage point across the street. From that distance she could see something of the warmly lighted rooms that faced the front, but nothing so clearly that she might identify any of the members.

"You should step a bit more lively, miss."

Some gremlin of perversity made her stop in her tracks. She did not pretend she hadn't heard his suggestion this time. Her position squarely at the bottom of the steps did not give her the high ground, yet her rigid stance yielded nothing. She stood there a long minute. It was too dark to gauge the frustration on his features. She hoped he was weighing the consequences of leaving his post either to forcibly remove her himself or get assistance to do the same. Either way he would have to abandon the door. It was then that she might have an opportunity to slip past him.

He was made of sterner stuff, it seemed, else he saw through her defiance to her plan. She huddled more deeply under her mantle and finally stepped back.

Rain beat a hard, noisy tattoo off the sidewalk and rushed along the cobbled street to the sewer. A speeding carriage marked its passage with a high spray of water that she could not avoid. The sodden hem of her gown dragged along the pavement, and her shoes were no longer proof against the wet. Her stockings were damp inside the leather, and water seeped in and out of the welts with every one of her steps.

It was the realization that there was really nowhere to go that brought her up short. She spun on her wet heels and marched determinedly back to the entrance of the club. This time she did not stop at the base of the steps, but went right up them, head held high in spite of the spirit-dampening elements.

"Now, see here, miss," the footman said in tones both flustered and affronted. "You can't come up here."

"What an absurd thing to say when it must be clear to even the meanest intelligence that I can and I have." She did not give him time to mount an argument. "You must see that you occupy one of the only places for respite from the rain. It would be churlish of you to refuse to share it."

"Churlish?" The creases about his eyes deepened as he squinted to get a better look. "Why, you're quite a pretty little baggage, aren't you? Take yourself off before I call for a runner. It's a nasty night for them to be out, and they'll thank you by putting you before the magistrate forthwith."

She averted her head, tugging on the hood of her cloak so that he might not mark her features to memory. "You would call for a runner because I've taken shelter from this abominable rain? They might put you before the magistrate for bothering them with such a trifle."

The footman wasn't gulled. "You wouldn't be the first of your kind to try to gain entrance here."

"My kind? You are referring, I hope, to the fact that I am female. You would do well not to paint me with any other brush." Glancing down, she saw his weight shift from one buckled shoe to the other. It seemed her words had unsettled him a bit. She would not allow him to assume he knew her business here. She was no man's cast-off mistress come to seek retribution, and she was not a whore looking for trade.

"There can be no harm if you allow me to stay until the rain slows."

The footman gazed up at the stormy sky. There was no evidence of either moon or stars this evening. The underbelly of the low, heavy clouds could be glimpsed by the reflection of thousands of London street lamps. Thick fingers of mist were drifting up from the Thames and soon every thoroughfare, park, and alley would be taken over by the shroud. It would be no different here in the West End. The fog was the town's great leveler, making no allowance for privilege or property. The architectural details of many of the finest buildings in the world would become so blurred as to be indistinguishable from the warehouses and brothels on the waterfront.

"The rain's not moving on anytime soon," he said, giving no quarter. "And the fog's coming on. You better find your way home now. Footpads and worse will be about soon."

She still didn't move. She could have told him that she'd only just arrived in London and that home was two long days' journey away, but she could see no purpose in revealing either of those things. "I'll wait," she said. "You must not worry that I mean to make a scene. It's just that I . . ." Her voice trailed off. "I'll wait," she repeated softly.

The footman's broad chest heaved once with the fullness of his sigh. He gave a bit of ground so that she might shelter more securely in the slender alcove. "Is there a message?" he asked. "I'll see that it's delivered directly."

She shook her head. A message might simply send her quarry off in another direction. It was the very reason she had not announced herself at his home. She was in no expectation that he would agree to see her. She could not even be certain that he would know who she was, let alone what the consequence of his knowledge or lack of it might be. Was she more likely to gain a moment of his time if he was aware of her identity or if he was wholly ignorant of the same? Might his interest be piqued, or would he dismiss her out of hand?

Her questions had led her here, to this bastion of male exclusivity in St. James, in the hope of forcing a meeting. She had no assurances that he was inside, but after watching his home for a time she had concluded he was gone from it. Given what she had learned about him, this seemed as likely a place for him to have come as any, and she had to begin somewhere.

She did not want to make his formal acquaintance at the funeral.

Evan Marchman, the newly titled Duke of Westphal, eyed his companions over the steepled points of his fingers. Stretched out as he was in the high-backed chair, his posture was not one of prayer, but rather of lazy contemplation. He and his friends made a somber foursome this evening. They could not rouse themselves to humor or find the wherewithal to make a wager of no consequence. They sat for long periods without trading conversation. They drank little. No one disturbed them.

The subdued air of their group was giving rise to glances in their direction and talk among the other members of the club. People acquainted with the news of his father's death would also understand he was not in deep mourning. "We're causing a stir, you know," he said at last.

East glanced around and saw it was so. He shrugged. "Must be South. He is looking rather disheveled this evening. Bound to cause talk."

Viscount Southerton roused himself enough to ask, "You are referring, perhaps, to the flecks of mud on my boots?"

Gabriel Whitney, Marquess of Eastlyn, could have named a number of other things that contributed to South's less-than-tidy person, but he settled for the mud-flecked boots. "That's right. Never say Darrow has left you."

"It is more to the point that I have left him," South said of his valet. His head rested against the back of his chair. Through half-closed eyes the color of polished steel, he regarded the tips of his offending boots. It had been a hard ride from the middle of nowhere back to the center of London. "It is a temporary state of affairs." He added this in the event East had some notion that he might tempt Darrow with an offer to come into his employ. "He is not available to you."

"Pity." Eastlyn sipped his port, and in due time his attention swiveled to Northam. "You are particularly introspective this evening," he said. "It cannot be solely on account of West's father."

Brendan David Hampton, many years now the sixth Earl of Northam, absently raked back his helmet of sun-bleached hair. "It's not." His slim smile communicated his apology to West.

For his part, West waved it aside. There was no reason to take umbrage with his friend's admission. He could hardly fault North for having little in the way of feeling for the passing of the late duke, not when his own feelings were similarly impoverished. West cocked his head to one side, his dark-green glance amused as Eastlyn poked a bit more at Northam, trying to discover the cause of that worthy's contemplation.

"Elizabeth, then," Eastlyn said. The words were no sooner out than he held up his hand, staying North's reply. "No, don't answer. I should not have asked. It is none of my affair."

West did not miss the visible change in the set of Northam's shoulders as he relaxed his guard. It seemed North did not mind that they knew things were not at all as they should be in his marriage, but that he had no desire to share the blow-by-blow. West could respect that. Just as they had all come together for him tonight, North must know his friends would rally if he required anything of them. He had only to look at Southerton to see the effort that would be made if necessary.

North inclined his head slightly in South's direction and caught his friend's eye. "Where were you when you heard the news?" he asked.

West wondered how South would respond. He had reason to know that South had been a considerable distance from

London, having helped make the arrangements for that journey's end himself. It occurred to West that South was taking pains not to let the strain of his hard travel show. He did not take South's presence here for granted, but acknowledged this as further evidence of the bonds of friendship that had been forged at Hambrick Hall.

West doubted that it had entered South's head for even a moment that he should go on to his destination rather than turn back to London. *Friends for life, we have confessed.* A stranger might not have recognized Southerton's taut expression for the deep weariness that it was, but he was among his boon companions now and they could not help but see the toll his journey had taken.

A small smile eased the lines of tension about Southerton's mouth as he prepared to answer North's question. "More than halfway there," he said quietly. "I was more than halfway there."

North's own expression was wryly appreciative of the enigmatic response. "So far."

"Indeed." South pushed himself upright in his chair. "I suspect the return will take somewhat longer."

Eastlyn chuckled softly, the first any of them had laughed since coming together. "Especially if your intention is to arrive at some end. You cannot travel halfway, and halfway again, and expect to get there, South. Or did they teach you something different on board His Majesty's vessels? If they did, I should like to know." He raised his glass of port, his expression sobering. "How long will you remain in London?"

"Another day," said South. "Two at the most."

East nodded. His voice dropped so that it could not be heard beyond their small circle. "You will call on us, will you not?" he asked. "If there is a need."

"If there is a need," Southerton repeated in the same grave intonation. "I would not have any of you compromised."

One of Eastlyn's chestnut-colored brows rose in a perfect arch. "So that's the way of it."

None of them needed to hear anything else to know that South was engaged in ferreting out a spy. It was the sort of work that was often laid in West's own lap, and for once he was grateful not to have pulled the assignment. It said something about the nature of the trap if South's peculiar talents were being put to good advantage. West clearly recalled more than one occasion at Hambrick where South had had to use considerable gray matter in evading their enemy, the bishops. For his part, West would have preferred another brawl, but Southerton liked to talk his way out of things.

West grinned as Eastlyn's next question showed he was drawing upon the same recollection. "You won't have to re-count the entire history of Henry VIII's reign, will you?" East asked. "If you have to extricate yourself from some exceptional coil, I mean. I don't think I could sit through that again."

North nodded. "I am with East there. You cannot expect so much of us this time, South."

West found himself moved to contribute to this observation. "No matter that it was a score of years ago. The memory resides painfully in my arse." That comment immediately drew three pairs of amused glances. He returned their gaze, his own innocent. "What? Cannot a duke speak of arses?"

"A duke may speak of anything he wishes," South said. "Especially one so recently acquiring the title, the lands, and the fortune."

"You mean some allowance will be made for a bastard son suddenly acquiring legitimacy," West said.

Southerton continued as if there had been no interruption. "But unless you want others to hang on your every word and have the same come back to you, it is usually a thing better done quietly."

"Bloody hell," West said under his breath. "Bloody, bloody hell."

His disconsolate manner first raised identical grins from the rest of the Compass Club, then their rousing laughter. They fell into the moment without examining it too closely, letting their laughter speak for them when they could find no words that would do so well.

* * *

The rain did eventually slow to a drizzle. Mr. Dunlop—for she had finally learned his name—was insistent that she vacate the stoop before members of the club began to take their leave. There was no point in arguing or pressing him for further information. She counted herself as fortunate that he had resigned himself to the inevitable of sharing his shelter. He had even become something of an amiable companion, lowering his guard enough to allow her to learn what she needed to know. For the first time since arriving in London, she permitted herself to hope.

Standing at the corner where an iron gate marked the perimeter of the property, she could see gentlemen stepping out of the club. They left alone or in pairs, all of them pausing on the lip of the first step to adjust their brushed beaver hats so the rain did not mark their faces. They wore kid gloves and caped greatcoats. Some of them carried walking sticks. Now that the rain had nearly subsided, it did not seem to inconvenience them overmuch. Occasionally there was a comment cursing it, but it presented little hardship as their carriages came forward on the street to collect them. From time to time she would see Mr. Dunlop step down to the sidewalk and call for a hack. One always came quickly, the drivers having been waiting for just this opportunity.

Her spirits flagged when an hour of this activity passed, and he did not appear. She could not imagine there were many gentlemen left inside. More than three score had already absented themselves from the establishment. It did not look so large a place as to accommodate another exodus of the same.

Dunlop opened the door and made a small, deferential bow of his head. "Your Grace. Shall I bring a hack?"

West wondered at what point he would no longer feel a prickle of alarm at being addressed in such a manner. *Your Grace.* He had been at the club only two days past and had been greeted politely but without this rather disconcerting obeisance. He really did want to plant someone a facer.

"I'm for walking this evening," he said. "It's bracing, don't you agree?" West could see that the footman thought he was quite mad to eschew the offer of a hack, but there was no opinion offered to that effect. There was a trace of mockery in West's tone as he said, *"Et tu,* Dunlop?"

"Me, Your Grace?" Dunlop swallowed hard. "I don't know what you mean."

West supposed that he didn't. "You are not so easy with me as you were two days ago."

"Have I given some offense? I assure you, I have meant none."

Seeing that he was making the man uncomfortable, West abandoned the subject. Dunlop couldn't very well point out that two days ago West had been a gentleman, true enough, but also a bastard in no anticipation of that ever changing. He sighed. He would have to depend upon South, North, and East to deal with him as they always had and make no allowances for this sudden change in the status of his birth and station. "My friends took to their carriages, I imagine."

"Yes," Dunlop said. "Indeed they did. Not above a half hour ago."

West knew very well when the others had left. He had assured them he was all of a piece and encouraged them to go back to hearth and home. He stayed behind to nurse the last of his brandy and consider what was to become of him in light of his father's surprising final declaration. It wasn't enough that the dying man made some explanation to those gathered at his bedside for the death watch, but West had it from the solicitor that the duke had composed a document a sennight earlier that told the whole of it.

Naturally, West had questioned the solicitor as to his sire's lucidity, hoping to hear that he had been, in fact, completely out of his senses. Mr. Ridgeway, not understanding that West was in no way desirous of the title, lands, fortune—or the responsibility—dashed his hopes by assuring him repeatedly that the old duke was as sharp as a tack right up until the moment he called for Meg and seemed to see her come for him at the side of his bed.

West was not the least softened toward his father upon hearing that he had cried out for Meg in the end. He remembered how often his mother had cried similarly for the duke and how rarely he came. If she *was* hovering at his bedside, West hoped it was because she intended to point the way to hell. She surely had not arrived to lead him to that part of heaven where she resided. Even the Almighty could not be so forgiving as to grant the late Duke of Westphal a place there.

West tapped the brim of his beaver hat so that it rested on his head at a proper roguish angle, set a wry smile on his lips, and started down the steps. He had a light tread and the patter of the rain was barely disturbed by it. He turned right on the sidewalk toward his home, his long stride marking the distance to the corner quickly. He paused as he stepped down to the street. It was the narrowest of hesitations, so slight that he doubted it had been noticed. Because of the thickening fog, he did not trust himself to see what manner of traffic there might be on the street. He cocked his head to one side and listened instead. He recognized the approach of a heavy carriage drawn by a pair of horses and a hackney pulled by a single animal. Neither conveyance was moving quickly and he judged he had time to cross without mishap. He was not at all concerned that the person following him might not be able to do the same.

West reached the other side of the street, made a sharp left, and continued swiftly to a point halfway down the block where there was an opening between two white brick residences. He stepped sideways into the dark mouth of the narrow alley and waited.

The steps that had been following him slowed, then finally came to a halt. Weapon in hand, West waited patiently to see what trick the cutpurse might get up to.

"Your Grace?"

Had he not been mildly astonished by the sweetly feminine voice calling to him, he would have had occasion to wonder if he had indeed been branded with his new title. The fact that he had been followed from the club by a woman did not mitigate the danger. It had been his experience that women who took to the street for their living could be every bit as treacherous as their male counterparts. He could also not dismiss that there might be a pimp nearby ready to help if she could not manage the thing herself.

"Please, Your Grace. I can no longer see my fingers at the end of my hand. Are you here?"

West stepped forward and stood safely at a long arm's length from her. He spoke softly, pleasantly. "Mayhap you can see this?"

"Yes." She blinked, recoiling from the blade that was thrust close to the tip of her nose. "Yes, I see it."

"Just so. You will have the goodness to remove your own weapon."

"I have none."

Her denial did not convince him. Lest he find a shiv between his ribs, or a bullet in his balls, West moved quickly, capturing her wrist and spinning her around so she was pressed against him. He frog-marched her into the alley and pushed her flush to the rain-slick wall of the southernmost residence. She turned her head sharply to one side so that her nose was not ground into the mortar and allowed her cheek to be imprinted by the brick. Other than an initial gasp, she did not make a sound. That was unexpected, for experienced thieves rarely came along quietly, preferring instead to protest their innocence at the top of their lungs, or better yet, make accusations of wrongdoing against the very person they were trying to rob.

"What do you want?" he asked.

For all that her response was nearly inaudible, it held the unmistakable tenor of a command. "I want you to remove your hands from my person."

"That is not what I meant." He continued his search without pause, drawing aside her cloak and running his hands impersonally along her narrow torso and under her breasts as he looked for a sheathed dagger or pistol. His large hands almost completed a circle about her waist, then spread apart as he covered her hips and the length of her thighs. He forced her legs apart and conducted an efficient search between them, all the while keeping his own knife at the small of her back.

When he was finished, he stood slowly and stepped away, returning his own weapon to the soft leather scabbard fitted inside his boot. "You can turn around." His tone was everything polite. "And you can tell me why you were following me."

She did not answer immediately, and West chose not to press, recognizing that a few moments' respite were in order for her to achieve composure. He took those moments to study her averted profile, a study that was impeded by the heavy woolen hood that covered her hair and fell low over her forehead. West reached out to push it back. She reacted as quick as an adder, striking his forearm with the flat of her hand to shove him away. She could not have moved him if he had not allowed it, at least not without a good deal more force than she applied, but he did allow it and slowly dropped his offending arm to his side.

"You will not touch me," she said, mustering quiet dignity, but also clearly mortified that she had struck him. "Not again." There was the slightest catch in her voice as she added, "Please."

It was being borne home slowly that he had made a grave error in judgment. This was no cutpurse who had followed in his wake. By the same token, the fact that she had suffered his touch as he searched her, offering no encouraging ribald commentary as he did so, made it very doubtful that she was a whore. West did not like to consider what possibilities remained. He had behaved less boorishly when he was Mr. Evan Marchman. Upon becoming the Duke of Westphal, it seemed he had taken leave of every sense of what was proper.

Just like his father.

The black, yawning mouth of hell might well be within his reach if he continued to apply himself in just this manner.

"Come," he said at last. "We will leave this place and I will find transportation for you. It seems to me that you should not be about this night." Or any night, the truth be told. He had glimpsed a fragile, fey look about her when she had offered up her soft plea to go unmolested. It was only in profile and blurred by shadow and fog, but the look of her appeared to be finely molded by a gentle hand. She had high, delicately defined cheekbones and a slender nose. The pale arch of her brow was a soft curve. It was not simply the lack of light that prevented him from determining the color of her eyes. She kept her lashes lowered so he had only a view of the thick, dark sweep of them.

West held out his elbow for her. He smiled a little grimly when she did not accept it, though it came as no surprise. They walked out of the alley together, he taking the lead, she just a half-step behind him, and came to a stop beneath a street lantern.

"I should like it," West said, "if you would state your business with me, but that is not a requirement for me to find you a hack. There *is* some business, I collect. You are not in the habit of stalking gentlemen." He paused the merest fraction and one dark copper brow lifted in a sardonic curve. "Or are you?"

She shook her head.

West wondered if she had lost the ability to speak, then he heard her teeth chattering and realized she was trembling with the cold and damp. He placed two fingers to his lips and whistled shrilly. The call brought an immediate response. From somewhere down the fog-bound street, a driver snapped his whip, and a horse clambered forward. West whistled a second time to guide the hack toward them. "Help will arrive shortly," he said. "Tell me where I might direct him to take you."

"No. 24 J-Jericho Mews."

West decided he could be forgiven for thinking he had not heard her correctly. He tilted his head toward her averted face and wished she would have done with the sodden shroud that made her more grim reaper than woman. "Pardon? I thought you said—"

"No. 24 Jericho Mews."

"Yes. That's what I thought I heard. There's nothing wrong with my ears, then. There's a bit of good news, isn't it?" He saw her head come up sharply as though she were arrested by his odd humor, but she did not swivel her face in his direction nor make a reply to his rhetorical question. "I feel I must point out," he said evenly, "that the address you mentioned is my own."

She nodded.

"That means I live there," he added helpfully.

"Yes, I understand that." A glimmer of a smile had attached itself to her lips.

"I see. You do realize *you* don't live there." West wondered if she were a bedlamite, then supposed it was of little consequence. No matter the outcome of this evening's encounter, it would make a diverting story in the retelling. After sitting with his friends at the club, he was more certain than ever that they were in need of a diversion. God, but they had been a glum lot. "Then you want me to take you to my home?"

"I have n-nowhere else to g-go."

West was not at all encouraged by that bit of intelligence. "Perhaps if you told me where you've come from? That would make a good start to getting you back there."

She did not reply. The hack had found them and was stopping. West hesitated, quickly identifying his options. He could leave her just where she stood and walk home himself, or he could take the hack and leave her to walk. He could put her in the hack and send her to perdition, but then what would there be to look forward to? It had been a considerably dull night until she had set her footsteps in his. He was of the firm opinion that leaving her would not change the outcome.

She knew where he lived and meant to go there. It would show a remarkable lack of manners if he forced her to make her way alone.

West opened the hack's door and gestured to her to climb inside. He gave the driver his address, then followed. The interior of the cab was dark and thwarted his attempt at a second study of her features. Even though he sat opposite her on the stiff leather bench, there was little he could discern. "You've yet to tell me anything of import," he said. "That will have to change, you know."

"I am M-Miss Ash-sh-b-by," she said around a bone-jarring shiver.

"Oh, I hope you are not," he told her, removing his coat. "That is a most unfortunate name. Far too many syllables to get the tongue around. It sounds foreign. Is it German?"

Her head came up sharply again, this time almost clipping his nose as West closed the space between them to unfasten her cloak. "You are quite m-mad," she said. "N-no one t-told m-me that."

He smiled, and even in the gloom of the carriage it was a bright enough beacon for her to see. "Then it is because you failed to ask the correct questions. I assure you, the lamentable condition of my upperworks is common knowledge. Now, Miss Ashby, remove your cloak and put this around you. You will find it considerably warmer."

West was pleased when she didn't pause to consider the merits of his suggestion. It was a measure of how deeply cold she was. He watched closely as she finally removed the hood from her head and shrugged out of the cloak. He could make out a heavy fall of pale hair and the slim stem of her neck. He knew from his search of her person that the fabric of her gown was bombazine and that it was only a modicum less wet than her outerwear. He doubted she could be induced to remove it as well.

His caped greatcoat swallowed her whole and he tucked it around her when her shaking hands prevented her from managing the thing herself. "Put your feet under you," he told her. When she was slow to obey, he added, "Unless you want to stretch your legs in my direction and let me warm your toes." He chuckled when she drew her feet up abruptly, amused by the alacrity with which she complied. "It seems," he drawled, regarding her once again from the opposite bench, "that I have found the chink in your armor."

She made no reply, not entirely certain if he was teasing her.

"So, Miss Ashby," West said, removing his hat and placing it beside him. He stretched his long legs and crossed his arms, his posture conveying a certain negligence as well as curiosity. "You will tell me now from where you've come. We will arrive shortly at my home, and I can assure you that for very little coin our driver can be persuaded to circle the mews for hours without stopping."

"G-gillhollow," she said with effort. "Are you fa-familiar?"

He was. He wished he had not been. There was a tightening at the back of his neck and his discomfited senses prickled with awareness. "Near Norfolk Broads."

"Yes."

"And Ambermede."

She merely nodded this time.

"I see," he said darkly. It was little wonder, then, that she had addressed him as *Your Grace*. Having recently come from the environs of Ambermede she would have been privy to knowledge of the duke's death and all the considerable changes his passing brought. She had come to London remarkably quickly. His father would not be interred until tomorrow morning. As a statesman of considerable note and long service to the Crown, the duke was being accorded the honor of a Westminster Abbey burial. West was already determined to suffer the ceremony; he was not looking forward to it. "You were perhaps his mistress, then?"

Miss Ashby blinked widely.

West felt himself relax a modest amount. "You are of an age, I think."

"F-four-and-tw-twenty."

"Then mayhap a bit old for his tastes."

"You are un-k-kind," she said. "T-to b-both of us."

He merely grunted. There were other questions he meant to put to her, but even in his current state of mind he was able to recognize the unfairness of it. She was in danger of sinking her teeth into her tongue for all the chattering she was doing. The least he could do was warm her up before he continued his interrogation. If he were fortunate, she would simply spill the whole of her sordid tale, and he would not have to rouse himself to make further inquiry.

The hack slowed, and West looked out. There was a lantern lighted outside the entrance to his town house, but at every window there was darkness. The servants were all abed, he realized. Even his valet must have decided he meant to stay from home tonight, for Finch could usually be counted on to greet him, no matter the hour.

The residence was red brick, trimmed in white, and of a middling size for this section of the West End. It had not the imposing presence of his friends' homes, but then until two days ago he had not had their deep pockets. His money had come from shrewd investments and enterprise, and while his wealth could not match that of Northam, Southerton, or Eastlyn, he marked himself as comfortable and wanted for nothing materially. Now, he supposed, he would be expected to move to a larger home, more befitting of his title and fortune. The *ton* would be in anticipation of his entertaining. There would be callers and hangers-on. It was all too depressing for words.

"Have w-we n-not arrived?"

For a moment West had forgotten he was not alone. He glanced in her direction, taking her measure again, wondering what trouble he was bringing down on his head by inviting her inside. It really didn't matter, he decided, because he was determined to do it anyway. "We have," he said. "We have indeed."

He opened the door and alighted, then turned to her and extended his hand. It took her some time to extricate her limbs from under his greatcoat, and his patience was sorely tested. She accepted his help and made only a small sound of protest when he lifted her by the waist and set her on the ground.

West retrieved his hat and her mantle from inside the hack, then paid the driver and waved him off. He started up the walk and was halfway to the door when he realized she was not following him. Expecting to find her standing, forlorn and fogbound, at the street side, he was taken aback to discover she was stooped over like the veriest crone and rooting around in his hedgerow.

"There are several fireplaces inside where you can warm yourself," he said. "No need to burrow here."

Miss Ashby made no reply. She stayed exactly as she was for several moments before standing suddenly to reveal a large, carpeted valise clutched in her arms.

"Aaah," West said, understanding. "You hid it there in anticipation of your return."

"You are very cl-clever."

He did not miss the faint sarcasm that edged her tone. "And you are very c-cold." Her mouth snapped shut, and West grinned. He turned and sprinted up the walk.

Once inside, he tossed his hat and her cloak on a table to the right of the door and lighted a candlestick before Miss Ashby stepped over the threshold. He relieved her of the valise, setting it down beside the table. It was not as heavy as it appeared when she dragged it from the hedgerow, and he decided she either had very few worldly goods or was not in expectation of remaining long in London. "This way." He saw her fingers move to the buttons of his greatcoat and he shook his head. "Do not remove it yet. Let us put you before the fire in my study first."

He led the way down the hall and pushed aside the pocket doors. Standing back, he ushered her inside. This was the one room besides his bedchamber where he knew he could depend upon a warm hearth. The fire that had been laid for him earlier was small now but it only required a little kindling and one log to bring it to a proper blaze. Satisfied with his effort, he motioned Miss Ashby forward and lifted his greatcoat from her shoulders.

She was hugging herself beneath the heavy coat, and this posture did not change when she was relieved of it. She came to stand as close to the fire as she dared and let its considerable heat flood her. Where her gown was damp, steam actually rose from the fabric.

Watching her, West was struck by how slim she was. She was not small of stature, only slightly built. The top of her head came as high as his nose, he noted, making her rather tall for a woman. She was reed slender, with rather more bosom than one might expect, given the delicacy of her frame. It was not that the severity of her black bombazine gown emphasized the curve of her breasts, but that West already knew the fullness of their shape by virtue of his earlier search. He would not have been able to guess at the perfect roundness of her hips and buttocks if he had not had cause to feel them in the cup of his palms. The mourning gown she wore defied even a careful observer to suppose what form of woman might be under it. He, however, had already discovered the length of slim legs and the lithe turn of her calves and ankles. In truth, West could not bring himself to be fully repentant of his earlier actions. She had carried no blade or pistol, but it didn't mean that she couldn't have.

Her hair was drying quickly. She had finally been moved to unwind her arms and raise her hands to untangle it. West thought it was even paler than it had looked in the carriage. It absorbed some of the reds and golds of the firelight, but that was only because, like sunshine, it had so little color of its own. Children sometimes had hair that was as light and fine a corn silk texture as this, but he could not recall seeing such a cascade on a woman grown.

Four-and-twenty, she had told him. Standing before the fire, tugging on the damp curls of her unbound hair with fingers made clumsy by an awareness of his open regard, she looked no more than six-and-ten.

"Perhaps you are Tenley's mistress," he said of a sudden.

Her fingers stilled in her hair. "No," she said quite firmly, if only on a thread of sound. "I am not your brother's mistress."

"Half-brother."

"Yes, of course, your half-brother. I was not his half-mistress."

A wry smile lifted one corner of West's mouth and a dimple appeared. "You are feeling more the thing, I take it."

"Yes."

Her stuttering had stopped, and he was heartily glad of it. "Good. Will you take a brandy?" He went to the drinks cabinet and found the decanter he wanted. "You would prefer sherry?"

"I prefer brandy."

"Just so." He poured a small amount into two crystal snifters and handed one to her. He watched her cup her hands around the bowl of the glass to warm the brandy, then sip delicately. "Better?"

She nodded.

"You will want to turn round," he said.

She stared at him blankly.

"To pull the dampness from your backside."

"Oh."

Seeing her flush, West found it difficult to believe she had journeyed all the way from Gillhollow to London unmolested—if one did not refine upon what he had done to her in the alley. He lighted several lamps in his study while she turned her back to the flames. He could feel her eyes following him, though each time he turned she quickly averted her gaze and regarded the floor.

Had she expected someone with the same imposing presence of his father? he wondered. Until the cancer had finally weakened him in the last months of his life, West knew his father had enjoyed robust health and the vigor of many men half his age. The duke had been tall and broad of shoulder. He had carried himself with a certain correctness of posture, as if he were always aware of his consequence and would have it that others were aware of it also. His countenance was severe but not unhandsome. He had aged well, the lines creasing his face at the eyes and mouth only adding to the definition of his character.

West had taken great pains to see as little of his father as was possible. That had been the duke's wish as well. Neither of them had been unhappy with the arrangement, and no attempt had ever been made to alter it. Still, his father had loomed rather larger than life. It was not possible to be unaware of him, given his services to the Crown. He might have been prime minister had it not been for Liverpool's deft handling of the opposition during the war with Napoleon. The defeat in the parliament had rankled him, West knew, and he imagined his father had been plotting a new stratagem when the cancer struck and made this final ascent to power impossible. England mourned. West did not.

He sat down in the comfortably worn wing chair situated not far from where Miss Ashby still stood. It was a restful place, this chair, or at least he had always found it so. He caught one leg of a three-legged stool and nudged it closer so he might place his heels upon it. Easing back into the chair, he cocked one eyebrow at his guest and bid her sit.

"I shall stand, if you do not mind," she said, looking around at row after row of books that lined the room.

"I do mind. I want to sit, and it is poor manners for me to be seated in the presence of a lady."

"My gown is still damp. I will ruin—"

"Sit."

She dropped to the upholstered bench on the edge of the Aubusson rug. The blood-red damask covering contrasted sharply with her black gown. She steadied the snifter in her lap with her fingers laced around the stem. Her back remained ramrod-straight as she waited him out.

Her eyes were blue-gray, he saw at last, and there was nothing youthful about them. She might appear to be six-and-ten in every other way, but not in her eyes. They were far older than the age she had given as her own—wise, perhaps, but also weary. The long journey to London could explain some of it, his harsh treatment of her earlier could explain still more, but neither of those things filled the whole of it. He wondered what these eyes had seen.

"Who are you mourning?" he asked, taking in the unrelieved blackness of her attire.

The question surprised her. How could he not know that now? "The duke, of course."

West's slight smile was humorless. "There is no *of course* about it. Is he your father also? You are another of his byblows, perhaps. Tell me, must I embrace you as my sister?"

She spoke softly in a carefully modulated voice that was no effort for her. "You mean to be horrid, I think. I was told that you would be, and you are."

"One endeavors not to disappoint."

"I did not say that *I* was in expectation of your rudeness, merely that I'd been told of it."

West wondered what he might make of that. He sipped from his brandy. "You had formed an opinion of me that was contrary to what you heard of my character?" he asked. "How is that possible when we can scarcely call ourselves acquainted?"

"We have met before."

"Now, there you are in the wrong of it. I have a happy talent for remembering faces and putting names to them. I would know if we had been introduced."

"I did not say there were introductions. Only that we have met."

He studied her face for a long moment. To her credit, she did not look away, but met his gaze directly. West suspected that she had kept her face averted before because she was afraid he would recognize her and have cause to send her away. Now that she had secured entry to his home, she was no longer so fearful that he would do so. He wasn't certain why she thought that was. He could put her back on the street as easily as he could have left her there.

His mouth twisted wryly as he set his brandy on the side table. But he hadn't left her on the street, had he? Like a bedraggled kitten, he had bundled her up and brought her home. He reluctantly concluded her confidence was not entirely misplaced.

"Then you are not my sister," he said at last.

"Not even your half-sister."

"Touché." He tipped his head forward in a modest salute. "We met in town?"

"No."

"Then it wasn't during the Season."

"No." She smiled faintly, amused that what had begun as an interrogation was now a parlor game. He had seventeen questions left.

"You are acquainted with Southerton?"

"No."

"Eastlyn?"

"No."

"Northam?" Before she could say no and tick off another point in her favor, he was inspired to ask a different question. "His wife, then, the former Lady Elizabeth Penrose?"

"No." She subtracted two more questions from him anyway.

West fell silent as he considered a different tack. He was reluctant to pursue their connection if it existed only through his father. It would be difficult to be kindly disposed toward her if she had been somehow enamored of the late duke. Her name meant nothing at all to him, but then he had not spent a great deal of time with the solicitor since learning of his father's passing. In point of fact, he had walked out on Mr. Ridgeway, although not before announcing bluntly that he preferred bastardy to dukedom. West fully expected in the coming days and weeks he would be learning the names of relatives who had never troubled themselves with any thought of him.

He had always been Westphal's bastard to them, as if he'd had no proper name of his own. He was the by-blow, born on the wrong side of the blanket. As a child he had accepted this last information in the most literal sense, assuming his mother had lain on the sun-faded side of a quilt when she gave birth to him. He could not imagine why he was treated so differently because of this oversight. He had finally been moved to ask her about it. It was the only time he could remember her striking him. She had cried afterward, of course, patently horrified by what she had done. There had never been any question that he forgave her, but he had also never forgotten.

There were things that could not be put from one's mind.

West removed his feet from the stool and leaned forward in his chair. His elbows rested on his knees and his fingers formed a steeple beneath his chin. A slight, vertical furrow appeared between his brows as his eyes narrowed. A slim lock of copper hair fell forward over his forehead, but he was too intent upon the pale crown of his guest's own hair to give it notice.

He had seen hair like that before.

"You are Ria," he said.

She marveled that he had won the game.

Chapter Two

"No one has called me Ria for a very long time," she said. "I wasn't certain you would know me by that name or any other. I thought I would have to explain so much more. You recall the occasion of our meeting, then."

West still had the stripes across his back and backside to keep the memory fresh. He did not tell her that. "I remember it well enough." There was little inflection in his voice to indicate any emotion. He picked up the brandy snifter and got to his feet. "Will you have another?" he asked, pointing to her glass.

"No."

He nodded curtly and retraced his steps to the drinks cabinet, where he refilled his glass, allowing himself considerably more this time than last. He was willing to risk a sore head in the morning for the pleasant numbness of liquor now. He did not return to his chair immediately but stood where he was, considering what he would do next.

"You are much changed," he said at last. It was an absurd things to say. Of course she was changed. A score of years had passed.

"As are you."

He shrugged. "How did you find me?"

"I inquired of Mr. Ridgeway. He gave me your address."

"As solicitors go, the man has a loose tongue."

"I pressed him rather urgently."

West had little difficulty imagining that, though by what means she had done so was a mystery. She was a thorough beauty with her sunshine hair and fine, perfectly symmetrical features. The blue-gray eyes were perhaps a bit too grave, but their color was splendid and the lashes that framed them were dark and long. She had not fluttered them once in his direction, yet West wondered if Mr. Ridgeway's experience had been different.

Ria was in no way comfortable as the subject of West's unwavering observation. She thought he had had sufficient fill of her in the carriage, then again in front of the fire. His repeated assessments were unnerving, though she hoped she gave no indication of it. It was not her wish to appear spineless.

She was more cautious in her study of him, confining herself to glances when she was certain he would not catch her out. It was not easy to accomplish as he rarely turned his attention from her. She wondered if he had not entirely absolved her of intending to do him harm.

It was not in her nature to harm anything. She would trip over her own feet rather than step on another creature, no matter how repellent the thing was. She had once allowed a great, hairy attic spider to crawl up her bare leg until she could flick it away rather than squash it with the book in her hand.

West would not know that about her, she realized. There was no reason that he should. To her knowledge he had not put his eyes on her in twenty years. It was astonishing that he had divined her identity after so much time had passed.

"How did you know me when I stepped out of the club?" he asked her.

Ria felt a wash of heat in her cheeks that could not be explained by the proximity of the fire. She dissembled. "I heard the footman call you *Your Grace*."

"Paladin was also at the club this evening."

She had no idea who Paladin was, except that he must also be a duke and therefore addressed in the same manner as Westphal. Her silence did her in.

"Then it wasn't Ridgeway who described me," West mused aloud.

Ria chided herself for not offering up that most simple explanation. She just hadn't thought of it. The truth was that while he had not been aware of her for two decades past, it could not be said that she was in ignorance of him. She did not tell him this, however. Instead she said, "Mr. Dunlop gave me a sign." Ria watched West mull this over. As a lie it was a good one, she realized, for he was prepared to believe he might be betrayed for some coin. It also explained her earlier dissembling as an attempt to protect the footman from retaliation. When West grunted softly she knew he had taken the bait and swallowed it whole.

How could she tell him that she had grown up asking after him? Although she was discouraged from doing so by those around her, it merely made her more curious . . . and more careful. On visits to Ambermede when her parents were still alive, there were always trips to the village, and in the village there were always those who were willing to talk about the duke's bastard. She'd heard about his wild ways and his fiery temper, compliments of his upbringing and his red hair, they'd said. She knew he had been sent to Hambrick Hall so that he would not cross paths with his half-brother Tenley at Eton. He had distinguished himself at cricket and rowing, but perhaps more so as a brawler. When she was yet in the schoolroom, he had gone to Cambridge and studied mathematics. The villagers allowed that he was recklessly handsome but still no better than he ought to be. They were suspicious of his successes, and not a little envious of them, telling wild tales of smuggling French brandy and debauchery on the Continent.

She had seen a portrait of him once and wondered immediately how he had been coerced into sitting for it. Ria amended that thought: he had not actually been sitting. As a young man, West had posed standing beside a great black stallion. The artist had been skillful enough to capture insouciance in every line of West's lithe frame, from the shoulder resting negligently against his mount's flank to the leg making a casual cross of the other at the ankle. There was carelessness also in the shape of his mouth, in the smile that revealed a profoundly wry appreciation for the vagaries of life. That particular placement of his lips carved a deep dimple in one cheek and merely hinted at one in the other.

It was the eyes, though, that had riveted her attention. There was humor suggested in the dark-green depths, but there was something else that was not so easily defined— and it made her shiver.

Ria had glimpsed it this evening, just moments before he had spoken her name aloud, and she wished she had been looking elsewhere. It was a glance that pinned her back and made her heartbeat trip. *Anger* was insufficient to describe it. *Rage* was rather more than it was. This was temper on a short tether, the desire to do harm and damn-the-consequences, masked by humor and a careless smile.

It made her less afraid for herself than it did for him.

Drink in hand, West returned to his chair. Instead of sitting, he hitched his hip on the arm and balanced himself with easy grace. She had been woolgathering, he noted, and wondered at the direction of her thoughts. She was not entirely comfortable in his presence—which he counted as a good thing—but neither had she made any noises about leaving him. He wished there was less trust and more wariness in her manner. What the devil did she want with him?

"So you induced Dunlop to betray me," he said consideringly. "Dare I hope it cost you thirty pieces of silver?"

"Not nearly so much as that."

"I was bought rather cheaply, then."

"I'm afraid so."

He nodded and sipped his brandy again. "To what purpose? You still have not explained yourself. You have made a rather long journey to arrive at just this end. Surely I am owed your reason for it."

"I require your help."

His smile was sardonic. "I am not so deep in my cups that I could not surmise that myself. The more salient point is, how much."

"A great deal, I should think."

"A hundred pounds? A thousand? You will have to name your figure." He observed that she was much struck by this. Her mouth parted and formed a perfect "O." "More than a thousand?" he asked. "Is it to be some blackmail scheme, then? You will be sadly out of it there. The wags have always been willing to say the worst of me, and there have never been any serious repercussions, save that I am not always invited to the best affairs. That, by the way, has always seemed a good thing to me."

Ria stared at him in fascination, her jaw having snapped shut when he mentioned blackmail. "You really are a most peculiar gentleman," she said at last. She added quickly, "I hope you are not offended by my plain speaking. I mean no offense."

He gave a short bark of laughter, genuinely amused. "You will have to expand your vocabulary considerably if you ever mean to give me offense, though you've made a good start by calling me a gentleman."

"Oh, but I didn't mean—" Ria stopped because she realized he was having fun with her. It was disconcerting, the way he could blow hot and cold, sometimes both at once. She raised her glass and swallowed a mouthful of brandy. Perhaps considerably more libation than she had consumed was required for full comprehension.

"I am not in need of funds," she told him, "as long as there is no interruption in my allowance. I can depend on you, can I not, to quickly take care of the matters Mr. Ridgeway puts before you concerning me?"

West found that his balance on the arm of the wing chair was suddenly precarious. Not taking his eyes from her, he carefully lowered himself onto the cushion. "Why would Mr. Ridgeway put what concerns you in front of me? And what do you mean about an allowance?"

"Surely you understand that you will control my allowance?"

"I surely do not."

"But it is one of the responsibilities of guardianship."

West did not like where this was going. If he could turn back the clock, he would once more be standing at the curb outside the club. On this occasion he would time his step onto the street differently. He would count himself fortunate indeed to be flattened by the approaching carriage and again by the hack.

"Then you must apply to your guardian," he said.

"That is what I am doing."

Even though he knew what was coming, it was not possible to brace himself for the blow. It was every bit as sharp as a jab to the ribs. He had traded punches in the ring at Gentleman Jackson's salon and not had the wind so cleanly knocked out of him. "You are mistaken," he told her bluntly.

"You are welcome to think so." Under her breath, she said, "But I am not."

"I heard that."

She made a slight, apologetic smile.

"You are four-and-twenty," he said.

"Yes."

"In what society is that not considered past the age of majority?"

Ria tempered the urge to smile more deeply. His frustration—or was it fear?—was palpable. "Your father had rather strict notions of what should be required for my independence. It was determined that I was incautious in my judgments, though I do not think many concessions were made for the fact that I was yet a child when my parents died."

"How old?"

"I was just shy of my tenth birthday."

"You were orphaned at once?"

"Yes. Cholera, I am told. My parents were in India. My father was assigned to the regiments in Delhi and my mother was with him. It had already been arranged for me to join them when word arrived of the epidemic. Not long after that, a second missive came informing us that they had died."

West thought Ria made this recitation with some effort to detach herself from it. He understood and appreciated what it cost her to do so. *"Us?"* he asked, prompting her gently to continue. "Who is *us?*"

"My great-grandfather. I was living with him when word came. His late wife was your father's mother's sister."

It was precisely this sort of revelation that made his head hurt. "The duke's aunt, you mean."

"Yes."

"You might have simply said so."

Ria regarded him from under the raised sweep of her perfectly arched brows. "I thought I did," she said. "Shall I draw the tree for you? Connect the—"

He held up one hand, palm out. "Pray, do not elaborate on that theme. We are family, then."

"Cousins."

"Distant," he said.

"To be sure."

West leaned back in the chair, closed his eyes, and pressed the crystal curve of his snifter against his forehead. While it had seemed warm in the cup of his hands, it was cool against his brow. He lowered the glass slowly and opened his eyes. Ria was still watching him intently, and he suspected she knew most of what was in his mind. He'd made no attempt to temper his reaction to her words.

"Why did you not remain with your great-grandfather?" he asked at length. "You were already in his care."

"Yes, but his health was failing, and no one expected that he would survive his own great-grandson. It is one of the reasons I was to join my parents in India, the other being there was no love lost between him and my father. Since he was not named my guardian in my parents' will and because they clearly specified that I should be placed elsewhere, that is what was done."

"What about other relatives? Your grandparents, for instance."

"Dead before I was born. My side of the family tree has few sturdy branches."

"So it would seem." He finished his drink and set it firmly on the table at his side. "More's the pity."

"The duke was made my guardian."

"Yes." West's slight smile held no humor. "I may have come at the thing rather slowly, but I have finally arrived."

Ria was uncertain if this were true. He did not look like a man who had gotten his mind entirely around the notion. "Shall I pour you another brandy?"

"Pray, do not try to be helpful. It is too little, too late."

She made no other offers, but sat silently and allowed him to absorb this further evidence of how his life had been altered by his father's passing. He was not taking it at all well, and she had yet to arrive at the purpose of her visit. It would occur to him sooner or later that she had not traveled all the way from Gillhollow to inform him of his responsibilities as her guardian. When she set out, she had supposed that Mr. Ridgeway had already done that.

West placed his thumb and forefinger on the high bridge of his nose and rubbed gently. Weariness was setting deeply in his bones. He imagined if he multiplied that feeling tenfold, he still would have only an approximation of the weariness in hers.

"It seems to me that whatever else must be said," he told her, "it will be said better in the morning. There will be time before the interment. You mean to attend the service at Westminster, do you not?"

"Yes."

"Good. Then you have no objections to postponing further discussion until tomorrow."

She did, but it seemed the wiser course not to raise them. In truth, the prospect of putting a pillow beneath her head was a tantalizing one. It was becoming increasingly difficult to fight back each urge to yawn. "No objections," she said. "We will speak in the morning."

West nodded, relieved that exhaustion seemed to have made her more biddable than recalcitrant. "Tell me. What arrangements have you made for your stay in London tonight?" he asked. "I will summon a driver to take you there." He saw the last vestige of color leave her face. "Oh no," he said, shaking his head. "Never say you thought you might remain here."

Ria decided that hearing it aloud made it seem remarkably cork-brained.

"It is becoming clear to me," he said quietly, "why, at the advanced age of four-and-twenty, you still require a keeper."

"That is unfair."

"On the contrary, it seems to put a neat bow on the thing."

"I traveled here with funds," she said. "I did not acquire a room for myself because I determined it was more important to find you at the outset."

"And I say to you again, Miss Ashby, that your poorly set priorities, as well as your manner of making my acquaintance, underscore the reasons you have yet to achieve independence. To point out that you have gone about this in a havey-cavey fashion vastly understates it. I might have cut you this evening."

Fatigue did not prevent Ria from lifting her chin. She spoke quietly, however, in softly clipped accents. "Your chastisement is unwarranted. You have not the least notion as to why I've sought you out. You would have me not speak of it until morning because it is an inconvenient hour, and yet this lack of knowledge does not halt you from a rush to judgment." She stood and was pleasantly surprised that she did so steadily. It was unfortunate, perhaps, that the hem of her gown was still so damp that droplets of water fell lightly on the rug. Ria resolutely ignored this sign of her shabby appearance and went on. "I will call on you at eight. That should present us with adequate time for discussion before we must go to the service."

West roused himself sufficiently to regard her with a remote glance, one eyebrow coldly cocked. The effect, he was gratified to see, dropped her right back on the bench. When she was seated, he nodded approvingly. "Very prettily said."

Ria's legs were shaking now, and she doubted she could pull herself to a stand a second time. Even the late duke had never been able to pin her back so deftly. West would not credit it, she thought, but with few exceptions his father had been more likely to indulge her than take her to task.

"You have nothing to say?" he asked.

She shook her head.

"Are there things you mean to tell me that must be said tonight?"

Ria hesitated. What could be accomplished if she were to tell him everything now? Her mind might be eased by unburdening herself, but she had known from the outset that he could not immediately come to her aid. He would have obligations that must be satisfied, first among them to see that his father was buried and that matters of the estate were well in hand.

West tried to gauge what Ria's indecision meant. "Are you in any way unwell?" he asked. "In danger? Threatened? With child?"

She was too startled to deny any or all of those things.

"No," he said, answering for her. "I can see none of these is the case."

For once Ria was glad that her thoughts were so clearly expressed on her face.

"It is too late to impose your presence on any of the suitable females of my acquaintance, therefore I will escort you to suitable lodgings not far from here. My housekeeper will choose one of the maids to accompany us, and she will remain with you as your companion." West paused long enough to allow Ria to put forth an argument. He hoped it was good sense rather than exhaustion that kept her from doing so. Rising to his feet, he said, "Wait here. I will make the necessary arrangements."

* * *

It seemed to West that his head had only touched the pillow when his valet was announcing it was time to rise. West ignored Finch until his bath was drawn, using the twenty minutes this required to fall into a second, deeper sleep.

"Will you take breakfast in your room this morning?" asked Finch.

West finished lowering himself into the tub. The water was blessedly warm, and it was like pulling the blankets over him again. "I always take my breakfast here. Why would today be—" He stopped, remembering of a sudden what caused this morning to be out of the ordinary. He rubbed his closed eyes with thumb and forefinger. When he spoke, it was more to himself than his valet. "Never say she is already arrived."

Finch wisely made no answer. He placed towels near the fireplace to warm them and moved the stool with sponge, soap, and the *Gazette* within West's reach. Disappearing into the dressing room, he chose West's clothes. Since there would be no bracing ride in the park this morning, Finch selected black trousers, a loosely fitting shirt, a black waistcoat with silver buttons, and a short black frock coat, all of it suitable for breakfast in the dining room. He arranged these items within West's easy reach, then applied himself to the change of clothes that would be necessary before West attended his father's service.

West was toweling his hair dry by the time Finch reappeared. He glanced up at his valet from between the tails of the towel, saw the unrelievedly black clothes Finch had chosen, and swore softly under his breath.

Not at all discouraged, Finch approached, handing one item at a time to West until all that was left was the frock coat. This he held out so that West could slip into it. Finch adjusted the line of the coat, pulling on the sleeves until the fit was without wrinkles, then brushed it off.

West suffered Finch's fussing in silence. The man was more of an age with the late duke, but acted like a mother hen with a chick. West had decided early on that it was no reason to upbraid him. The valet performed his duties conscientiously and West never feared making a cake for the way he was turned out. Because Finch tended toward portliness these last few years and experienced shortness of breath and knees that creaked alarmingly when he climbed stairs, West felt it was incumbent upon him to make certain the man remained employed.

"I am all of a piece?" West asked, turning toward the cheval glass and making a quick assessment.

"Your Grace must not doubt it," Finch said.

"I should like a headache powder."

Finch nodded, his oddly cherubic countenance perfectly inscrutable. "I will have it brought to you directly."

"In the breakfast room, Finch."

"Very good."

Ria was wearing the same black gown as the previous night. Water stains and flecks of mud that had circled the hem had been removed by a vigorous washing. The gown was neatly pressed and looked none the worse for wear. Still, she felt at some disadvantage when West entered the breakfast room and she saw him freshly turned out. Last evening he had looked vaguely disreputable. This morning he looked—every inch of him—to the manner born.

His expression, while lacking the haughtiness that was the hallmark of his father and brother, was neither warm nor welcoming. The smile was slight and the angle of that damnably raised eyebrow suggested a certain remoteness, as if he were exercising the right to be more observer than participant in whatever drama would occur. Most telling was that neither dimple was in evidence.

Ria was of the opinion that gravity did not sit easily upon West's shoulders and that the countenance he presented her was somewhat forced. She could not conceive that he had adopted this mien out of respect for his father. It was more likely that he had decided his responsibilities as her guardian must be discharged in an overbearing, high-handed fashion.

She thought she might prefer that he hold his knife to her throat.

West's head dipped a fraction in greeting as his eyes surveyed her. "You are looking well. The accommodations were satisfactory?"

"Yes, thank you. It was kind of you to see to everything."

"It was not kind, but necessary."

So it was to be like that, Ria thought. He did not mean to support an easy communication between them. It seemed that if an opportunity presented itself to reproach her for what he still considered her precipitous behavior and poor judgment, then he would make the most of it.

West indicated that Ria should precede him to the sideboard. Once there, he uncovered the dishes and invited her to take her fill. Tempering his amusement, he watched her crowd her plate with slices of bacon, tomato, and toast with jam. When they were seated at the table, Ria chose a soft-cooked egg, cracked it expertly with the bowl of her spoon, then began to peel back the shell. It was at this point that she looked up and realized West had yet to help himself to anything but his coffee.

Ria slowly lowered her spoon. She had been about to set upon her meal like the veriest street urchin.

"What are you doing?" West asked.

What remained of Ria's dignity was shattered when her stomach growled with considerable ferocity. The apology she had been about to put forward simply died on her lips and she flushed hotly.

West did not waste gray matter on determining when Ria had last eaten. Clearly, it had been too long since her last meal. "Eat," he said, his tone brooking no argument. "Do not stand on ceremony. I do not."

Mortification made Ria's eyes slide away from West's direct gaze. She stared at her plate, then her lap. Her fingers loosened around her spoon enough to allow her to set it aside.

"Never say that something so trifling as a lapse in good manners makes you come undone," West goaded her gently. He regarded the warm muffin and strips of crisp bacon on his plate. "I would not have anticipated that, given the rousing defense you mustered last evening." Watching her out of the corner of his eye, he split the muffin and lightly spread sweet butter on the halves. When she still was not roused to begin eating, he raised his soft-cooked egg, set it in its cup, and thwacked the crown loudly with his spoon. He took it as a good sign that the noise gave her a start, but she still would not raise a morsel of food to her mouth. There was nothing for it but that he tuck into his meal. He bit into a muffin half and hoped it would be enough to encourage her as he had little in the way of appetite.

Ria picked up a triangle of toast and put it to her lips. She was careful to take small bites.

"God's truth, but you are stubborn." West offered this simply as an observation, without rancor. "I believe you would starve rather than break your fast before me. It seems rather oddly done by you."

Looking at him askance, she sighed. "You mean to go on about it, don't you?"

"I am of a mind to do so, yes."

It was his perfectly arid accents that made the corners of Ria's mouth turn up ever so slightly. She could not have predicted that he would have this agreeably curious sense of humor, nor known that she would find it so much to her liking. There had been so little of late that could raise her smile, she did not begrudge herself this response.

Ria forced herself to eat slowly without regard for her hunger. Occasionally she pressed the hand resting in her lap against her midriff to quiet an embarrassing rumble, always darting a look sideways to see if he was taking measure of her success. It seemed to her that he had lost interest in teasing her, in spite of his words to the contrary. He ate more slowly than she, she noticed, and drank three cups of black coffee to her one of hot cocoa. She wondered that he did not come out of his skin with the effects of the bitter brew, but in truth he appeared no more than casually watchful from under his heavy-lidded glance.

West was grateful to see that Ria required no invitation on his part to help herself to more toast and tomatoes. He could not finish his own first serving, let alone take more of the same to his plate. He did not press her to discuss what manner of crisis had prompted her to take leave of both her senses and Gillhollow and journey alone to London. There was time enough yet for that, though he hoped the explanation she served him was more diverting than tedious. The day stretched long before him, and it would be filled with a surfeit of tedium, beginning with his father's funeral service. He was certain to be the object of far too many stares and whispers there. There would be no possibility that he could hang back as was his wont in all gatherings of the *ton.* Circumstances—and the heavy, manipulative hand of his father—had contrived to push him front and center. It was enough to make anyone lose their appetite.

West set down his cup and pushed his plate away. He allowed the footman to take it up, then waved the fellow off. Unlike many others of similar position and modest or better income, West was conscious of the presence of servants in his home. He had never been able to pretend they were not about when they so obviously were, and it was his habit not to discuss just anything in front of them. He knew firsthand what manner of secrets could be learned by the maids and footmen in the course of serving dinner. Between the sorbet and the port, a great many things were often said that were overheard by ears no one at the table seemed to notice. Playing the footman himself, West had had occasion to come by intelligence in just such a manner. Hiding in plain sight was how he'd explained his tactic to Colonel John Blackwood, his mentor in the foreign office.

It had been a very long time since spy work required climbing a chestnut tree.

West waited until the door to the breakfast room closed behind the footman before he spoke. "You have someplace to begin your account, I collect. I should like to hear it now."

Out of West's sight, Ria's fingers pleated the napkin in her lap. On her way to his home, she had mentally rehearsed a pithy speech that would put the facts before him so straightforwardly they could not be lightly dismissed. She could not remember a word of it now. "One of my girls is missing," she said.

West considered this. "Very well," he said. "You mean to begin in the middle, or perhaps it is at the end. It is not often done, but both approaches have their supporters. Will I discompose you by asking how you have come to have any girls at all in your possession?"

Ria had allowed the maid to ruthlessly scrape back her thick hair this morning and fashion it into a smooth knot. Now, as her head began to ache, she had no idea if it was the tightness of her scalp that prompted the condition, or West's wry commentary. If she had to choose, she thought it might be the latter. It had not escaped her notice that one of his eyebrows was raised a fraction, and that with very little provocation he might actually laugh at her.

Ria's nostrils flared slightly and her sweetly curved mouth flattened. "I am headmistress of Miss Weaver's Academy for Young Ladies in Gillhollow. I have been a teacher there these last six years and headmistress since January. And before you inquire, no, there is no Miss Weaver."

It hadn't occurred to West to ask after the academy's namesake, but now he could not resist. "There is no Miss Weaver now, or there never was?" He wasn't entirely surprised when Ria did not deign to answer. She was learning when she must ignore him, which he counted as a good thing. "Go on, Miss Ashby, you have explained to my satisfaction why you think of the students as your girls, but it begs the question as to how you came to Miss Weaver's Academy. Last night you mentioned an allowance. I cannot reconcile that with your taking a position at the school. Did the duke provide so little for your care?"

"His Grace provided a generous allowance," she said. "The choice to engage in respectable employment was mine."

West had learned to listen for what it was that people did *not* say. He thought he heard something between the lines now. "My father did not approve of your enterprise."

"No. He did not forbid it, but neither was he in favor of it. He insisted that I continue to accept the allowance."

Here was another thing she was not quite saying, West decided. "Which you do not use for your living expenses," he said, eyeing her serviceable gown, "but for sustaining Miss Weaver's Academy."

"There are always students who can ill afford to pay the tuition."

"These are students with little in the way of consequence and with few prospects of acquiring any. Why educate them at all? What can be the sense of it, especially as they are females?"

It was an argument Ria had heard before. Usually it frustrated her. Now, coming from this man, it merely disappointed. "That is one view," she said in carefully neutral accents. "Mine is considerably—" She stopped because she was finally able to comprehend the perfect blandness of his expression and know he was putting significant effort into affecting such a countenance. "You do not believe that at all, do you?"

West smiled a little then. "No, I do not." He leaned back in his chair and stretched his legs comfortably. His hands were folded loosely on the edge of the table. He tapped the balls of his thumbs together. "But I do not think I am such a reformer as you. Indeed, I am not a reformer at all. It's a messy business, better left to politicians, who like to wallow in it, or women, who cannot help but take a broom to it."

"I think you are a cynic, Your Grace."

"And I make no apology for it." He regarded her thoughtfully. "There is much more here I want to know, Miss Ashby, but mayhap you should tell me about your missing girl."

"Her name is Jane Petty, and she is but fifteen years old."

"Then she is no child."

"No, but—"

"Have you considered there is a young man? Perhaps she has fashioned an attachment to one of the local fellows and gone to Gretna."

"I don't think so," Ria said, shaking her head. "I could find no evidence to support it."

"Then you did admit the possibility."

"Let us say I did not want to overlook it. Jane is rather more trusting than is strictly good for her, so I could envision that such a thing had come to pass. Yet she is not a restful girl, and one has to consider that maintaining secrecy around an elopement is wholly out of character."

"You are perhaps understating it when you describe her as *not restful?*"

With an almost imperceptible nod of her head, Ria conceded the point. "Jane is a chatterbox," she said, her tone giving clear proof of her fondness for the girl, "and her movement is not confined to the workings of her jaw. She is rarely still. She chafes at inactivity and suffers the strictures of the classroom because she must. Outside of it she flits about like a hummingbird, pausing here and there, but never settling for more than a few moments. She fairly thrums with energy, and she cannot do a thing quietly. Something is invariably overturned or at least set askew. One always knows when Jane has been about." The recollection raised a faint smile that quickly disappeared as Ria continued. "But it is not only her physical path that is marked by disarray. Jane manages to do the very same thing with the girls. She cannot seem to help herself. There is always some drama in her wake."

"Then she is not well liked."

"No, that is not it at all. She is popular with the others—it is just that it requires so much effort to accommodate her presence."

"I had forgotten how appreciative females are of high drama. They will make a great many allowances for it."

Now it was Ria who lifted an eyebrow. "Surely neither the appreciation nor the allowances are exclusive to females."

West thought of his friends and the intrigues they reveled in at Hambrick Hall. "I stand corrected," he said. He caught himself in time to keep from saying that it was all part and parcel of one's youth. How, then, could he reconcile that statement with the fact that he and his friends still regularly engaged in intrigues? It would not stand up to much scrutiny, and West wisely kept his silence. "How long has Miss Jane Petty been missing?"

"Sixteen days."

West was careful not to let his dismay show. He had hoped to hear it was much, much less. "There has been no word at all? No hint?"

"Nothing. It is yet another reason I have dismissed the idea that she eloped. I believe she would have written by now. She was not a thoughtless child."

"Pray, temper this tendency you have to name her a child. It is not helpful. You cannot yet acquit her of responsibility for her own disappearance."

"I can," Ria said softly. "You do not know her as I do. I will not believe she is gone of her own accord."

West chose not to argue the point. She was right—he did not know Jane—but he was also right, characterizing Jane as a child was not helpful. "What is it you would have me do, Miss Ashby? Have we finally arrived at the reason you set yourself in my path yesterday? You might have ridden to town with Tenley and his brood if you had only meant to attend the service and inform me of my responsibilities to you as guardian. It seems you should set the matter before me in very plain language."

"I want you to help me find her."

It was *almost* what he had expected she would say. "Help you?" he asked. "Do you mean that you would assist me in determining Miss Petty's whereabouts?"

"No," she said firmly. "I mean that you should assist me."

He did not like the sound of that at all. It was with some effort that he voiced no objections. He decided they could wait, as he was not yet prepared to give her an answer. "I am finding it hard to imagine that had the duke's health not been a concern, you still would have applied to him with the same request." When her eyes slid away from his and she remained silent, West knew he was right. "I would hear it from you."

"I would not have gone to him," she said at last. "It is not that your father would have been unsympathetic, only that he would have seized the opportunity to lecture me about the school. He would have had me abandon my duties."

It was considerably difficult for West to believe the duke would have had even a *soupçon* of sympathy, but he let this pass. It was borne home to him again that Ria's experience with his sire was vastly different from his own. "Miss Petty disappeared more than a fortnight ago. That was before any of us knew what revelations the duke was preparing to make. You might have gone to Tenley with your concerns. At that time you could have properly expected that he would be your guardian."

"Your brother would not be inclined to help me." She hastily added, "There is no animosity between us. It is just that Tenley is not often inclined to extend himself."

West chuckled and watched as Ria's fair complexion colored. "That is a damning defense you offer. I hope you will never make a similar effort on my behalf."

"I only meant—" She stopped before she made it worse. He knew perfectly well what she'd meant; his view of Tenley could scarcely have been more complimentary.

Pushing back his chair, West came to his feet. He felt her

anxious eyes marking his progress to the fireplace where he poked at the logs while he considered what he might say to her. He glanced out the window to the garden. It had started to rain again, this time with a gusting wind accompanying it so there were diagonal etchings on each pane of glass. Occasionally splinters of ice fell among the raindrops, a clear sign that the weather was turning colder. These ice needles hit the window at a different pitch than the rain and dissolved slowly, sometimes collecting visibly on the sill before they melted.

He replaced the poker and turned back to Ria. He ran a hand absently through his copper hair. "I am not certain what you think I can do for you."

"I have said as much, haven't I? You can help me find Jane."

"In what way?" he asked. "Is it money you require? Assistance hiring someone to do the investigation? Perhaps you mean that I should interview candidates for the position and weed out the fellows that are likely to take advantage of your naiveté."

"I could hire anyone," she said. "I want you." She watched both of his eyebrows lift in response to her directness. "I can say it no more plainly than that."

"No, that was perfectly frank. You seem to have gotten the hang of it."

Ria refused to be turned from her purpose by his light mockery. "I can offer you compensation, though you will understand that it means I will only be returning my allowance. If you want more than what you give me, then you shall have to give me more."

West wished he had not stood up because it was just that sort of logic that set him reeling. She looked as if she meant to explain herself, and he held up a hand, palm out, to forestall her. "It will be a kindness if you do not repeat yourself. It is my experience that this rarely results in clarification, yet one tends to speak more loudly the second time."

Ria felt a tendril of hair flutter against her cheek. The distraction as his eyes fell on it was not welcome. She tucked it behind her ear quickly. "What is your answer to my proposal?"

"Forgive my obtuseness, Miss Ashby, but I am no more clear as to why you think I *can* help."

"Your Grace is being disingenuous or modest or both."

"I don't know what you mean."

She could not very well call him a liar, though it was a temptation. "You have a position in the foreign office."

"Yes. That's true enough."

"Then you have connections."

"I suppose that is also true, though how they can be of use in finding Miss Petty remains a mystery."

"Have you learned nothing at all?"

West rubbed his chin with his thumb and forefinger. "I know something about drawing up legal documents. That is how I spend my time, after all, reviewing and revising documents that pass from one person to another person to yet another person. Dull stuff, but I do it in the service of my country."

"I don't believe you," she said. "About the documents, I mean."

"I'm a clerk, Miss Ashby, though I suppose the Westphal inheritance will put a period to that. Perhaps they will allow me to pen the documents myself in the future. I imagine there is a Westphal seal. I may be able to use it when I put my signature to paper." West saw the line of Ria's slender shoulders droop. Her blue-gray eyes were no longer suspicious, but resigned. "What, precisely, is it that you imagined I did at the foreign office?"

She shrugged. "I'd heard things."

"Do not make me strain to hear you."

"I'd heard things," she said more audibly this time.

"What sort of things? Not that rubbish about smuggling French brandy, I hope."

So it wasn't true that he had been a smuggler. Ria allowed that she was disappointed to hear it. The tales of debauchery on the Continent were probably false as well, though she had never set much store by them. "I'd heard that you were instrumental in providing intelligence concerning Napoleon's movements during the war."

West replaced the poker and regarded Ria with ill-disguised amusement. "My dear Miss Ashby, never say you have conceived the notion that I was a spy. Oh, but I can see that you did. You are perfectly crestfallen to have it denied and no doubt even more worried about Miss Petty. It is true that I was attached to Wellington's camp, but such intelligence as was gathered was done so by others and merely passed on by me. If I called myself a courier it would still be puffing the thing up. To say that I was instrumental means only that I was a cog in the wheel, as clerks often are. Had I performed my duties with less diligence, perhaps there would have been a company without proper rations, but I doubt the outcome at Waterloo hinged on whether there was enough salted beef in the camp."

"You tallied foodstuffs?" she asked, her eyes widening a shade.

"I tallied most everything that an army requires to move and fight and move again. Mathematics, after all, is what kept me prisoner at Cambridge for more years than I care to remember."

"That was mathematics," she said. "You are speaking now of . . . of *adding.*"

"Yes, well, one does what one is asked to do. If you are Wellington, you want to know you can rely on the accuracy of the count. Rifles. Cannons. Pistols. Men. Uniforms. Wagons. Boots. Horses. Saddles. Bayonets."

"Salted beef," Ria said. "Yes, I understand the importance of it, I just thought you did something . . ." Her voice trailed off.

"Something more?" he asked. "I think you have conceived some romantic notions about what is required to win the day.

I do not blame you. No one who is not on the field can know what hard, bloody work it all is."

"I didn't mean to disparage your contribution," Ria said hastily. Embarrassed by her insensitivity, she was contrite. "It is only that . . ." She had no words again.

West returned to the table and his chair. "You are burdened by your worry for Miss Petty, and I have done nothing to relieve you of it."

Ria managed a faint smile as indication that she was resigned to the weight of it now.

"Tell me," he said in a tone of only mild interest. "This thing you heard about me being instrumental in the effort, how did it come to your attention?"

She could tell him honestly, for this was information she had never set out to learn. Indeed, he would have been a very poor spy if it was common knowledge that was his business. "I was staying with the duke in London," she said. "It would have been five or six years ago, around the time Wellington entered Madrid."

"Six years, then," West said.

Ria thought about that. "Yes, I do believe you're right. It was just before I accepted the position at the school. As I was saying, I was in London at the duke's residence and he had a visitor. I was not introduced, as I was not seen on the stairs, but I could see that Westphal was glad of his visit and offered him refreshment in his study. That struck me as peculiar because your father rarely entertained and seemed to suffer those occasions rather than enjoy them. This was decidedly different."

"So you were made curious."

She nodded. "I listened on the other side of the door, though I should not admit it. I was certainly of an age to know better. Long past that age, in fact, so it does not speak at all well of me. I meant only to learn the man's name and perhaps later find an opportunity to ask Westphal about him. The name I heard, though, was yours. It was confusing at first because the man did not call you by either your Christian or surname."

"Oh?"

"He called you West."

"I see." Nothing about West's expression changed, though the pain he felt was real enough. "That was indeed confusing for you."

"Yes. I'm afraid I spent considerably more time at the door than I meant to in order to work it out."

"But you did."

"In the end. It was clear to me they were speaking of you when you were also referred to as the duke's son. I knew better than to suppose they meant Tenley. He was not on the Continent, but enjoying himself in the gaming hells at the time. Perforce, it had to be you."

West's only acknowledgment of this was a soft grunt at the back of his throat.

"They had talked at length by then, and I learned something about your work in the foreign office."

"Not enough, apparently. You did not even realize I was in Madrid."

"Well, no, but then I was not able to ask questions, and neither man was entirely straightforward. It is easy to suppose they knew what they were talking about, but it was not as clear to me."

"So you filled in the gaps with twaddle about spies and intrigues."

"I did not conceive it was twaddle," she said quietly, "but yes, you have summed it up."

"Sums," he said succinctly. "My forte." West closed his eyes a moment and rubbed them. "This man, the one who spoke of me as West, do you recall his name?"

Ria thought back. "I remember he carried a walking stick," she said, "and that it was no affectation. He leaned heavily on it to get to the library doors."

West nodded. That bit of information was every bit as good as having a name.

Ria's head lifted sharply as she snapped her fingers. "Blackwood. Colonel Blackwood. What do you think of that?"

West knew that she was looking for approval for having remembered the name from so long ago, but he could not give it to her. "What I think," he said with quiet menace, "is that I will do murder."

Chapter Three

West wished himself anywhere but where he was. The service at the Abbey had been interminable and he had not been wrong to anticipate the attention he received. He had intercepted more furtive glances than he cared to think about, and there had been almost a constant hum of whispering at his back. Now those closest to him, those who had known him as well as he permitted anyone to know him, were gathered in his home. It was not to mourn the late duke that they came—because there was no one present who had been particularly fond or forgiving of the man—rather, they came to pay their respects to the late Mr. Evan Marchman, who now and forever would be known as His Grace the Duke of Westphal.

It was not to be borne.

Yet, what choice did he have? Entailment being what it was, he could not give the title to Tenley no matter how much his brother might covet it as his own birthright. Neither could he give his brother legitimacy, for that had been taken away from Tenley the moment the duke had revealed the truth about his marriages. Whether Tenley might be able to apply to the Prince Regent to have the question of legitimacy raised again was still unclear. West hoped that his brother would have that recourse and that Prinny would be generous. Tenley could find some small solace that he remained the earl, a title that came to him from his mother's side of the family and was not subject to the same strictures as the duke's title and holdings. Unfortunately, there was little in the way of money or lands that accompanied the honor of being the Earl of Tenley. It was not that Tenley was destitute, but that his circumstances and prospects had been vastly reduced.

Seeing Tenley at the service had been deuced uncomfortable, though West thought that each of them had comported themselves well enough. At least there had been no pistols drawn, and West counted that as a good beginning. He could allow that Tenley's adjustment was harder than his own and was not without sympathy for him. Every one of his brother's expectations had been dashed, while he had long ago decided that survival meant having few of them, especially as they related to others.

West's contemplation ended when Lady Benton-Reade came determinedly to his side and engaged him in conversation. Standing on the opposite side of the drawing room at the green-veined marble fireplace, was Southerton. West was careful not to allow his attention to be diverted in that direction overlong, but from between the swaying plumes of Lady Benton-Reade's bonnet, West thought he glimpsed evidence of South's unholy gleam. It was proof that he could not expect rescue from that quarter, and he resigned himself to enduring the soliloquy that passed for the lady's conversation.

He did eventually manage to excuse himself as Northam and his wife came to offer their condolences and announce they were leaving. Looking from one to the other, West could not help but be aware of the strain that existed between them. Was it only last night at the club that North had been teased for being distant and contemplative? It seemed that nothing had changed since then. Although everything in North's manner was correct, West could not help but wonder if anything was as it should be between Elizabeth and her husband. The countess's complexion was pale and her eyelids were faintly swollen. It was grief he saw in her face, and he knew very well that it was not this solemn occasion that had brought it about. North's own countenance gave little of his thoughts away, which in itself was telling to those who knew him. West counted himself among that set. Watching these two, their combined pain so palpable, he felt very much like an intruder in his own home.

He made them as easy as he could, escorting them to the door himself so they would not be waylaid by his other guests. When he returned to the drawing room, he saw immediately that South had disappeared. It did not require any special talent to know where he'd gone. West could see that the door to his study was closed and understood that South would have made his way there to speak to the colonel. Northam and his countess had been in conversation with Blackwood earlier, and when West glanced over at Eastlyn, it seemed to him the marquess was looking as if he meant to have a turn with the colonel as well.

That was all right, then. West knew he could afford to give his friends first crack at Blackwood. Perhaps it was even better that the others saw him first. The colonel might be moved to take his leave when West was finished serving him a few home truths.

John Blackwood, that adviser in the foreign office who directed the activities of the Compass Club, tucked a rug about his thin legs, then pushed his wheeled chair closer to the fire. He had allowed himself to be persuaded not to attend the services for the duke this morning, but neither his doctor nor his valet could keep him from West's home tonight.

Now he wondered if he shouldn't have listened to them, not because they were right that the evening away from home would fatigue him almost beyond bearing, but because so little good had come of his presence. His dear Elizabeth, not to put too fine a point on it, had abducted him from the drawing room and wheeled him into West's study. Short of making a scene, he could not have stopped her and wasn't certain that he wanted to.

She had argued with him, pleaded even, to turn her husband away from the assignment he'd been given to find the Gentleman Thief. He, who thought there was nothing he would not do for her, could not grant her this boon, nor could he tell her anything that would ease her mind on the matter. The thief must be caught and it must be done soon. North was in every way the man for the task. To place that considerable responsibility in someone else's hands would set them back months, and so he had refused her.

He was very much afraid she would not speak to him again.

On the heels of that encounter, South had begged a moment of his time. The colonel smiled a little grimly as he poked at the fire. *Demanded,* not *begged,* was the proper word for it. South had demanded his time and called him a bloody bastard, a term usually reserved for the late duke. The viscount had been witness to the unhappy tension between Elizabeth and Northam and wanted absolution for having played even a small part in bringing about their union. The colonel was slightly more optimistic than South that all would be made right in the end, but he absolved South of responsibility anyway, just as if he were a priest, and took it upon his own less-than-robust shoulders.

The interview had not ended there, for there was still South's assignment to be managed. What South had managed to do was set all of London talking about the disappearance of Miss India Parr. The most beloved actress at the Drury Lane had missed two performances, and her devoted audience, largely male, had almost not been prevented from burning the place down. If it became known that Southerton was responsible for Miss Parr's absence, he would be run to ground, then drawn and quartered. There were moments during his discussion with South that he had contemplated leading that charge.

He had only just dismissed South when Eastlyn arrived to take up the empty chair. The marquess had himself in the very devil of a coil, compliments of a spurned mistress, and had no simple way to extricate himself. The rumors of his engagement to Lady Sophia Colley would not be silenced and presented yet another obstacle to the completion of his assignment. There was nothing for it but that he be taken to task.

The colonel jabbed hard at the fire again, his knobby knuckles perfectly white with the strength of his grip on the poker. He had not tread lightly with East, but forced the younger man to examine his situation carefully and come to a decision of how he meant to go on. Matters related to his task of martialing support for the East India Company could not be accomplished without East putting his own house in order. Indeed, it seemed that success demanded that East place one before the other. Blackwood sympathized but did not relent.

The colonel had just replaced the poker when the door opened. He did not look up. "I've been expecting you."

"I thought you might be," West said. "The others have had their audience. It seems only fair that I have a turn myself."

Blackwood did not think he was imagining the chill edging West's tone. His dark eyes narrowed faintly as he wheeled around and took measure of the man stepping into the room. No line of West's trim frame conveyed that he was in any way easy with himself. The rigid set of his shoulders made his carriage stiff, and his long-legged stride had none of the casual grace he might otherwise have affected. There was a tautness to his mouth, and the gravity of his thoughts had drawn the skin of his face tightly over the bones. He looked gaunt. It would not be hyperbole to say he looked vaguely haunted.

The colonel pushed his chair to the drinks cabinet. "Will you have a whiskey?"

"No." West saw the empty tumblers left by his friends. It seemed Blackwood had been successful in plying them all with alcohol, no doubt enjoying the opportunity to imbibe freely himself. His doctor and his valet restricted him as much as was possible in his own home. "But you must help yourself," he said.

Blackwood shook his head. "I've already done that. I am quite aware of my tolerance and find that I have reached it."

West sat down as the colonel pushed his chair closer. Blackwood was still a handsome man; the wasting disease that had laid siege to his legs had not robbed him of his fine looks nor dulled his mind. His reflexes were slower now and a tremor could sometimes be spied in his hands, but he held his own, fixing his quarry with a dark glance that was at once an appraisal and a challenge. Though no longer muscular, he was still fastidious about his appearance and took some pains to make certain his stock was folded in the latest fashion.

West knew the colonel's legs were weaker than they had been, even this summer past. Then Blackwood had been able to travel to the Battenburn estate for North and Elizabeth's wedding and make his way down the center aisle, aided by two sticks and the wiry strength of his own arms. Only five months later, West doubted that such a thing would be possible, though he would not underestimate the colonel's tenacity. There was evidence enough of that in the pronounced creases at the corners of his eyes, the faint frown that was present even in his relaxed state. Except for a light thinning at the crown and a few seeds of gray, the colonel's shock of black hair was not conceding either to his illness or his advancing years.

Blackwood lowered his gold-rimmed spectacles over the bridge of his hawk-like nose and regarded West with a surprisingly gentle smile and an invitation to proceed.

"Everyone is gone?" he asked.

West nodded. "I have just now come from bidding farewell to South's parents and North's mother. Lady Winslow and Sir James left only moments before."

The colonel was not surprised that East's family had also lingered. It had been like that since West's own mother died when he was yet at Cambridge. Long before then, a connection had been made to each of the other families, perhaps, Blackwood thought, because West was, for all intents and purposes, fatherless. No less a personage than the dowager Countess of Northam had been moved to call the duke a bloody bastard, championing West even though she still took umbrage with him for breaking the nose of her son when they were but boys at Hambrick.

The corners of Blackwood's mouth were lifted as he considered the temper and aggressive posture that had put West in conflict with every one of his schoolmates. He wondered what he would have made of young Evan Marchman if he had known him in those days. Would he have been as rigidly uncompromising as the Hambrick house masters, or would he have seen past the boy's fiercely held fists to the pain and confusion that made him so belligerent?

West did not recline in his chair. Instead, he sat forward slightly and rested his forearms on his knees. His fingers were loosely intertwined, and as was often his habit, he lightly tapped the pads of his thumbs together. He did not engage in pleasantries, but came immediately to the point.

"Why did you never tell me you visited him?"

Although the colonel had no difficulty divining West's meaning, the question still surprised. "I have never thought it necessary to apprise you of the names of even a quarter of the people I visit. Why should this have been different?"

"Do not pose a question to me that you can answer yourself."

Blackwood gave West a sharp look over the rim of his spectacles. "Actually, I am not certain I *can* answer it. Being Westphal's son did not entitle you to know every occasion I had to visit him. Indeed, given the estrangement between you, it seemed to me that you would be uninterested in my dealings with him."

"It is a different matter when you used those occasions to discuss me."

"I have never thought of you as someone prone to exaggerating his own importance. We also discussed things wholly unrelated to you."

West would not relent. "But you *did* share my activities with him."

It was rare that Blackwood hesitated, but he did so now. "Sometimes," he said finally. "Yes."

West straightened a little then and sat back. He did not know there was more hurt in his glance than there was accusation. "Why?" he asked softly. "Why tell him anything at all about me? Have you been as forthcoming to Lord Redding about South's activities over the years? I cannot imagine that you have ever informed North's mother about the things he has done, and continues to do, for you. And East? I am quite sure he would not thank you for apprising his—"

"I take your point," the colonel said. "And you are right. I have made it a point to say very little to others."

"Then why? Why would you—"

"They have never wanted to know. Lord and Lady Redding. Sir James and Lady Winslow. The dowager countess. All of them are more at their ease not knowing the particulars, and they will tell you as much if you press them. The duke *wanted* to know, and to the extent that he could be informed, I informed him. Your father was highly placed in the government, West. He came within a hairsbreadth of being made prime minister after Perceval was assassinated, and he had many supporters this last time around. Do you imagine he could not have found out whatever he liked? I should think you would prefer that he received his information from me. You can depend on the accuracy of my accounts."

"What I depended upon," West said without inflection, "was your silence."

Uncharacteristically at a loss for words, Blackwood offered silence now.

West eyed the whiskey decanter on the drinks cabinet and realized he had not the wherewithal to go there. He could not recall a time when he had been so lacking in energy, so boneless as he was now. The events of these last three days had conspired to tap both his strength and the soundness of his judgments. "He had not earned the right to know what I was about." In spite of surging emotions, his voice remained remarkably steady. "I thought that had always been understood between us. It was not for you to say, but rather for me. The duke should have addressed his questions to me."

There was no point, the colonel decided, in stating what they both knew to be true: West would not have responded to any question put to him by his father. Blackwood remained silent, offering no defense for his actions.

"You have nothing at all to say?" West asked.

"Save for an apology, I can think of nothing that you will wish to hear on the matter."

West waited, but the colonel's apology was not forthcoming. "Then you do not regret it?"

"I regret that I did not listen to my own counsel and inform you that your father was making inquiries."

West's eyes narrowed faintly as he regarded his mentor. "Why not?" he asked. "Why not trust your own judgment? Isn't that what you demand of us?"

"It is." His smile was rueful. "I can do the wrong thing for the right reason as often as any man. It is only in hindsight that any of us can know how wrong it truly was."

"And what of speaking to the duke about me? I have not heard you offer any regret for that."

By saying nothing, Blackwood said everything.

"I see," said West. He slumped more deeply in the chair so that he was almost reclining now and stretched his long legs before him. "Did you never wonder at the consequences?"

"Of course I wondered what you would make of it. I had hoped you would endeavor to understand."

"Understand? What I understand, Colonel, is that he's made me his bloody heir. He wouldn't have done that if he thought I was only a clerk in the foreign office. That's what I understand. You filled him with nonsense about some instrumental task I performed in Wellington's camp and—"

"Nonsense?" Blackwood bristled at the idea he ever spouted such. "I spoke nothing save the truth. I did not tell him one-half of what you were able to accomplish for Wellington at Fuentes de Oñoro and Aluera. A year later you were in Madrid ahead of the army, taking considerable risk out of uniform."

West turned one hand over in a gesture that communicated both modesty and indifference. "I moved documents. Wellington moved an army. My contribution was—"

"Essential," the colonel said.

"I was not fishing."

"And I am not flattering. I am speaking the truth."

West wanted no more of this conversation. He knew what he had done was important work and he was proud of it, but he did not consider it more or less singular than the contribution made by others. He roused himself enough to come to his feet. Ignoring the decanters of whiskey and brandy, West walked to the window instead and drew back the heavy velvet curtains. The rain had finally turned entirely to sleet and the tattoo against the window was sharp and steady. He wondered about the road to Gillhollow, how difficult the travel might be for a coach and four. He wondered if Ria had gone on alone or taken her place with Tenley and his family. He wondered . . .

West allowed the drapes to fall back and turned away. Belatedly, he was aware that the colonel had wheeled his chair around and was watching him closely, seeing something more than he had ever meant to reveal. West plowed his fingers through his hair, discomfited by the scrutiny, out of patience with himself for lowering his guard. "You were saying?"

"Indeed," Blackwood said dryly. In truth, he had been silent, but he was not about to allow West's prompt to go begging. "I was hoping that you would humor me, and tell me the source of your information. I can think of no one save your father who was aware of my visits."

"The servants."

The colonel shook his head. "I did not forget to take them into account, but it is not possible that they spoke to you. They would not speak of it to anyone."

West could not entirely temper his smile. He shrugged to draw attention away from it. Blackwood had forgotten, however briefly, that he was now in the company of the Duke of Westphal. Those servants who had been loyal to his father were, for the time being, in his employ. They might have reservations about relating certain events to him, but they would not hold their tongues if he pressed.

"You will not explain it to me?" asked the colonel.

It seemed to West that he was being small by not telling Blackwood what he wanted to know. Getting a little of his own back was not a particularly pleasant feeling. "Miss Ashby," he said finally, watching the colonel's reaction closely. "I will not ask if you know who she is. I can see that you do."

Blackwood struck a thoughtful pose, cocking his head and tapping the right side of his nose with his forefinger. "She was at the Abbey today for the service?"

West nodded slowly. "In addition to the title and considerable fortune the duke has left me, I have also inherited a ward. What do you make of that, Colonel? It seems he was possessed of a sense of humor after all."

"I had not thought of it in that light."

"What else can I do but find the bloody humor of it?" asked West. "He is already dead, so however much I wish to do so, I cannot kill him."

The colonel thought it was a good sign that West's own sense of humor had finally surfaced, no matter how black it was. "I cannot conceive that Miss Ashby will upset the equilibrium of your existence. She can be the very least of the responsibilities you have inherited."

Both of West's eyebrows lifted. "She is a person. She is female. Female persons are always more difficult to manage than land and money. You smile, but you know it is true. You cannot help but have noticed that North is deuced unhappy with Elizabeth. And East? He has got himself between Mrs. Sawyer and Lady Sophia and would welcome a cup of hemlock at this juncture. Even South, who can be bloody brilliant on occasion, has been acting most peculiar. Mark me, there is a woman involved, for he pressed me to loan him my cottage near Ambermede for a trysting place."

West saw that the colonel did not blink an eye at this last bit of intelligence. "Hah! You know about that, do you? I thought I detected your fine hand in the thing. Then it is not a tryst at all—or not *only* a tryst—but an assignment from you." He held up a hand. "No, I do not want you to confirm it."

"And I will not. The very last thing I need is the four of you tripping over one another. It seems to happen in spite of my desire that it be otherwise."

"It is rather remarkable that East has not shot one of us by now."

Blackwood's dark eyes dropped to West's boot. "More remarkable that you have not stabbed one of them."

"They say that very thing from time to time."

The colonel did not doubt it. "Tell me about Miss Ashby," he said. "How did you come to learn about my visits to the duke from her? I have never had occasion to meet her."

West related what Ria had told him. "Does she sound as if she is not a handful? She listens at doors, if you can credit it. That is just the sort of thing that causes no end of problems."

Since West was called upon to do it frequently in the course of his work, the colonel thought he was being somewhat harsh in his assessment of Miss Ashby. "I doubt it is her practice to engage in eavesdropping."

"I couldn't say. She only apprised me of this one instance."

The colonel coughed to cover his chuckle. "Careful, West, your tone puts me in mind of Northam at his most priggish. You would do well to avoid that comparison. Even his own mother can't stand him when he adopts that tone."

West was much struck by that. "Then you see firsthand what Miss Ashby is capable of, for no one has ever accused me of priggishness."

"Indeed," Blackwood said softly. "Your ward has had an unsettling influence."

That described it very well, West thought. He returned to his chair and hitched one hip on the arm. He waited for the colonel to turn himself around before he spoke. "You might well wonder how we had such a conversation at the service. In truth, we did not exchange a single word there. Miss Ashby arrived on my doorstep last evening—*sans* chaperone."

"The devil you say." The colonel did not try to conceal his surprise. "I confess I know little enough about your ward, but it seems unlikely the duke would have countenanced such behavior."

"The duke is dead."

"Aaah, yes—well, there you have it."

"There can be no getting around the truth of that." West's chest rose and fell, his sigh inaudible. He decided then that he would tell Colonel Blackwood everything.

Ria hugged Amy Nash to her breast. The girl was inconsolable, and it did not help that Ria felt very much like giving in to a frenzied bout of weeping herself. Instead her expression was bleak, although this was only evident while little Amy's face was buried against her. Each time the girl looked up to gauge Ria's reaction, Ria masked her anxious concern with a fair approximation of an encouraging smile.

"You did the right thing by coming to me, Amy." Ria stroked Amy's untidy russet hair with her fingertips. "It is better late than never. You were very brave to step forward when you thought there would be a punishment." There was so much more Ria could have said—an entire lecture was unfolding in her mind—but she bit it back. Amy knew very well that she should have stepped forward immediately with her information. She also knew she could have offered that same information at any time in the last six weeks. Ria decided it made no sense to belabor those points. Amy had finally come to her, and this was cause for thanksgiving, nothing less.

"Come," Ria said. "Have done with these tears and show me your pretty face."

Amy raised her face and allowed Ria to examine it. Her tears were gently wiped clean with a handkerchief that smelled of lavender. When she was ordered to blow, she resisted soiling the linen and sniffed loudly instead.

Ria chided her. "It can be washed, Amy. Blow, please. Let me hear Gabriel's trumpet." She covered Amy's watery smile with the handkerchief and held it there while the girl blew hard. "That's so much better, isn't it?" She folded the linen and pressed it into Amy's hand. "You may keep it, and if you feel as if you must cry, you will squeeze it very hard and it will stay the tears."

Amy's dark chocolate eyes were both luminous and vaguely suspicious. "Shouldn't I press it to my eyes?"

"Only if you want to catch the tears. If you want to stop them, you should squeeze. It's rather like magic." Ria was grateful Amy was still young enough that she could be appeased by magical handkerchiefs. "Good girl. Now, from the beginning. I must have it again, without sobbing this time. I want to be certain I understand everything."

Nodding, Amy closed her fingers tightly around the handkerchief. It really did seem to help. "Jane said I mustn't tell. We made a blood oath." She held up her forefinger to show Ria where she and Jane had each pricked themselves with a needle from their sewing baskets. There was no scar, but she offered the finger for inspection anyway. "I promised her, Miss Ashby. It was a solemn vow."

"I understand, but you are not wrong to break your promise. It is very important that we find Jane." Ria thought that if Amy had been but a few years older, she might not have held so strongly to her vow of secrecy. At eight, the girl was too young to weigh the consequences of keeping a promise against the consequences of breaking one. Even when Amy could see that so many others were worried about Jane, she clung to Jane's words that all would be fine and that she musn't give up the secret. Ria wondered why Jane had shared any part of her plan with Amy, then acknowledged another prayer of thanks that she had. Perhaps Jane had found the adventure she meant to take as simply too exciting to be kept to herself; perhaps it was only that she wanted to impress Amy with her self-importance.

Ria gave Amy's fingers a squeeze and prompted her. "You said that Jane told you she was going with a gentleman."

"A proper gentleman."

"Yes, a *proper* gentleman." Ria could not imagine what that meant to either of the girls. Jane's idea of a proper gentleman might very well be one who cleaned the dirt from beneath his fingernails, or carried a walking stick with a crystal knob. Jane had not the breadth of experience with any gentleman from which to draw upon. "What did she say about her proper gentleman?"

"She said very little, Miss Ashby. Very little."

"But something, Amy." Ria wanted to shake the girl, rattle her hard and make the words spill out of her like coins from a bank. "Think. Think *hard.*"

Amy Nash's brow furrowed deeply. "She said he was handsome. He wore a fine coat, soft as brushed velvet, she told me, with brass buttons."

"What about the color of his eyes? His hair?"

The little girl merely shook her head.

"His age?"

Amy's lower lip trembled. She bit down on it and clutched the handkerchief more tightly. "She didn't say."

Jane probably had no idea, Ria thought. It was equally useless to inquire about the man's height. To Jane, petite as a doll, every man she encountered was likely to assume the proportions of a Titan in her mind. "Did Jane ever say where or how she met him?"

Amy shook her head again.

"It's all right. Don't fret yourself. Tell me what you *do* know."

"She loves him truly, Miss Ashby. They are married now. I am sure of it. Jane wanted ever so much to be married."

"Did Jane ever mention Gretna Green? Can you remember that, Amy? Gretna. Green."

"No. She never said a word about that. Where is it? Shall we look for her there?"

Ria heard the hope in the child's voice, and it squeezed her heart. "Gretna is in Scotland. You have seen the map in the classroom. Do you recall where Scotland is?"

"On top."

"Something like that. It requires a journey of many days to go there, and it is not likely that we would find Jane or her beau in residence." Ria leaned against the rails of the stiff ladderback chair. Amy was a small armful, but she managed to occupy all of Ria's lap. After almost one half-hour of securing her, Ria's legs had little in the way of feeling. Still, she didn't ask Amy to move to the stool at her side, and she didn't deceive herself into believing that her decision was only for Amy's sake. "Jane took no clothes with her," Ria said. "What do you make of that?"

"Oh, but I know. Jane said she was to have a new wardrobe. He would take her to the dressmaker's on Firth Street and order her—"

"On Firth Street, Amy? Is that what Jane said? Are you quite certain?"

Amy's brow furrowed again, then cleared. "Why, yes. It is *precisely* what she said."

The candle on the dish beside them began to sputter. Without jostling Amy, Ria reached for another on the table and lighted it before the first went out. She set it carefully in a ball of warm wax, holding it there until it could stand without support. It was not accomplished without difficulty. Her fingers trembled.

Ria watched the play of shivering shadows and light caused by the flickering flame. Could it be true? she wondered. Had she finally come upon a detail that might lead her to Jane? "Firth Street is in London, Amy. Perhaps there are other Firth Streets, but I know there is one in London."

"Then it is good that I remembered?"

"Very good." She gave Amy's shoulder a light squeeze. "Let us see what else you can recall, shall we?"

Although Amy was game, she was unable to produce anything Ria defined as significant. When the little girl began to yawn in earnest, Ria knew she had pressed as much as she dared. She rang for assistance, and Miss Jenny Taylor appeared within moments to escort Amy to her bed.

"Poor dear," Miss Taylor whispered, lifting Amy into the comfortable shelter of her plump arms. "She's worn herself out crying."

Ria nodded. "But she's provided a clue, I think."

"How clever you are, Amy." Miss Taylor's voluptuous figure cushioned the squeeze she delivered. "Off to bed with us, then." Over the top of Amy's dark head, she asked, "Is there anything you require, Miss Ashby?"

"Nothing. I am also for bed. In the morning I shall have to consider whether to go to London myself or send Mr. Lytton in my place."

"London? Is that where this little one says our Jane has gone?" Miss Taylor's bosom rose and fell dramatically in concert with her heavy sigh. "London's terribly big. And Mr. Lytton hasn't been very helpful, has he?"

Both of Miss Taylor's observations were true enough. "Firth Street is not overly long. There cannot be more than a score of shops there and less than half of those are dress-makers. I should think that narrows the possibilities so that even Mr. Lytton can discover something that will satisfy." Ria noted that Miss Taylor remained skeptical. Thus far, Mr. Oliver Lytton had not impressed with his investigative skills. Miss Taylor, in particular, was disappointed with his lack of success. She had been the one to suggest Mr. Lytton when Ria returned from the duke's funeral service and announced her intention to hire someone to find Jane.

"We shall see, Miss Taylor," Ria said. "I have not yet made my decision."

Miss Taylor's smile evinced confidence that Ria would do what was best. "Good night, then, Miss Ashby."

"Good night."

Ria spent the next twenty minutes making notes about the day's activities, in particular the revelations Amy Nash had disclosed following vespers in the chapel. She couldn't be certain what had touched Amy so deeply that the child could no longer keep her silence, but she had started sobbing as soon as they formed the line to file out of the chapel, and none of the usual tricks worked to quiet her.

They had all tried. The board of governors for Miss Weaver's Academy employed three teachers in addition to Ria. They each took a turn at trying to calm Amy. Mrs. Abergast, the most matronly among them, found her advances spurned. Miss Taylor, with her plump arms and ample bosom, was similarly rejected. Even Miss Webster, well known among the girls as the teacher most easily softened by a pitiful smile, found that her own tears could not halt Amy's. It had been left to Ria to bring the thing about.

Ria closed her journal and began making preparations for bed. As headmistress, she was given use of a suite of rooms, none of which was large, but all of which were comfortably appointed. In addition to the bedchamber and adjoining dressing room, she had a sitting room for receiving guests to the school and a study where she could meet privately with teachers and students and make her reports to the board. There was no part of this last that she particularly enjoyed, but she suffered it in order to influence the operation of the academy.

Since Jane Petty's disappearance, Ria thought she had good reason to wonder how long she could expect to continue her employment, at least as headmistress, but the governors continued to evince their support of her management. Not only did they acquit her of responsibility for Jane leaving the school, they seemed to be no more than mildly concerned by the incident. Ria supposed it was the insulating effect of distance that moderated their response. The governors made only the occasional visit to the school, choosing instead to provide oversight of their charitable work from London or their country estates. It had the consequence of giving Ria free rein in many decisions affecting the academy, but provided little in the way of direction when she required such.

The governors had, however, and with nary a dissenting vote, approved her suggestion to hire Mr. Oliver Lytton to investigate Jane's disappearance. It was, perhaps, the most she could hope for in the way of involving them. She understood very well that they were protecting themselves from the possibility of scandal. The very last thing they desired was to find their names connected with something considerably more substantial than a nine days' wonder.

Sighing heavily, Ria dropped to the edge of her bed and began pulling a brush through her pale hair with unenthusiastic strokes. Out of the corner of her eye, she could see her movements reflected in the cheval glass. She avoided looking in that direction. Nothing about her appearance at present inspired confidence, and she could find no purpose in making yet another inventory of all the things that were wrong.

"You look like the very devil."

Ria did not startle immediately. Given the direction her thoughts had just taken, it merely seemed that she had spoken them aloud. A moment was required for comprehending the fact that the voice was very much unlike hers. Her head snapped up, swiveling toward the door in the same motion.

West chuckled at the delay in her response. She put him in mind of a marionette whose strings were being inexpertly pulled. Even as he thought it, he watched her brush fall through nerveless fingers and drop to the bed. He did not mind her staring at him, for it gave him opportunity to return her regard—and he did not like what he saw. She was as insubstantial as a wraith, an observation that could not wholly be accounted for by her white cotton nightdress. It was West's opinion that she had dropped nearly a stone in weight, none of it that she could properly afford to shed. Her face was thin, with the cheekbones achieving an unattractive prominence. Violet shadows beneath her eyes made them appear sunken. Her unbound hair held little luster, in spite of the fact that candlelight from the bedside table washed over it. Perhaps if she had been dressed in the same serviceable bombazine mourning gown she'd worn in London, he might have been fooled into thinking she had some shape to her, but he didn't think so.

"The very devil," he repeated for good measure.

"I quite heard you the first time." Ria snatched up her flannel robe lying at the foot of the bed and threw it around her shoulders.

West stepped fully into the room but did not close the door behind him. "By all means, take time to put it on. It is not very warm in here. I suppose that is because you were preparing to nest under all those covers." Without invitation to do so, he went to the fireplace and added a log. Brushing off his gloves, he turned to her. "That will keep the chill in abeyance until your return."

"My return?" Ria found it more than passing strange that she could offer any speech at all. She felt as if she were running to catch up with him, and her oddly breathless response and racing heartbeat seemed to confirm that this was true. "Where am I going?"

"To your sitting room, I hope." West took off his hat and coat, folded the latter over his arm, then began removing his gloves. "Unless it is your habit to conduct interviews in your bedchamber. That presents a bit of a dilemma for me, though, and surely you must see it. While I am often at the forefront of any movement or protest that will give society's conventions a proper tweaking, I find that as your guardian I cannot support you entertaining gentlemen in such an intimate setting. Furthermore, I cannot even recommend myself as a gentleman. The nutshell of it is this: if you do not remove yourself to the sitting room with due haste, I shall be forced to consider whether I can throw myself out."

Ria wondered that she could be so befuddled, yet know without a doubt that she was *not* dreaming. She could not even find the wherewithal to be affronted or to offer a defense. Rising to her feet, she slipped into the flannel robe, belted it, then made one point for clarification. "You do realize, don't you, that I did not invite you in?"

"You're rather late coming to that. You might have said something when I was still standing in the doorway."

It was difficult to argue that particular objection. "This way," Ria said, extending the invitation she had not made earlier. Taking up the candlestick, she led him back into the sitting room and lighted the candelabra on the mantelpiece. West assumed the duties of bringing the dying flames in the fireplace around to a full blaze. He stood in front of the hearth for some moments, seemingly in contemplation of his handiwork, while Ria placed his coat, hat, and gloves on a rack inside the door. She thought he had no notion any longer that she was in the room, yet the moment she sat on the sofa behind him, he pivoted on his heel to face her. Though he stood several feet away, she still had to look up at an uncomfortable angle.

"Is it your intention to keep the benefits of your labor to yourself?" she asked.

West frowned, trying to comprehend her meaning, then came to the realization that his presence squarely in front of the fire was blocking its heat.

Ria was grateful when he stepped aside. More important than the obstacle he presented to her, the light coming from behind him had thrust his features into deep shadow. When he had announced that she looked like the very devil, it was most definitely the pot calling the kettle black. "Thank you," she said. "Will you not sit? It is preferable to hovering, I think."

The suggestion of a smile played about his mouth. "Preferable for whom?"

"I can own that it is more to my liking."

West looked around and chose the chair with the emerald brocade seat and back and dark walnut trim. It was by far and away the least comfortable of the upholstered offerings, but at this late hour and after so long a journey, West was not desirous of comfort. He would retire to his room at the inn in Gillhollow for his sleep; he had no wish to nod off here.

"Would you like some refreshment?" Ria asked. "I can offer you tea or wine. I have not much else in the way of spirits."

"Nothing, thank you." His eyes narrowed faintly as he regarded her. "You have rather more than your fair share of aplomb, I'm thinking. No hysterics. No demands. Very little in the way of reaction, in fact."

Ria glanced at the mantel clock. It was gone eleven, even later than she had supposed. Little Amy had been swept away to bed more than an hour earlier. It did not seem possible she had stayed awake so long after, writing and making plans. "I will have a fit of the vapors directly if it will hurry your explanation along."

A ghost of a smile flitted across his features, acknowledging her wry riposte. "I do apologize for coming to you at this hour. I would not have let myself in if you had been abed, but I saw you pass in front of your window and knew you were awake."

"You were watching me?"

"Actually, I was observing the school. There must be a dozen ways an enterprising girl can come and go without attracting notice. A lattice is always a suitable ladder if it is sturdy enough. You will be pleased to know your lattices are solidly constructed. Downspouts can be shinnied in either direction if they are secured properly to the masonry. Yours are. There is also an easy exit from the attic windows, across the box gutters to the ladder propped against the east wall."

Ria's lower jaw sagged a fraction. "Roof repairs," she said on a thread of sound. "An ice dam lifted the slate."

"Yes, I thought that might be the way of it. Perhaps you will want to instruct the laborers to remove the ladder when they are finished for the day." He went on, ticking the points off on his fingers. "Inside, the doors swing on well-oiled hinges, which is invariably a good thing when one wishes to move in and out of the school or between rooms. The floors in your corridors do not creak overmuch and the stairs, while noisy in places, offer a wide, polished banister as a neat, speedy alternative. I assume all the windows can be latched, though this is only moderately effective for keeping intruders out. It does nothing to keep your girls in."

While Ria's mouth was no longer agape, her eyes had widened considerably. "It is a *school,* Your Grace, not a gaol. The young ladies here are students, not prisoners."

"Then you don't mind if they leave."

"No. Yes. Of course I mind if they leave unattended or without permission." She waved her hand impatiently. "That is not the point at all. I hope you mean to apprise me of your manner of entering the school."

If she had hoped to make him defensive, she was sadly mistaken. West said easily enough, "I used the front door."

"It was locked."

"It wasn't barred."

"I put the bar in place myself before vespers."

He shrugged. "That is my point, isn't it? A bar works to

deter intruders; it does not present any obstacle at all for the inmates."

"It is a school," she said again, *"not* an asylum. You are pur—" Ria stopped, considered what he was telling her in a different light, and began again. "What are you saying? That the door was no longer barred because someone here removed it?"

"Wasn't I clear?" he asked. "I thought I was clear. Yes. That's what I'm saying. One of your students slipped out the door and met a lad by that stand of beeches not a hundred yards from the school. She did not remain there long, though I should think there were some passionate words exchanged, oh yes, and I saw a note pass between them. You will not credit it, but there was no kissing. I believe your girl was all for it, but the lad had his wits about him and kept her at a distance. I cannot say why he did so, though one supposes he imagines himself in love with her and regards carnal denial as chivalrous. But then," West added, his tone mildly ironic, "I am judged by my friends to be a romantic."

Ria could not rouse sufficient breath just then to call him mad.

"No wind in your sails?" West asked. "Perhaps you would like a glass of wine yourself? You are markedly more peaked than you were moments ago. That does not bode well." He held up one hand to stop her from rising and got to his feet. "I shall get it. Do you keep the wine in the sideboard?"

She nodded.

West poured a half-glass of red wine and carried it to her. "Here. It can do no harm."

Ria had difficulty not draining the glass. "Has she come inside?"

"Your young lady? Yes, she didn't tarry once her beau took his leave." West returned to his chair. "She hurried back, dutifully barred the door, and, I believe, went straightaway to her room. By then I was already inside, so replacing the bar was of no consequence."

"I see." She didn't, not entirely, but it seemed appropriate to report some understanding. It occurred to her that she should inquire as to the identify of her student, though she had a very good idea who it was. "Can you describe the girl? I shall speak to her in the morning."

"Certainly I can describe her, it is just that I have no intention of doing so. No harm has been done, and the boy looked to be a decent enough sort. I don't believe you will have any trouble from that quarter." Especially, West told himself, after he hunted down the lovestruck lad and had a few words with him. "It seems to me that your girl can be spared a lecture."

"Surely that is *my* decision. I am responsible, after all, and her actions had the lamentable consequence of opening the door to you."

"I believe I mentioned there were other means by which I could have entered the school."

"Yes, but at least you might have broken your neck using one of those."

"Aaah," he said. "You would have preferred to find me lying sprawled in the hedgerow at morning light."

"I would have liked it better if you missed the hedgerow."

West laughed outright at that. "You, Miss Ashby, are decidedly coldhearted."

Ria pursed her lips to temper her smile. His easy laughter was its own invitation, and she found it hard not to join him. "It will have been Emma Blakely that you saw," she said. "She has been known to flirt with the village boys." Ria finished her wine and set the glass down. "What brings you to Gillhollow, Your Grace? You were careful to leave me with no expectation that I might depend upon your help, and indeed, I have not."

"That is true."

"Never say you have changed your mind."

"Let us say that what assistance I have determined to offer shall be offered on my terms."

"What do you mean?"

West leaned back, crossing his arms in front of him, the posture both relaxed and watchful. "I have set it in my mind to join the board of governors of Miss Weaver's Academy for Young Ladies."

Chapter Four

"You are serious," Ria said.

"You say that as if exactly the opposite were true. I assure, I *am* serious. The list of governors for the school is impressive. Why should I not lend them my name in this charitable enterprise?"

"My, but you have become full of yourself. And in so short a time. It really does give one pause." To press that point, she paused. "There, it is passed. Goodness, but it is a relief to have that done with."

He cocked one eyebrow. "You are not taken with the idea."

"Your Grace has a happy talent for understatement. I abhor the idea. Loathe it, in fact."

"Pray, do not mince words. You must say precisely what you think."

Ria did smile then, albeit softly and without the passion of humor behind it. "Forgive me. You are generous to tolerate my sharp tongue."

"Now you disappoint, Miss Ashby. It is not in my mind to punish you for speaking yours. Tell me why I should not apply to the board."

"What would be the purpose?" she asked. "You already

enjoy considerable influence as my guardian. Must you hold sway in this aspect of my life as well? Your father was good enough not to interfere in this manner."

With some effort, West let this mention of his father pass. He could not very well encourage her to speak freely in one moment, then press her to be more cautious in the next. "My intention is not to exert my will on you. Am I wrong to suppose that you still desire my assistance? Miss Jane Petty has not returned to the school, has she? The last inquiries I made before leaving London indicated that she had not."

"You made inquiries? How? Of whom?"

"I believe you were the one who pointed out I must not be without connections in the foreign office."

"Yes, but—"

"I applied to them, Miss Ashby, on your behalf. I regret they were of no help in divining Jane's whereabouts, but some use might yet be made of them. What I learned was enough to bring me here."

Ria blinked. She felt strangely weepy of a sudden and hoped she would not embarrass herself or him by crying. "Thank you," she said, working the words past the lump in her throat. "Thank you for that."

"Save your thanks for when I announce I have accomplished something." He tilted his head slightly to one side as he continued to take her measure. "Apart from the control you feared I will inflict upon you, is there some other reason I should not apply to the board?"

"I suppose not, though I don't understand what can be accomplished by it."

"Humor me, Miss Ashby."

"I have not placed a knife at your throat, have I?"

He gave a shout of laughter and ignored her attempt to shush him. When he caught his breath, he said, "That is proof indeed of your charity toward me."

"You must lower your voice. Someone will hear you."

West shrugged. "It is just as well that I am your guardian,

then. We will be acquitted of arranging a tryst in your apartments."

Ria regarded him skeptically. "You are not serious."

"Correct. I am not. But the thing of it is, it is vastly entertaining to watch you try to work it out." West wisely shifted subjects. Ria looked as if she might like to go searching for a blade. "It seems to me that I can be of most assistance by having unrestricted access to the school. While I could use my position as your guardian to do that, it is not a proper fit. I believe it will inspire comment, especially since the former duke did not deign to visit you here."

"He visited." She watched his eyebrow arch and amended her statement. "Once. He visited once."

"Yes. That is what I've heard."

Ria wondered if Tenley was the informant. Tenley would not have shared this information as a kindness. He begrudged his father any time spent with her. "Then you must also know that the governors are not in the habit of coming here."

"But they tour the school."

"Certainly."

"And if they desire to visit, it is an acceptable practice."

"Of course."

"They can come and go if they please."

"Yes."

"Then it will serve nicely as a means of doing all of those things without comment. Now, have off with trying to dissuade me. I have my own reasons for being set on the matter."

"Shouldn't you like to tell me what they are?"

"No."

"But—"

"No," he repeated. "There is no predicting what you would make of them. I have not forgotten that you traveled to London without benefit of escort, armed only with the most improbable notion that I was some sort of spy and the odd conviction that I could lend you assistance."

"Yet here you are."

He gave her a sharp glance. "Because it amuses me. You would do well not to make too much of it beyond that. I found myself at sixes and sevens in London with all of my friends engaged, one of them literally, in their own imbroglios. It seemed good sense to make myself scarce. There is also the matter of acquainting myself with the estate at Ambermede. Tenley is still in residence, and he and I will have to discuss how we mean to go on."

It occurred to Ria for the first time that West had probably never stepped foot inside the manor. As the duke's ward, she had had opportunity to become familiar with the house, while he had not been allowed to cross the threshold. "Will you demand that Tenley leave?"

"No. For now it is his choice if he comes or goes. I have no immediate plans to take up residence beyond a few weeks."

"Then you mean to be a frequent visitor to Gillhollow?"

"Not the village," he said. "But here at the school. I plan to visit Mr. Beckwith at Sunbury first and express an interest in the academy. I understand he is there now, settling in for the winter. It is not so far. We shall see how that goes."

"I do not believe you will find him so overcome by the honor of your visit that he will invite you to join the board."

"Perhaps he has not heard that I am no longer a bastard."

"I do not believe there is a person in all of England who has not heard the story of the duke naming you his true son and heir." She paused. "Oh, I see, you were making light of it."

"I was." West's green glance fell on the small smile that hovered on her lips. She had a sweetly generous mouth that demanded attention be paid to it. West was inclined to give it its due. "I think Mr. Beckwith will hear me out and mayhap be persuaded to accommodate me." He saw that Ria remained unconvinced. "Am I so objectionable, then?"

"No," she said hastily. "That is, I do not think so. It is only that as a group the governors are singularly insular."

"Really?" West was confident that Ria knew next to nothing about the men who governed Miss Weaver's Academy—

nothing, that is, but the face they put before the public. "How do you mean?"

"Well, the school is a very old institution," she said. "It was founded in 1725 by a group of London gentlemen who were forward in their thinking about the education of females. The governors today are largely comprised of the third and fourth generation of those founders. This social responsibility has been passed on as a legacy to the sons, their sons, and their grandsons. So it goes. Your father's family was not part of that tradition. That is why I do not think they will welcome you into their fold."

"You may be right. I will allow it presents a challenge, but I am not unaccustomed to standing at the bakery window with my nose to the glass. If there is a sweet I desire, I usually find my way inside."

"As you did tonight." Ria flushed as she realized how her words might be interpreted, and her eyes slid away. "I did not mean . . . that is . . ."

"You did not mean that you are the sweet? Is that what you are trying to take back?" He chuckled deeply at the back of his throat, the sound of it perfectly wicked. "You are blushing, Miss Ashby, and it suits, for you are far too pale without it. However, your discomfort is so palpable that even I cannot continue to tease you at this juncture. In the future I hope you will take yourself in hand, else you will prove to be tedious company."

Her chin came up and she glared at him.

"Oh, you have rallied nicely. Very well done."

"You are incorrigible."

"That is the considered opinion of those who know me well."

"My, and I have arrived at the same conclusion after only a short acquaintance. I *am* clever."

West grinned. "Now you most definitely have your feet under you, Miss Ashby." He leaned forward and set his elbows on his knees. "Enough about the governors. Tell me about that fellow you hired . . . Mr. Lytton, I believe is his name . . . I understand he has not yet proved his worth."

Ria shook her head, no longer in surprise that he knew what he did, but simply as a response to his statement. "It is true that he has been a disappointment. I was hopeful at first, but there is nothing he has been able to discover on his own."

West was compelled to point out, "There may be nothing anyone can discover. You must admit to that possibility. Miss Petty might be lost to you."

"I have considered it," Ria said, though she was loath to admit she had lost faith, however briefly. "But this very evening, Amy came forward and has told a story which holds out some promise."

Glancing sideways at the clock, West realized he had kept Ria from her bed far longer than was his intention. He had no regrets about coming to the school straightaway, but he had meant only to have a look at the lay of the land, then retire to the inn. Miss Emma Blakely's departure from the house had inspired him to step inside for no other reason than to prove that he could, then demonstrate the same to Ria. He had overstayed a welcome that was only grudgingly given in the first place, and now she was teasing him with this tidbit of information from someone named Amy as artlessly as Eve had tempted Adam with the apple.

West did not try to resist. He bit down hard. "Who is Amy?"

"Miss Amy Nash. She is also a student."

"Of an age with Miss Petty?"

"Amy is eight."

West was disappointed but careful not to show it. Ria obviously considered the girl a reliable informer, and he did not disabuse her of that notion. "Amy knows where Miss Petty is?"

Ria shook her head and began to relate what Amy told her. West listened patiently to the story without interruption. When Ria concluded with Amy's disclosure of the dressmaker on Firth Street, West merely nodded.

"Are you not encouraged?" asked Ria when West made no comment.

"It is something worth investigating, but it does not warrant so much enthusiasm."

Since Ria thought she had offered a carefully tempered explanation of events, West's comment stung. "I am aware it may come to nothing."

"It was not my intention to dash your hopes, merely to maintain perspective. Your information is from someone who, unlike Miss Petty, may properly be called a child. I have not the experience you have with them, but from having been one myself, I know something about the lack of reliability."

"Amy is not a liar."

"I did not say she was. It is likely she believes the few details she told you and no doubt has spent weeks guiltily reviewing Jane's conversation with her. I should not be surprised if she has convinced herself of particulars that were never shared between them. It is just as well she could provide no description of Jane's proper gentleman, because it would be of little use."

"I had already thought of that," Ria said quietly. "What is to be done?"

"I will question her myself tomorrow. That is the first thing. If she tells me Jane has gone to Gretna we shall know how suggestible she is. You planted that seed with her."

"Then I should not have mentioned it?"

West shrugged. "We shall see."

"And what of the dressmaker's?"

"You will provide a description of Jane as well as a decent sketch of her. Perhaps there is a portrait of her already? A locket?"

Ria shook her head. "No. Jane had nothing like that. But Miss Taylor teaches watercolors and is credited to be our best artist. I believe she gave Mr. Lytton a sketch such as you want. I shall have her prepare another."

"Have her prepare two . . . and the same number of descriptions also. I will send one of each to London and keep the others."

"Then you will not be going to Firth Street yourself?"

"Miss Ashby, I have only just arrived here. I cannot traipse all over England in pursuit of every lead. Besides, other than presenting the portrait to every dressmaker on the street, I haven't the least idea how to go about it. I told you I was a clerk. I have no training in the subtleties that this work requires. I suspect that interviewing your eight-year-old student will tax my abilities. You must allow me to use my connections instead." West's grin surfaced briefly as he considered how eagerly the colonel would embrace this opportunity to assist him. The boot was on the other foot, as it were. While it happened on occasion that one of the Compass Club was in Dutch with the colonel, it was not at all the usual thing for the colonel to be in Dutch with one of his own men. West thought there was little Blackwood would not do to extricate himself from that uncomfortable position. In hindsight, discovering the colonel had met regularly with the old duke was proving to be more help than hurt.

"Something amuses you?" Ria asked, watching West's smile flicker across his face. The deep dimple came and went, teasing her. She tried not to stare but felt rather like a moth to the flame each time it appeared. "I confess, I can find nothing—"

West held up one hand. "It is a wayward thought that amuses. I apologize for the poor timing of it."

Ria knew herself to be disarmed again. It troubled her that he had accomplished the thing so effortlessly. It seemed that it was not always necessary for him to brandish his weapon. "When will you arrive on the morrow?"

Her question was, in effect, a dismissal. West rose from his chair and stood, feet planted slightly apart, hands clasped at his back. "If it is convenient, I should like to come before the noon hour."

"That will be fine." Ria also rose. "Will you take your luncheon with us?"

West tried to imagine eating a meal surrounded by dozens of young ladies, three female teachers, and their headmistress. He could not. "Perhaps another time."

"The governors do, you know. When they visit, either individually or together, they always sit at the head table for a meal. All of them have lived to tell the tale."

Recognizing a challenge when he heard it, West raised one brow. "You think I'm afraid."

"You blanched, Your Grace."

He grunted softly, acknowledging her dry riposte. "Very well, I shall join you, Miss Ashby."

"Oh, bravo! You do credit to all the scriveners in the foreign office by showing this measure of backbone."

Ria did not know she had gone too far until West closed the distance between them in a single, silent stride. His hands caught her at the waist and drew her sharply toward him. When her head fell back, he adjusted quickly, cupping it in one of his palms while his other arm circled her back and closed the embrace. Her face was very near his own, her lips but a hairsbreadth from his. When he spoke, his breath tickled her mouth.

"And what of your backbone, Ria? Will you not show it to me now?"

Without conscious thought, she stiffened a little. She had known instinctively what he meant. He was not daring her to resist him, but daring her not to. To that end she held herself very still and let her heavy lashes flutter closed.

The touch of his mouth was light, without real pressure at first. She felt it at the corner of her lips, then sliding over them. The contact was warm, slightly humid, and firmness was slowly applied. Her own mouth parted in response. Her reward was the damp edge of his tongue tracing the opening.

Ria's hands hung at her sides, and she did not lift them to mirror his embrace. It was not fear of what he would do if she reciprocated in kind, but fear of what she might allow. He was right to suspect that she trusted him, but not herself.

West lifted his head and drew back slowly. He held her steady, the fingers of one hand threaded in her silky hair while the other hand was splayed against her back. She was not trembling, but neither was she entirely steady on her feet. Her response had been something more than sweetly innocent. It held the promise of real passion at the end of a surprisingly short tether.

He smiled, the curve of his mouth perfectly wicked now, and bent his head quickly to kiss her again. This time her body came flush to his without any encouragement. His hands and fingers did not tighten their grip, nor did they move for better purchase. She was the one who reached for him, digging into the shoulders of his frock coat with her fingertips and holding on with the tenacity of a limpet. Her sumptuous mouth fitted itself to his as she pressed herself against him. It was no wraith that he held but a woman as light and supple as a sapling.

West pressed his advantage and deepened the kiss. His tongue made a sweep of her upper lip, dipping along the honeyed underside, then sliding across the ridge of her teeth. She bit him very lightly and all the blood in his head pooled suddenly in his groin. He felt her jerk in response to this pressure against her taut belly but she fit herself to him again once she understood the nature of it.

West set her firmly from him this time and did not attempt to steady her. "I cannot tell if it is too much courage or foolishness that you possess, but you can trust me not to toss down the gauntlet a second time."

She blinked at him, her equilibrium too strained to hide that he had wounded her. "By all means," she said with credible dignity, "I shall depend upon you to demonstrate good sense and a cool head. As your ward, it is only proper that I defer to your better judgment."

"A direct hit, Miss Ashby." In point of fact, the blow was so low and barbed so sharply that West felt his tumescence shrivel. There was a lesson here for him as well. "I most humbly beg your pardon." Without waiting to hear if she would accept his apology, West took up his coat, hat, and gloves and exited the room. He paused just once on the other side of the threshold to remind her to bar the door after him, then he was gone.

The inn at Gillhollow was not without certain creature comforts, one of whom crawled into West's bed in the middle of the night and wrapped herself around him. He allowed her to pleasure him with her mouth and hands, then reciprocated in kind, but would not mount her. This refusal nettled his companion, for she made no secret that she wanted a stiff, hard one in her pocket. Still, West was of no mind to explain that it was not his habit to risk populating this shire, or any other, with his bastards. In the end she flounced from the room, and he did not begrudge her lifting the coin lying at his bedside. Her technique was smooth, but she was no adept like himself.

His valet woke him at the agreed-upon hour and West cursed several times without any real feeling for doing so. As was Finch's way, he suffered this in silence, having accepted long ago that this cross nature in the morning was his own cross to bear.

"Will you want another night's lodging here?" Finch asked. He wiped West's neck and chin clean of shaving lather and scrutinized his handiwork for the stray nick.

West removed the towel from around his neck and handed it to Finch. "You have not sliced my throat, have you?"

"As always, I resist the temptation."

"Good man." West stood and picked up his frock coat. "We will not be staying here tonight. I think I prefer to go to Ambermede. You will inform Beedle and the tiger that we will be leaving Gillhollow, most likely at nightfall. I will take my mount out to the school. I have not yet decided if my ward will accompany us, but you should anticipate that she will and plan accordingly."

Finch did not indicate by so much as the flicker of an eyelash that he was in any way rattled. "Of course. I shall fetch the leg irons directly."

West shot his valet a sideways look. "I was thinking more that you would arrange the luggage so that hers might easily be accommodated." He paused. "But I find your idea about leg irons inspiring and will let you know if such will be required."

"As Your Grace wishes."

West could detect no hint of amusement in his man's dry delivery, but he did not think he was wrong that it was there. "You continue to surprise, Finch."

"Oh, I hope that is not so. It is my aim to be in every way reliable. Surprise does not suit, for it means I have failed to impress on some earlier occasion."

Two deep, vertical creases furrowed the space between West's eyebrows. He stopped shrugging into his coat and regarded the portly figure of his valet with some suspicion. "One of them has put you up to this," he said slowly. "That's it, isn't it? One of them is playing puppeteer to your marionette."

"I cannot think what Your Grace means."

West's expression cleared as he realized the truth of it. He gave a shout of laughter. "Your denial will not serve, Finch. I have not imagined the fine note of impertinence in your tone since I inherited this damnable title. It was most decidedly lacking when I was Mr. Evan Marchman. I absolve you of coming to it on your own, not because you wouldn't think it, but because you wouldn't express it aloud. Now, which one of them is paying you to needle me proper?"

"I couldn't say, Your Grace."

"No, I suppose you can't. Perhaps if I hazard a guess, you will give me a sign. A nod. A wink."

Finch cleared his throat and offered in the same arid tones that he had made all his other observations, "I am certain you would not want me to wink."

"No, you are quite right about that. A nod will do, then."

The valet nodded.

"Is it Northam?" When there was no response from Finch, West amended his thoughts. "No, perhaps he has become too priggish for tricks of this nature. What about Eastlyn?" Again, no answering nod. "Well, he is squirming in his own damnable coil, so it may be that he has empathy for mine. That leaves South. He has wrung extensive enjoyment from watching me swing at the end of the old duke's gibbet." Neither of Finch's chins lifted by a fraction. "Is it none of them or only that you do not intend to respond?"

This time Finch nodded hard.

West threw up his hands, though he was not clear whether it was done in frustration or surrender. If it was the latter, it was only temporary. "I will find out, Finch. Until then, you should carry on. I am certain you are being well paid for your trouble."

"It is no trouble," Finch said. "Of all the queer ideas quality gets from time to time, this is one of the better ones."

West actually rolled his eyes as he picked up his hat. "Good day, Finch." He left quickly, somewhat surprised he had managed to have the final word.

Miss Weaver's Academy for Young Ladies was an imposing gray stone manor some two miles distant of the village. The sylvan setting was pleasant enough in the spring and full summer with slim silver beeches, mature chestnuts, oaks, and tall pines dotting the perimeter of the open acreage around the school, but in the winter it was a rather bleak edifice. A groundskeeper kept the hedgerow trim and a small flock of sheep did the same for the lawn. Those sheep poked lazily on the edge of the semicircular driveway looking for spots of grass in the snow as West approached on his mount. A few lifted their woolly heads and bleated dolefully, most did not. The groundskeeper paused in sweeping clumps of wet snow from the hedge and doffed his hat, recognizing in West a person of some consequence.

In the light of this day, West had a better view of the out-buildings from Draco's back. He steered his Arabian stallion away from the crushed-stone drive and toward the east side of the school. The ladder was still leaning against the build-ing, but it was in use now, and Draco shied as icicles and pieces of slate fell from the roof and shattered on the ground near his hooves. West quickly drew the stallion away from the site and waved off the apologies of the two laborers on the rooftop.

Rounding the school, he saw that the carriage house and stable were both larger than had been his impression the night before. He wondered how many people were employed in addition to the teachers and groundskeeper. There must be grooms and drivers, maids and a housekeeper, a first and second cook and two or three helpers besides. The girls themselves were probably assigned various tasks, but West could not imagine they scrubbed floors or emptied chamber pots.

West rode out to the stable and paddock and saw no prime flesh among the cattle, but no nags, either. Further afield, there were cows huddled around bales of hay that had been placed there for them. Chickens dashed from the coop into the yard as Draco passed. The tips of their fluttering wings stirred up eddies of snow, and they rushed the fence in antic-ipation of a proper feeding.

West guided Draco around the school and dismounted at the front entrance. A groom appeared to take his horse and West noted this was no young man who had the responsibil-ity, but a fellow some thirty years his senior with stooped shoulders and a friendly smile that revealed several missing teeth. West grinned himself. It made sense that the school would not employ temptation in the guise of strong, strap-ping lads in the first awkward stages of manhood. That would have surely led to more elopements than Miss Jane Petty's.

Taking the steps two at a time, West found the door opened to him before he reached it. A woman wearing a white mobcap and apron stepped forward and bobbed a curtsy. There were hints in her flickering, uncertain smile and darting glance that she was tempering the warm welcome she typically extended to visitors. West suspected that she feared effusiveness would not be appreciated and was striving for something more dignified. He obliged her assumption by offering his chilliest smile, the one that Southerton said could halt a glacier's advance.

"Miss Ashby is expecting Your Grace." She accepted his hat and coat and moderated her tendency to shift nervously from one foot to the other while he removed his gloves. "This way. I will take you."

West thought the housekeeper would escort him to Ria's suite, and he almost made the error of turning in the direction of the stairs. He caught himself, pretending to take a moment to study one of the portraits in the main hall. "This is one of the founders of the school?" he asked.

Mrs. Oldham paused in her step and turned to draw near. "Yes, that is Sir Anthony Beckwith."

"Beckwith." West repeated the name softly. "Would he be a relation of the same Beckwith who now is one of the governors?"

"Indeed. You mean Mr. Jonathan Beckwith."

"Yes. He resides in Sunbury, I believe."

"That's right, at least half the year he takes his residence there. Sir Anthony was his uncle, though several generations separate them, to be sure."

"To be sure." West regarded the portrait a moment longer. Sir Anthony was a very cold fish, with eyes as lifeless. The man's expression was severely constrained. One could easily imagine he had posed with clenched teeth. "Is there a resemblance to Mr. Beckwith?"

The housekeeper considered that. "Only about the eyes and mouth."

Bloody hell, West thought. It would be a cheerless interview with that man. He turned away, but not before glancing at the other portraits lining the hall. It seemed to him that every one of the academy's governors had sat at least once before an artist's easel. As the housekeeper led him forward, he spied what he surely supposed was Jonathan Beckwith. He was posed similarly to his founding ancestor, against a stately marble column, his countenance severely and self-importantly drawn. If the man had been panicked, West could have better understood that emotion. It was akin to what he felt as he was escorted to the large dining room where twenty-nine girls stood in response to his appearance on the threshold. At the head table, Ria and three teachers also rose to their feet and the hall fell absolutely silent.

West could not help but be put in mind of dining at the great tables at Hambrick. He could recall occasions when they had been visited by dignitaries and friends to the school, and how those visits had inspired awe and more than a little fear that one would split the silence with a belch or giggle, or worse, by breaking wind. It was difficult to suppress his laughter at the thought of it.

He mustered dignity enough for the assembly and inclined his head toward Ria. "Miss Ashby," he said. "It is good of you to invite me."

Ria quickly left the table and came to the door, dropping a graceful curtsy in front of him. Behind her, all the others immediately did the same. "The honor is ours. We are very pleased to have you visit our humble school."

Butter wouldn't melt in her mouth, he decided. He could detect no hint that she was saying the words but remembering his late visit to her rooms. There was no blush to suggest that she was thinking of their kiss. He could admit that her self-possession piqued him. "The pleasure is mine."

Ria led him to the head table and introduced him to Mrs. Abergast, and the misses Taylor and Webster; then she turned and made a formal announcement to the girls. "Will you not say something to them?" she asked. "I am certain they will appreciate such advice as you are prepared to give them."

"And I am certain they will not," he said under his breath. So this was how she meant to take her pound of flesh. It was brilliant, really, a completely admirable strategy. He would do well not to underestimate her. "But I shall endeavor to impress." West did not miss the flash of uncertainty in her eyes as she began to consider what he might actually say to her girls. North's grandfather had a series of lectures prepared for such occasions, and West had heard them all at one time or another. He wondered if he should give the one on the unfortunate consequences of sowing one's wild oats or the responsibilities of a woman to her husband.

West offered a restrained smile as his glance moved smoothly to the students at all three oaken tables. They stared back politely, just as he had at Hambrick, but he knew that they were counting the seconds until they might sit. "Ladies, it is my experience that a luncheon postponed is a luncheon grown cold, and no one is the better for it. Please, won't you be seated and enjoy your repast?"

The girls dropped to their benches with such alacrity that West's restraint was sorely tested. He lost the battle with himself and his bland smile became a boyish, light-hearted grin. The deep dimple appeared, along with its less showy twin, and somewhere among the girls a spoon clattered to the stone floor and a whisper campaign began. Most of them had opportunity to glimpse that roguish smile before West reined it in.

Beside him, Ria sighed.

"What?" he asked, taking his seat.

"You have no idea of the havoc you have wrought."

West picked up his spoon and dipped it into the steaming lentil soup. "With no time to prepare, you cannot have expected a more erudite speech. What it lacked in pomposity, it acquired in pithiness."

Ria smiled evenly when she noticed that Miss Taylor was watching her with some concern, and lowered her voice so she could not be overheard. "I was not referring to your speech."

"Oh, then what?"

"Did you have to look at them in that particular manner?"

"In what manner?"

"Grinning as if you had swallowed the sun."

He flashed her that same smile but asked, "You would rather I had glowered at them?"

"Infinitely preferable," she said tersely, forcing her own sweet smile to the forefront.

West considered this as he took another spoonful of soup. "Perhaps when I am one of the governors, you will explain your thinking to me. I admit I find your methods peculiar. I have not seen you glower." He chuckled quietly as she suppressed the desire to fix him with her angry stare. She was caught neatly between the devil and the deep blue sea, unable to vent her frustration without alarming her fellow teachers or her students. "The soup is excellent," he said. "You know what they say about a luncheon postponed."

"I know what *you* said."

"It is gratifying to know you were listening. Tell me, how do you think my birth-out-of-wedlock speech would have been received?"

After the meal, West and Ria retired to her study. He held the door open for her and allowed her to pass before him. "Are you certain you are feeling quite the thing?" he asked. "I thought you would strangle on that mouthful of soup."

She could cheerfully strangle *him*. His seemingly artless question had caused her to aspirate a spoonful of broth and cost her the pleasure of drawing a single breath. She had choked and wheezed and gasped, stuffing her serviette against her mouth to keep from spraying the table, all the while having to suffer the flat of his hand on her back, thumping her as if she were an infant in need of burping. The dining hall had fallen silent again, except for the gurgling that rose from the back of her throat. West had taken it upon himself to assure everyone that she would be fine, never once pausing in the application of steady percussion to her back.

"You beat me like a kettledrum," she said.

"An efficacious remedy and I make no apology for it. I may have saved your life."

Ria's sour look told him more eloquently than words what she thought of that. There was no time to point out that he had been the cause of her choking fit in the first place as she heard Amy Nash's distinctly pitched voice in the corridor. "Mrs. Abergast is bringing Amy now," she said. "Will you want me to leave while you speak to her?"

"No, I think she will be more comfortable if you are present, but I require that you say very little. I do not want the child looking to you for answers or being influenced to respond as she thinks you want her to." He looked around the room and saw a well-worn reading chair in one corner. "If you will sit there when we begin, I think it will do. Amy and I will sit here." He pointed to the chair behind her desk and the one opposite it.

Ria offered no advice about this arrangement, though she thought it was unlikely that Amy would be comfortable with West asking her questions from across the desk. "Here she is." Ria turned smoothly and invited Amy inside. "There is nothing else, Mrs. Abergast. I will send for you if I need you."

The teacher nodded once, accepting her dismissal, and hurried away.

Ria started to take the girl's hand, but she caught West's quick, negative shake of his head and resisted the urge. She made introductions again and watched in some amazement as West made a courtly bow and lifted Amy's hand to his lips. The child was immediately in his thrall, and Ria had the honesty to admit it was not so different for her. Excusing herself quietly, she slipped to the corner of the room. Amy, she noticed, did not glance once in her direction.

"Come, child, will you not sit down?" asked West. "Or shall I play the frog for you?" He dropped immediately to his haunches and met Amy at eye level. "I confess it is deuced uncomfortable. Will you not have some pity and take Miss Ashby's chair behind the desk?"

Giggling, Amy accepted this direction. She skirted the desk and climbed onto the Queen Anne chair. With its decorative carved shell on the top rail, gracefully curved splat, and ball-and-claw feet, it required little imagination before it became a throne. Once she was situated on the horseshoe-shaped seat, her mien was condescension itself.

"May I?" West asked, indicating the chair at his back.

"Please," Amy said, inclining her head just so.

The child was the equal of the great Mrs. Siddons, West thought as he took his place. In fact, she may have been able to teach that actress something about embodying a role. "I understand that you requested my presence so that you might tell me about Jane's disappearance. Is that correct?"

"Yes, it is." Amy's voice was properly grave, and she kept her hands folded neatly on the edge of the desk. "Shall I begin, then?"

"By all means."

Nodding once, Amy launched into her account of everything Jane had confided. When she was finished, she regarded West expectantly. "Shall you find her now?"

"Is it your command that I do so?"

"Yes. Yes, it is."

"Then I can hardly refuse to begin the search," he said. "But I cannot promise that it will be resolved quickly."

Adopting the royal *we*, Amy said, "We are nothing if not patient."

"That is gratifying to hear." Keeping his tone one of polite interest, he asked, "What can you tell me about the gentleman's means of transportation? Jane told you he promised to take her to Firth Street. How do think he meant to get her there?"

"By carriage, of course."

"Not horseback?"

Amy shook her head. "Jane does not ride. She is afraid of horses."

"I see. Then you do not know if her gentleman had a carriage, only that she would not ride to London on horseback."

"I know he has a carriage. Jane said he would wait for her at it." Amy seemed to hear herself say this last and was properly abashed. Beneath the desk, her legs began to swing. "I did not say so before, did I?"

"Your Highness has many things to occupy her mind. She cannot be expected to remember every detail all at once."

Amy's legs slowed and finally stopped. "That is true."

West continued questioning Amy for twenty minutes before he judged she was grown weary of it. By carefully maintaining a manner of neutrality, he had been able to gather more in the way of particulars than Ria had the night before. More importantly, Amy had not once mentioned Gretna Green. To West, it was a good sign that she was no more susceptible to suggestion than any other child might be.

When Ria returned from escorting Amy back to the classroom, West had moved from her study to the sitting room and was in a partial recline on the sofa. "It is not your intention to sleep here, I hope."

He roused himself enough to open one eye. She was standing over him, legs stiffly planted, arms slightly akimbo, every inch of her the headmistress. "I was rather late retiring last evening." He closed the eye and placed his forearm across both of them for good measure. If he was being strictly honest with himself, this was done in aid of hiding from her flinty blue-gray stare. He had been wrestling with a vague sense of having been unfaithful to her since the serving wench had crawled into his bed, though why it should be so was not immediately apparent to him.

It was not as if he owed her fidelity. They had shared nothing beyond a wicked kiss. Even Ria, with her genteel sense of what was correct, could not fault him for taking advantage. And was he not two-and-thirty and unattached?

Certainly of an age and circumstance where he might enjoy a woman at his leisure without fear of repercussion.

What he owed Miss Ria Ashby, according to the lady herself, was a quarterly allowance. He had discharged that responsibility by seeking out the solicitor to make certain it continued without disruption. Now he was here, offering his assistance when he was not obligated to do so, and she had not done much more than upbraid him for announcing himself without notice, scold him for trespassing, reproach him for winning favor with her students, and now wanted to deny him a few moments of well-earned respite.

Except for that appealing kiss, she was singularly ungrateful.

"Are you asleep?" Ria nudged West's shoulder with her fingertips. "You are not sleeping. You cannot have fallen asleep so quickly."

"Not with a magpie chattering so sweetly in my ear." He let his arm fall away and pushed himself upright. "You do not mean to stand there, do you, hovering like a hummingbird?"

"You are mixing it up badly. I cannot be both magpie and hummingbird."

West gave her a crossways look that put her firmly in the nearest chair, then he was all for the task at hand. "How did you find Amy's recitation? Is it your opinion that she did her best to remember accurately?"

"Oh, yes. She was very forthcoming, I thought. You made it almost effortless for her, treading as lightly as you did. I confess, I did not realize you would suggest that she sit in my chair. She seemed to think she was controlling the interview."

"She was. I merely posed questions that followed the weave of her story."

He did more than that, Ria thought, though she could not clearly identify what it was. He had managed to engage young Amy within moments of meeting her, not as a friend her own age might, but as an adult who might be depended upon. It was skillfully done, and watching him from the back of the room, Ria had been filled with admiration. "And her answers?" asked Ria. "They will be helpful to you?"

"I think so, yes. The carriage, in particular, was useful."

"How? The description Jane provided Amy was unexceptional. There must be a score of well-sprung carriages in this part of England with brass fittings and plump leather squabs. As one approaches London, the number will be multiplied tenfold. You probably traveled to Gillhollow in such a conveyance."

West did not deny it, though she was wrong about the springs. They were too stiff to be accommodating on the rutted roads, and he had elected to ride alongside the carriage for most of the distance. "You are missing what is salient," he told her. "Jane's description suggests that she had ridden in the carriage at one time. Else how would she know if it were well-sprung? The brass fittings she could view from the outside, but the squabs? How would she know if they were plump if she had not rested her head against one? Of course it would be very neat if Jane had recounted the details of a family crest on the carriage door to Amy, but I doubt there was any such brand upon it. Therefore, we must endeavor to examine what we have been given."

West made a steeple of his fingers and tapped the pads of his thumbs together as he thought. "What opportunities were there for Miss Petty to enjoy a carriage ride?"

Ria considered this for a time before she answered. She did not know that her lush mouth had flattened or that a crease had appeared between her brows. When a tendril of silky hair fell forward at her temple and she worried the inside of her cheek, she looked as young as Amy. "She has ridden in the school's carriages, naturally, but they have always been accounted for. Neither of them is particularly comfortable, but there you have her point of reference." Ria shook her head and batted back the wayward lock of hair impatiently. "I cannot think of a single opportunity she had to ride in a better appointed conveyance. We closely supervise our students. It is the sort of thing that would have been noted by one of the teachers or reported directly by the other girls."

"As I noted Miss Emma Blakely's elopement last night?" he asked wryly. "Or as Amy reported directly?"

Flushing at the soft rebuke, it was all Ria could do to hold West's steady gaze. His green eyes were not accusing, but neither was this a tease. "You are right, of course. There must have been many opportunities of which I am unaware."

"Do not whip yourself for it," he said, a smile touching his eyes now. "You are hopelessly outnumbered by them. What one girl does not think of, another will, and when they join forces in pairs or threes or fours, it is only by experiencing a most damnable run of bad luck that they will not outwit you."

Ria held up one hand, palm out. "You must stop," she said, striving for firmness. "Else I will be forced to resign my position immediately. I wonder that I ever considered myself competent to take it."

"Madness," West said succinctly. "The explanation lies there."

Ria felt the corners of her mouth lift. How was it that he could chide her for her naiveté in one moment, then take the sting from it in the next? It was somewhat humbling to realize she was as pliable in his hands as Amy Nash, but she could hardly lay the fault for it at his door.

"Tell me about Jane," he said. "Have you the sketches I asked for?"

"Yes, and the descriptions also." She rose and went to the adjoining study to retrieve them. "I think you will find them satisfactory," she said, handing them over. Her fingers brushed his as the papers passed between them. There was heat in that touch, but she suffered it so that she would not appear cowardly. She could not say if it was the same for him, only that he did not pull back, either.

West skimmed the written description, then studied the skillfully rendered watercolor portrait. "Is it a good likeness?" he asked.

"I think so." Ria perched on the edge of her chair and smoothed the folds of her gown over her knees. She had chosen a dark-gray day dress with lace edging at the scooped neck and hem. It was serviceable, and satisfied her desire for plain, simple lines. In observance of mourning, she wore a wide black band on the upper sleeve of her right arm and covered her shoulders with a black, fine woolen shawl. "She is very pretty, as you can see."

West nodded. "It is perhaps what brought her to the gentleman's notice." Jane Petty's likeness stared back at him and he felt the pull of the girl's leaf-green eyes. Here was a hint of mischief. She had a clear complexion, if he was to believe Miss Taylor's painting. No spots marred her fair skin. Her hair was a dark honey-brown, cut short, and curled forward to frame her heart-shaped face. In the portrait she wore a green ribbon hair band the same shade as her eyes. It was a loving detail supplied by the artist that West knew would distract someone looking at the watercolor for the first time. It was doubtful Jane was wearing that hair ribbon any longer, or even that she had worn it when she disappeared.

"What about her family?" he asked, putting the papers to one side. "You have said nothing about them."

"Because there is nothing to say. She has none. Jane is one of the school's charity students. She was plucked from a London workhouse when she was Amy's age, and brought here."

"Plucked?" West's glance narrowed a fraction. "Plucked how? By whom?"

"I should have to look at the records, but I think it was Lord Herndon—he has a seat on the board—who found her and thought she showed promise. He sent her here. That was before I joined the school, but I can check my facts if you wish."

"I most definitely do wish."

Ria heard something in his tone that prickled the back of her neck. "Why?" she asked. "What is it you think you know?"

West was a long time in answering, weighing the consequences of doing so. "Let me ask you a question first, Miss Ashby," he said slowly. "What do you know of the Society of Bishops?"

Chapter Five

"The Society of Bishops?" Ria repeated. "It is not familiar in the least. Are they clerics?"

West laughed at that, though without genuine humor. "Hardly, though they have been known to demonstrate a certain religious fervor." He glanced at the clock and saw there was time enough to relate his information, though perhaps not with a guarantee of privacy. "I wonder if you would be willing to accompany me to Ambermede in exchange for particulars regarding the bishops."

"Accompany you?" She could not have been more surprised. "To the manor? Whatever for?"

"You ask a great many questions at once, you know, but the answers are yes, yes, and because I wish it."

"Well, as long as you wish it, then I must hold my objections, mustn't I?"

West winced a bit, knowing this softly spoken statement was but a precursor to illuminating every one of the reasons she must not join him. Before he could inject his plea that she should restrain herself, she was already off the leash. He took some solace from the fact that she did not nip and yip at him. She made her argument to the logic of the thing, not the emotion. When she had finished, he nodded once, then asked, "Will an hour be long enough for you to collect your things?"

In the end it didn't matter but that he would have his way. Ria had been able to fashion a compromise in which she was allowed to have an hour and one-half to pack her portmanteau and valise and an additional hour to set her house in order. The latter involved meeting with her teachers, placing Mrs. Abergast in charge temporarily, and dividing her responsibilities for instructing geography and history among them. She left drafts to pay the laborers for the roof repairs and, in the event Mr. Oliver Lytton made an appearance, specific directions that he should leave immediately for London to investigate the leads Amy provided.

She had been in favor of dismissing the man, but when she mentioned it to West, he had been adamantly opposed. It was yet another thing she conceded to him without knowing the why of it, but not before she had wrested a 200-pound-per-annum increase in her allowance.

West returned with the carriage remarkably close to the appointed time, given the onset of darkness and the poorly maintained road between Gillhollow and the school. Snow had also begun to fall, and the graying, bulging underbellies of the clouds promised it would not remain a light scattering for long.

Ria's bags were secured to the roof of the carriage, and West's mount was tethered at the rear. The liveried groom offered Ria and West rugs for warmth, then took his seat beside the driver. The carriage rolled slowly at first, then with more speed as its own momentum carried it forward.

Inside, Ria tucked one of the rugs around her while West fiddled with the lantern so it would remain securely on its hook. When he was done he sat back and propped his feet on the bench opposite him, which put the heels of his boots just beside Ria. She glanced at them pointedly, but said nothing, and he did not remove them. He was not the sort of man one took to task for these lapses, she realized, though he did not seem to mind when she tried. On the contrary, it appeared he found her censure mildly amusing and gave it no more due than he would if she'd told him his stock was askew.

"You are staring at me," she said. "Has no one told you it is rude?"

"Everyone, in fact, has told me."

She raised one gloved hand quickly to her mouth to cover her smile.

"Why do you do that?" he asked.

Ria's blue-gray eyes widened above her hand as she spoke from behind it. "What?"

"Cover your smile. Why do you try to hide the fact that I make you smile—or dare I say it?—sometimes even make you laugh?"

His observation sobered her, and she lowered her hand to her lap. "I think it best not to encourage you."

"Why not? If you are of a temperament that appreciates humor, then why do you not seek more of it? You really should be encouraging me, instead of the opposite."

"You have never seemed to require any encouragement," she said. "Surely it is my prerogative to withhold it."

West ignored that. "Is it because laughter is an intimacy?"

Ria gave a small start that could not properly be blamed on the jouncing carriage. "I don't know what you mean." But she did, and he most likely knew it. In fact, he had nailed the thing perfectly, and she did not thank him for it.

"You have never impressed as thick-witted—endeavor not to do so now."

"We are not moving so fast that I cannot jump without fear of injury," she said, "nor so far from the school that I cannot walk back to it. You have never impressed as insufferable—endeavor not to do so now."

West used his index finger to raise the brim of his beaver hat a fraction so he might better observe her. Her equanimity had been sorely tested, but she was improved for it. There was high color in her cheeks, and he had struck sparks in the flint-colored eyes. Her wide mouth was slightly parted and the pearly ridge of her teeth was visible where she had clamped them. He would never have cause to say that she was beautiful in a temper, but temper had stripped her of artifice and left her features beautifully animated. This latter state was infinitely preferable to the former.

"It occurs, Miss Ashby, that if you married you would have no need of a guardian."

Ria was no longer reactive to the abrupt shifts in his conversation. "Your Grace is a mathematician—therefore, you must study the equation. On one side there are but eight months before my twenty-fifth year and independence. On the other side there is marriage. If we agree that marriage is for a lifetime, and I might reasonably expect to live to see my sixtieth birthday, that is—"

"Four hundred twenty-eight months," West said with nary a pause. "If you marry tomorrow."

"I shall trust your figures," she said. "That is four hundred twenty-eight months that I must endure without being accorded my natural rights. It is not a difficult decision to make. If you thought you hit upon a plan to rid yourself of me, you would do well to revise it. Are you carrying your knife?"

West gave a shout of laughter so loud the horses were startled. The carriage pitched alarmingly until the driver got them under control. It required somewhat longer for West to rein himself in. "By God, Ria, but you are a piece of work. I cannot remember when I have been so entertained."

"Outside the company of your friends."

"Perhaps," he said thoughtfully, sobering a bit, "but I did not qualify it. What do you know of my friends?"

"Precious little. I was only informed that wherever you gather there is certain to be a stir."

"Tenley." He did not wait for her to confirm it. "It is like him to say so."

"Is it true?"

"On occasion, yes, though to say we cause a stir is an exaggeration." West remembered that it was only this summer past that he and his friends had cut up at a picnic at the Battenburn estate. They had engaged in so much ribald humor over the peculiar feminine properties of a peach that South had nearly choked. Then there had been that business at the theater when they had stopped the play with their laughter and were taken to task by the lead actress, Miss India Parr herself. That had been but a few months ago. And how much humor had they wrung from East's predicament with Lady Sophia? It would have been a kindness if they had ejected themselves from Lord Helmsley's reception. "Then again," West said, "Tenley may be in the right of it."

"I thought he might be."

"Yes, well, we conducted ourselves with due gravity at the Abbey."

"You must have. I did not know your friends were there."

"They have never not been there when they were needed."

Ria could think of one time, but it had been many years ago, and perhaps they had not been his friends then. She wondered if they would have been willing to throw themselves on his back to protect him from his father's cane. "Is it true you have a name for yourselves?"

Tenley again? West wondered. Or had she learned it from the duke by way of the colonel? It was not commonly known, though people remarked on their names often enough. "At Hambrick Hall we called ourselves the Compass Club. Northam. Southerton. Eastlyn."

"And you are Westphal."

"Now. Then I was Evan and my friends were Brendan, Matthew, and Gabriel. The titles came later. It was my contention that if enough people experienced an untimely passing, they might each take up a title. A little ghoulish, perhaps, but it is the thing boys get up to when they are bored. When we realized what connected the names, it was not long before someone suggested the Compass Club. They called me

West because it fit the theme, and they meant to include me, but we all knew I would never be Westphal. It was not only that I was a bastard, but that the duke had so little to do with me."

"You bear an uncanny resemblance to him."

"I hope you do not mean that."

Ria could not determine if he was teasing her. His voice held no inflection and his glance was remote now. She chose not to offer support for her comment and asked him to continue instead.

"It would not matter if, God forbid, I had been a stamp of him," West said. "The truth is, without his public acknowledgement of what everyone knew to be the truth, I could never inherit. He supported my education at Hambrick, later at Cambridge, and he arranged a quarterly allowance for me. None of it, though, was done in his own name. My benefactor was Mr. Thaddeus Hood."

"Mr. Hood? But I am certain he was your father's solicitor before Mr. Ridgeway."

"Yes, I know. I don't think there was anyone who didn't comprehend that the duke provided for me, but no one said so."

"You will allow it is peculiar."

West had said as much as he wanted to say on the subject and he was not anxious to hear Ria's opinion. He brushed her comment aside as though it were of no import and resumed telling her about the Compass Club. "Matthew became Viscount Southerton while we were yet at Hambrick. For East it was not long after, I think. Brendan's father and brother died while he was with the regiments in India. He had to sell his commission and return to England."

"So all of you were wrong," Ria said after a moment. "You told me you all knew you would never be Westphal, yet exactly that has come to pass."

"You not only stick the point with a sure hand," he said dryly, "but you insist on twisting it."

This time she did not try to hide her cat-in-the-cream smile. "How is it that the four of you have remained friends for so long?"

West shrugged as if he had never given the matter any thought. "Similar interests, I imagine, and East, North, and South are often invited to the same affairs, so they are in one another's company whether they like it or not."

"And you?"

"They torture me by inveigling invitations on my behalf. Even among the *ton,* there are always those hostesses who are not squeamish about a bastard rounding out the numbers at the table."

"You cannot possibly respond to all the invitations that will come your way now. Your plate must already be full. You will be the guest of honor, I suspect, no longer the one assuring the numbers are even." Ria saw West shift as though discomfited, and she realized how slow her wits had become of late. "That is why you've come to Gillhollow, isn't it? It has little enough to do with your amusement and everything to do with your fear. You are running from the *ton.*"

"Hardly running."

"That is because you can afford a horse and carriage."

"True. There is something to what you say."

"You do not mean to deny it?"

"Why? I can freely admit that I would rather take my chances walking alone in Holbern late at night than sit through one of Lady Stafford's interminable musicales. I am not sure fear characterizes my feelings about the latter, but there is certainly a pronounced aversion to those affairs."

Ria tucked the rug around her legs where the carriage's jouncing had loosened it. "Well," she said with emphatic finality, "I do not care what has motivated you to come here—the fact that you are willing to assist me in finding Jane is enough."

West decided that nothing good could come of arguing the point regarding who was assisting whom. Ria had already demonstrated that she would fall in with his plans—for a price. He just had to make certain she did not bankrupt him in the process. It was difficult to imagine a more lowering circumstance than applying to her for an allowance.

Though she could not divine his thoughts, Ria saw that he was amused again. She was learning that while it took little enough to divert him, he was possessed of a most singular mind. "Why did you not want me to instruct Miss Taylor to give Mr. Lytton his marching orders? You know very well that he has not been helpful."

"He has had little enough to work with until now. It hardly seemed fair. He may prove his worth in London."

"I don't believe you, you know. There is something more."

West shrugged. "Certainly you must make up your own mind. I will not try to convince you of the truth of it."

"I should like to hear about that society you mentioned. I am here, after all, and you did agree to tell me if I accompanied you to Ambermede."

"I've not forgotten." He considered removing his feet from the opposite bench and sitting up, perhaps tipping his hat back into place, then decided he would not surrender his comfort to the bishops, even to give them the consequence they were due. "For almost as long as there has been a Hambrick Hall, there has been the Society of Bishops. Like Amy and Jane, they have their blood oaths and secrets, though I believe considerably more than a single drop of blood is involved, and their secrets largely remain just that." He held up one hand, forestalling the question he could see hovering on her lips. "Yes, I know some, and no, I will not speak of them."

Ria feigned indifference. "It does not matter. They are only boys—I have some idea of the mischief they get up to."

"No," West said. "You don't. There is very little in the way of mischief done by them and much in the way of cruelty. They are bullies and blighters. It may be that individually they would not provoke others, but as members of the Society they do not act alone. They hold themselves as superior to everyone outside of their circle and admit members only after they have proven their worth by some arbitrary standards."

"Your Grace is describing the *ton*."

"Am I?" He reflected on his words, then shook his head. "No, even I acquit the *ton* of the sort of organized viciousness the bishops promote."

Ria wondered if that were entirely true. He had never demonstrated any tolerance for the foibles and mores of the *ton*. It was most telling that while he found humor often in the unlikeliest of places, he never found it there. She suspected he would have to care much less in order to enjoy himself more.

"Did you never want to be a bishop?" Ria asked. Seeing his derisive expression, she defended her question. "It is a perfectly reasonable poser. You must allow that envy stirs some to hold others in contempt."

"Sour grapes, you mean?"

"Yes. Sour grapes."

"You must judge the truth of this for yourself—I never had the least desire to become one of them. Once they promised North he could join their Society if he would approach a certain fortune-teller performing at the local fair and ask to see her—"

Ria regarded him, curious that he broke off so abruptly and now looked discomfited. "Yes? See her what?"

"It would be deuced improper of me to say."

"Because you are my guardian?"

"Bloody hell, Miss Ashby. It is because you are a woman."

"Unless I have misunderstood, so was the fortune-teller."

His eyes narrowed, taking her measure. "No," he said finally. "You cannot provoke me. It was a good effort, though."

She sighed. "Not good enough. Will you not at least tell me what Lord Northam did?"

"Of course. He met the challenge and invited South, East, and me to share in the accomplishment. We reported our success to the bishops and they predictably reneged on their promise. In fact, they were furious that we had done what they could not. We were fortunate to escape. They sincerely meant to hurt us."

"I see." But she did not, not clearly. "It still seems rather more mischief than criminal."

"And it was . . . right up to the point when they came at us with slingshots and pellets."

"Oh."

"Indeed." He removed his hat and pointed to a spot in his hairline just above his right temple. "Do you see that dent, Miss Ashby? That was from a glassy blue-green cat's eye measuring one-half-inch in diameter."

She did not see the crease in his skull but she had no reason to doubt his word. "It is fortunate, then, that you are remarkably thickheaded, else you might have been killed."

It was not quite the sympathetic response he had hoped to elicit, but he supposed it would do for now. He chose to ignore her characterization of him as thickheaded and go on. "Then you fully comprehend the problem."

"They are complete ruffians."

He smiled faintly at this description. "That is still rather too kind, but it captures their essence. Barlough—he was the archbishop of the Society for most of the years the four of us were at Hambrick—took it upon himself to collect a tax from anyone who wanted to cross the courtyard or use the common areas. He seized whatever struck his fancy, and it was not the material things he craved, but the distress he caused by relieving others of their possessions. He demanded prized tin soldiers from the youngest boys, French postcards from the older ones, coin from those who had it, and sweets from Eastlyn."

"Sweets?"

"Iced cakes. Muffins. Tarts. That sort of thing. East had a fondness for them in those days and received a parcel almost every week from his mother. I can tell you, he parted with them most reluctantly." West did not return his hat to his head but placed it on the bench beside him. "The bishops' tribunal once forced South to steal the questions for a history examination and give them over. That caused quite a row when it was discovered."

Ria considered what she had been told. Absent from these descriptions was how the Compass Club retaliated, if indeed, they had. "I think you are not telling all. What response did you and your friends make?"

West grinned. "Something with wit attached. We threw peaches at the fellows with the slingshots, stole Barlough's chamber pot and named our own price for its return, and South, being South, did not steal the examination but committed it to memory, then recited his long-winded answers to the tribunal."

Ria's brow furrowed. "I'm afraid the wit escapes me."

"Perhaps if you were to hear it from the others," he said, shrugging. "I am not accounted to be the best storyteller, though if you apply to South for the particulars, you must be prepared to make a day of it."

She smiled, for there was no mistaking from his tone that he held his friend in high esteem. "You make me regret that my own education was confined to the schoolroom at the manor. It was all very dull. My tutors and governesses did not inspire me to make mischief. In any event, there was no one but the servants to bedevil, and that would have been unworthy of me."

"Tenley?"

"He was often away. I saw surprisingly little of him." Ria did not want to linger on the subject of Tenley. "While I found your discourse edifying, I fail to comprehend what the bishops of Hambrick Hall have to do with Miss Weaver's Academy. We have no society like them at the school. The girls form clutches and circles that sometimes exclude others, and while I discourage it, there seems not to be the same mean spiritedness as your bishops. At least, I hope not. I shall be very disappointed in them if you are about to tell me that you know it is otherwise."

"I have no knowledge of that."

"Then you do not suspect Jane's classmates of having a hand in her leaving the school."

"No." West could not miss her palpable relief. "I apologize. I did not realize your thinking had taken that turn."

"What have I misunderstood? I thought you were warning me about the girls by way of comparison to your Society of Bishops."

"Not at all. I was warning you about the Society."

"That is not helpful," she said in clipped accents. "What have boys from Hambrick Hall to do with my girls, and most particularly, Jane? Is one of them responsible for enticing her away? Is that the sort of vicious rite of passage they practice with their initiates?"

West leaned forward and took Ria's gloved hands in both of his. He held her glance and spoke softly, forcing her to ignore the continuous creaking and rumbling of the carriage, and concentrate on the sound of his voice. "I have gone about the thing badly," he said. "It was not my intention to advance either of the ideas you have mentioned because, in truth, I had not considered them. I assumed when Jane spoke of a proper gentleman, she was speaking of someone who had reached his age of majority, not a schoolboy. It bears thinking that you may have hit the mark closer than I."

Ria looked down at her hands, then back to him. "You are not quelling my fears. You know something that you have yet to say. I wish you would be out with it and—"

"Every member of your board of governors is a member of the Society of Bishops."

Ria blinked. Her mouth parted, closed, then parted again.

"You are gaping."

"I am incredulous," she said. "Gaping is required." Studying his fine, patrician features, seeing no hint of amusement in the curve of his mouth or any deepening of the faint lines at the corners of his eyes, Ria realized he was perfectly serious. She could not match his gravity either in tone or expression. "You are in earnest. I could not have imagined this is where you were leading me."

"You don't believe me?" He had not considered that she would doubt his word. He had not given her reason to think him a liar.

"No. No, that is not it at all. Of course I believe you. It is just that I do not attach any importance to it. You don't know these men. No matter what they might have done at Hambrick Hall, they are not those boys any longer. All of them have position in a society far removed from that Society of their youth."

Ria slipped her hands from between his, no longer in need of his steadying clasp, and waited for him to sit back. She noted that he did so slowly, as if not so certain as she that his intervention would not be required. "Can you not conceive," she asked, "that maturity and time would eventually influence the purpose of a group like the bishops? Look at the charitable work they have done on behalf of Miss Weaver's. Surely that speaks to a change in what is important to them. I would imagine their shared experience as bishops at Hambrick provides a lasting bond very much like the one you enjoy with your friends."

West said nothing for a long moment. "I regret, then, that I have alarmed you. My experience with the bishops is such that it is difficult not to be concerned when I discover them together, especially when their interests exclude outsiders. I have most likely made too much of their connection to your school. As you said, they are engaged in charitable work and should be commended for their effort on behalf of your students."

Ria said slowly, "It is probably only coincidence that they were once bishops."

"I'm sure you're right."

She was feeling less so by the moment. His immediate capitulation was unexpected. She had supposed he would expend some breath convincing her his suspicions were warranted. "These are not the same men you knew at Hambrick, are they? Didn't you say the bishops have a long tradition?"

"A very long tradition. So does Miss Weaver's Academy." He let her think about that a moment, then went on. "But you are quite correct—I was acquainted with none of these men at Hambrick."

"Then you will concede that it might have been only the bishops you knew who were bullies and blighters."

"If it is important to you that I concede it, then I will."

Ria frowned. "You are patronizing me."

"I am Westphal. Patronizing is required."

She turned away from his remote, hooded glance and stared out the window to collect her thoughts. The interior lantern turned the glass into a black mirror, and she saw only her own pale, vaguely insubstantial reflection. The carriage moved more quietly now than it had at any time since their journey began. It was the snowfall, she thought, cushioning the wheels and horses' hooves. "I do not think I understand you at all," she said quietly.

"There is no requirement that you should do so."

She looked at him askance. "But there is. I cannot shake this sense that you are angry with me."

"I am not."

"Disappointed, then. Frustrated." Ria paused. "Annoyed."

"And if I am any or all of those things? What can it matter? Please say you will not subvert your own judgment to accept mine. If you are willing to do that, I shall marry you off to a plump country squire of only moderate means by Boxing Day. It is exactly what you will deserve."

Ria's smile was grimly humorous. "I think you delight in being perverse."

He shrugged, picked up his hat, and tipped it back on his head. The brim came low over his eyes as he leaned back against the squabs. Lifting his feet, he returned them to the seat beside Ria, then folded his arms comfortably across his chest. "We still have some way to travel, Miss Ashby. It occurs to me that I should like to pass these last miles in silence."

* * *

When William Fairchild, Earl of Tenley, learned his half-brother had already been shown to the library and that rooms in the north wing were being readied for him, he merely nodded and informed the first butler that he should carry on. His shock, though, was visible when he was further told Westphal was accompanied by Miss Ashby. After sending the butler out, Tenley picked up one of the Egyptian artifacts on the mantelpiece—in this case, a small, bronze figure of a cat—and hurled it hard onto the floor. As an outlet for his rage, it did not satisfy. The feline bounced on the carpet and rebounded sharply so that it actually struck Tenley on the knee. He winced and looked to the remaining statuettes on the mantel for a better second choice.

He took so long making a selection that the urge to break something passed. It might be more the thing, he decided, to break Maria's neck, for surely she deserved it. Her deliberate disregard for his wishes was not to be borne, yet that was precisely what he must do. Hadn't he promised he would visit her at the academy as soon as it was politic to do so? His wife had been very cool to him since he had permitted Maria to accompany the family back to Ambermede from London. She could not suffer Maria's presence without making his own life a hell, and it had been very nearly that since the Abbey service.

Tenley stooped, picked up the bronze cat, and turned it over. An emerald chip that had been the cat's left eye was missing. This piece was a favorite of Margaret's and she was bound to notice the absence of the eye within twenty minutes of retiring to this salon. There could be nothing else for it, he thought, returning the figurine to the mantel, but that one of the servants would have to accept the blame.

West turned from his casual study of the library's tomes as the doors behind him opened. He inclined his head toward his brother but waited for him to say something by way of greeting.

"Taking inventory?" asked Tenley.

Ignoring the snide remark, West responded pleasantly, "Good evening, Tenley."

Grunting softly, Tenley closed the doors. "Will you have a drink?"

"No. But you must please yourself."

"I do."

West watched his brother pour a generous portion of whiskey into a crystal tumbler and seize the glass so forcefully that it might have been a rope thrown to a drowning man. It occurred to West that he did not know Tenley well enough to speculate about his drinking habits but was hopeful his brother found only occasional solace in his cups. He did not blame him for clutching his drink now. There was nothing about the situation in which they had been thrust that was comfortable.

Tenley took a large first swallow. "So, you have come. Should I be informing my wife and children we will be leaving with due haste?"

"If you do, it will be because you want to. I am not here to evict you from the estate." West felt his brother's keen regard as if it were a palpable thing. It had never escaped his notice that he and Tenley shared some similarities of manner and feature, and this remote study of another person, done specifically to take their measure and discomfit them, was certainly something held in common.

West wondered why he had never considered that it might be a practice inherited from the duke. Thinking on it now made him vaguely uneasy. It was less troubling to acknowledge the similarities of resemblance. They were of the same height, easily within a stone's weight of each other, and both were possessed of a like profile: strongly defined jaw, fine patrician nose, and a broad brow. At a distance, with their heads covered by hats, they might easily be mistaken for twins. Their coloring was an obviously distinctive feature. His own darker hair took its copper shades from his mother, while Tenley's fair locks and complexion favored the duke.

Tenley smiled thinly, and West could not miss the fact

that his brother had not been plagued by dimples. On the other hand, West saw that in the absence of this feature, the set of his brother's lips was petulant rather than wry.

"You are not here to toss us out today," Tenley said. "That is what you meant."

"Is it? I do not think so." West shrugged lightly. "I seem to recall that you have always liked to insist on having your way. I do not suppose there can be much difference in determining what games your friends should play as children to assigning meaning to another person's words that was not intended."

It was no effort for Tenley to put a chill in his glance. His eyes were glacier-blue at the outset. It was left, rather, for them to influence the temperature of his smile, and in a moment it was frosty. "What the devil are you talking about?"

"It is unimportant."

Tenley did press himself to think about it but went straight to the heart of the matter. "If, as you say, you have not come to give us our walking papers, then what may we infer from your presence?"

"You may infer anything you like, but I am here to set some of my affairs in order. It makes no sense to set up lodging anywhere else."

"I suppose you have no use for the cottage any longer."

"In fact, I do. It is just that I have lent it to a friend for the time being." West made a point of looking around the large library with its vaulted ceiling and ornately sculpted plaster work. "I believe the whole of the cottage could be fit in this room. Will you find it so onerous to have me underfoot, Tenley?"

"Why have you brought Maria?"

West did not miss the fact that his brother had not answered the question put to him. It was response enough, he supposed. He could not blame Tenley for wishing him gone. If positions were reversed, he might very well be of a similar mind. "Quite frankly, I brought her because I did not know what sort of reception I could expect. I knew she was familiar with the estate and could act as a guide and mentor should you not be of a mind to do the same."

"Hopper will do that. He is the steward."

"Of course." He paused, noting that the tips of Tenley's fingers had whitened a bit where he pressed his glass. "Have I presumed too much by inviting Miss Ashby to accompany me?"

"You are duke now. You may presume anything you like."

"I will adopt that cast of mind in time, I suppose. You certainly have."

Tenley's smile was without humor. "If you meant to offend, you did not. That you think you could by such a remark merely shows how ill-suited you are for the responsibilities that attend your new station."

"We were not speaking of responsibilities. We were speaking of a certain disposition toward others."

"A disposition that is bred in the bone."

"Pray, do not remind me."

If anything, Tenley's smile became a fraction cooler. "You think I am speaking only of our common sire. I assure you, I am not. My mother was the daughter of an earl while yours was—"

West waited. When Tenley chose to take another swallow of his drink rather than finish his sentence, West did it for him. "While my mother was not. That is what you meant to say, isn't it? Your mother was the daughter of an earl while my mother was not."

After a long moment, Tenley nodded. "Yes," he said. "That is it."

"I thought it might be. There can be no faulting the observation—it's true enough."

Tenley finished off his drink and set the tumbler down. "You might have sent word around of your intention to visit, especially of your intention to bring Maria with you."

"So there *is* a problem. She gave no indication that she would not be welcome."

"Did you ask her?" He did not wait for West to reply. "How did you come to be in her company? Have you been to Miss Weaver's, then?"

West nodded. "Once I learned that Miss Ashby was my ward, I thought a visit to the school was in order. I could not get away from London until a few days ago."

Tenley gestured with his hand to indicate the pair of wing chairs turned at an angle toward the fireplace. He let West choose one, then took the other. There was no sense in squaring off like fighters at Gentleman Jackson's. "What is your opinion of the school?" he asked.

"My visit was brief, but it seems to be fulfilling its promise to educate young ladies. It has not the breadth of resources of Eton or Hambrick Hall, but the teachers appear adequate to the task and the girls are eager to learn."

"You realize Father did not countenance Maria taking a position with the academy."

"She told me. It seems he did not forbid it, though."

"He was infinitely indulgent with her."

"You did not approve?"

"No. I thought she should be made to marry."

"On my short acquaintance with Miss Ashby, she does not impress as one who can be made to do anything."

"Long acquaintance will not alter your view. She is singularly wrongheaded."

West's lips twisted wryly. "Naturally, it is for the rest of us to know what is in her best interests."

"Naturally."

Here was another difference, West thought. His brother had no sense of the ironic. It seemed Tenley could not find humor with a map and compass. It was a pity, really, because it might have been something worth sharing with him—infinitely more important than the cut of their features, the breadth of their shoulders, or the way they both sat with their legs stretched lengthwise before them.

"Was there some particular candidate for Miss Ashby's hand?" asked West.

Tenley's hesitation was brief but telling. "I seem to recollect there was a Mr. Butterfield who came up to snuff. And a Mr. Abbot. She would have neither of them, of course. Set her cap for independence."

Remembering the views Ria had expressed during their journey to Ambermede, West was hard-pressed to keep his chuckle in check. "I believe she's read Wollstonecraft's *Vindication of the Rights of Women.*"

Tenley waved this comment aside, anxious to make his point. "The thing of it is, she is not independent at all. Not with an allowance that would beggar most men trying to support it."

Ria's allowance was not so great as that, West thought, but perhaps his brother begrudged her the use of any funds at all. "I believe it is her wish to *become* independent. She will have control of her inheritance in eight months."

"To throw away on the school. Mark my words, she will bankrupt herself providing for those girls."

"Mayhap she will." West turned over one hand in a gesture of indifference. "Mayhap she is only demanding the right to do so."

"You do not foresee a problem? She will announce herself on your doorstep and apply to you to provide the solution."

"Pay her creditors, you mean? Somehow I cannot imagine that she would. What of the board of governors? Wouldn't she be more likely to go to them?"

"She might, but that won't keep her from coming to you. The board charges her with operating the school on what they give her. They aren't likely to dig deeply in their pockets on her behalf."

"Oh? I thought there was a rather generous endowment."

"I couldn't say. I have never inquired. What I know is that Maria seems to think there is never enough money."

West chose not to pursue this with Tenley. He realized his brother had never had sufficient curiosity about the school to be able to answer his questions. It meant seeking out Ria again on this subject, something he had hoped to avoid, since she made it clear she did not share his views of the governors. He was prepared to inquire on the health of the countess and Tenley's children, when the door to the library opened and Ria stepped inside, a child in the crook of one arm and two others trying to lay claim to her free hand.

"Never say you have brought them here," Tenley said, visibly annoyed by the interruption. "Where is James's nanny? William? Caroline? Where is your governess?"

William stopped batting his younger sister's hand away from Ria's and came to attention at her side. At six years of age, he felt it was incumbent upon him to speak up. "Mrs. Burke is not feeling well, Father. She is resting."

"What of Chapel? Is she abed also?"

Ria ruffled William's toffee-colored hair with her fingertips, forcing up the cowlick he had taken pains to squash earlier. "James's nanny has gone to the kitchen to inquire about the children's supper. They are of the opinion that it is late, and they are likely to starve if trays are not delivered promptly." She glanced at Caroline for confirmation, her eyes encouraging. The little girl offered a rather uncertain nod, pale blue eyes darting between Ria and her father. "Oh, you must be more sincere in your approach, Caro, else your papa will think I have put you up to it."

"I think it anyway," Tenley said. "Whether they support you or not. Take them back to the nursery and see that they stay there. Find one of the maids to sit with them until Nanny Chapel returns."

West thought Ria looked more disappointed than surprised by this edict, though even that emotion was couched quickly so the children might not see. He gave her full marks for making no comment. She also did not insist upon a demonstration of affection between any of the parties, as that would have been uncomfortable in the extreme. She did, however, make a formal introduction of the children, something Tenley appeared reluctant to do himself.

"They are handsome children," West said when Ria had taken them from the room. "You are a fortunate man, Tenley."

"You will understand if the circumstances of late have made me think otherwise."

West nodded faintly. "What made him do it?"

Tenley shrugged. "I have asked myself that a hundred times since coming away from his deathbed. Perhaps you think there was some quarrel that put me out of favor with him, but that was not the case. He was distant of late. I thought it was in aid of coming to terms with the fact that he was dying, and I might not have been wrong. However, I could not anticipate that his reflections would lead us to this pass. You, the duke. Me, with reduced circumstances."

"You know I did not ask for this."

"Of course I know. Do you imagine that matters a whit? What's done is done. I will tell you frankly that I have inquired as to the legalities, but it seems he was thorough in his documentation. Mr. Ridgeway reports that everything is in order and there is nothing to be done regarding the duke's wishes save carry them out."

And that is what they were doing, West supposed: parsing out their words carefully, practicing something that passed for civility, gauging weakness and strength. There had been no love lost between them, but then how could it have been otherwise? They had never known each other except in a remote sort of way. "It has been distressing for your wife?"

"Distressed is what she is when soup is brought cold to the table. There is no word that adequately describes her mood now that we have arrived at this pass."

This comment might have been lifted to the level of a jest if West had not already learned his brother was humorless. He matched Tenley's gravity. "I am sorry to hear of it."

Whatever Tenley had begun to form as a reply was cut short by Ria's return. He did not rise as she entered the room, but favored her with his glacial blue stare. "That was not well done of you, Maria, bringing the children here. You know I cannot abide that sort of interruption. I will not have it encouraged."

"Forgive me, Tenley," she said with some effort at contriteness. "I cannot imagine what I was thinking."

"You weren't. That is precisely the problem. You know I don't hold with your notion that children should be underfoot."

"That is not my notion. I merely think that they should be out of the nursery on occasion and—"

"They are. Nanny Chapel and Mrs. Burke often have them in the garden."

"You did not allow me to finish. I also think they should be in the company of their parents."

"Why? They are wholly uninteresting."

She was tempted to inquire if he was referring to himself and Lady Tenley or his children. Thinking better of the jibe, she said, "That you could think so proves how little time you spend with them."

"I don't deny it."

West listened to this exchange with growing amazement, though he took pains not to reveal it. He had been around South and his sister Emma often enough to recognize the sparring that was part and parcel of being siblings. If it were not the subject of the children that brought them to loggerheads, they would have found something else. The teasing that was often present in the matches he observed between Southerton and Emma did not exist here, but West decided it was because Tenley was so lacking in the ability to laugh at himself.

It was also not possible to miss that there was some strain between them. It was suggested in the slight rigidity of Ria's carriage and the tightness about Tenley's eyes and mouth. The cause of it was not so easy to discern, but West was developing a hypothesis he meant to test in the future. If he was right, it would go a long way to explaining things he did not currently understand.

West offered Ria his chair, but she chose the sofa instead. "I did not mean to interrupt your coze."

Tenley's upper lip curled. "Yet you have done so twice now. Still, it is preferable to listening at the door."

"I do *not* listen at doors."

West coughed politely into his fist.

"Are you certain you won't have that drink?" asked Tenley.

"Thank you, but no. It is nothing."

Tenley shrugged and stood. "If you will excuse me. I mean to inquire after my wife."

West nodded and said nothing until Tenley was out of the room. "Do you suppose he will take his cue from you and press his ear to the door?"

"Unfair," Ria said. "I did it once and am heartily sorry for it. I wish I had not told you."

"You probably should not have. It is the sort of thing I am likely to hold over your head now and again." He held up his hand, staving off her reply. "Tell me why Lady Tenley has not greeted us yet."

"I cannot say why she has not bid you welcome, though if I were to venture a guess, it would be that news of my arrival has put her directly in her bed with a megrim."

"She is not an admirer, I collect."

"No."

"You did not mention this when I asked you to accompany me to Ambermede."

"Your recollection is at odds with my own. I do not remember being asked."

"Very well. When I *insisted* that you accompany me. Does that satisfy?"

Having made her point, Ria nodded serenely. "The objections I did offer counted as nothing. How could I know this one would?"

"You misunderstand. I did not say it would have altered the outcome, only that I would have liked to have known. Surprise is highly overrated."

"I shall remember that."

West inclined his head a fraction. "Just so. Now, tell me why Lady Tenley is not among your admirers. You must know each other passingly well. You were still at home when Tenley married."

Ria took in a short breath and let it out slowly. "I think Your Grace knows the answer. It cannot be important that I say it aloud."

"Then I shall, if for no other reason than to put the matter plainly before us." He paused the span of a heartbeat. "It is because Tenley has conceived a passion for you."

Chapter Six

"Conceived a passion for me?" For once, Ria did not try to hide her amusement. "It is as you said—you are a romantic."

"And you are trying to put me off the scent. Tenley is in love with you."

Ria sobered. "He *imagines* himself to be in love with me. It is an old habit, thoughtless and difficult to break, like always putting on one's left shoe first. Long ago he applied to his father for my hand. I was sixteen at the time."

"The duke considered you too young?"

"I don't know. He did not speak of it to me. Neither did Tenley. I only discovered his suit when he went to his father again the following year. This time, when the duke turned him down, he came to me."

"And you thanked him for the honor of his proposal, et cetera."

"Something like that, though I hope I was not so perfunctory. I would like to think I had compassion for his situation and some sensitivity to his feelings."

"God's truth, I hope not. Men don't want women feeling pity for them—it is completely lowering. Stomp hard on the heart once and have done with it. We can recover from that. The other is torture."

Ria stared at West, gauging how serious he was. "That is extraordinary. Do you mean it?"

"I do."

"You have experience to draw on?"

"No, but it is what I would want. And I think I can safely speak for my friends. More to the point, did what you say to him change his intentions toward you or merely set him on a course to change your feelings for him?"

"The latter."

West raised one eyebrow to punctuate his point. "Well, there you have it."

"Tenley is like a brother," she said.

"Yes, that is my observation also. The pair of you are more in the way of siblings than lovers."

Ria flushed to the roots of her hair but managed to give West a quelling look. "A very good thing, since he is married."

"My thought, too. I believe you were in the right of it— Tenley only imagines himself in love with you. How did you describe it? An old habit, difficult to break? Something about a left shoe?"

"Yes. That is what I said."

"That must not set well with the countess. She cannot be oblivious to the undercurrent that exists between you and her husband."

"There is no undercurrent."

"I beg your pardon, but the damn thing is like a riptide. Thought I would lose my footing and be sucked under. Tenley treats you as a sister, but he has not been quite able to think of you as one." West saw that Ria was occupied by some thought that had her worrying the inside of her cheek. He ventured a guess that would explain the tenor of her thoughts. "Perhaps Tenley's behavior toward you is not always brotherly. Is that it?"

Ria stopped worrying her cheek, but she said nothing.

"So he has not tempered his pursuit. Has he tried to force himself upon you?"

"No!"

"Compromise you, then. Has he made his attentions uncomfortable for you?"

Her eyes slid away from West to stare at a point past his shoulder. She considered what she might say, then decided against any response.

"Do not press yourself," he said. "Your silence is eloquent."

"My silence is no answer at all. Do not assume you know what it means."

"Of course." Although he offered this agreeably enough, it did not mean he had changed his mind. "Your arrival in the library, accompanied by the children, begins to make a different sort of sense. I think you wanted to speak to Tenley but not entirely alone. The children were a shield—and unnecessary, as it turned out—because I was already with him. It spared you from being alone, but neither could you speak to him plainly."

"You have a piquant sense of the absurd."

West grinned. "I shall treasure that."

"Fool."

"Perhaps, but fools are not always wrong. In fact, as observers of the human comedy, we may be without peer."

"Is there no insulting you?"

"There is, but you do not seem to have the knack for it."

"Something to strive for, then."

West's deep grin softened. "You would not like the consequences if you hit the mark." He saw that his warning, casually offered but completely sincere, caused Ria's chin to come up a fraction. "I was not issuing a challenge," he said. "Pray, do not take it as one." He indicated the door behind her with a lift of his hand. "Tenley will return shortly, I suspect, and most likely with his wife. I suggest you use this time to tell me what I might expect."

Ria collected her thoughts quickly. "Margaret will be everything gracious. Her absence thus far is highly unusual and must have been influenced by my presence. There is no slight intended toward you."

"Really? Does she hold me in such esteem, then? I would not have credited it."

"At the risk of jabbing at your Achilles' heel, it is most likely your title that she holds in esteem, not you. Margaret is nothing if not practical."

"I am relieved to hear it."

Ria sighed audibly, unaccountably eased that she hadn't insulted him. There was no predicting how his mind might work. Truth be told, she was no longer certain of her own. "She will be civil toward me," Ria said. "But that is only in front of you. She will avoid me outside of company, and if she cannot, I will do well to avoid her."

"She sees you as a threat to her marriage?"

"Yes, though I have given her no reason to view me in that light."

"But Tenley has."

"I cannot say. I am not privy to what manner of conversation passes between them. All I know is that from the very beginning, she has been suspicious of me."

"Is she jealous by nature or circumstance?"

Ria did not understand, and her puzzlement showed clearly in her expressive eyes. "You will have to explain that to me."

"Some people are jealous at their very core. They want what they do not have simply because they do not have it, and rarely is need a consideration. There is also jealousy that is predicated by the fear of losing something that has been acquired. Circumstantial, if you will."

"Then Margaret is the latter. Not petty by nature, but afraid Tenley will be unfaithful."

With good reason, West thought, for it seemed his brother had something more of their father in him. "Tenley says that she is easily distressed."

"He is right. Her nerves are pulled taut, and it requires very little to upset the balance, yet she was not always thus."

"You left Ambermede soon after Tenley set up residence with his countess."

"Yes, but it was entirely my idea."

"Westphal and Tenley did not support it, though. Did Lady Tenley?"

"She was . . ." Ria paused, searching for the right word. "Encouraging."

"And you have stayed away since then?"

"No. Your father remained at Ambermede for at least four months out of the year, so I never stopped visiting. However, I preferred to go to London when he was there and Tenley was not. I have an affection for the children that Margaret does not begrudge me, though she is wary of it." Ria's shoulders rose and fell with her sigh. "I have often thought that if Tenley were to recognize the truth of what it is that he feels for me, Margaret and I could count ourselves as something close to friends."

"Something close to friends?" he asked. "Why not friends?"

"Such friendship as we might enjoy would always be tempered by what has come before it. I accept that. There is also the matter of our different interests. Margaret enjoys pursuits that are considered wholly feminine, while I am for embracing ventures that—"

"That tweak the boundaries between men and women?" West asked with wry inflection. "Yes, I am beginning to appreciate it."

"That is probably for the best," she said, ignoring his mild sarcasm. "It will help us deal well together."

West very much doubted it, but he did not offer that opinion. "I am all for tweaking boundaries," he said, rising from his chair. He closed the distance to the sofa in two lithe strides and dropped to the cushion beside her. Surprise kept her immobile long enough to allow him to set his arm along the curved back and close to her shoulders. "Will you trust me?"

"Of course, but—"

West knew that was no answer that she had given him. No matter how she meant to finish the sentence, the addition of *but* negated what had come before it. He accepted it as affirmation anyway and turned slightly toward her, dropping the arm at her back so that it embraced her shoulders, and circling her waist with his other. He pulled her close, the action so swift and strong that she could not counter it. Her arms were trapped neatly at her sides, and when she stiffened in reaction, it merely brought her flush to his body.

He hesitated a fraction of a second, his head cocked to one side, then lowered his mouth to hers. "Trust me," he said again, his voice something less than a whisper, husky and intense. Then his lips covered hers.

West realized his memory had served him false. This kiss was more of everything he remembered—sweeter, hungrier, deeper, greedier—and his own reaction was as unexpected as it was unwelcome. He had not meant to break his promise that he would not throw down the gauntlet a second time.

Of all the ill-conceived plans . . .

That thought flickered through his mind as wildly as a candle flame caught in a draft. He could not steady it, yet it would not be extinguished. He closed his eyes to it instead and kissed her with more urgency, listening for that thing outside himself that would call a halt, knowing that he did not want to.

"Oh my!" Margaret Warwick Fairchild, Lady Tenley, stepped into the library ahead of her husband. She knew his view of the pair on the sofa was unobstructed, because her height was not sufficient to block it. She wished that she might turn and gauge his reaction to what they were seeing. It was certain he would be struggling to put an indifferent face on it.

West did not permit Ria to break away in a guilty start. He lifted his head slowly, steadied her with a long, significant look and a roguish smile, then drew back his hand at her waist. He kept his arm about her shoulders, while his head swiveled in the direction of the door.

"It seems we are caught out," he said with considerable sangfroid. "That was unanticipated."

Ria knew it was a lie but not because she heard it in his voice. Those carefully modulated tones of his gave nothing away. She suspected now that he'd heard Tenley and Margaret approaching before they ever twisted the door handle. He had meant to be caught out.

Lady Tenley raised one hand to her lips to help stifle her smile. "Apologies are in order, I think." She hurried to the sofa as West released himself from Ria's side and came to his feet. "You should be able to expect a measure of privacy in your own home. The manor is that, now, is it not?"

"Let us not make too much of it," West said graciously. "I know I am the interloper, and you are kind to make us welcome."

Ria watched Margaret flush becomingly and could hardly credit how the warmth transformed her sharply cut features from haughty to charitable. The difference was so striking that Ria actually blinked. This was something more than she could have anticipated, and she knew very well that Margaret was not merely responding to the title of the man before her, but the man himself. Risking a sideways glance at West, Ria could not discern that he found Margaret's reaction in any way out of the ordinary, yet she was quite certain this was a new experience for him.

Ria accepted West's hand when he held it out to her and permitted him to help her rise. It was less easy for her to be drawn toward him, but she followed his lead and tried not to show her relief when he kept the distance between them perfectly respectful. He released her fingertips and favored her, then Margaret, with a smile that held a question in its curve. Ria was the first to answer that smile's prompt.

"Margaret," she said softly. "I regret that I have imposed upon your hospitality. I hope you will accept my apology for being unable to give you notice of our arrival."

Lady Tenley rose to the challenge and offered a public

peace. "There is no apology necessary. I think we all comprehend that our altered circumstances require some flexi-
bility of thought and action. Notice is not required. We are
family, are we not? There is no imposition."

Ria thought Margaret's tone could have been a shade less
cool, but it was a good effort, and mayhap a good beginning.
She promised herself that she would not take it to heart if
she learned later that Margaret meant little or even none of
it.

Margaret laid her hand lightly on her husband's forearm
and smoothed the sleeve of his black frock coat. "Have you
nothing you wish to add, my lord?"

"I have already welcomed them," Tenley said. His eyes
darted between Ria and West, then rested on his wife. "Why
has no one announced supper?"

Ria resisted making a jibe. Tenley was in a snit, and she
wished above all things that she might needle him for it.
Commenting, though, would be unwise; it was certain to set
an uncomfortable tone for the meal.

Margaret graced Tenley with an indulgent smile, then ignored him. She engaged Ria and West in conversation, inquiring about their journey, London, the academy, their
health, and finally, the weather. By the time they were seated
for supper, she had made them easy for silence—except
Tenley, who had said little and was, in fact, praying for it.

Supper was lightly seasoned potato soup, warm, thick-
crust bread, and baked trout. The fare satisfied at this late
hour and Lady Tenley was delighted to accept West's compliments for the cook. Conversation resumed in fits and
starts. Politics. Theater. Books. Art. By unspoken mutual
agreement, they avoided the subject of anything that could
be construed as personal, most particularly the interrupted
kiss. That topic was held in abeyance until the sexes divided
after the meal: West and Tenley remained at the table for a
glass of port; Ria and Margaret excused themselves and advanced on the salon.

Ria could freely admit that she was dreading being alone

with Margaret. Their usual pattern following supper was to leave the dining room together and immediately find separate diversions. When they had no choice but to retire to the same room, they engaged in solitary interests, and such conversation as passed between them was scrupulously polite and invariably cool.

Lady Tenley was a fierce warrior, a fact that was often lost on people of short acquaintance. Her dainty, doll-like figure, porcelain complexion, small chin, and wide, aquamarine eyes served to influence assumptions that she was somehow lacking in spirit, perhaps even spine, and that she was best wrapped in cotton wool. It was naught but an illusion. She was, in fact, definite in her ideas, protective of her family, impatient with incompetence, and did not suffer fools. Those delicate features could become severe, even arrogant, when she was feeling threatened, and she had a way of drawing herself up that made her diminutive stature irrelevant.

"You will explain yourself, I hope," Margaret said once she and Ria were alone. "Do you imagine you have developed a tendre for him, or he for you? I would not have supposed you could be so lacking in good sense."

Ria sighed. "Can I not indulge a whim?"

"A whim? You will be fortunate if Tenley does not march you to the altar."

"How is that fortunate?"

"Surely you know he has a reputation of a certain kind."

"What I know is that you do not call him by name. He is Westphal, Margaret, and whatever his reputation, it will be reevaluated in light of that."

"He is your guardian. He must not take advantage."

"And he has not," Ria said firmly. She came within a moment of admitting her confusion to Margaret. The tenor of this interview was not what she had expected. Where was Margaret's relief that her affections were engaged elsewhere? Had she seen through West's charade, or was she merely testing the waters, wanting to be convinced? "I like him very much, Margaret, but you must not worry that I will allow myself to be compromised. I would not bring that shame upon the family."

"Westphal might not share your scruples."

"You are too harsh." There was no reason Margaret must know about the weapon he carried, or his trespass into her private apartments, or his insufferable high-handedness. "He has been everything kind and decent."

Margaret's eyes sharpened as she considered this. "He is not Tenley," she said at last.

Ria frowned. "I don't understand. What do you mean by that?"

"He is not his brother," Margaret said. Her pause was uncharacteristically long as she measured her words. "I do not wish to be disagreeable by broaching this subject, but I must point out that you cannot satisfy your tendre for Tenley by substituting his brother."

What could she say that would be believed? Ria wondered. Denying that she had any tender feelings for Tenley, beyond that of a sister toward her brother, seemed unlikely to convince Margaret. If Ria had ever required evidence of the depth of Margaret's feelings for her husband, she had it now. Margaret could not conceive that a woman would choose another man over Tenley.

It also seemed vastly inappropriate to discuss Tenley's feelings. While Ria understood that Margaret was aware of her husband's interests, she also knew Margaret had too much pride to admit it aloud.

Ria decided there was only one direction she might take, and it was West. Neither the wordplay nor the reality of it amused her. "You will account me as shameless," she said slowly, as if the words were being taken from her against her will. "I have not known His Grace but a few days, and you are fully aware that his existence was rarely mentioned in this house, but from the outset it has been as if I have never *not* known him. Mayhap you are right, and it is the passing resemblance and manner he shares with Tenley that makes it seem so, but I do not believe it is only that. What I feel for him in my heart surpasses anything I have known. I cannot say if it is love, only that I think it might be, because my heart trips over itself when he is in the room, and my thoughts scatter like wild seed in the wind. He is irritating and arrogant and must always be right, yet I forgive him all of it, not because I want to, but because I cannot seem to help myself."

"Oh my," Margaret said softly. She lowered herself onto the sofa, perching on the edge like a wren. "You do not forgive Tenley those things."

Ria pretended to think about this. "No, I do not. I never have. What do you make of that?"

"When Tenley was courting me, I forgave him those things also."

"Then the urge passes," said Ria. "That, at least, is good."

Margaret's features were softened by a slim smile. Her gaze went past Ria to the mantelpiece where she saw the Egyptian cat was missing one of its emerald eyes. "I still make allowances for him."

Ria nodded. "You love him."

"Yes."

"Is it love, then, that I feel for Westphal?"

"I think it might be."

Ria sighed heavily and sat herself. "You must give me advice, Margaret, for I haven't any notion of how one goes on from here."

West was a light sleeper. It served him well during the Spanish campaign when he had to take his rest wherever he could find it. He had once wedged himself in a rock crevice and woke at the approach of a French patrol some one hundred yards distant. He'd slept curled on the damp floor of a wine cellar and come awake at the sound of a cork easing itself out of a bottle. He'd spent one memorable night lying on his back in a whore's bed, bolting upright when she unsheathed a dagger from beneath her corset.

He never worried that he would not wake up. He always did.

That is why he was surprised when he snapped to attention and Ria said, "You sleep like the dead."

Unable to capture his bearings immediately, he simply blinked at her. She stood at his bedside holding a candlestick, and the wavering flame illuminated her cheek and the underside of her chin. Her eyes fell in shadow, making them impossibly dark, almost as if she were wearing a mask across the upper half of her face. Her brushed flannel robe was cinched tight around her waist, but the opening at her throat revealed the white scooped neckline of her nightdress and the hollow of her throat. The candle flame flickered madly again, and West realized it was caused by Ria shifting her weight from one foot to the other. She was fairly dancing in place, and it made him curious enough to lean over the side of the bed and have a look.

"Where are your slippers?" he asked.

"That is what you have to say to me? I have arrived in your room in the middle of the night, and you only inquire after my slippers?" She stood perfectly still for a moment. "You will allow it is most curious."

Groaning softly, West closed his eyes and leaned heavily against the bedhead. He ran one hand through his hair before he risked opening a single eye. When he confirmed that she was still standing there, that under no account was this the result of sharing too much port with Tenley, he took stock of the situation and found it so wanting of common sense and seemliness that for a moment he could not think what he might say to impress this upon her.

"Bloody, bloody hell."

Ria gave her head a toss and the pale, braided rope of hair that lay over her shoulder fell down her back. "I do not usually hold with cursing," she whispered. "But you have captured the essence of my own thoughts."

"Oh, good," he said dryly. "It is a relief to know. I was sore afraid I would never comprehend the workings of a woman's mind. To discover differently—at this hour, no less—well, you can see that I am buoyed by the news."

Ria's mouth flattened disapprovingly. "I see you mean to be unbearable."

"You collect there is some other manner I should adopt?" he asked coldly. "I should like to know what it is. It is gone midnight. You are here without invitation. Tenley and his wife sleep within a stone's throw of my bedchamber. We are both in our nightshirts. And—this may be the most salient factor—there is no bloody fire! Can you not conceive there might be a better approach, mayhap one that does not have a march to the altar as its consequence?"

Ria turned slightly and sat, hitching her hip on the edge of the bed. "I wish I had been as clearheaded when you appeared in my room at the school. The situation was not so different, though I think we might have avoided marriage. The most likely consequence of you being discovered there would have been my dismissal. I understand that you would not regard this as the same tragic ending as marriage, but it would be of like importance to me."

At the moment Ria sat, West had been of a mind to plant his foot hard against her bottom. He thought better of it now and eased it back.

Ria caught the movement under the comforter and said, in faintly accusing accents, "You were going to shove me onto the floor."

"I was going to push you off the bed. Whether or not you went as far as the floor would be up to you."

She could hardly credit that he did not lie about his intent. "That is something, at least."

West's brow furrowed. "Pardon?"

Ria did not realize she had spoken aloud. "It is nothing. I was musing."

West decided it was better to let that pass. He sighed. "Will you not come to the point? Why are you here?"

"How can you not know?" she asked. "You are certainly responsible. It is that cork-brained scheme you enacted in the library that must be put to rights."

"Put to rights? What is wrong? I thought it went very well. Tenley is sullen, and Margaret is relieved. My brother will recover his heart soon enough, and Margaret will be less prickly. She was everything cordial during dinner. I judge that kiss to be a success."

"Margaret was pleasant at dinner because she would not have you think ill of her. You failed to comprehend that while she was hopeful that I might have formed an attachment to you, she was still reserving judgment. Once we were alone in the salon, she challenged me. At first I could make no sense of it, then I realized she wanted to be convinced."

"Convinced?"

Ria's short sigh communicated her impatience with him. "Convinced that I no longer had a tendre for her husband. Convinced that I was not agreeable to your advances simply because you are Tenley's brother. Convinced that I would not be compromised. Convinced that my feelings were deeply engaged. In short, convinced that what she saw was not a sham."

"I see," West drawled. Then he went straight to the part of her exposition that he found the most striking. "Am I to understand that Margaret considers me an inferior substitute for my brother? That really is the outside of enough."

Ria glared at him. "Can you not be serious?"

"Yes, but not about this. You are making too much of her doubts."

"My point, Your Grace, is that she no longer has any doubts. I *convinced* her."

"Good. Then it is an agreeable ending to a long day. Will you take yourself off now?"

"I convinced Margaret because I told her I *love* you." Ria felt an acute sense of satisfaction when that intelligence garnered all of West's attention. It was difficult to discern in the candlelight, but she liked to think his normally healthy color had gone ashen. "That's right," she said. "I told her I love you."

"There is nothing wrong with my hearing. Once was quite enough."

"Just so. Now that you know all of it, I shall leave." She started to rise and found her wrist seized in a sure grip. The tug was wholly unnecessary because she was already sitting down. "Yes?"

"Gloating does not set at all well on your face."

Ria did not make a very good effort to remove her smile. "Will you not release my arm, Your Grace?"

West glanced at the spot where his fingers circled the fragile bones of her wrist, then back at her. "And will you not call me West? I am heartily sick of the other." His eyes lifted, and he saw hesitation clearly marked on her face. "This one thing," he said, "and I will not press you for any other favor." He released her wrist to prove that answering her request was not predicated on her responding agreeably to his.

"Very well," she said, sobering. "If it pleases you. West."

"Good." He reached out and took the candlestick from her hand and placed it at the bedside. "Now, as to the other, this matter of you loving me, that is a Banbury tale, is it not?"

"Your panic is not flattering."

"You misjudge my feelings. It is not panic, but terror." At another time the sound of Ria's laughter would have pleased him. Now it seemed inordinately loud and certain to attract notice. He shot forward quickly and placed his palm across her mouth. "Have a care," he whispered in her ear. "Else you will bring Tenley running to this room."

Over the top of his palm, Ria's eyes were wide. She nodded jerkily a few times to show her assent. When the pressure on her mouth eased, she added an apology in the same husky whisper as he. "I'm sorry. You understand, don't you, that it is not Tenley we have to fear. He is not likely, as Margaret suggested, to insist on a march up the aisle. It is Margaret who would want to see us leg-shackled."

"A fair point," he said, dropping his hand, "but I should like to have an answer to my other question."

Ria had to think a moment, uncertain what he had asked her. "Oh, you are referring to what I told Margaret. Ease your mind. It was a fabrication, nothing more."

What quite amazed West was that his mind was not entirely made easy. "That is good," he said, though he wondered why he had to force conviction into his voice. He decided it did not bear scrutiny now, if it ever would, and he resolutely suppressed the niggling sense that all was not quite as it should be. Ria, he noticed, appeared to be untroubled. "Margaret has not pressed you to set your cap for me, has she?"

"She has advised me on all the ways I might encourage you to propose marriage. You will be relieved to know that if I follow her instructions, when the thing comes about, you will be convinced it was your idea."

"She is diabolical, then."

"Completely."

"Perhaps you should not have been so convincing."

"I did not see an alternative. You *did* begin this, you know. I did not tell her that you returned my feelings."

"So she thinks I am a thorough scoundrel."

"Of course, but that is neither here nor there. You are still the Duke of Westphal."

He nodded slowly, as though reluctant to confirm the truth of it. "What is to be done?"

"It is simple, really. Now that Margaret fully comprehends my feelings for you and is no longer fearful I will turn to Tenley, it is important that I not appear too eager for your advances."

"Were you too eager? I hadn't realized." What West did realize was that he was enjoying himself enormously, not playing at that emotion, but genuinely in its thrall. It occurred to him that the eight months Ria had remaining until she was legally independent of him was not so long a time as he'd first thought. "You mean to spurn me, is that the way of it?"

"Spurn you? No, that is too harsh. Margaret advises more subtlety than that. She says you would see through the pretense if I were suddenly to affect no interest. It would also lead to raising Tenley's hopes and give him reason to pursue me again. Neither of us acknowledged this particular point to the other, but we understood it well enough."

"It seems as though you mean to walk a tightrope, then. I intend no offense, Ria, but I am not certain subtlety is your strong suit. Have you considered what you will do to resist without refusing me? I can be persuasive, you know."

She did not deny it. "Then you must endeavor to be less so."

"How?" Under the covers, West drew up his legs tailor-fashion. "It is very much in my nature."

Ria offered up her most disapproving countenance: slightly pursed mouth; narrow, flinty eyes; and locked jaw.

West's brows lifted. "I take that look to mean I should stand in opposition to my inclinations."

"Good." The muscles of her face relaxed and she smiled, not softly enough to erase her seriousness, but without the severity of one pressing a point home. "You understand perfectly."

"I don't see how it could be otherwise. That headmistress manner you adopt would put a period to the advances of the *ton's* most determined rogues, and I am not accounted to be one of them. As South might say, it is an expression that will repel all boarders."

She sighed. "It is as you have pointed out, then. I have not the talent for subtlety. I am not supposed to repel you."

"There you have the conundrum. Perhaps what Margaret means is that you should lead me to water but not allow me to drink."

"Yes. Yes, of course. That is it precisely."

West grinned and made himself comfortable against the

polished walnut bedhead again. Folding his arms across his chest, he made a considering study of Ria. "It is all well and good that I should be right, but it is not the same as knowing how to—" His abrupt stop was prompted by the fine tremor in the bed's frame and the cause for it. "Look at you. You are freezing." He lifted one corner of the covers and offered her shelter under it. "Your shivering is likely to eject me from my own bed. Get in."

"It is only because I am that cold," she said. "Not that you are the least persuasive in this instance."

"You may have it however you wish, but please climb aboard quickly." He moved a few inches toward the middle of the bed, raised the blankets a fraction higher, and looked pointedly at the space beside him. "You will find it warmer here."

Ria slipped under the covers and waved off his help to tuck them around her. She rubbed the soles of her bare feet against the sheets. The friction added a pleasant rush of heat at the end of a violent shiver. "This is most improper."

"I believe I noted that when you were still hovering at my bedside. Now our position is choosing to be hanged for a sheep instead of a lamb. Still, I shall count on you to dive under the bed in the event someone approaches."

"Of course."

"You are being uncharacteristically accommodating."

She shrugged. "Perhaps it is because I really do not expect an interruption. I locked your door."

West lifted his head an inch, then let it thump back against the bedhead. For a moment he closed his eyes. "Damnation, Ria, that is not the sort of thing you tell a man who has just invited you to share his bed."

"Oh, did you mean to be a gentleman? I thought it was all in aid of making another advance."

"Well, if it was, I'm not likely to say so, am I? And if you thought I was offering warmth as a lure, why did you not have the good sense to refuse it?" He held up one hand, staving off her reply. "Never mind. It cannot be important now. I cannot tell whether you trust me so much or so little."

Ria did not know the answer to that herself, so she was glad when he did not pose it as a question. "Shall I leave now?"

"Stay or go. It is your choice."

It did not feel so very much like a choice. Stay or go. There were arguments for both sides of the matter, yet her innate sense of honesty compelled her to admit that she was not interested in those points that would influence her to leave. "I want to stay."

West sighed and glanced sideways at her. She was cocooned in the blankets, but they were protection only against the cold, not him. "Are you a virgin, Miss Ashby?"

Ria's entire body jerked. It was not simply the question, but the manner in which he asked it that repelled her. Something chilly had crept into his voice and there was no evidence of genuine curiosity. Rather it seemed to her that he was indifferent of the answer and asked it more to gauge her reaction than receive a reply. The fact that he had called her Miss Ashby when moments earlier she had been Ria, was also telling of the distance he meant to put between them.

"Well?" West asked.

"I think I will leave after all."

He nodded. "As you wish."

Ria shivered once as she flung off the covers and set her feet on the floor. Her fingers trembled slightly until she had her hand firmly around the candlestick. "I can think of no reason I should have to trouble you again," she said quietly. "This night or any other."

"Then you underestimate yourself. I'm certain something will occur to you if you apply yourself."

Ria bit back a reply, but did not move away from the bed. She hovered there much as she had when she'd first entered West's room. Sleeping, he had looked far younger than his years, vaguely innocent of life's petty cruelties, untroubled by thoughts that there was anything he might not conquer. It was naught but a fancy on her part; she suspected that even as a youth, his sleep had been disturbed by restlessness and fear. There was nothing to be gained by remembering the boy he had been when this was the man he had become.

"Yes?" he asked. "There is something you wish to say?"

"You will still find Jane, won't you? You do not mean to change your mind about that."

West was silent for a long time, considering his answer. "It pains me that you are uncertain," he said at last. "But it occurs that I have myself to blame for that. Yes, I mean to find Jane. Whatever our grievances with each other, Jane is separate from them."

Ria nodded once, then left as quietly as she'd come.

West left for Sunbury shortly before eight. The servants had long been about, but neither Tenley nor Margaret had risen. Ria was also abed. All of this made West's departure easier. He penned an explanation for whoever was the first to inquire after him and left it with the butler. That the explanation bore little in the way of details did not bother him. Ria would probably deduce his destination, and Tenley and Margaret did not need to know.

The tidy and charming village of Sunbury lay thirteen miles southwest of Ambermede. West had chosen Mr. Jonathan Beckwith as his first contact on the academy's board of governors because of his proximity to both the school and the manor. He was in no expectation that his visit would be welcomed beyond what was afforded by his new station. If Ria was correct, he would be politely denied a seat on the board of governors, no matter what influence he brought to bear. She understood that much without knowing the board had connections to the Society of Bishops. What made West hopeful that they might entertain his application was that at their center, they were suspicious to a fault. If he piqued their interest just enough, they might draw him in to observe him. Keeping him close and under their watchful eye was better than allowing him to do as he pleased.

It had been a favorite tactic at Hambrick. West doubted that time had changed the Society's fundamental approach to keeping their secrets.

West's arrival without announcement or invitation, without a letter of introduction, and finally without an entourage, created the greatest stir for everyone residing at the Beckwith estate. Currently that numbered twenty-eight: the confirmed bachelor Mr. Jonathan Beckwith and twenty-seven servants, including the grooms, who had their sleeping quarters at the back of the stable, and the estate steward, who had very pleasant accommodations above the newly built carriage house.

Mr. Beckwith was about to spread butter on his toast when West's presence was announced. Beckwith immediately ordered his breakfast tray to be taken away and his clothes set out. West should be made comfortable in the gallery and invited to breakfast, he told his man; then, after they knew the purpose of the visit, they would decide what must be done to make everything agreeable for the new Duke of Westphal.

West was in no hurry to make his host's acquaintance. He accepted the invitation to wait in the gallery with equanimity and used the time while Beckwith was making his ablutions and fussing with his stock to tour the room and study the host of paintings on display. The traditional and unexceptional landscapes, still lifes, hunting scenes, and family portraits were not terribly interesting to him, but taken as a whole, they created a broader picture of the man Beckwith imagined himself to be, or at least the one he wished to show his guests. West thought the choice of the gallery as a place for him to cool his heels was most deliberate, and one that had probably been used to great success before as a way of introducing Beckwith to his guests. Here was the pretense of intimacy, for it was infinitely less intimate than being shown to a man's study, where one might see what sort of books he read, the type of cigars he preferred, his tastes in liquor, and what importance he placed on his own comforts.

West was determining how he might create the opportunity to see more of the house, especially the less public rooms, when Beckwith entered the gallery. They exchanged greetings, with Beckwith waving aside West's apologies for the abruptness of his visit.

Jonathan Beckwith stood half a head shorter than West and possessed a slender frame well suited to the current fashion for clothes that were elegant but not ostentatious. He made a good leg in his long, narrow knitted pantaloons, white stockings, and blue tailcoat. His cravat was carefully knotted, but not intricately so, suggesting that he had no use for the fussing required of a more complicated pattern, or that he had been impatient to make his way to the gallery. His one conceit was his hair, for he had taken the time to make certain his heavy brown locks were in studied disarray and that the thinning spot at the back of his head was concealed. It was seldom that he was mistaken for a man approaching his forty-third year; most often he was thought to be a full decade younger.

West took the time to politely inquire after some of the paintings, successfully delaying Beckwith from delving into the purpose of his visit. Because West wanted to control the interview, he was able to engage his host in circumnavigating the gallery before agreeing it was time to accompany him to the breakfast room.

"I had not heard you were up from London," Beckwith said after they had been served baked eggs and thin slices of ham. "I find that plainly astonishing. Word usually travels more swiftly. One always knew when your father was in residence at Ambermede."

"I had not realized his coming and going invited such interest. He was not one for entertaining."

"You are right, but that did not stop people from speculating that he might. There was no figure more widely known in these parts than your father." Beckwith continued in the same vein, expressing his condolences at the duke's passing and treading carefully around the change in West's own circumstances. "Your journey was uneventful, I hope."

"It was." West took a bite of his eggs. "I imagine I will be making it several times a year now, so I find it a good omen that this one went well. You must be speculating on the reason for my call."

"It has been a question in my mind," Beckwith said, raising a triangle of buttered toast to his mouth. "You honor me by singling me out for a visit, for I am not, after all, what one can properly call a neighbor. It occurs to me that Miss Weaver's Academy might figure into the explanation for your arrival."

"Very good," West said. "Then you know that Miss Ashby is now my ward."

"I was not certain, actually. I knew, of course, that she was your father's ward, but I was not privy to the details of that arrangement following his death. It did not come up in her recent correspondence as it had no bearing on her position at the academy. Is there a problem? You are perhaps not similarly inclined to allow her to continue her employment as headmistress? I feel compelled to point out that it would be a great loss for the students and her fellow teachers, but I would understand if that was your decision."

"Then you realize it was an indulgence on the duke's part to permit her such latitude when he could have insisted that she marry."

"Naturally." Beckwith lifted his teacup and studied West over the rim before he sipped from it. "It was remarked upon from time to time."

"Remarked upon? By whom?"

"By the board of governors. We were always pleased to have Miss Ashby at the academy, but it would have been irresponsible not to question our good fortune." He smiled faintly, in the manner of one sharing confidences with an old friend, then replaced his cup in its saucer. "One always wondered when the duke would set his mind on another course for her. Miss Ashby's association with your father was not exploited by the school, but neither was it overlooked. It lent a tacit importance to Miss Weaver's Academy that the school had not enjoyed before."

"I wonder what you will say to my proposal of a more direct connection," West said, gauging Beckwith's reaction while he continued to tuck into his meal. "I am of a mind to allow Miss Ashby to remain at the school. She has expressed no interest in marrying, and I have no wish to insist that she should. However, I am not willing to indulge her as excessively as my father did. I have made it my concern to learn more about the school and have been largely pleased with the particulars. I have decided I should like to lend the consequence of my title to the good efforts being made on behalf of these students."

"And if your involvement with the academy provides you the means to keep Miss Ashby on a short tether, so much the better."

West swore that Beckwith almost winked at him. Suppressing his desire to put the man's face in his eggs, West offered a faintly conspiratorial smile instead. "You have it almost exactly."

"Almost?"

"In light of the recent disappearance of one of the academy's students, I am as concerned for Miss Ashby's safety as I am for shortening that tether."

"Aaah, she has seen fit to inform you of the girl's elopement. I cannot say that I like it."

"I'm sure it is the sort of situation your board of governors wishes to keep quiet. All of the girls are not charity students, after all, and there are parents enough who might very well raise questions."

"Which would lead to Miss Ashby's dismissal," Beckwith said. "She is the one with the most to lose by not keeping confidences." He waved this statement aside immediately.

"Though it is misplaced, her concern—and, might I add, yours—is admirable."

"Misplaced? How is that?"

"Though it defies common sense, there are always those girls who do not appreciate their good fortune and choose to leave. This most recent one . . . Miss Petry . . . she is not—"

"Petty," West said. "Miss Jane Petty."

"Yes, that's right. As I was saying, Miss Petty is not the first to take her leave of the school without notice. It is hardly a regular occurrence, but it happens now and again. Miss Ashby has informed you that we are employing someone to look into the girl's disappearance?"

"Yes. And also that nothing has come of it. I am considering making inquiries of my own."

"I am certain that is not necessary. She will turn up soon enough. Soiled goods, unless I miss my guess, mostly likely with a swollen belly to show for it, and without benefit of banns having been read or a special license."

"That will be a relief, I think, for Miss Ashby," West told him. "It is Miss Petty's cold remains that she fears will turn up."

Chapter Seven

By West's reckoning, it was nearing two o'clock in the morning when he saw the manor at Ambermede again. His view from the back of Draco was unobstructed at this curve in the road, and the silvery cast of the full moon's light illuminated every snow-covered hillock, valley, and open field. The manor was positioned like a jewel in a deep bed of white velvet, a diamond itself with the moonshine glancing off its stone walls.

West tugged on Draco's reins, slowing the mount to a walk, then halting him. Looking around, West realized what it was about this particular view that tickled his memory. Off to his left was the lake, iced over now but still visible by the outline of its banks. There, too, was the stand of trees—beeches, firs, oaks—and the venerable and stately chestnut that he had loved to climb in his youth.

A slight change in the pressure of his knees was all the encouragement Draco needed to start walking, this time turning off the road toward the wood. When they reached the chestnut, West stopped his horse again and looked up. The branches of the tree were perfectly limned by moonlight and snow, and West could follow the route he had taken to the top. Accounting for the growth of the last twenty years, West realized he had not much exaggerated the height and breadth of this great tree in his own mind. He had no trouble finding the peculiar cradle of the branches that had held him safely while he surveyed all of the countryside. Seeing the precariousness of that position now, and the considerable distance it was from the ground, West wondered that he had not broken his neck either in an attempt to reach it or leave it.

He lowered his head and let his gaze fall on the lake. Without quite realizing that he'd signaled Draco to do so, the stallion began heading in that direction. Draco carefully picked his way along the edge of the bank until West stopped him. Judging the distance from the woods and the perspective of the lake from this angle to be the right one, West was satisfied he had come upon the very spot where he had jumped into the water to pull young Ria out.

All these years later, it was still a question in his mind if he had really been the cause of her tumbling into the water. Was his effort to pull her up short the thing that made her take the spill? If he hadn't left the tree, would she still have run into the lake? He knew how he remembered the incident, but on occasion he wondered if his memory played him false. Why had no other person seen what he had? If he was innocent, why had his father flayed the skin from his back?

A shiver that had nothing to do with the chill in the air or the frozen landscape made West turn Draco away abruptly and set off for the road and Ambermede.

Ria could not sleep. She had managed to hide her concern regarding West's long absence from Tenley and Margaret, but that had been during the day when there were activities to occupy her, chief among them avoiding being alone with Tenley. The children helped by being eager for her company and willing to do whatever she suggested. With the assistance of the groundskeeper and one of his lads, they built a snow castle with crenelated embattlements. Caroline wanted to live there in relative peace as princess; William wanted to lay siege to it. William's warlike inclinations triumphed, and the ensuing flurry of snowballs caught each of them at one time or another.

Building and battling in the snow could not occupy the whole of the day, however, and when tempers wore thin, Ria moved the children back inside for their lessons. While they were attended by their governess, Ria enjoyed a short visit with the infant James, then sought out Margaret for adult companionship. There were questions about West's enigmatic missive and subsequent departure to be carefully turned aside, but it was not too difficult to accomplish as Margaret was certain the cause of it lay with the previous evening's kiss and West's discomfort with the tendre Ria had developed for him.

"You have given the game away," Margaret had scolded her gently, "by being entirely too forward."

Ria had agreed this was probably the way of it and let Margaret speak at length on the cowardly nature of men when they were confronted by a woman's tender feelings. During Margaret's argument, Tenley joined them briefly, and Ria noted that he offered nothing in his defense, or in defense of his sex. He backed out of the room as quickly as possible after seizing a book that he'd supposedly come for.

When the doors closed behind him, Margaret had given Ria a significant, knowing look, and neither of them could contain their laughter. It was the first time in Ria's memory that she and Margaret had shared such a moment of abandon and delight. That it should come at Tenley's expense seemed rather more right than wrong.

Hours and hours had passed since then, every one of them devolving into the next with excruciating slowness. Dinner filled up some of the time, and Margaret's recital at the piano following the meal engaged still more. At the end of the day, however, there was nothing for it but to retire to her room with all of her own questions unanswered.

Ria had prepared for bed by taking a steaming bath in lavender-scented water. When it had seemed that she might fall asleep there, she roused herself enough to be dried and dressed and directed to the comfort of the large four-poster. She was in anticipation of immediate slumber and turned on her side, one hand under her pillow, the other folded into a light fist and nestled close to her lips. She was vaguely aware of the maid extinguishing the lamp and quietly exiting the room, then conscious only of her own soft intake of air.

Twenty minutes later, she was still conscious of her breathing. It did not matter that her eyes were still closed—she was as thoroughly awake as she had been before she'd taken her bath.

"Bloody hell," she said under her breath. It was a credible imitation of the intonation West used when he had occasion to curse. She found it deeply satisfying. "Bloody, bloody hell."

Pushing herself upright, Ria relighted the lamp and picked up the book she had taken from the library after breakfast. Scott's *Guy Mannering* had held her interest through three chapters this morning, but now she could not gather sufficient concentration to go on. After reading, then rereading, the same half-dozen pages, Ria finally gave up and set it aside.

She threw back the covers and took her flannel robe from the foot of the bed and put it on. Her slippers had been placed at a practical distance from the bed so that all she had to do was step into them. The fireplace was her immediate destination, and she chose a poker from among the fire irons and jabbed at the logs until a great flame jumped from between them, and they were burning evenly again.

Satisfied she would not catch a chill, Ria turned her attention to the window. The heavy maroon velvet drapes denied her a view of the starkly beautiful winter landscape. Through a slender parting in the panels, she could see that the moonlight was uncommonly bright this evening. The hem of her own nightdress was frosted by silver-blue light wherever it was touched by one of the slim bands of moonshine.

Ria pulled back each panel and secured it against the wall

with the matching velvet sash. She knelt on the upholstered
window bench and rested her arms on the narrow sill. Her
breath clouded a pane of glass at first, then slowly disappeared.

The breadth of the landscape never failed to astonish her.
This panoramic view of the estate was at once familiar and
foreign, the former because she knew every curve in the ribbon of the road and in the lay of the land, the latter because
each time she visited this place, the exploration of the countryside seemed as novel to her as the first.

Compliments of the recent snow and this full moon's
light, the fields were awash in crystalline splendor. The crests
of drifted snow sparkled, and the long boughs of the firs
were swept gracefully downward by the weight of the snow.
Several deer wandered cautiously away from the wood in
search of food. Farther still in the distance was the lake. Iced
over, it was almost indistinguishable from its surroundings,
but Ria knew where to look for it. She stared at it for a long
moment, trying to make out its perimeter, when a movement
along its southern bank captured her attention.

At first she thought it was deer come looking for water.
The size, though, puzzled her. She rubbed at the glass with
the sleeve of her robe to erase the last vestige of condensa-
tion. When the clarity of her view still did not satisfy, Ria
threw open the window.

The air was bracing, and the first icy gust shivered the
drapes and flattened Ria's robe and nightdress against her
chest. A moment later, the wind stilled, and Ria could draw a
full breath. She leaned out the window, her pale braid falling
forward over her shoulder so that it hung like an icicle.

Eyes narrowed, her stare intent, Ria was able to make out
the shape of horse and rider. She could not be sure that it was
Draco and West, but intuitively she knew it to be true. To
what purpose would a stranger detour from the road and go
down to the lake? Moreover, to that particular curve in the
lake's bank? She wondered that he had the courage to go

there. It must be a place fraught with unpleasant memories. She had not often gone back, and her memories were rather more vague than she suspected his would be.

Ria's right hand lifted absently, and she massaged the back of her neck. When she realized what she was doing, she smiled a trifle wryly and let her fingers fall away. An old habit, she thought, one that gave her an odd sort of comfort when those uncertain and unsettling memories came to the forefront of her mind.

She watched for as long as she could withstand the cold. She followed West's progress away from the lake and back up to the road and lost sight of him in one of the curves. By the time he reappeared, she was shaking with the effort to stay in the open frame of the window. Her fingers were stiff and clumsy when she reached for the latch, but she managed to secure it after a few attempts. Hugging herself until she reached the fireplace, Ria thrust her hands as close to the flames as she dared. Droplets of water fell to the floor from where the end of her damp braid had actually frozen and was now melting. Ria unplaited her hair and combed through it with her fingers.

He was finally returning. The realization had the power to ease Ria's mind as well as disturb it. She remembered his clipped and chilly accents from the previous night when she told him she could think of no reason she would have to trouble him again. *Then you underestimate yourself,* he had said. *I'm certain something will occur to you if you apply yourself.*

God's truth, but she was out of patience with him for being right.

West let himself into his room and found Finch was waiting up for him, or nearly so. The valet was snoring softly in a wing chair that had been pushed close to the fireplace. Finch's plump arms rested comfortably on the curve of his belly, and his feet were propped on a three-legged stool. West woke him by stomping his boots rather loudly, because to let him sleep on would have been the graver insult.

Finch was at the ready immediately, and West pretended not to have noticed there had been a moment's inattention to his duties. They had gotten on well for years in such a manner, and West was confident that so it would go.

"Was there much in the way of speculation regarding my absence?" he asked as Finch unwound his stock.

"Enough that I felt compelled to start a wager book."

West ignored that dry retort. "Did Miss Ashby ask after me?"

"No."

"That either proves that she is learning some restraint or that she concluded for herself where I had gone."

"I suspect it is the latter," Finch said as he assisted West out of his frock coat. "She impresses as being capable of deciphering your cryptic missive."

"I also suspect it is the latter, but that is because I cannot conceive she has mastered restraint."

"She has not yet bloodied your nose. That is always a good sign."

West frowned. "You will have to explain that remark. I have treated her in every way respectfully. She has had no—" He stopped because Finch's rounded countenance was clearly skeptical. "What have you heard below stairs? No doubt there is gossip."

"It seems you were caught out in a provocative pose."

"Provocative? What the devil does that mean? I was kissing her."

Finch shrugged. *"Provocative* is how they're telling it in the kitchen. Mr. Hastings—he is the first butler—has been disapproving of such talk, but it goes on outside of his hearing. Some of the speculation is that you went off to secure a special license."

"Swear you are jesting."

"If you insist."

West groaned softly. "You did not encourage that kind of talk, I hope."

"I did not participate."

"Except for initiating the betting book."

Finch's smile was maddeningly inscrutable. He turned back the covers on West's bed and inserted a warming pan at the foot. "Will there be anything else, Your Grace?"

"No. See to your own comfort, Finch. I am for sleeping late and taking my breakfast here."

"Then I shall see that you are not disturbed." He gathered up West's clothes for laundering and pressing and laid them neatly over his arm. "Good evening." It seemed to him that his employer was asleep before he had exited the room.

Ria waited until she heard Finch's retreat in the direction of the servants' stairs before she stepped into the hallway. It had been a narrow thing, for she had almost been at West's door when it had opened. She ducked into the nearest available room—Margaret's private reading salon, as it turned out—and remained there until it was safe.

She slipped into West's bedchamber as silently as she had the night before and approached his bed. He was sleeping on his side, facing the fireplace. That golden glow highlighted the angles of his face, the thrust of his jaw, the patrician cut of his nose, the sculpted line of his cheek. There were faint shadows beneath his eyes and another shadow that was this day's growth of beard across the lower part of his face. He did not have the look of one in an easy sleep. In contrast to the night before, he appeared older than his years, more world-weary than simply tired.

Ria stood there for more than a minute as she debated the wisdom of waking him. He was unlikely to appreciate the anxious state that had prompted her to leave her room. He would expect her to act more circumspectly, or better, not to act at all. They were very different in that way. Unease pushed her to do something, while discomfort quieted him physically and roused his dark humor.

She wondered what she might learn from him. Was it possible she could sleep as deeply as he was now? She turned to go, and that was when she saw the slim book lying on the table just inside the door. Curious as to why he would place it so far from his bed if he meant to read it, Ria crossed the room to pick it up. She tried to read the gilt lettering on the spine by holding it up to the firelight. It was not lettering at all, she realized within a few moments of studying it more closely, but decorative embellishment, like scrollwork in the mantelpiece and wainscoting. There was nothing on the cover to indicate the contents.

She walked closer to the fireplace to take advantage of the light and opened the book. If she had bothered to suppose what might be contained inside, Ria would have said it was verse. It wasn't, as it turned out, nor was it anything she might have had imagination enough to guess.

Heat rose in her cheeks as she stared at the illustration confronting her. Curiously enough, though it seemed to span both pages and little in the way of margins remained, the picture on the left was upside down. On the right a beautiful young woman lay in a pose of complete abandon. She was not naked, but her clothing had been arranged to make her very nearly so. Her arms were raised overhead and she grasped an iron headrail with her fingertips. The scooped bodice of her gown had been cut away along with her corset and chemise, and her full, sweet breasts lay bare, the nipples puckered and ripe as though for plucking. The hem of her skirt and all of her petticoats had fallen back to the level of her waist. Her hips were angled upward, supported by two large pillows that had been placed there for such a purpose. Her thighs were parted and the dark hair of her swollen mons glistened.

Ria's eyes swept upward to the woman's face, every detail

masterfully rendered there by the skilled artist's hand. Her eyes were not entirely closed, but lowered to half-mast, shaded by long lashes. Her mouth was parted, the lips were dewy, and the tip of her tongue could be seen either in advance or retreat. The long, slender neck was arched, her chin thrust upward. The woman's ebon hair lay in a tangle about her head and influenced the look of her as untamed, almost feral. The effect of the whole was an agony of delight or pain; it was not possible to know.

Kneeling at the foot of the bed and between the woman's legs, was a man of such perfect proportion and well-defined masculinity that Ria thought he must be the artist's idea of a god stepped down from Mt. Olympus. Unlike the woman, he wore no clothes at all. The muscles of his arms were sculpted, as were his buttocks and thighs. One of his hands rested on the woman's right knee, the other grasped his considerable erection as though he meant to guide something more than his courage to the sticking place.

Ria placed her knuckles against her mouth to stifle the nervous giggle this last errant thought produced. Because she had been slow to react and some small sound had escaped her throat, she quickly glanced over her shoulder to see if West had awakened. She sighed, relieved that he had not.

Ria was discomfited by what she held in her hands, but mature enough not to believe she would experience all the fires of hell for examining it. To that end, she turned the book around so the picture that had been upside down was now righted. It was a different couple on this side of the page. Here a man stood with his back to a marble column. He was wearing clothes that had been in fashion more than a score of years earlier: a coat lined in satin with braided cuffs and large buttons, a heavily embroidered waistcoat, and black, tight-fitting breeches with white stockings and buckled boots. On her knees in front of him, face and arms raised as though in supplication, was a woman whose powdered hair was carefully coifed in curls and ringlets. She wore a gown with a cinched waist, laced bodice, and flared sleeves. The man's pelvis was thrust forward, the flies of his breeches open, and he held her raised head between his large hands. In profile the intent of his actions was clear. He meant for the woman to take his jutting, swollen cock in her mouth.

Another partially strangled sound escaped Ria's throat, and she felt a stirring between her thighs that was more unwelcome than unpleasant. She did not know how to think about her disappointment when she turned the page and found it was identical to the one before it. She turned another and another and found they were all alike. It was the same when she reversed the book again and regarded the woman and her Greek god on the bed. Every page was like every other.

"Can you not determine how it works?"

The book fell from Ria's nerveless fingers and thudded to the floor. She spun on her heel and glared at West. He was reclining on his side, his head propped on one elbow. His coppery hair was a crisscross thatch, and his eyes had a certain slumberous appeal, but he looked perfectly at his ease, in no way weary as she had noted earlier. It seemed, no matter how improbable, that he was enjoying himself. Ria did not think she was mistaken that it was amusement lifting the corners of his mouth.

"Bring it here," he said.

"I . . . I wore my slippers."

West's grin deepened as his eyes dropped to her feet. He could not recall that Ria had ever been more off her stride than she was right now. "Yes, I see. It was good of you to remember." He pointed to the book. "Go on. Pick it up and bring it here."

Ria stooped. She continued to regard West somewhat warily as her fingers searched out the book's smooth leather binding. She caught one corner, edged it closer, then took it in hand as she stood again.

West indicated the space in front of him at his bedside. "Here." He noted that she walked forward slowly, with all the enthusiasm one might rouse for those final steps to the gallows platform. "I won't show you if you'd rather I didn't. I shouldn't anyway, so some encouragement on your part will be required."

Ria reached the bed and held the book out to him. "Did you find it here?" she asked. "Is it Tenley's?"

"If I found it here it could have been the duke's," West said. "Do not worry, though. I did not pluck it from this library." He took the book from her hand and opened it to a random page. His brows lifted a fraction as he regarded it, then Ria. "It is rather explicit, is it not? I gather from your expression that you have not seen the like before."

Ria shook her head. "I didn't know such things existed."

"That is because you had governesses and tutors while I went to a school for boys where things like this are as treasured as sacred relics."

"Then it's yours."

He chuckled. "No, not mine. I have borrowed it, so I suppose it is mine for the time being." An expression he could not quite define flitted across Ria's face. "That disappoints? Intrigues?"

"Confuses."

"That is all right, then, because I am confused as well. What are you doing here? I can safely assume you did not come for this." He watched her eyes stray to the open book, then lift quickly. Her curiosity was a palpable thing, but he pretended he had not observed it. He casually closed the book around his index finger. "I only arrived a short time ago. I should have thought you would be enjoying sleep at such a time. Were you perhaps waiting for me?"

"If you mean was I staying awake in anticipation of your return, then no, I was not."

"You are a very poor liar. I would wager that if you sucked on a lemon, your features would not pucker so severely."

"I was disturbed from my sleep by a noise in the hallway, and I rose to investigate."

"I admire the way you do not back down from the lie. It is a good strategy if one starts off well, but I have already informed you that you did not. Still, carry on as you wish. I am a rapt audience."

Ria sighed impatiently. "Will you not show me the workings of the book?"

West grinned. "Of course. We will get to the other later." He pointed to the bedside table. "To fully appreciate this, more light is required."

Ria was not certain he was talking about her appreciation of the book, but rather of his appreciation of her reaction to it. She wondered at what point she had become his entertainment. "Perhaps not."

"Very well. As I said, I should not do it." He removed his index finger and set the book beside the unlighted candlestick. "We have come again to the point of your visit. I make it to be less that twenty-four hours since you left my bedchamber in a high dudgeon, vowing never to return."

"That is an exaggerated account. I was not so dramatic, either, in manner or phrasing."

West moved closer to the middle of the bed to make room for her on its edge. "Come, else I shall have a kink in my neck."

Ria sat down much as she had the night before, turning slightly sideways so she might face him, and drew up one leg. "I want to know what occurred while you were gone. Tenley thinks you were meeting with Mr. Ridgeway on pressing matters regarding the estate. Margaret thinks you suspect my strong feelings for you and panicked. I think you were in Sunbury making the acquaintance of Mr. Beckwith."

"All intriguing possibilities. If it was Lady Tenley who believed I had taken off in such cowardly fashion, who is it that thought I was procuring a special license?"

"I had not heard that. You didn't, did you?"

"As you suspected, I was in Sunbury with Beckwith."

She nodded. Her relief that there was no special license was tempered by her concern that his introduction to Mr. Beckwith might not have gone well. "Am I still employed at the school?"

"Yes. I did not interfere, though he suggested he would understand if I did. If he is representative of the entire board of governors, then they are not quite as progressive in their thinking as you led me to believe. Apparently they are pleased to employ you, but cannot fathom that the duke permitted it."

"I am well aware of their confusion on this last count. I am only the second woman to have the position as head of the school since its founding. Except for my immediate predecessor, all the others have been men."

"What about Miss Weaver?"

Ria shrugged. "I cannot say. I've told you the school was founded by gentlemen. If Miss Weaver existed at all, she was simply a namesake. There is no record that she was ever headmistress. Pray, do not miss my point—the governors take small steps, but they are always moving in a forward direction."

"That is your opinion. One might take the position that permitting women to find purpose outside the drawing room and bedchamber is likely to bring about the collapse of society. That is hardly a forward direction."

"One might take that position," she said, "but you don't. It is far too late an hour to argue the devil's convictions. Tell me what became of your bid to join the board."

"No invitation was formally made, but I believe Beckwith intends to speak or write to the other governors about my interest. I have reason to hope." The dim light did not prevent West from glimpsing Ria's uncertainty. "You do not find this a helpful development?"

"I am not at all confident that anything will be gained by you joining the board. Jane Petty is my concern, not the board of governors."

"Miss Petty is also my concern. This is not a means to keep you on a short tether."

"I am very glad to hear it."

West grinned at her clipped accents. Clearly, she was offended by the notion. "Those are Beckwith's words, not mine. I have to say I did not care for the manner in which he said it. I think he has given some thought to the fashion in which he would like to restrain you."

Ria frowned. There was a meaning in his words that she did not quite understand, something that was being said but not being said plainly. "I do not comprehend why Mr. Beckwith believes I require restraint of any sort. In what way does he think I have overstepped myself?"

West realized he had just put forth an idea that Ria was not fully prepared to hear. For all that she had initiated this second encounter in his bedroom, she was not worldly. These overtures were prompted by her belief that they were both necessary and urgent, and they were done on Miss Petty's behalf, not out of some carnal self-interest. He would do well to remember that, he decided, though it was a damnable temptation to pretend it was otherwise. Miss Ria Ashby had a splendidly kissable mouth.

West understood he would have to respond to her question only so far as she could accept the answer. "Beckwith thinks that you should not have told me about Miss Petty's disappearance. He believes your worries are excessive."

"Excessive? But—" She stopped because West held up one finger.

"He is of the definite opinion that she will reappear, most likely pregnant and unmarried, remorseful but with her hand out. You must admit that it is a distinct possibility, especially in light of what Amy told us."

"If it comes to pass, it is because someone took advantage of Jane. He must be made to account for his actions. Does Mr. Beckwith think nothing should be done?"

"He believes he is doing it. There was approval to hire Mr. Lytton."

"But there has been no progress."

"I do not think that concerns Beckwith. He believes the governors have done their duty by Miss Petty."

"That cannot be true," Ria said. There was a slight catch in her voice and an ache behind her eyes. "You must have misunderstood."

Offering no argument, West continued to regard her steadily.

"He was so supportive," she said. "I have his letter at the school. He responded quickly when I wrote to him about Miss Petty, and he shared all of my concerns."

"Then you are probably right. I must have misunderstood."

Angry tears made Ria's blue-gray eyes steely. "Why do you do that? Why do you offer your opinion, then not stand behind it?"

He shrugged. "It is not so important to me that I convince you that I'm right."

"But I don't want you to surrender your opinion if I am wrong."

One corner of West's mouth lifted, but his eyes remained perfectly grave. "I don't surrender my opinion, Ria. I simply allow you to have yours."

A tear fell from the corner of her eye. She wiped it away impatiently. "You are maddening. Mayhap I want to be convinced."

His smile deepened a fraction. "I don't think so."

Ria's next breath came shakily, but she managed to suppress a shudder. On a thread of sound, she asked, "What will happen now?"

"Beckwith will speak to the other governors. If we are fortunate, they will decide it serves them better to make me a member."

"When you told me you meant to join them, I thought you would offer them money to secure a seat. But that was not your plan at all, was it?"

"No. They would not be moved by money."

"Then what is it that you're offering?"

"Power." West sat up and pushed a pillow behind his back

to lean against the bedhead. He raked his hair with his fingertips. "I told you Beckwith is not pleased that I will take it upon myself to determine what happened to Miss Petty. It is natural that he will want to have a measure of control over what I do. He can't have it unless he invites me to join them, and he can't invite me without speaking to the others. What I am offering them, Ria, is an opportunity to eliminate me as a threat and protect their positions."

Ria absently laced her fingers until her hands formed a single fist. Raising that fist against her chest, she rested her chin on the knuckles. Her regard of West was candid. "You still think of Mr. Beckwith as one of the bishops."

"He *is* a bishop. I cannot pretend it is otherwise."

She nodded faintly. An argument formed in her mind, but she held it back, adopting his manner of not trying to change his opinion when it was at odds with her own. He seemed to know the battle she was fighting with herself because a faint smile lifted the corners of his mouth. She returned it. "I never said I could not learn something from you."

That raised West's wicked grin. "Indeed," he said dryly.

Ria could do nothing about the flush pinkening her complexion from her throat to her cheeks. "You have taken a meaning I did not intend."

"Indeed."

"Intolerable."

His grin deepened. "The slight would be more effective if your eyes were not straying to that book."

"I was looking at you."

"You were *thinking* about that book." He took Ria's small sigh as a sign of admission. "What do you want to know about it?"

"Where did you get it?"

"Beckwith's study."

Ria hardly knew what to say. "How extraordinary."

"I suppose it must seem so to you, but not all men find the poetry of Byron and Shelley to be an adequate aphrodisiac."

He gave her a quizzing look. "You do know what an aphrodisiac is, don't you?"

"Of course I do," she said coolly. "It is derived from Aphrodite, the goddess of love and beauty to the ancient Greeks. An aphrodisiac is something that excites the manner in which one thinks about love and beauty."

West nodded slowly, hard-pressed not to laugh. "Yes, well, that is one definition."

"If there is another, I should like to hear it. I have no liking for being kept in ignorance."

"And I am not your bloody tutor."

Ria did not take issue with either his assertion or his way of expressing it. She merely stared him down.

"Very well. An aphrodisiac is something—usually a food or a drug—that excites the blood." He sighed heavily when she merely furrowed her brow at him. "It rouses sexual desire. I cannot say it more plainly that that."

"You don't have to. I understand perfectly." She paused a beat, then added, "Thank you."

It was Ria's thanks that undid West. The crisp accents were so entirely at odds with the heat in her cheeks that the presentation was comical. He wasn't moved to laughter, though. His inclination, instead, was to kiss her.

He leaned forward and slipped one hand at the back of Ria's neck before she properly determined his intent. His mouth settled on hers, lightly at first, then with more pressure when she did not resist. Her lips were soft and sweet and warm. They parted for him on a breathy little sigh.

He slid closer until his hip nudged hers. She turned into him, seeking better purchase on the edge of the bed. Her hands rose to the level of his shoulders, hovered, then were lifted higher so she could thread her fingers in his hair. The first tentative touch of her fingertips wrested a low, throaty growl from him and quickened his blood. He felt her press herself flush to him, and he could make out the shape of her swelling breasts against his chest.

She tugged lightly at the curling ends of his hair. This small encouragement was all he required to lower her to the bed. He followed her down, mouths fused, eyes closed. The kiss deepened; his tongue plunged into her mouth, teasing hers, pushing, tasting, sucking.

West pushed at the blankets tangled between them. He found the sash of her robe and untied it. The brushed flannel fabric fell away on either side of her waist, leaving only the thin cotton of her nightdress as a barrier to his touch. He laid a hand on her abdomen and felt her skin retract. His palm slid upward and she drew in a ragged breath in response to its advance. When he cupped her breast and dragged his thumbnail across the turgid nipple, her hips lifted off the bed.

He tore his mouth away from hers and steadied himself. They were topsy-turvy on the mattress, their heads at the foot, their feet at the head. The warming pan was dangerously close to tipping, and he moved it safely away. One of the pillows had fallen to the floor, along with both of Ria's slippers, and the blankets were bunched in a mound in the middle of the mattress. He was aware for the first time how cold it was outside of the quilts, although cold had little enough to do with the shiver that shuddered through him.

She was watching him through eyes no longer steely, but the color of smoke. Her expression was not vague or unfocused, neither slack nor slumberous. Rather, she was watchful. Desire, as it was cast on Ria's face, was a conscious act of will, perhaps even a bit defiant. Here was wanting emboldened by curiosity, need made lively by the intelligence of a sentient being.

Whatever he might do to her now, it would not be against her will.

West touched Ria's forehead with his own. He closed his eyes, and his smile hovered just above her mouth. "Perhaps I shall be your bloody tutor after all," he whispered.

Her own smile was faint as she repeated words she had

spoken earlier in a different context. "I never said I could not learn something from you."

He said nothing to this, kissing her once instead, then lifting his head again and rolling away so that he lay on his back. Out of the corner of his eye he saw Ria turn on her side and stretch lengthwise beside him, propping herself on one elbow and adopting much in the way of the pose he had earlier.

"I have given you disgust of me," she said quietly.

"No."

"Then why are you not kissing me?"

"I am not certain I want the responsibility."

She rubbed her bare feet against each other, warding off the chill. West started to reach for one of the blankets to give her, but she stayed his hand. "You do not have to take responsibility," she said. "For anything." She leaned over, found a corner of one of the blankets, and dragged it across them. "I would not ask so much of you as that. I would not even want it. If it is that you are my guardian that gives you pause, then—"

"It has nothing to do with that bit of nonsense."

"Then what is it?"

"You are without experience."

"But that is exactly my point. I am four-and-twenty. I am resolved that the time has come to acquire some."

"Your confidence is misplaced. You don't know enough about the inclinations of men to say that."

Ria sat up and turned her back on West while she lighted the candlestick on the bedside table. She picked up Beckwith's book and lay down again, this time on her back. Opening the book, she held it up so they could both view the illustrations. The drawing of the woman on her knees in front of the man was the one that was right side up.

"Tell me about this, then," she said. Though it was her intent to be bold, the slight catch in her voice gave her demand a slightly tentative edge. Having managed that much, however, she was determined to persevere. "She looks as if she means to put the whole of him in her mouth."

West could not recall that he had ever had a conversation such as this with a woman. The tone of it, though, was not unfamiliar to him. Ria communicated the same uncertainty and awe he remembered from his Hambrick days when he and the rest of the Compass Club had seen pictures such as this one for the first time.

"I believe that is her intent, yes," he said carefully.

"She might very well choke. It is uncommonly large, is it not?"

West made an effort to concentrate on the illustration and not on the part of him that she might term uncommonly large. "It is of the length and girth one might expect for an aroused male." He was pleased he could address her question in such a composed manner. "As to whether she will choke, that depends on whether she has the knack of it."

"The knack of it? I take that to mean it requires some special talent and practice." She fell silent as she considered this, then offered thoughtfully, "I saw a Gypsy fellow once swallow a flaming sword almost to the hilt. It must be rather like that."

West realized he might very well choke on nothing more than his own spit if he did not take Ria in hand. "Yes, I suppose it is."

She glanced at him, frowning slightly. "But you're not certain?"

"You will perhaps comprehend that I have had neither occasion to swallow a sword nor suck on a—" He stopped short, knowing he had said entirely too much. So much for taking Ria in hand. That caution was best applied to himself, and after she left he was determined to do it in the most literal manner possible. "I think enough has been said," he told her. "There is no sense in talking a thing to death."

Ria held the book away when he would have taken it from her. "If this is the only way I am to acquire knowledge, then you should not deprive me of it. Now, tell me if it is a thing to be enjoyed by both of them."

He groaned softly and placed his forearm across his brow. "By the man, certainly. By the woman, sometimes."

"Why only sometimes?"

"It depends on what enjoyment she derives from giving pleasure."

"I see," she said slowly, loath to admit she was still uncertain of his meaning. "You know this from your own experience?"

West lifted his forearm just enough to give Ria a quelling glance. He was satisfied when she blushed deeply and went back to studying the illustration. There were limits to what he would tell her, he thought, and she had just pushed that question against one of them.

Ria's fingers trembled slightly as she turned the page. She regarded the next drawing for a long moment before she spoke. "This one is just like the one before it. I fail to understand the point of that."

"Not *exactly* like the one before." He reached for the book again, and when she was hesitant to give it up, he asked for it. "May I? I promise to return it." He plucked it from her hands when she held it out to him. Angling it until her view was better, West grasped all the pages between his thumb and forefinger, then let his thumb slip from the edge of each successive page so they flew by quickly.

Ria blinked widely, fascinated and a little frightened as the figures of the man and woman were set into motion by the rapidly flipping pages. The woman was pulled forward, swallowing the man's erect member as deeply as Ria recalled the Gypsy taking in the fiery sword. "To the hilt," she said under her breath, scarcely aware she had spoken aloud.

"An apt description."

Ria took the book back and held the pages just as he had, then let her thumb slip. The movement of the figures was jerky, almost comical, but there was no denying their purpose. "How is it accomplished?"

West chuckled. She was more curious about the method the artist used than the content. "As I said, each page is not identical to the one before. There are subtle differences that account for the movement when the pages are thumbed through quickly." He directed her to open the book to an illustration that was at the midpoint. "You can see the differences between this one and the one at the beginning. Now look at the final illustration. The woman has released him again."

"You must allow that it is very clever."

"That is what South said the first time he saw a book like this."

"How old were you?"

"Eleven. Perhaps twelve."

She nodded, sighing. "And I am twice that age. Boys are more fortunate, I think, to know of these things early."

"I do not remember having that opinion when we were caught out."

Ria smiled. "Well, perhaps twelve is rather young. Still, girls would be better able to secure their place in society if they knew what they might be asked to embrace or endure."

"Embrace or endure," he said softly. For all that Ria was inexperienced, he thought she had neatly captured a woman's dilemma. It had certainly been his own mother's. He watched her face as she riffled the pages a third time. Her features were no longer awash in color, and every aspect of her countenance was set in concentration. There was a fine crease between her fair brows, and her eyes had narrowed a fraction. Her lips were flattened and twisted slightly to one side. He had no difficulty imagining she had applied the same formidable intelligence and consideration to her studies in the schoolroom, a student much prized by her teachers.

Ria turned the book around, understanding at last why the other illustration was printed in the opposite direction. Grasping the fore edge of the paper between her thumb and finger, she let it fly past. Even though she knew what to expect, it was still startling. The man thrust himself into the woman and pumped himself in fits and starts between her open thighs. The woman's head was thrown back first, then her fair-haired lover's.

West managed to catch the book before Ria dropped it on her head. He closed it and put it aside, out of her reach. Turning on his side, he rested on one elbow while he regarded her. "Have you seen quite enough?"

Ria felt a peculiar quickness to her own heartbeat and a queer, unsettled feeling deep inside her. The response she made was a trifle breathless. "Quite enough, I think. It looks to be a rather clumsy business."

"It is." West was happy to encourage this line of thinking.

"It seemed as though it might be painful."

"A perfect agony."

The glance she cast in his direction was suspicious. "It cannot be so terrible, else no one would ever engage in it— even for procreative purposes."

"One endures a great deal to continue the species."

"I don't believe you."

West shrugged.

"I liked it well enough when you kissed me."

"Kissing is meant to lull the senses to what comes afterward."

Ria was a trifle less certain than she had been moments earlier. "What about giving and receiving pleasure? You mentioned that before."

"I may have overstated that aspect. In truth, there is precious little pleasure to be had."

"The poets speak favorably of it."

"They speak of love. You are speaking of . . ." His voice trailed off as he searched for the proper word. "Mayhap you should continue this discussion with Lady Tenley."

"Coward." Ria turned toward him. "Can you not say *fornication?* That is what the couples are doing, are they not? Fornicating. You may as well say so."

"Of course," he said with an ironic lift to his brow. "I seem to offend your sensibilities when I least mean to do so."

Ria's expression was grave. "I know you have respect for me," she said quietly. "It is not necessary to consider your words so carefully."

"Ria, you flinch when I say *bloody hell*."

It was a valid point, and she did not deny it. "It is just that sometimes you think I do not know my own mind. That is what I find truly offends my sensibilities. I wish you would not try to protect me from myself. I wish your respect for me was not predicated on a fact of biology. I am a woman, true enough, but that might be cause for celebration, not a reason to set me from you."

"And it is not because you are a woman that some distance is in order. It is because you are a lady."

"Bloody hell."

West's laughter rumbled softly at the back of his throat. "It will require more than colorful language to make me treat you like a strumpet."

Ria sat up and drew back the blanket. His erection made a tent of the fabric of his nightshirt. Before he knew what she was about, she straddled his legs and pushed the material upward as far as his thighs. "Then mayhap this will be enough to encourage you."

Chapter Eight

West caught Ria by the shoulders as she began to bend toward him. The centers of his eyes were so dark and large, the emerald edge of his irises had almost disappeared in response to wanting her. His heart hammered in his chest, and the thundering he heard was the roar of blood in his ears. "You don't know what you're—" He stopped because Ria was shaking her head slowly, and he knew he was lost when it took no more than this subtle movement to set him from his own course.

"Then you'll have to teach me," she said. "Or allow me to learn it for myself."

He had no doubt that she had deliberately misinterpreted what he'd meant to say, but neither was he proof against that soft and sumptuous mouth or the way her words parted it. His hands fell away, and he watched her continue her downward descent. At the first touch of her lips, he felt his entire body go taut. It was too much and not enough. His hips jerked as she opened her mouth around him, drawing back his foreskin with her hand so that her tongue could sweep over the silky, sensitive head of his cock.

Her pale braid fell forward over her shoulder, and the tip of it brushed his thigh, swinging back and forth like a pendulum as she moved over him. Her hands went to his hips, and she stroked him with her fingertips, running them lightly across the firm flesh of his buttocks, using her thumbnail to score his skin with a pale pink line.

He wanted to close his eyes. He wanted to watch her. It was erotic either way, and for a while he did one, then the other, until she drew back at last, her breathing husky and slightly ragged, and asked for more. At first he did not understand, but then her eyes fell on his arousal, and he realized it was more of him that she wanted. Like the illustration. To the hilt.

He sat up and turned to the head of the bed, drawing off his nightshirt. The room's chill did not penetrate now, not with his blood heated to the temperature of molten lava. He leaned back against the headboard and held out his hand to her, inviting her to come to him as he had not done before.

Ria knelt before him, and this time when she bent to him she started at the smooth curve of his neck and shoulder and worked her way down. His skin was warm and taut, the muscles defined by planes and angles that seemed carved with a sculptor's eye for detail of the human form.

She drew her mouth along his collarbone and made a damp trail with the edge of her tongue. The taste of him was both unfamiliar and tantalizing. Sweet and salty, musky and humid, it seemed to Ria that she should know it, yet it was wholly new to her, a combination of tastes and scents that teased her own senses. Her skin prickled, and her nostrils flared. She felt something hot and sweetly urgent uncurl in the center of her. Ribbons of sensation followed the path of her blood until her fingertips tingled. Between her thighs she was damp. She felt a pressure there, but also a void, and the effect of both was that she wished he would touch her.

He did not, though. His fingers curled in the sheet on either side of him instead.

She ran her fingertips down the length of his arms until they reached his wrists, then they curved like talons, and she took him captive while her lips and tongue, and finally her teeth, made a separate exploration.

Her head dipped lower. She felt the catch of his breath and then the vibration of his hum of pleasure. She took him in her mouth again, and everything about the taste and scent of him here was more intense. This act of giving pleasure struck her as profoundly intimate, a thing done in which she was both master and supplicant, at once powerful, yet in the service of him.

It seemed to her that he sensed these things as well, for it was no different for him. He could command that she stop or surrender to her. The pull of both kept him exactly where he was, straining slightly under the pressure of her hands and mouth, but not so much that he would remove her. He was still except for those movements he could not help, and the fact that she was responsible for each small stirring excited her almost beyond bearing.

She suckled him more deeply this time, helped by their altered positions and his hoarsely whispered instructions. The cry she wrested from him was her own name, and the sound of it was so pleasing to her that she determined she would hear it again.

West slipped his wrists free of Ria's loose grip and lifted her hands to his hips. With no more encouragement than that, her fingers trailed along his inner thighs. She found the base of his shaft and added the rhythmic massage of her hand to the steady suckling of her mouth. One of his hands captured her loose braid and wrapped it around his fist; the other found purchase in the sheets. He felt the change in the cadence of his breathing. It was ragged now, and harsh. Things that he wanted to say came to his mind in disjointed phrases; words simply lodged in his throat. His hips surged upward, and then she had all of him, and his fist around her hair held her just so. He knew himself to be incapable of removing her at that moment. He was riding a wave of pleasure so sharp that its crest was like a finely honed blade. It was not beyond the realm of possibility that he would be split from balls to brains by it—then thank her for having done it to him.

There was something about this last that caught his sense of humor. Whereas laughter usually left him weak, this time the effect was exactly the opposite. His pleasure was so whet by it that he felt the quickening of his pulse and the urgency for release more acutely than he had moments before.

Swearing softly, his words hardly intelligible to his own ears, he lifted Ria's head away and guided his seed to the sheets, aware all the while of her surprise and deeply fascinated study. Feeling rather like an insect with its wings pinned back for examination, West yanked on a blanket to cover himself as he set his feet over the side of the bed. Without a word, he disappeared into the adjoining dressing room.

West poured water into a basin, though whether he should use it to make his ablutions or drown himself was not entirely clear. He stared at his reflection in the mirror above the washstand but saw nothing there that helped him understand what had just transpired. His sense of honor was deeply offended by what he had allowed Ria to do, yet there was no denying that his pleasure at her hands and mouth was unlike any he had ever known. Other women had shown greater skill—the barmaid at the inn, for one—but none had been so determinedly interested in every aspect of his response. Perhaps it was Ria's very innocence that made her curious, but West suspected it was more than that. From the outset, she seemed to be aware of him in a way few people were. She was sensitive to his mood, to his wayward thoughts, even to his contrary humor. Was it so unlikely, then, that she would be so keenly perceptive about what gave him the sharpest pleasure?

West unhitched the blanket at his hips and threw it over a nearby bench. He washed himself, removing the scents of lavender and musk from his skin. The icy water made him draw in a quick breath, but it had the desired numbing effect on that part of him that was still stirring.

Water splashed his chest when he dropped the sponge

back into the basin. He wiped it away with a negligent flick of his fingers, then turned to take a towel from a brass hook beside the door. His line of sight into the bedchamber did not include the head of the bed where Ria sat. The candlestick cast sufficient light for him to see that most of the blankets had been pushed from the middle of the bed to the foot of it, and the warming pan was set where it could finally do some good. Ria's slippers were still on the floor, but the pillow that had fallen there earlier was gone. He also did not see the book.

For a moment West braced his arms on the marble edge of the washstand and hung his head, not so much in the manner of a man avoiding his reflection, but in the manner of one reflecting. After a long moment in this position, West pushed himself away and straightened. He raked his thick hair with his fingertips, leaving it furrowed at the temple and crown, then grabbed the towel and dried himself. When he was done, he tossed the towel aside and went to the highboy dresser to root out a pair of drawers.

His tread was almost soundless as he padded back to the bed. Ria was indeed sitting comfortably at the head of it, surrounded by a throne of pillows and still modestly attired in her nightdress and flannel robe. Her knees were drawn up and propped on them was the erotic treasure he had stolen from Beckwith's private library. She was studying the illustration of the pair engaged in more traditional coupling, though even that description of their activity was suspect, given certain aspects of the drawing that Ria seemed to have failed to notice.

West grasped the book by its backboard and spine and removed it from her hands. She did not resist his interference. Closing it, he set it on the table. "I think you've had enough book learning today." He was gratified to see that she was still capable of blushing. He did not like to think that her experience had already hardened her against it. It pained him that she might become so changed by it that she would be indifferent to all sensibilities. "I want you to go now."

Ria had been expecting this. She nodded faintly, but it was only an indication that she heard him. She made no attempt to leave the bed. Instead, she moved one of the pillows from her side and pressed it against the headboard, inviting him to sit beside her. "I have questions I am learning a book cannot properly answer."

"And I have already suggested you apply to Lady Tenley."

"I think broaching this subject with her would be a mistake. How would I explain my interest?"

"Don't women discuss these things among themselves?"

She lifted one eyebrow in an incredulous arc. "I have never been privy to conversations of that nature, and you can be certain no governess ever thought to educate me. It is not a subject broached at the school, even among the teachers who have been married." Ria folded her hands and rested them atop her bent knees. "Therefore, it falls to you."

It was precisely this sort of responsibility that he had been trying to avoid. His sour, impatient look reminded her of that. He took the blanket he was carrying over his arm and rolled it lengthwise. Before he sat down, he placed it beside Ria so that it would be between them. It was an inadequate physical barrier, but as a reminder of the need for distance between them, it was more than sufficient.

"I am not ashamed," she said. This was offered somewhat defiantly as he crawled in beside her. "You can't expect that I should be."

West yanked on the blankets still mounded at his feet. He snapped them out and pulled them up over his legs, offering Ria a portion of them to tuck around her. She accepted them so gratefully that he realized she had been waiting for this invitation. Apparently she would not be moved from his bed until she was ready, but neither would she nest there without his permission.

He did not comment on whether he thought she should be ashamed or not, but let it lie with her. "What is it you want to know?"

"You are angry with me."

It was no question, but a statement of fact. "Yes," he said, "but you seem to be impervious to it." No part of his response was completely true. That she mentioned his anger at all showed she was not immune to it, and it was more to the point that he was angry with himself, not her. "You mentioned a question, I believe?"

"Why did you take the book from Mr. Beckwith?"

It was not at all what he'd expected her to ask. He could not decide if this line of questioning was preferable to the other. "I took it because I know someone who publishes books—not of this type, to be sure—and I thought he would be able to tell me about the origin of this particular one. I was curious what I might learn from it."

"You told me it is not uncommon."

"It is not uncommon for gentlemen to own books with an erotic content, but the breadth of Beckwith's collection sets it apart from what one might consider ordinary. This particular type of book is relatively rare. The fact that the illustrations were printed on both sides of the page makes it rarer still, yet I had no trouble finding two others like it on Beckwith's shelves in a very short period of time. Finally, there is Beckwith's taste for such fare that is a curiosity. There are certain peculiarities of content that make his collection so unique."

"Peculiarities?" She frowned. "I thought what I saw on those pages was naught but what was in the nature of men and women."

"If you allow that violence is sometimes in the nature of both, then it is just as you thought."

"I don't understand."

No, she didn't, he thought. Her inexperience had caused her to focus her attention on the illustrations' more striking features. She had not regarded them as a whole nor comprehended precisely what she was viewing. "Both women were shackled," he said. "One to the iron bedrail, the other to the column that supported the man's back."

Ria's head snapped up. "That cannot be right."

West sighed. "I wish you would find another manner of expressing your astonishment that was not a challenge to my every word." He held up his hand, stopping her from reaching across him for the book at his side. "I will show you." He retrieved the book, opened it to a random page featuring the couple on the bed, then used his hand to cover every part of the drawing except the woman's hands curled around the iron rail. He held it up for Ria to see and watched her face for comprehension.

She stared at it, blinking once, then accepted what she was seeing. West turned the book, covering the other drawing in the same fashion, and showed her the woman's wrists were indeed manacled to the column. These were not heavy irons that held the woman in place, but delicate bands that might have been gold or silver. The links from the wrist cuffs to the rings that secured them were almost invisible, so lightly were they drawn, but Ria saw them once she knew where to look.

West closed the book and put it aside again. Ria's face held a little less color than it had a few moments earlier. "You must have some opinion," he said. "I should like to hear it."

"No, you're wrong. I don't know what to think . . . about the illustrations or the fact that the book belongs to Mr. Beckwith."

He allowed that it would require considerable effort on her part to take it all in. "There are men who find pleasure in the subjugation of others. In this case, it is women who are made their slaves. To further complicate your mind, I must tell you that not every woman would object to being used in such a manner, though it is not the artist's intent to show this. His drawings have a particular purpose and that is to create excitement in the person viewing them. The appeal may be to the act itself or it may be to the themes of domination and helplessness. There is restraint in the illustrations, literal and figurative."

When Ria spoke this time, her voice was almost inaudible. She continued to stare at her folded hands. "I thought the women were wearing bracelets. Bangles. I thought they were Gypsies." She shook her head slowly, feeling weak and vaguely ill of a sudden. "But I think some part of me understood there was something more that I was seeing, something I was responding to without being fully sentient of it. When I was . . . when I was touching . . . that is, when you and I were forni—" Ria bit off this last word, no longer certain it was the most appropriate one.

"When you were pleasuring me," West said. "Let us call it that and dispense with more graphic descriptors—unless it offends you to do so."

On the contrary, Ria was grateful for his suggestion. She cleared her throat, but her speech was still impaired by a tightness there, and she had to force out a shaky breath to give the words sound. "When I was pleasuring you, I was struck by . . . by this odd notion of being both in command and subservient. I never . . . I never experienced anything like it before and I . . . and I think I rather enjoyed the conflict of it. I am very much afraid that it excites my blood."

West might have found this confession piquant if she had not been so earnest. Clearly she was troubled, and he could only imagine what it cost her to make the admission. In the course of a single evening, she had been roused by a fierceness of passion unknown to her before, and now she was discovering the complicated truth of its birth. He turned slightly so he might see her better. It was not her usual way to avert her eyes, but she was doing so now. He reached across the barrier separating them and touched her chin with his fingertips.

"Look at me, Ria." He nudged the point of her chin until her head swiveled slowly in his direction. "What you experienced is not something to fear. It was you who put forward the idea that a woman should know what she must embrace or endure. What occurred between us is meant to be embraced, and if it seems otherwise to you now, then you are denying your own nature. Do you think I did not share in the same thorny emotions? Was there perhaps some other proof you required to know that my blood was also excited?"

The shake of Ria's head was almost imperceptible. She drew in her lower lip and worried it between her teeth, concentrating on the pain she inflicted in order to keep her eyes steady on his. It troubled her that she felt so young and so thoroughly vulnerable, yet this was Evan Marchman come to save her from the consequences of her own recklessness, and the knowledge that there was safety here righted the world.

The pad of West's thumb passed across Ria's lower lip, drawing it out so the fullness of its line was visible to him again. "I cannot say, as you can, that I did not understand the whole of those drawings. I knew what they were when I took them from Beckwith—indeed, I selected the book for precisely that reason. I did not mean for you to see it, but having seen it, I should not have teased you with the contents. I bear a measure of responsibility for what happened, whether I want to own it or not, whether you want to give it to me or not. I understood it is the very nature of fire to burn and blister, even if you had not the same experience."

"You are speaking again of protecting me."

"I suppose I am, and I cannot say that it will ever be different." She surprised him by not insisting that it should be. He brushed back a wayward strand of hair at her temple. "Nor can I say that I will never fail. That I should be your guardian has a certain fox-guarding-the-henhouse bent to it." West saw that this raised her slight smile, and he was glad for it. "I am certain Tenley has thought so from the beginning, and Margaret is coming to that conclusion. My valet wonders what I am about, bringing you here. My friends would be exchanging significant looks between them, each thinking they knew the answer."

"What is the answer?" she asked softly. "I do not know myself."

"Don't you? You quite accurately have pointed out that I am a coward. I did not want to face down my brother and sister-in-law alone."

"Oh."

"You are disappointed?"

"No . . . yes . . . a little, I think."

West caught her eyes shifting from his again. He tilted his head a fraction to hold her glance. "You have not truly developed a tendre for me, have you?"

"No."

"That is good. I like you enormously, Ria, but certain finer feelings can make things between us hopelessly complicated."

She nodded. "I understand. You needn't concern yourself. I like you well enough—I don't suppose I should have been able to pleasure you if I did not."

West was glad to have positioned himself toward the middle of the bed, else he might have fallen out of it. While he was generally appreciative of frankness, Ria had a way of practicing it that invariably disarmed him. His throat felt unaccountably strangled. "Yes," he said hoarsely, "there is that."

"Are you all right?"

Because she looked as if she meant to pound his back, West stopped her by catching her wrist. "I'm fine." He eased his grip but did not release her completely. "You comprehend, don't you, that there will be no repetition of tonight?"

"I did not, but I can see that you are set on it."

"I am. As to that second illustration, there will be none of that, either."

"With you, you mean."

"What?"

"With you," she repeated. "You cannot dictate that I should never engage in sexual intercourse with another man."

Although West was gratified she was no longer using *fornication* to describe the intimate activities between men and women, he could not say so without losing the point he meant to make. "Has your thinking on marriage changed?"

"No."

"Then you will not engage in sexual intercourse with *any* man."

Ria gave this all the consideration she believed it deserved and answered without hesitation. "You mean to be perfectly tiresome about this, don't you?"

"And you mean to be deliberately provocative."

The smile she flashed him was rather smug. "Are you certain?"

He could admit to himself that he was certain of nothing where she was concerned, but he would suffer all the tortures of the damned before he'd admit the same to her. "Yes, quite certain. You take fair delight in needling me."

"Perhaps," she said. "But then again, I might only be getting a little of my own back."

"Touché."

The smile she offered him now was faintly rueful. She glanced down at his fingers circling her wrist, then spoke in soft, deliberate accents. "You don't think you're being unreasonable? Whether or not I invite another man to my bed is not something you can decide for me. How can you hope to enforce such a thing? In eight months you will discharge the last of your responsibilities for my welfare, and I will be independent of your influence." She slipped her wrist free of his fingers and teased him with his own words. "You have not developed a tendre for me, have you?"

"No."

"That is good, then. For both of us, I think."

It seemed to him there was but one way of answering, though he was no longer certain of the truth of it. "Of course."

"Then it is settled."

It wasn't, but he could think of nothing that would make it so. He chose to remind her that he could make his influence felt for the present. "There are still eight months remaining."

"A little less than that now, but I will not refine upon it."

"Naturally," he said dryly. "At the risk of winding you up again, are we done with your questions?"

"Almost. I should like to know if I had the knack of it."

It required a moment for him to understand what she was talking about, and when he did, another moment was required to recover himself. "God's truth, but you say the most astounding things. Do you never temper your tongue, or is your every thought made available to the public?"

She merely regarded him gravely, giving no inkling of the workings of her mind.

"Yes," he said at last. "You had the knack of it."

Ria nodded slowly, thoughtfully. "And at the end . . . what was it exactly that happened at the—"

West let his head fall back and thump the headboard. He closed his eyes and swore softly under his breath. It occurred to him that he would not be in this position if he had let her drown in the lake twenty years earlier.

"Perhaps you regret saving my life," said Ria.

Opening one eye, West regarded her carefully. The suspicion that she could read his mind was finally confirmed. "What happened exactly was that you milked me dry."

This description, both apt and astonishing, made Ria's head snap around. Her eyes were owlishly wide, and her mouth was parted on a quickly snatched breath. She managed to choke out a word. "Milk?"

"That was my seed." He bit off each word with a pause in between for emphasis. "I gave it to the sheets instead of you."

"Then there will be no child."

Sighing heavily, he grabbed the book and opened it. He jabbed his finger at the drawing of the couple on the bed. "This is how a woman is got with child."

Ria was relieved to hear it. "Then it is just the same for us as it is for other animals. I wasn't entirely certain."

"Well, now you can be." He snapped the book closed, almost catching the tip of his finger. This time instead of putting it on the tabletop, he opened the uppermost drawer, dropped it inside, and slammed it shut. When he turned back to Ria, he caught the narrowest glimpse of her smile. "Amused?" he asked.

"Only at your expense."

"Then it is a good thing I can afford it." He pointed to the door. "I swear I will put you out myself if you do not take your leave."

Ria threw off the covers and threw her legs over the side of the bed. She walked around to the other side, found her slippers, and stepped into them, then secured the belt of her robe again. "Good night, Your Grace."

West did not invite her again to address him with more familiarity. He simply nodded and kept his eyes on the direction he meant her to go. When the door closed behind her, he lay back in bed, dragged a pillow across his face, and held it there. His choices seemed clear: he could suffocate himself or die laughing.

West slept late and had breakfast in his room. Finch said nothing about his request for fresh bed linens, but West did not miss the slightly arch look that rose above him in the mirror. After he bathed and dressed, he dismissed Finch and locked the door. From far beneath the bed he retrieved two rolled lengths of canvas and set them on the mattress. He was not satisfied with this hiding place, not with the maids coming soon to put his room in order, and certainly not with Ria inviting herself to visit as the whim struck her. Had she truly taken it in her head to dive under his bed, there was no doubt her curiosity about these items would have caused him considerably more trouble than the damnable book.

He removed the string on one of the canvas cylinders and carefully unrolled it. The colors of the painting were so vibrant as to make him blink. There was the deep sapphire blue of a damask-covered chaise longue and the brilliant metallic gold-and-platinum threads of a woman's hair lying resplendently across its curved back. Rich velvet drapes the color of rubies hung in the background and their heavy folds swept the floor. The woman had one slender arm extended toward them as if she might draw them back and let a narrow beam of sunshine enter. It reminded West that there was no source for the light in the room the artist had painted. No lamp. No candles. No fire.

Instead it was the woman herself who was the wellspring of radiance. She was stretched naked along the length of the chaise, one leg raised, an arm flung above her head. Her skin had the luster of mother-of-pearl. Her eyes, slumberously hooded, hinted at the dark glow of polished onyx. Her back was slightly arched, her moist lips parted. The tip of her pink tongue could be seen teasing the ridge of her teeth. Her pale breasts were raised, the nipples puckered. Between her thighs her pubis glistened with the evidence of her arousal and the spendings of the men who had already taken her.

She was not alone in the exotic, jewel-toned room. The artist had placed three men with her. Two stood at the edge of the room with only their naked backs presented to someone studying the painting. The third man stood at the foot of the chaise, his cock rampant, his knees slightly bent as he leaned forward. In the next moment he would grasp her ankles and pull her toward him, raising her hips just as he fell to his knees. Her long legs would wind around him and he would push himself into her. Hard. Grindingly hard.

West could admire the painting for the artist's talent, but the subject troubled him more than a little. He sat on the edge of the bed and rolled it up, then replaced the string. This was exactly the manner in which he had found it in Beckwith's study, not framed and mounted on the wall—for where could one properly display this art?—but residing in a stand made expressly for the purpose of holding this cylinder upright and a score of others like it. It was no way to store a valued painting, and hairline cracks were already appearing in the brushstrokes. A better method of storage would have been a map drawer, and West wondered what Beckwith would say if he suggested it.

His host of yesterday was probably yet unaware of the things West had taken from his home. With some luck, he would remain in ignorance until they could be returned. It had not been West's intent to remove anything from the private library when he entered it. The idea of actually playing sneaksman and investigating the room occurred to him only after Beckwith made excuses for himself and cut the interview short. Beckwith did not have the manner about him to accomplish the thing smoothly, but West pretended not to notice. He had bided his time, watching the manor from a distance, and observed Beckwith leaving his home on horseback. He had followed for a while, but it was a dangerous and tricky thing to do when he could be so easily spotted. He turned Draco around when he realized that Beckwith's route would take him to Gillhollow. Whether Miss Weaver's Academy was his destination, West could not know, but the man's business in that direction was certainly intriguing.

West had doubled back and patiently waited until nightfall, then let himself into the house and into Beckwith's inner sanctum. Having no clear thought as to what he was looking for, nor for what he might find, West's search was done in the most casual manner, unhurried but thorough, just as the colonel had taught him. He applied mathematical constructs to his work, seeking out the value for the unknown factor that was Beckwith and balancing the equation forming in his mind.

It did not take him long. The desk was a repository for uninteresting documents: letters, bills of sale, estate affairs, inventories, a character for a departing servant. West made short work of sifting through it. It was when he turned his attention to the bookshelves that he came across Beckwith's rather startling collection of erotic works.

It was not every book that contained such themes. Beckwith also collected the writings of Fielding, Jonson,

Swift, Cervantes, and Marlowe. His library was remarkable for the breadth of the works he had acquired, though West had to wonder if part of it was to prove that his tastes were not confined only to things beyond the pale.

Choosing books at random, West had come across the Marquis de Sade's *La philosophie dans le boudoir.* Farther along the same row, he had stumbled upon de Sade's *Justine.* There were more writings of a similar nature by men less infamous than the marquis but with his same penchant for confusing sexual pleasure with blood sport.

West's final selection of the illustrated volume as the one to take was based on its relative uniqueness and the likelihood that it would not be missed. It was tucked away with other untitled books on the uppermost shelf and seemed an unlikely choice for Beckwith to make unless he was looking for it specifically.

The paintings, however, had been something else again. He had looked at three among a score and determined there was nothing that could be learned from them. As evidence of the artists' talents, they were of middling quality, something he might paint himself if he were so inclined. He could not say with any certainty what made him unwrap the string on the fourth.

The vibrant colors held his attention at first. There was a mysterious light that made the woman's nude body the focal point of the painting and drew his eye to her. She was in a cool and sterile place—a temple, perhaps. The graceful Ionic columns, the polished floor, and something that was probably an altar were all cut from the same green-veined marble. Her wrists were cuffed in gold chains, and she was stretched tautly between two pillars. Behind her was a man wearing nothing but the head of a great horned bull. The artist had rendered this mask with enough detail to show the fierce expression in its drawn mouth and flared nostrils. That the animal's head rested on the naked shoulders of a fully aroused male made the image as powerful as it was obscene. It might

have been Hades come for Persephone, the very devil in want
of his reluctant bride.

West's eyes strayed back to the woman held between the
columns. Her pale, unbound hair was like a beacon of light.
The fine strands formed a madonna's halo about her face and
made her seem almost at peace with what was to be her fate.

At first glance he thought he was seeing Ria, and he was
struck by such an urge for violence that it was painful to rein
in. When that haze of blind emotion receded and he was able
to think and see more clearly, he realized that he was mistaken. The woman was not Ria, but he knew her nonetheless.

She was India Parr.

The shock of it was a physical thing, pushing West down
in the chair behind Beckwith's desk. Miss Parr was easily
the best-known actress in London, famed as much for her
sense of communicating the absurd as for her beauty. His
own acquaintance with her had been brief, limited to the
time he saw her on stage at the Drury Lane, then standing in
the doorway of her dressing room afterward to witness her
cuff South solidly on the chin for interrupting her performance with his ill-timed laughter.

There was gossip circulating in London that Miss Parr
had come under the protection of a Lord M—, and the *on dit*
was that she had gone abroad with her lover. Occupied by
the problems that Ria served him, he had paid little attention
to the particulars of Miss Parr's absence from the theater, not
even taking the time to place a wager in the betting books as
to the identity of the enigmatic Lord M—.

Now he wondered if he should have learned more about
her. Southerton was not far away, but West did not want to
trouble him with this. It was unlikely that South would appreciate an interruption at the cottage when he was using it
as a trysting place with his latest bit of muslin. The bit of
muslin would probably not appreciate it, either.

After finding Miss Parr was the centerpiece of one painting, he had to go through all of the others. He only found

one more in which she was featured, and he decided he would take it also. These oils were vastly superior to all the others in Beckwith's collection. The artist had not signed his work, but West doubted it was because he did not deem the paintings worthy of a signature. It was an extraordinary talent that had put these brush strokes to canvas. What this master had chosen as his subject, however, suggested a mind that was dangerous with dark humors. It bore consideration that the artist himself was Miss Parr's mystery lover and protector, Lord M—.

West looked around his bedchamber for a better place to stow each of the paintings. He would have to take them to London and show them to the colonel. Blackwood was the person best suited to know what could be done—indeed, if anything should be. The colonel sat at the center of an intricate web that stretched the length and breadth of London and beyond. It brought him information from the palace at St. James and Holbern's meanest streets, and he filed it all away in his steel trap of a mind. Blackwood's slender, silky threads reached across the channel to Brussels, Calais, and Amsterdam, then were spun out to Paris, Madrid, Rome, even Moscow. It had been several years since West had sent his coded messages from abroad, but he remembered the intricacy of the network and the speed with which the colonel gathered his intelligence.

West wished there was someone else he might depend upon to take the book and paintings to Blackwood. There were no couriers here, however, and this was not a wartime mission. He was not even in the colonel's service at the moment, but was reversing their long-established roles and asking for his assistance. Blackwood had already been helpful in identifying the academy's board of governors as members of the Society of Bishops. West hoped he could depend on more of the same.

The disappearance of Miss Jane Petty was opening Pandora's box.

* * *

Ria had schooled herself to be able to face West in the breakfast room. When he did not join them for the meal, she was made more anxious than relieved. It meant that this first encounter of the day would not necessarily be on her terms. It was important to her that she not appear to have any regrets about the previous night. He would pounce on her for those sentiments like a cat on a canary. There was no question in her mind but that he would misinterpret her feelings in that regard. The regrets, from his perspective, would be all about what she had done. It was not likely to occur to him that her regrets were for what she had been unable to encourage him to do, namely, apply himself to the particulars of illustration number two.

Before falling asleep, Ria arrived at the somewhat humbling conclusion that she had not the ways of a temptress and was unlikely to acquire them. She was the headmistress of Miss Weaver's Academy, not a courtesan, and she did not aspire to be the latter. What she wanted was the full experience of being a woman without the trap and trappings of marriage, nor did she want to gain that experience in the bed of just any man. It must be someone whose discretion and manners were above reproach and could be depended upon not to take her to his bed, then name her a whore for being there. When she considered the whole, it seemed rather a lot to expect.

The idea of being done with her virgin state was not one that had been long in her head. Tenley's single-minded pursuit had provided ample opportunity for Ria to be relieved of her virginity if she had been so inclined. In truth, she had not even conceived of such a notion. She had not lacked for partners during her first Season, and there had been a proper number of rakes and rogues among them. The duke's watchful eye would not have been enough to keep her safely out of their arms had she been determined to be in them. The fact of it was, she had not been interested.

Ria did not hold West responsible for putting so many

contrary thoughts in her head, but she believed he should be made accountable for stirring them. It seemed a certainty that but for his provoking, they would have lain dormant for the length of her life. She might have carried on in blissful ignorance, unaware of her baser needs, and secret yearnings would have remained secret, even from herself. It seemed to Ria that West had shown a certain disregard for her with the reckless use of that wicked smile, then underscored that carelessness with a kiss of the very same nature.

Ria found that if she refined upon it too long, her temper required some outlet. To that end, she plunged knee-deep into the snowbank beside the hedgerow and began preparing her arsenal. "We shall lay siege to a real castle today," she told Will and Caroline. "Do you think you can throw as high as those windows?"

West almost toppled from his stool when the first snowball thumped loudly against the glass. He managed to right himself by grasping the beveled cornice on the armoire, using the toe of his boot to tip the stool back into place. He made certain the canvas rolls were not visible from any angle before he stepped down and approached the window.

The next snowball exploded on the pane directly in front of his face. Even at the risk of taking one on the chin, he threw open the window and leaned out. The children appeared patently horrified. Ria, he thought, was looking rather pleased with herself. If he'd harbored any doubts as to the identity of the one pummeling his window, they were gone now. "Beware!" he called down to them. "I have cauldrons of boiling pitch, and I will be pouring them on you directly."

Will and Caroline swung around to face Ria, their eyes as large a sovereigns. "It is a fib, is it not?" asked Caroline. "There is no poiling bitch."

"Nor boiling pitch, either," Ria told her. She touched the little girl's rosy cheek with her gloved fingertips and erased a dusting of snow. "Come. He has already closed his window and will be upon us more quickly than you can imagine. We need more weapons and a better place to fire them."

Will took charge then and led them to the garden, where the statues and topiary provided protection and the terraced landscape offered opportunity to seize the high ground. In spite of the advantages they had, West managed to sneak up on them from the rear and mount an effective attack.

Caroline was the first to defect. She took up a position behind a scalloped fountain on West's side of the battleground and packed snowballs almost as fast as he could throw them. At first Will ridiculed his sister for abandoning them, but had cause to reconsider when she sent one flying that caught him in the open mouth. After that he hunkered down and applied himself to her demise. That was when Ria realized it was safer for Caroline if Will was allowed to join West's flank. She waved Will's white neckcloth to signal a temporary truce and demanded parley. In exchange for giving up young William, she received as many snowballs as she could carry in her skirt.

Although the outcome was never in doubt, Ria did not surrender until she was lying on her back in a snowdrift with West, Will, and Caroline standing over her. Even then, she capitulated with ill grace.

West held his snowball at the ready and allowed Ria to consider her options. "Even at Waterloo, Napoleon did not force Wellington and Blücher to such a pass as this," he said. "The man knew when to yield."

Will glanced up at West. "I say, it is very bad of you to compare Aunt Maria to Boney. She is a right'un, through and through."

This pronouncement, delivered in tones that lent it importance and sincerity, had the effect of raising Ria's most beatific smile. At the first glimpse of it, West thought he might go down on his knees. He managed to steady himself, but only by the narrowest margin. Maintaining his balance on the stool in his dressing room had been easier. Offering peace, West held out his hand to her.

Without the slightest compunction, she pulled him down,

rolling away at the last possible moment to keep him from landing on top of her. He fell on his face in the drift, and the children immediately pounced. Ria saw that he didn't try very hard to fight them off, and when he finally gave in, it was with grave good humor. Yet another thing she could learn from him, she thought. Surrender did not have to be met with resistance.

Will and Caroline ran off in the direction of the kitchen immediately afterward, in want of large mugs of hot chocolate. Ria and West followed more slowly, brushing themselves off as best they could before conceding they required some help from the other to make a good job of it.

"To do what I must do next I will need to return to London," he said without preamble.

Ria's steps faltered, but she recovered quickly. More difficult to manage was the way her spirits plummeted at this news. "Of course."

"It is this business of Miss Petty that takes me away." He did not know if an explanation was required, but he thought he should offer it.

"Yes, I understand. I did not think otherwise."

"Shall I accompany you back to the school?"

"No. Christmas will be upon us soon and more than half of the girls will be leaving for their homes. For the others it will be time away from the classroom. I have not spent Christmas at the manor since Tenley married Margaret. I think I should like to stay this year, if they will have me."

"You will not be uncomfortable?"

"No." Her smile was a trifle lopsided, slightly rueful, but her chin came up, and she managed to infuse her voice with carelessness. "I shall be perfectly credible as one who is missing you. That will make Margaret's mind easy and keep her at my side to offer condolences and more sage advice."

"While Tenley will remain at a distance."

"If he chooses, yes. I do not think he will have occasion to find me without Margaret nearby. I will return to the academy after Boxing Day but before the new year." She turned to him as he opened the door for her. "How soon will you leave?"

"As soon as the roads are passable for the carriage. Even Draco would find the going hard after the snowfall these last two nights."

"Then let us hope for a quick thaw, for Miss Petty's sake."

"Yes," he said quietly. "For Petty's sake."

Three days passed before West judged the roads to be in tolerable conditions for traveling. It was not with an eye toward his own comfort that he waited, but to ease the journey for Finch, who suffered a painful attack of gout and could not endure the jouncing and hitching of the carriage for long. Although the valet protested vociferously against the accommodations that were made for him inside the carriage, West would have his way.

They left at daybreak and made frequent stops. West often rode ahead of the carriage, ostensibly to make certain the way was clear, but in truth, to be out of hearing of Finch's pained grumbling and alone with his thoughts.

He had left presents behind for Tenley, Margaret, and the children. It was the first time he had ever made any gift to them, and he was uncertain of the rightness of doing so now. His feelings were not precisely those of a brother, uncle, or even a cousin. He could not say with assurance that he felt anything familial, only that he was not so indifferent toward them as he used to be. The children, he realized, he liked well enough, especially when they were in Ria's company. They were spirited then, playful and energetic, up to every trick that she would entertain. They laughed easily in her presence, and she in theirs. It was only when he came upon the three of them unexpectedly that she grew more restrained.

West did not dwell on this now. He considered the subtle changes in the way Margaret conducted herself and realized that a thaw was not only a characteristic of the weather. Margaret was no longer so determinedly gracious or affable, rather she had become genuinely so, seeming to find pleasure in his company that was not predicated on his inheritance of the title. Her nerves, while not entirely settled, were stretched less tautly when she comprehended he did not mean to send them packing.

As for Tenley, there was no ignoring the strain between them. Neither of them mentioned it or acknowledged that a second seed had taken root now. West decided he could be tolerant of his brother's temperament, though it would have been easier had Tenley possessed even an inkling of what was darkly comic about their circumstances. That Tenley was put out with him for removing Ria from his path was infinitely more understandable.

He'd left Ria a present also, something that he'd carried with him from London: William Blake's *Songs of Experience*. The slightly mad, mystic poet appealed to him in a way the romantics did not, but he treasured this particular volume because it had belonged to his mother. On the frontispiece, Blake had penned his name as a favor to the man who had meant for her to have it. West never considered that his own father might have been an admirer of Blake's bold, sometimes violent images, or that he had presented the book to his mother with any thought save to get her in his bed. Gifts like this one were rarely offered in penance of the grievous wrong he had done her, but as inducement that he be allowed to carry on without consequences.

That was not West's own purpose in presenting this book of verse to Ria; rather, he hoped she would appreciate that the well-thumbed copy was important to him and that the title made it apropos of their short acquaintance. There was some part of him that wished he could see her face when she unwrapped it and another part that was relieved he would not. If she was disappointed in his peace offering, he did not want to be witness to it.

Ria had not been wrong to name him a coward.

Chapter Nine

Blackwood motioned to West to remove the pictures from his sight. West carefully rolled both and slipped the strings back on to secure them. He laid them on the sideboard and returned to his chair. The colonel, he noted, was visibly agitated by what he had seen. It was not a state that West observed very often, and he could not fathom what it was about the paintings that had prompted this reaction. The colonel was a man of the world. He had been to Africa and India, toured all of the Continent, studied at Harrow and Oxford, could speak intelligently on the campaigns of every great commander since Alexander, and held his own when the topic turned to literature, music, or art.

West could not conceive that the colonel had never seen paintings like Beckwith's before. That was not to say Blackwood could not be offended by them—West certainly was—yet it was something more than offended sensibilities that had the colonel wheeling sharply around his chair in search of the decanter of whiskey.

"What can you tell me about the artist?" asked West.

Blackwood poured his drink and knocked back a large swallow before he answered. "Besides that he is a bedlamite and a bloody talented painter? Nothing whatsoever." He added another finger of whiskey to his tumbler to replenish what he'd drunk and turned around slowly. "How did you come by those? I thought when you left London your destination was your ward's school and then the manor at Ambermede."

"It was, and I went to both places. The paintings came from neither." He explained where he had found them, as well as the why of it, then handed the colonel Beckwith's book.

Blackwood reluctantly parted with his whiskey to have a look at it. He riffled the pages first one way, then the other, before he tossed it back to West. "I haven't seen one of those since I was a schoolboy, and never one that would make de Sade himself blush. Mr. Beckwith's proclivities are certainly apparent—not that I judge a man harshly for such things—but that he is on the board of governors of a school for young ladies is perhaps worth noting."

West nodded. "The same had occurred to me. I thought I would show the book to East's father. Sir James might be able to tell me something about it—when it was published and by whom, who could have done the original engravings. It is not one of a kind, I think, but there cannot have been many printed."

"I agree. You must speak to him. If he does not know the answers, he will direct you to someone who does."

It occurred to West that Blackwood was more comfortable discussing the book than the paintings. Still, something had to be said about them. "You recognized the woman in the paintings."

The colonel was aware that West hadn't posed a question, but made a statement. He sipped his drink, then nodded. "Miss India Parr. She is not easily mistaken for anyone else."

West did not inform Blackwood that Miss Parr and Ria bore a passing resemblance to each other or that he had been nearly moved to kill because of it. "What do you make of it?"

"Nothing. It is unfathomable."

"I have heard there is a certain Lord M—who has become her protector."

Blackwood's chuckle held little humor. "You surprise me, West. I did not think you attended the gossip."

"Sometimes it comes to me whether I want to hear it or not. Do you know anything about this Lord M—? I believe he was mentioned in the *Gazette.*"

"That is the same paper that printed that East was engaged to Lady Sophia Colley—and you know the falseness of that report. The pages of the *Gazette* should be liberally sprinkled with salt before they are ingested as food for thought."

West remembered the story well enough. It had caused Eastlyn no small amount of embarrassment. "Where is East?" he asked, for the moment willing to be moved from the purpose of his visit. "I called for him at his home, but he is gone from there. No one would say where he had taken himself."

"And you think I will?"

"If you don't, it's because he is either engaged in an assignment for you, or you don't know where he is. If it is the latter, then I suspect he is running Lady Sophia to earth. The engagement might be false, but of late I am of the opinion that his feelings for her are not."

Blackwood sighed. "It is the latter. I have no idea where he's gone."

West did not bother to temper his amusement. This state of affairs was in no way to the colonel's liking. "He'll be around directly. He always is. Whether he'll have Lady Sophia with him is less certain." Stretching his legs before him, West let his head fall back against the chair. He regarded Blackwood from beneath his lowered lashes. "About Lord M—, do you suppose he might be the artist?"

"He cannot be both the artist and Miss Parr's protector. It defies logic."

"But then he is mad—you said so yourself."

"An expression, nothing more, though it would not surprise if it were true. The bold brush strokes . . . the use of those brilliant colors . . . the incandescence of Miss Parr herself—there is genius in the presentation, but something very dark that guides it."

West realized the colonel's thinking mirrored his own. He wished it were otherwise; there would be some hope then. "Can you make a guess as to when the paintings were made?"

Blackwood glanced at the sideboard. "I should think they were done in the last three years, perhaps the last two. They would not be in such relatively good condition had they been stored so carelessly for longer than that. They are taken out and regarded frequently, though. You realize that, don't you?" The colonel waved aside his own question. "I can see that you do not. The paint at the edges of both pictures is wearing thin in very particular places. It is Beckwith's thumbs, I believe, that are causing the damage. He unrolls the painting, then holds it open to regard it, like so." Blackwood demonstrated with his hands spread on either side of an imaginary canvas. "He will destroy it with his admiration."

West did not care about that. He cared more that Beckwith might miss the thing before too long a time had passed. "I will have to return them soon, then," he said, more to himself than the colonel. "I believe I will have that drink now." Rising, he went to the drinks cabinet and poured himself a generous tumbler of whiskey. Not one to knock it back as the colonel had, West savored the smooth, fiery taste. He did not return to his chair, choosing to hitch his hip on the colonel's desk instead and remain there half sitting, half standing. "What opinion do you have of Miss Parr? Not as an actress. I mean, as the subject of these paintings? Do you think she posed willingly?"

"You cannot be certain that she posed at all." The colonel wheeled his chair toward the fire. "You will allow that her face is known to many. Her admirers number a legion, and Prinny himself is one of them. You have seen her but a few times, I believe, yet were able to recognize her as the woman in the paintings. As to the form that supports that face, it might be anyone's."

"And it might be hers."

"Yes," the colonel said reluctantly. "That is always a possibility."

"How can I discover the truth?"

"Why is it so important that you do?"

West was surprised the colonel would pose that question. "Because if she did not pose for the artist, then she may be unaware that the paintings exist at all. She has a right to know what madness has been inspired by her beauty."

"I doubt she will thank you for it."

West doubted it as well, but if the paintings were done without the actress's knowledge, she would want to take measures to protect herself. "If she knows about the paintings, whether or not she posed willingly, I want to learn more. How Beckwith acquired two of them, for instance. Who the artist is. What market exists for these things. And how it all might have touched Miss Jane Petty."

"That is quite a leap you are taking to suppose India Parr will lead you to that missing girl."

West shrugged. "I can begin at any point on the road to see where it leads. What I want to know is if you will help me. How can I discover the truth about the paintings?"

Blackwood was a long time in answering. "I suppose you shall have to ask Miss Parr yourself."

"How is that possible? She is on the Continent."

"I warned you not to take gossip as fact. She is not abroad. I suggest you apply to Southerton first. He will advise you on the wisdom of broaching this with her."

"South? South knows where she is?" West was patently incredulous and did not trouble himself to hide it.

"He'd better. She is his assignment."

"Does he realize this? You know, don't you, that he has borrowed my cottage near Ambermede for use as a—" West stopped. "God's truth, but South gets the plum assignments. He is with Miss Parr even now, isn't he?"

"You are not usually such a slow top," the colonel said. "You did not suspect?"

"No. Can you doubt it? I would not have come here first. The damnable thing is that I was so close but a few days ago. Now I shall have to take myself off again." He would see Ria, though. The thought tumbled through his mind quickly, and he did not try to hold it. The colonel was certain to be suspicious of a sudden shift in his mood. "Are these paintings connected to what you have asked South to do?"

"Perhaps. I don't know. I was unaware of their existence until you showed them to me. I cannot say what Miss Parr knows or has told South. You must speak to him first—I am firm on that."

West nodded. "Agreed." He knew there was a great deal the colonel was concealing, most of it about the actress. Therein lay the explanation for Blackwood's agitation when he was presented with the paintings. West did not press to learn more. Whatever information applied to the disappearance of Jane Petty, he would get from South first.

Regarding the colonel over the rim of his tumbler, West asked, "Have you received the portrait of Miss Petty?"

"And the description," the colonel said. "They arrived in yesterday's post."

West made a disgusted snort. "I could have made the delivery almost as quickly myself. Someday you will explain to me how intelligence from Rome can arrive at your door faster than a missive from Gillhollow."

"All roads lead to Rome," Blackwood said dryly. "While there is but one to—"

"I take your point." West sipped his whiskey. "Then there has been no time to make inquiries of the dressmakers on Firth Street."

"On the contrary, I sent someone around immediately."

"And?"

"I expect to hear from her directly."

"Her? You sent a woman?"

Blackwood chuckled. "They are dressmakers, are they not? I judged a woman as likely to have better success."

West felt the skin prickle at the back of his neck. "Might I know the identity of this woman?"

"Of course. You will want to thank her, no doubt. It is Elizabeth."

"Lady Northam." West could not believe it, and yet he was hardly surprised. That he could adopt both those positions at once seemed in perfect concert with every other dilemma he was facing. "You sent North's wife on a mission for information about a missing girl?"

"She was going to the dressmaker's, regardless of whether I sent her or not. It was merely providential that she came to my doorstep first." The colonel touched the bridge of his spectacles and drew them lower on his nose so he might regard West over the top. "Need I remind you that I have known Elizabeth all her life? Neither you nor her husband can make that same claim."

"Then North knew what she was about?"

"I can't say. I have no idea whether she told him."

West groaned softly, certain he was to be in Dutch with North if that worthy found out. "Northam will have my head."

Blackwood dismissed that notion. "He will have mine first."

"The order that he comes for us makes little difference when he means to put us on the chopping block."

Chuckling, the colonel finished his drink and set his glass down. "I think Elizabeth will say nothing. She is desirous of getting some of her own back for this business with the Gentleman Thief."

"Then it is done? North has found his man?"

"In a manner of speaking, but there is a plan in the works to end it soon enough. After you have met with South, it is important that you return to London. There will be need of your particular skills."

"What can I do that the others cannot?"

"Soldier. Sailor. Tinker. Spy. Which one are you?"

West sighed. The colonel was amusing himself. "You

know perfectly well. If that is the way of it, who am I to watch?"

"The French ambassador."

That announcement, delivered with such matter-of-fact intonation, caused West to finish what was left of his drink. He actually contemplated pouring another. "I have promised Miss Ashby I will find her missing student. I cannot be here and there and here again. I was delayed in going to Gillhollow after the duke's funeral because Northam needed help when Elizabeth left him."

"And they both need your help now, although I am the one asking for it."

West could not recall there had been a request. He supposed it didn't matter in the end. He knew he would do whatever was needed because it was not in him to do anything else. It didn't matter that the colonel was counting on that; this was about a pledge made long ago at Hambrick Hall. "Friends for life we have confessed," he said softly. "Yes. Of course."

"I will give you the particulars later. All is not ready." Blackwood gave West his darkest, gravest glance. "This will require due care. You cannot be caught."

"I can be, but I will not be."

"Good. Your part must be done before the ambassador's winter ball. I believe he can be made cooperative, but it will fall to you to assure all the details are correct."

West allowed he was more intrigued than alarmed. "And this plan of yours? Will it put a period to the Gentleman Thief's reign of terror on the *ton?*"

"Their boudoirs and salons will be made safe again. Ladies will be able to wear their finest jewels and leave their paste with the creditors."

Grinning, West stood. He took his leave after the colonel had asked for and received his promise to join him on Christmas Day for dinner. It was not a difficult promise to give. West already knew there was only one other place he'd rather be.

* * *

Perceval Bartlett, The Right Honorable Viscount Herndon, rose slowly in greeting as West was ushered into his conservatory. The air was redolent of the rich, black planting soil, drooping ferns, and hothouse flowers. Until West entered the room, Herndon had been stooped over a potted orchid, examining the delicate pink petals for flaws. Now his palm gently cupped the corolla, and his thumb lightly passed over the stamen. The impression, from West's vantage point, was of a man reluctant to leave his lover, for there was something unmistakably intimate about the way Herndon caressed the plant.

West doubted that it was an accident that he had observed this. Herndon meant to elicit a response from him, to test his reaction. To that end, West obliged, feigning an appreciation of the gesture and communicating that he understood what it was in reference to.

"Aaah, Westphal," Herndon said. "So you have come after all. I had heard you would be returning to your estate at Ambermede after the new year."

"The new year is only just upon us. There is time enough to make the journey. Did you not receive my reply to your invitation?"

"Yes, I did—then I heard the rumors and became unsure of your intent."

"My intent," West said with a proper chill in his voice, "is to keep my word. You have me, Herndon—now what will you do with me?"

Herndon cut an angular figure. He had a narrow face and tight, square shoulders. His long arms ended in bony wrists, large hands, and elegantly tapered fingers. His full mouth was the exception to the perpendicular lines that defined him. Here he was soft and thick, the lower lip jutting forward in something that resembled a woman's sensuous pout. It thinned, drawing as fine a line as it was capable of, as his lordship considered West carefully.

"There can be no doubt that you are your father's son," he said. "Devil a bit, if you don't sound just like him."

West chose not to take umbrage. He could not afford to overplay his hand. Herndon's invitation was as unexpected as it was timely, and he meant to take advantage of it, not spurn it. "You knew the duke well?"

"As well as any, I would venture to say, certainly better than you."

West was witnessing what his icy tone had cost him. He would have to suffer the razor-sharp edge of Herndon's tongue if the man could not be placated. It seemed the best way to accomplish that was by appreciating the man's passion. He spent the next thirty minutes touring the conservatory and making proper noises of awe and respect for Herndon's greenery.

The subject of Miss Weaver's Academy was never broached. West could admire the man's patience, even as he disliked being thwarted by it. Patience was not a characteristic he often associated with a member of the Society of Bishops, but he supposed it could be affected when it suited their purpose, especially by one who had held the exalted position of archbishop. For three years at Hambrick Hall, Herndon had been the Society's leader. Now, more than thirty years later, he could still enjoy the benefits of that station as chair of the board of governors.

At the end of the tour, suitably placated, Lord Herndon bid West join him in the music room for tea. After it was served, his lordship came to the point of his invitation. "I have recently received a letter from Mr. Beckwith of Sunbury in regard to your concern about the school at Gillhollow. He indicates that you are interested in a seat on our board."

"I expressed that to him, yes."

"Good, then there is no mistaking the matter. You are aware, are you not, that none of us takes compensation for our contribution? It is more often that we must contribute or find others who will do so. This is a charitable indulgence on our part. The school is barely solvent most years."

"I am very well aware."

Herndon nodded, his dark eyes shrewd in their appraisal.

"No doubt Miss Ashby has informed you that she spends a considerable portion of her own funds on supplies for the students. What I wonder is if you can appreciate that she indulges them?"

"It seemed to me that a seat on the board would provide opportunity to remedy both those things."

"Your father could not take her in hand."

"I am not in every way the duke's son." West underscored this with a knowing smile that spoke of confidences between two intimates. "Beckwith suggested I might want to keep her on a short tether. After due consideration, I have come around to his manner of thinking. A tether would suit her very nicely."

"The tighter the better, eh?"

"Indeed."

Lord Herndon rubbed his chin. "Miss Ashby is a treasure. If it is your intention to interfere with her running of the school, it would not be wise for you to sit with us."

"You've spoken to the other members?"

"Most, not all. Those who are in London only. There has been correspondence with the others." He sipped his tea. "There is agreement among us that you will be an asset in our endeavors. There is a long history of good works here that we should like to continue. You will appreciate that we are breaking with tradition by inviting you. Seats on the board have always been given to those who have had a member of the family serve before them. New blood is in order, we think."

West wondered if he would be required to spill his own. "You do me a great honor. I had not permitted myself to hope. It seemed unlikely, given that you did not extend the same invitation to my father."

Both of Herndon's salted brows lifted a fraction. "I was not aware you knew he had inquired about a position on the board."

"Miss Ashby knew. She told me."

Herndon said nothing immediately. "She encouraged you to approach Mr. Beckwith?"

"Discouraged me, actually."

"I see." There was a pause as he set his cup and saucer on the table at his side. "But she has said other things, I believe. About the student who left the school?"

"Yes, she mentioned it. She is naturally concerned . . . as I am."

"Then you will be pleased to learn that Mr. Lytton, the man we approved hiring to find the girl, has recently been to every dressmaker on Firth Street. I believe the instruction to do so came from Miss Ashby and was based on some particulars she learned from one of her students."

"And?"

"And he has recently made a report to me. I am certain there is also a written one going by express post to the academy. Mr. Lytton tells me that Miss . . . " His eyes lifted as he tried to recall the name. When he grasped it, he returned West's level stare. "That Miss Petty was indeed seen at several of the shops. She was in the company of a young gentleman who indicated he was her brother and guardian. He was purchasing her traveling garments, nightclothes, and other intimate items. Miss Petty has no brother. I think we can safely conclude that she has put herself under the protection of a man who can afford her, but can afford no better than she. Miss Ashby will be vastly disappointed to learn of it, I think, but she cannot hope to influence every girl to comport herself in a decent fashion. It is to be desired that she will not blame herself."

"Yes," West said quietly. "That is an outcome I would also desire."

West waited in a stand of trees and watched the flicker of light in the upper window of the cottage. It was cold, and he stamped his feet in place and blew on his cupped hands to ward off the piercing chill. The ride to Ambermede had been a hard one, almost without pause. Snow squalls made the journey doubly trying, preventing him from seeing the road ahead or even much of what was under Draco's hooves. He had persevered because he did not know how to do otherwise.

It would be a relief to speak to South about the paintings, then quit this place and continue on to Gillhollow. Visiting the cottage was never to his liking, though Mrs. Simon from the village always kept the place in good order for him. He was never certain why he kept it up after his mother died. She had not asked it of him; he could have let it fall into disrepair. Of late he had begun to think he'd held the property to keep it vivid in the duke's memory, not his own. His interest in maintaining it had waned almost immediately upon hearing of his father's death. That was a sure indication that his motives were spiteful, not high-minded. If South had not asked to use the place, West felt sure he would have already spoken to the solicitor about selling it.

A slim beam of moonlight penetrated the canopy of pine boughs and slanted across his gloved hands as he raised them to his face. He took a single step backward and was swallowed by shadow again.

It was likely that South and Miss Parr were sleeping. That was a state he longed for himself. He thought of Ria and wondered what manner of sleep she was enjoying. Peaceful? Fitful? Dreamless? He would wager the answer would have a great deal to do with whether she had received Mr. Lytton's report from London. Moreover, if she was in possession of it, whether or not she believed it.

Either way, West knew he was going to be the bearer of news that would be difficult for her to accept, and she was unlikely to be grateful to him for bringing it.

Rather than think on the consequences of that, he let himself into the cottage and waited to be discovered. Until it happened, though, he decided to avail himself of the settee.

It looked infinitely more comfortable than the saddle that had been his home of late.

South's tread on the stairs was light, but not without sound. West heard him try to time each step so that it accompanied the intermittent gusts of wind that buffeted the cottage.

"You may as well announce yourself with a cry from the crow's nest," West said dryly. "Land ho! Avast, ye mateys. Or whatever it is one cries from the mainmast."

South stopped in his tracks, one foot on a step, the other hovering above the next. "Bloody hell, West. I might have shot you."

West regarded the pistol in South's hand, unconcerned. "Not if you were aiming."

"If that is evidence of your wit, pray do not strain yourself."

West shrugged. It was an awkward gesture, given the fact that he was still laid out on the settee as if it were a stiff hammock, his head propped at one end, his feet at the other. He sat up slowly, stretching as South finished his descent. He reached for the oil lamp on the end table and turned up the wick. "I apologize for waking you. Not at all what I meant to do. I thought I could come in from the cold and get a few hours sleep before daybreak." That had not been his first plan, but once he was stretched out, it had seemed a better one.

"You didn't stop on your way here?"

"No. I came straightaway from London."

Both of South's brows rose. He ran a hand through his hair and managed to suppress a yawn that would have cracked his jaw if he had given in to it. "Then I take it you are not here to look after your recent inheritance. That business cannot have been so urgent."

"No. I may go there later. Have you been to the estate?"

"I rode past it yesterday morning. Your brother is in residence, I believe."

West nodded. "Unless it is your intention to shoot me still, you might put down the pistol."

South looked down at his hand. The pistol was indeed leveled in West's direction. Grinning, but unapologetic, he set it on the table beside the oil lamp and pulled up a stool. "Is it Elizabeth?" he asked.

West shook his head. "No. She is back in London with North. I have not seen them yet, but the colonel says they are indecently happy."

"That is good, then."

"It may be, yes."

South smiled faintly. "Why have you come, West? If it is not that you mean to wrest all of the Westphal keep from your brother, then what is it?"

West pointed to where he had placed his satchel against the opposite wall. "There," he said. "I came across them in the course of some work I am doing for the colonel. When I showed them to him, he sent me here to you." It was not a thorough lie, West thought, but definitely pressing that boundary.

South shifted on his stool to get a better look. "What are they? Maps?"

"No. You need to see them for yourself." South started to rise, but West leaned forward and laid one hand across his forearm. "I will get them." He rose and crossed the room. "Miss Parr is sleeping?" he asked.

"If we have not awakened her." Belatedly, South realized that West should not have known who he brought to the cottage. "Did the colonel tell you it was Miss Parr I had here, or did I make some misstep?"

"It was the colonel. Offered quite reluctantly, I assure you. I had no notion of it. You can be a deep one, South." West bent and picked up both cylinders, one in each hand, and carried them back to where South was sitting. "I did not know what to make of these. The colonel thought you might." He placed one in South's open palm but did not release it. He glanced once in the direction of the stairs, then back to his friend. "Perhaps it is better that you heard me come in. I think it would have been more difficult in the morning."

"Because of Miss Parr's presence, you mean."

West nodded. He watched South take the canvas and lay it crosswise on his lap. When he started to unroll it, West took a step backward, giving his friend a modicum of privacy.

"Oh God." South spoke the words under his breath, part prayer, part curse, as the painting was unfolded before him. He stared at it for a long moment, then swore softly and shoved the canvas off his lap.

West plucked it out of the air and rolled it up quickly. "Do you wish to see the other?"

"Should I?"

West could not school his troubled expression. The painting with the bull's head was more grotesque than the one South had already seen. Still, South should not have asked the question. It was not a decision West could make for his friend.

South held out his hand. "Give it to me."

West hesitated. His friend's complexion was ashen. Clearly he had some feelings for Miss Parr, else he would not have been affected so deeply by what he saw.

"It's all right," South said. "I want to see it."

West placed the second rolled canvas in South's extended hand. He looked away this time.

South opened it and gave it little better than a cursory glance before he returned it to West. "Where did you get them?"

"I stole them."

"Can you say more?"

This time West lied willingly. There was no reason for South to know the personal nature of his investigation. "I can tell you I got them from one of the ambassadors."

"They are not the sort of works of art likely to be reported missing."

"That's what I thought." West returned both paintings to

where they had previously stood against the wall. As he considered what he must do next, he rubbed the back of his neck with his palm. Strands of dark red hair were lifted from his collar to lay lightly at his nape. "You will not credit it, South, but what I am uncovering appears to have something to do with the bishops."

South's head jerked upward. "The bishops? Are you speaking of the Society?"

"I am."

Shaking his head slowly, South glanced toward the rolled canvasses again. "But not the Hambrick Hall boys."

"No. At least I hope it doesn't end there. Men are at work here, not children." West's voice dropped a fraction lower. "Not yet."

South nodded once. "What do you require of me?"

Ria sat curled in her favorite reading chair in the corner of her bedroom, the soft folds of her nightdress spilling round her. The book in her lap was unopened, but this was not her first reading. She had already memorized some of the verse, and as she rested her head against the back of the chair and closed her eyes, the words of *The Lily* came to the forefront of her mind.

> The modest Rose puts forth a thorn,
> The humble sheep a threat'ning horn:
> While the Lily white shall in love delight,
> Nor a thorn nor a threat stain her beauty bright.

She was no Lily, Ria thought, nor even a modest Rose. More an *im*modest one, if she wanted to be strictly honest with herself—which she did not. Of late she had concluded there was no aspect of honesty that was inherently virtuous, especially in an examination of one's own character. Delusion and denial served better. At least she was finding it so.

While the Lily white shall in love delight. The words

drifted through her mind again as she considered whether it would ever come to pass that she would *in love delight.* Most likely it was a state of being confined to mad poets and young girls. No doubt Jane Petty had thought herself in love. She must have been filled to overflowing with the possibilities it presented to her, the realization of her every dream. It would be cruel to have that love crushed, crueler still to have it done by the very person one loved above all others. That was Jane's most likely fate.

An ache formed at the back of Ria's throat. She was becoming familiar with that pressure, the clog of tears that lodged there, the others that pressed at the back of her eyes. Blinking, she lifted her chin and turned her face toward the window. This winter's day sunlight was pale. There was barely strength enough in its transparent beams to push through the occasional fissure in the clouds.

The students would be rising soon. Ria could already hear the movement of the housekeeper and maids in the corridor. Cook and her young helper would have the porridge bubbling in the big cauldron, and the misses Taylor and Webster would be taking the last steps of their early morning constitutional. Mrs. Abergast disliked both porridge and walking, so she slept a few minutes past all the others and swore she was better for it.

Ria found that routines comforted. It eased her mind to know what she might expect in the next hour, day, even in the week. For the immediate future, she wanted to go forward as if by rote. What thought she could apply to this business of living would be given over to functions as dull as choosing what dress to wear or counting the number of brush strokes she applied to her hair.

Embracing the familiarity of these rituals would serve another purpose. Boredom, perhaps, was what she required to sleep deeply again.

A distinct *thump* in the adjoining sitting room caught Ria's full attention. This noise was followed by a softly pronounced curse and a flurry of movement in aid of making right whatever had gone wrong. Ria fairly catapulted out of her chair to get to the open doorway.

West did not look up, but continued to rub his thigh where the sharp corner of an end table had caught him solidly. "This table is not where I remember it. You moved the furniture."

"I hope Your Grace is not accusing me of laying a trap," Ria said. A smile edged the corners of her mouth upward. "It is daylight, after all."

Grinning, West lifted his head. "True enough."

It was not his reckless grin that made Ria's own smile collapse, but the condition of every other part of him. Indeed, the slightly wicked curve of his mouth was all about him that was familiar. She hurried forward, only to be stopped by the arm he put out.

"You should keep a distance," he said. "I am not at my best."

Ria's wide, blue-gray eyes swept the length of him, then made the same assessment from toe to head. She bit the inside of her cheek, holding back intemperate words. That he described himself as not at his best was a nice bit of understatement. Streaks of soot and sweat made his face almost unrecognizable. His features were drawn, the eyes infinitely weary. He smelled of smoke, and a lock of hair that had fallen over his forehead was frizzled and singed. There were black streaks also on his nankeen breeches and ash on his boots. She suspected that when he removed his caped greatcoat, she would see more of the same. Only his hat seemed none the worse for his adventure.

All manner of questions occurred to her, but she asked only one. "What can I do for you?"

"Help me out of this coat, then find a sheet to cover a chair so I might sit."

It was a good measure of his complete exhaustion that he required assistance to remove his greatcoat. Ria gave it willingly, placing the coat over the back of a rocking chair while West tossed his hat aside, then gingerly stretched his stiff limbs and slowly rolled his neck. She disappeared into her bedroom and returned quickly with a sheet. It did not matter to her in the least that his soot-smudged clothes would mark her furniture; she supplied the sheet because he would not sit down if she didn't.

West dropped into the armchair behind him as soon as Ria covered it. As tight and sore as he had been moments before, now he melted. His legs splayed, and his arms fell loosely on either side of the chair. He tipped his head back and closed his eyes.

He did not stir for so long that Ria thought he had fallen asleep. Several minutes passed when there was nothing but the light sound of his even breathing. She was preparing to rise from the bench beside him when his fingers caught her wrist.

"No," he said. "Sit with me a while longer."

Ria sat. For reasons that were not immediately apparent to her, she wanted to weep. She looked down at his blackened knuckles, at the smear of soot that crossed the back of his hand, but felt only the gentleness of his touch. She blinked back tears.

"What is it?" he asked.

She had not even realized he was watching her. "You make me afraid for you."

"I do? I assure you, it is not my intent."

Ria found it difficult to suppress the quaver in her voice. "You are pushed past the point of exhaustion, yet you are here. I cannot imagine what has befallen you, but it seems to me that you were fortunate to survive it, and still you have pressed on. Of course I am afraid for you. You demonstrate the good sense of a bag of beans."

With only the slightest encouragement from him, she was in his lap, her arms around his neck. The folds of her billowing white nightshift were quickly blackened with soot, but she was careless of those stains. No lily, she reminded herself, but an immodest rose.

She kissed him as if her life would have no significance if she did not. Her mouth slanted across his, parting his lips with the pressure of hers. Her arms slid forward, and she cupped his face lightly in her palms as she moved her mouth to the corner of his, then to his cheek, his temple, and finally along the line of his jaw. She caught him again, deeply this time, her tongue pushing against his. She felt her breasts swell even before his arms circled her back and pressed her closer. His woolen frock coat was gently abrasive against her cotton shift, and the buttons pulled at the material. The air between them was warm, but it threatened to become charged with heat.

His fingers wound in her unbound hair; it was like dipping his hands into cool spring water. He kissed her hard, needy for the taste of her, eager to be rid of the stale scent of smoke that was in his nostrils, and breathe in the sweet fragrance of lavender and mint that was peculiarly hers. It did not matter that she was in his arms—he felt that he was more in hers. If he had meant to shelter her by drawing her close, then he had not fully comprehended what she would give him in return. She was the one with the sheltering heart.

The knowledge threatened to overwhelm him.

Sensing that something had changed, Ria broke off the kiss and buried her face in the smoky folds of West's neckcloth. She held him tightly a moment longer while her uneven breathing quieted, then she raised her face. "I hope you are not in want of an apology."

He found he still had the wherewithal to chuckle. "And I hope you are not in want of a flannel. You will need several to clean your face."

Ria touched her cheeks, then regarded her smudged fingertips.

"Here, too," he said, placing an index finger against her lips, then showing her the evidence. "You are as soot-smeared as any chimney sweep."

She arched one brow at him, reminding him how she had come to be so. Her reproving look did not last long, however. She held out her hand to him. "Come. I know what is needed now."

Minutes earlier he would have sworn truly that he was incapable of rising to his feet, let alone rise in any other manner. He had underestimated both the pull of Ria's siren's smile and his response to it. It seemed very little effort was required on her part to move him. He could not even be unhappy about it.

Ria led him into the bedroom and closed the door. Without a word, she helped him out of his frock coat, his shirt, then guided him to the bed, bade him sit, then grappled with his boots. The more she touched him, the sootier she became, and never once did she try to avoid that end.

West lay back on the bed, naked save for his drawers, and watched her boldly strip off her nightdress before she climbed into bed with him. Her pale breasts were tipped in pink, and they brushed invitingly against him as she moved close. He looked at his hands, then showed them to her. "I will mark your skin if I touch you with these."

She said nothing, but caught his wrists and brought his hands to her breasts. She allowed his fingertips to graze her skin and his thumbs to pass across her nipples. The trail of his hands left the faint smudges he predicted. Ria raised her solemn gaze to his. "And I will be made beautiful by them," she whispered. "Everywhere you touch me."

He could have told her she was already beautiful, but was not confident of her accepting it. He showed her instead, rolling onto his side and pressing her back, then placing his mark on her, first with his hands, then his mouth.

He swept back the hair at her temples, sifting the silky strands with his fingertips. His lips found the soft hollow where her pulse beat so faintly and he kissed her there. Her skin was warm, flawless. He kissed her forehead, the corner of her eye. His head dipped, and he caught her earlobe with his teeth and tugged, then his lips touched that spot. He flicked it with the tip of his tongue and heard her breath hitch.

His smile imprinted itself on the skin of her throat. He nuzzled the curve of her neck and sipped lightly on her flesh.

It left a mark that was different from his fingerprints on her breasts, but no less proof of his intimate possession. He kissed the stamp he had left on her skin, then made another.

She moved restlessly against him, urging him without words. He sensed her impatience but would not be hurried. In this, at least, he would have his way. She could not appreciate it now, but she would thank him for it later.

"You're amused." The words came from deep in Ria's throat, a husky, heavy whisper that was foreign to her.

"Mmm." West lifted his head and nudged his mouth against hers, parting her lips. Her breath was warm, sweet. "Always," he said. He kissed her for a long time, holding her still with nothing but the pressure of his mouth on hers. He made that kiss an end in its own right, sucking on her full lower lip, her tongue, tracing the ridge of her teeth, licking at the sensitive, velvet underside of her lips, making them wet, making the whole of her mouth humid and hot.

She seized his neck when he would have drawn back and would have held her to him if he had permitted it. What he did was remove her hands and place a kiss in the heart of each palm; then he let them fall away and find purchase in the sheets as he bent to her again.

This time his mouth settled at the hollow of her throat. He made a damp trail to her breasts. Her heart beat a steady tattoo that he could feel against his lips. He kissed her there, then again at the curve of her breast. He took the puckered aureole into his mouth and suckled her. Her nipple was as perfectly formed as a rosebud and equally tender; he rolled it between his lips, flicked it with his tongue.

His hand fell on her hip, steadying her as she rose off the bed in a catlike arch. "Shhh," he said, not to quiet her, but to calm her. "I have you. I shall always have you."

He saw her mouth part as though she meant to say something, then she merely shook her head. Her eyes were dark at the center, her expression wondering. He thought he might even know what she was thinking, though one could never be certain about the bent of Ria's thoughts. "When you come to the precipice again," he told her, "I will let you fall. Then I will catch you." She nodded, not because she understood, he thought, but because she trusted him. The enormity of what he would do to her, what she would *allow* him to do, squeezed his heart and stole his breath.

She saved him from himself. He had no doubt of it as her fingers wound in his hair and gently tugged. That intuitive sense of hers, the one that linked her to him and allowed her not only to see his soul, but to be unafraid of it, had divined his faltering resolve. It was not that he did not desire her still, but that he did not want to desire her. He wondered if she could distinguish the difference when he could barely do the same.

He felt her tug again and saw the corners of her mouth lift in a shy smile. No siren's tasty curve this time; no coy, flirty beckoning. She made herself vulnerable with her honesty, and in doing so made him want to be her equal. "Witch," he said, then he bent his head and took her other breast into his mouth.

West was glad for the slim bars of sunlight that touched the bed and lay their transparent splendor across Ria's body. He slid his hand under one, stroking her hip, letting his fingers trail lightly along the curve of her bottom. She stirred again. His hand moved upward to her waist, his thumb passing over her abdomen, dipping slightly when her skin retracted in response.

She fit him perfectly, as if every curve was made to fill his hand. He made a slow study of her, learning the shape of her shoulder, her arm, the delicate depression at the inside of her elbow. Her breasts spilled over his palms, firm and taut; her skin had the blush of a ripening peach.

His hands slid along the length of her thighs, the back of her knees. The pressure of his fingertips, light but insistent, made her part her legs for him. He slid down her body, no longer making a trail with his hands, but with his mouth.

West stripped off his drawers and pitched them over the side of the bed. He urged Ria's knees upward as he bent be-

tween them. That she found a way to hook her legs over his
shoulders was her own doing, but it meant the intimate kiss
he pressed to her mons began as a smile.

He felt her give a start at the first touch of his lips, and
again when he applied his tongue. She was warm and humid
here; desire had made her damp. Now he used his mouth to
make her wet.

All around them were the sounds of the school stirring:
the chatter of students on their way to the dining room, followed by the occasional admonition to be quiet; the march
of girls in the corridor and in the stairwell; the housekeeper's
scolding of one of the maids; the more determined step of
the teachers as they herded stragglers to breakfast; and finally, the knock on the door to Ria's apartments and the concerned inquiry from the other side as to the state of her
health.

Ria heard none of it above the sound of her own breathing
and the dull, distant roar in her ears. West was aware of it
only peripherally; the sharpest focus of his attention was
Ria. They might have been ten leagues distant, for all the im-
pact it had.

West lifted his head. From the quick sips of air, the tension in her frame, the way her back curved, and her soft lips
parted, he judged that she was ready for him. He raised himself up, dropping one shoulder to let Ria's leg fall, and
cupped her bottom. She helped him, lifting her hips, but her
eyes remained on his face.

Her body was better prepared to receive him than she
was. West found her hand and guided it to his erection.
"Watch," he told her. "Watch what we shall do together."

Chapter Ten

Ria did exactly as West instructed her: she watched his first thrust and the lift of her own hips taking him. She closed her eyes then. She could not help herself. For a moment she thought she would not be able to bear the pressure or the openness necessary to accommodate his entry. Her hands went to his forearms and gripped him tightly. She bit her lower lip so she would not embarrass herself by asking him to let her go.

"Ria?" He spoke her name as a question. "Look at me."

Her lashes fluttered upward. He was in her as deeply as was possible for a man to be. To the hilt, she thought, exactly as it should be. There was no pain now; she could not even say that it was precisely pain that she had felt. There was discomfort, but there was also the sense of an ache being massaged that made her think the discomfort would pass.

"I can stop now," he told her. "But only now."

His voice came to her from the back of his throat, both smooth and rough, like honey over sand. It prickled Ria's skin and made her shiver. "I know what I want," she said on a thread of sound. "And it's not that."

His hips jerked in response, withdrawing and plunging

again. He leaned over her, resting his weight on his fore-arms, and slowly this time, exercising a degree of restraint he did not know he had, he taught her the rhythm that would pleasure both of them.

She was tight around him, but she fit him here as she did everywhere else. When she rose and fell, her breath quivered. He had prepared her to take him deeply and hard—she knew that now. When he had kissed her, every invasion of his tongue was a foreshadowing of what he was doing to her at this moment. He had thrust and withdrawn, thrust again. He had made her reach for him, not just welcome his touch, but need it. Nothing had changed.

Ria reached for him, looping her arms around his back, splaying her fingers across the faint ridges that still striped his flesh. She felt him stiffen, then shake it off, accepting that she, of all the women he had known, had a right to touch him here. The tapered tips of her nails scored a light crease on either side of his spine from the small of his back to his nape, then down again. The shiver that slipped under his skin became hers as well, and when she felt herself being edged toward all that was unfamiliar about this pleasure, he was as good as his word, pushing her to experience the lightness of falling from a very great height, then sweeping her safely into his arms at the very moment she would have shattered.

He moved between her open thighs a minute longer, his strokes becoming short and quick, rocking them both hard. The last test of what remained of his strength and resolve happened as he felt his own release. He jerked away from her, withdrawing, then collapsing beside her, giving up his seed to her naked hip and flat belly and finally to the sheets.

"So there will be no bastard," he said quietly.

Ria nodded. Her throat had closed, and she could not have spoken if she wanted to. She lay very still for several long minutes. His milky seed dried on her skin. She thought of this final mark on her and wished it made her feel as beautiful as all the others.

"You understand, don't you?" West turned on his side and raised himself on one arm. He placed a hand on her shoulder. "Ria?"

"Yes, of course." She worked the words past the tightness in her throat. "It was unexpected, that is all. You were right to think of it. It speaks to your experience, I suppose, and my lack of the same."

Before he could reply, Ria edged herself off the bed and stood. "Allow me to wash and dress, and then I will have a bath drawn for you. You can sleep here. No one will disturb you. Mr. Dobson is bound to have seen your horse by now. He, at least, knows you are about." She picked up her night-dress and held it in front of her. "I will explain that you rode out from Ambermede and were sickened by a megrim."

West raised an eyebrow. "A megrim?"

"You have another ailment in mind? Scarlet fever? Typhus? The influenza?"

"A megrim will do," he said, surrendering to the idea. She was taking him in hand now, and the tartness of her approach warned him he should proceed cautiously. "Eastlyn suffers from them on occasion, though he does not always take to his bed."

"Then he is a stalwart fellow." Ria felt some of her prickly humor fade and her heart twist a little as she saw the effort West was making to hold his head up. "More stalwart than you at the moment," she said in a gentler vein. "Let me care for you, then I shall hear your explanations. There will be some, I collect."

He nodded. There were no reserves remaining for him to brook an argument. Deprived of sleep for more than twenty-four hours, he could feel his eyelids begin to droop before Ria was out of the room.

The sun set early at this time of year. It was already dark, but not terribly late when West woke. He stretched slowly, feeling the aching pull of every one of his muscles. He was reminded of that unpleasant night outside Madrid, the one that he'd spent curled in a rock crevice waiting for the French to pass over his head. This was like that, only worse.

Opening his eyes a fraction, he stared blearily at the fire. What he could see of the room was not immediately familiar to him. He could not recall that he had ever owned bed curtains the exact color of wheat fields blanketed in sunshine, and was certain he did not secure each one to the posts of the bed with braided silk cords. An armoire that was also certainly not his, stood on claw feet between two shuttered windows. There was a large armchair near the fireplace, turned slightly more in his direction than toward the fire. He could still make out a faint depression in the cushion. A book lay on the arm of the chair, its spine turned toward him. He could not clearly see the lettering, but the burnished leather binding was one he knew from hours of holding it in his hands.

With a soft, throaty groan, West fell on his back, put a forearm across his brow, and stared up at the ceiling. It was then that Ria bent over the bed and into his view.

"Aaah, so you are awake," she said softly. "I wasn't certain."

As quickly as that, West thought, his world was righted, his balance restored. He smiled up at her, the curve of his mouth more drowsy than weary. His eyelids felt heavy, but his vision was finally clear.

Ria had drawn back her flaxen hair in a loose knot. The tails of a navy blue grosgrain ribbon rested on the ruffled collar of her muslin gown, and fine tendrils of hair that could not be tamed brushed her cheek and temples. Her eyes were bluer now than gray, bright with intelligence, and made even more luminous by the depth of her concern. She might have been an angel, save for a mouth that was too sweetly generous and a chin that was too stubborn. She was, in a word, lovely. He tried to recall if he had ever thought otherwise and chose to believe he had not; it was only that he was allowing himself to appreciate it now.

He remembered bits and pieces of the miracle she had wrought in making him human again. She had somehow co-erced him out of bed after a bath was drawn for him in her dressing room. She bullied him into the copper tub and threatened him with a proper scrubbing if he was not up to managing the thing himself. From time to time she checked on him, always at a point, it seemed, when he was ready to fall asleep. She produced warm towels and a clean night-shirt, then pushed and prodded until he made good use of them. It was abuse of a kind and caring nature—or at least that was what she told him.

West pushed at the blankets that were neatly turned down across his chest. He was indeed wearing a nightshirt, and it happened to be his own. "You found my bag."

"I did."

He came rather late to the realization of what else she found. His bag had been fixed to Draco's saddle, and fixed to the bag were Beckwith's paintings. "I don't suppose you checked your curiosity."

Ria's expression was genuinely regretful. "It probably will not matter to you, but I resisted for the better part of an hour."

"You're right," he said, pushing himself up. "It does not matter. What have you done with them?"

She pointed to her armoire. "I put them inside where they will not be found."

West pressed his thumb and forefinger to his eyes and rubbed. He wanted to shake off the dregs of sleep and was finding it absurdly difficult. "Did you ladle laudanum down my throat?"

"Only a little. Don't you remember? You complained the megrim was becoming quite real."

In point of fact, he did not remember, though he sup-posed she would not lie about it. "What is the time?"

"Not much after five, I should think." She anticipated his next question. "Evening, not morning. Can it be so important? You do not mean to go now, do you?"

West ran a hand through his tousled hair, leaving it unimproved by the effort. "No, not just yet. Draco has been cared for?"

"Hours and hours ago. He is in the stable now."

"Good. Thank you for seeing to him."

"Mr. Dobson did that." She hesitated, thinking perhaps she had sounded too acerbic. "You're welcome."

Looking up at Ria, realizing he had made her anxious and that nothing was proceeding as he had hoped, West sighed deeply. "God's truth, but I did not want you to see those paintings."

"I know."

"You looked at both?" He saw the affirmative answer in her clearly expressive eyes. "It's not important," he said after a moment. "I don't suppose I really thought it could be otherwise."

Ria sat on the edge of the bed. "I didn't want to see them, either, but I didn't know it until I had."

"If there is logic there, it escapes me." He held up a hand to forestall an explanation. "No, it is the sort of thing that only becomes more knotty when one tries to unravel it."

She nodded, accepting the truth of it. "Shall I bring you supper? It is roast beef tonight and Mrs. Jellicoe has made plum pudding."

"Not just yet." He reached for her hand and threaded his fingers through hers. "Have I been short with you? I did not mean to be. I apologize."

"And I accept."

"Is there another apology I should make?" he asked. His clear green eyes held hers. "Should I speak to your regrets?"

Ria shook her head. "I have none."

"Even at the end?"

"No," she said firmly, willing him to believe her. "I did at first, but I have had time to think since then. I was naive to suppose it would end any differently. I would be frantic with worry if you had done otherwise."

West's head tilted to one side as he continued to regard her. "Then you would not want a child?"

Ria chewed on her bottom lip as she considered her reply. It was no longer as simple as saying yes or no. That option did not exist anymore, and hadn't for some time. "What I do not want," she said, "is to present you with a bastard."

She allowed him to make of it what he would and gave his hand a squeeze, letting him know she would say no more on the subject. "Now, will you tell all, or must I apply thumbscrews? Where were you before you came here?"

The abrupt shift in the conversation made West blink, but he answered truthfully because he knew there was no help for it. "Not far away at all. I was near Ambermede. There is a cottage at the edge of the estate that the duke deeded to my mother years ago. You might know the one I mean. It has been mine since her death. That's where I was last night— visiting my home."

Though it answered her question, it barely qualified as an explanation. "You will have to say considerably more than that."

West didn't doubt it. Surrendering to the inevitable, he made room beside him on the bed. When she was settled there, he began with how he had found the paintings in Beckwith's study, the reason he had removed them, and finally the purpose of taking them to London. His relationship to the colonel required a bit of roundaboutation, but it was no more than he was used to doing when someone showed too much interest. If Ria no longer believed he was a clerk in the foreign office, she did not say so.

She proved to be a very good listener, asking questions infrequently and only for clarification. He could see there were things she wanted to know that he had not fully explained, but she let him proceed with the story in his own way. He kept his discourse to the paintings, not mentioning his visit to Lord Herndon or Lady Northam's own findings from the dressmakers on Firth Street.

"Miss Parr joined us shortly after I finished showing South the paintings," West said. "I think she might have been listening above stairs. She was very composed when she came to stand with us. It pains me to admit I did not give a lot of thought to how difficult it would be for her to look at them, or how hard it would be to watch her do the same, but I can tell you it is not an experience I will soon forget. Southerton, either. It was doubly painful for him, I am certain. Miss Parr admitted she knew the paintings existed. There are apparently more than forty of them, all with similar themes."

Ria shivered. "They are about her degradation."

"That is what I thought also," West said. "Miss Parr says the artist's intent is not so easily explained in that light. The paintings are meant to show that she is deserving of worship."

"And of sacrifice," Ria said softly. "She must know that the paintings show her as a sacrifice."

West was taken aback by how clearly Ria saw it. He and South had not had that same perspective until India explained it to them. "It may be that it is already begun," he said quietly, resting his head back. "She asked me to make her a gift of the paintings. She wanted to destroy them herself, to make certain they could not be made public. I couldn't allow it, and South knew I couldn't. I don't think you can imagine how difficult it was to say no to her. I thought—"

"I can imagine," Ria said. She rested her hand on his forearm and stroked it lightly. "You are decent. And good. A gentle . . . man." She smiled a trifle crookedly. "No, I have not forgotten our meeting in the alley outside your club, nor that you still carry a blade in your boot, but neither of those things negates the others. They do not change the fact that you can feel despair at having to refuse her request. I know you mean to return the paintings to Mr. Beckwith—you really have no choice."

West's shoulders rose and fell in tandem with his inaudible sigh. "I explained to Miss Parr that there were no other paintings concerning her in the collection I found, but she was clearly discomposed that any at all had left the hands of the artist. I had already learned from South that the paintings were not done with her permission, that she was, in fact, drugged. She was never posed with anyone in the room save the artist himself. Everything else he painted was born of his imagination."

"Except those rooms," Ria said. "The rooms are real enough, I think."

West had never doubted the sharpness of her wits, and here was further proof. "You recognized them. I wondered if you would. I was rather slow coming to it myself."

"I have passed those portraits in the corridor almost every day for six years. You cannot have seen them more than twice."

"Three times, actually. I took a moment to study them before I came in here this morning. The identical Ionic marble columns are in several of the portraits of the school's founders. The capital on each is the same as the pair in Miss Parr's painting. So is the fluting on the shaft. It is the frieze, though, that makes them truly identifiable. It is on the marble altar as well. Have you ever looked closely at it?"

"I have not made a study, no, but I remember thinking it was suited to the school. Young Greek maidens studying their scrolls. Horses, I think, grazing nearby."

"Nymphs and satyrs." He turned sideways to gauge her reaction. Ria was staring at him, openmouthed. He reached over and placed a finger under her chin, gently closing it. "At least you did not tell me I cannot be right. That is an improvement."

She removed his finger. "It is only because you closed my mouth. Are you quite certain? Is there no room to suppose you might be mistaken?"

"The frieze is very cleverly done, and I understand why you didn't give it more than cursory attention. It is not, after all, the focal point of any of the portraits, merely a background. This morning I studied each of the friezes to compare them with the one in Miss Parr's painting. I do not have any doubts about them now, but you are free to decide differently."

Ria fought the urge to quit her rooms and go to the entrance hall immediately. It was not that she did not believe him; it was only that it was something she needed to see for herself. "You did the same for the other painting?"

"The couch and draperies are not as distinctly unique as the other, yet you had no difficulty recognizing them. There is only one portrait that features those things in the background—a relatively recent one, I think. The colors of the fabrics are still the same, though not as vibrantly realized as they are in the painting of Miss Parr. It struck me that he thought the sapphire chaise longue was a good complement for his eyes."

"You are speaking of Sir Alex Cotton. He is the one sitting on the chaise with the open book at his side, and he does have rather piercing blue eyes." Ria plumped the pillow at the small of her back. "He is also the last person to join the board of governors."

"How long ago?"

"Since I've been here. It was February, I think. Two years ago."

"Miss Parr said that painting was done three years past."

"She was in that room?"

"No. Nor the other. She has only seen them as part of the paintings."

"But they must exist," Ria said. "The portraits of the founders and governors were not done by the same artists— at least one of them with the Ionic columns is nearly one hundred years old—and none of them were done by the artist who painted India Parr."

"I agree. The rooms exist."

Ria realized there was nothing he could say beyond that. He did not know any more. Whatever else had happened at the cottage, it was not connected to those rooms or Miss Weaver's Academy. "You have not accounted for the fire," she said.

"It happened as I was explaining the impossibility of leaving the paintings. Miss Parr smelled the smoke first. South sent her out of the cottage to safety and he and I went upstairs to find the source of it. We used what we had at the ready at first. Blankets. My jacket. I thought we would be defeated by it. Flames crawled up the ceiling and across the mantelpiece. The window to that room was open, and gusts of wind fanned the flames across the floor. We retreated once because of the smoke. I hauled buckets of snow from outside, running them up the stairs, taking the steps two and three at time. South threw them at the fire, and then I would run out again."

West sat tailor-fashion and rested his elbows on his knees. He steepled his fingers, and as was his habit, he tapped the pads of his thumbs together. His head bent, and he felt Ria's soft touch at his nape. She stroked the back of his neck, laying down the stubborn curls with the lightest touch of her fingertips. It was almost as if she knew what he had to tell her and how bloody hard it was to do so.

"We put out the fire that round," West said, "but by then we'd lost what was important. Too late, South realized the fire was a diversion. I should have known myself. All those mad trips outside to get more snow . . . you would think I'd have seen that Miss Parr was gone. We searched for her as best we could, on foot for the first hour because our horses had been sent off. Even the pair of grays that South used for his carriage were missing."

Ria's fingers stilled in West's hair. She hesitated, then finally broached her question. "I'm not sure I understand. Did Miss Parr set the fire to get away from your friend? Was she with him against her will?"

"No." He stopped tapping his thumbs a moment. "Most definitely no to your first question. The answer to your second is more complicated, I think, and not mine to share. Can you be satisfied with that?"

"Your discretion makes you an honorable man. I can be satisfied with that." She ruffled the hair at the back of his head again. "You did not find her?"

"No. The horses found us eventually, but by then the trail was colder than the day. Southerton returned to London. I offered help, but he would not accept it. He knew I had somewhere else to go, though I do not think it was only that."

"This is what you meant about Miss Parr being sacrificed, is it not? She is in grave danger, then."

West nodded. "South believes he knows where she can be found. He was meant to die in that fire. Perhaps he would have if I hadn't been there, but I cannot shake the feeling that I led Miss Parr's abductor to the cottage myself. South says I did not, but then he is the kind of man who takes everything upon his own shoulders."

"Unlike Your Grace," Ria said in unmistakably wry accents, "who is so eager to share responsibility and deals blame as blithely as he deals cards. No, you have nothing in common with your friend."

West gave her his most chagrined smile. "If your point were any sharper, it would draw blood."

Ria's eyes fell to the deep dimple carved at the side of West's mouth. Impulsively, she kissed him.

"What was that in aid of?"

She shrugged. "You will not want to know."

"I asked."

Ria shook her head. She could be discreet also, especially about the secrets that resided in her own heart. "Will you eat now?" she asked.

He realized his appetite had returned and was about to say as much when Ria's stomach rumbled indelicately. Chuckling, he nodded. "I think it would be best if you joined me."

They sat at the drop-leaf table that Ria opened in her sitting room and ate the same fare the students had had for their dinner. The roast beef was thinly sliced, pink in the center, and served in its own juice. The small potatoes and turnip medallions were boiled and glazed with lightly salted butter. There were fresh hot rolls, honey to spread on them, and finally, Mrs. Jellicoe's steaming plum pudding for the sweet.

West did not need to be encouraged to eat his fill. By the time he dressed and the meal was served, Ria's rumbling stomach was no match for his own. Afterward he sat back in his chair and regarded Ria over the rim of his wineglass. "How was it you were able to stay with me today?"

"I did not spend the entire day watching you sleep," she said. "That would have been very dull indeed. I taught my classes and came in as my time allowed. You never stirred." She took a sip of her wine. "The staff and students are curious, but no one has reason to doubt my word regarding your arrival here and even less reason to suspect me of untoward behavior."

West might have choked if he'd been drinking. "Just so," he said mildly.

"I cannot say what they might suspect you are capable of."

"Very amusing."

Ria merely raised one eyebrow and smiled.

West wondered if he dared take her back to bed. She looked as if she would go willingly, perhaps even eagerly. He quelled the temptation by reminding himself of the reason he had come here.

"Do you know," Ria said, "that if Adam had had but a thimbleful of your resolve, we would still be living in Eden?" She frowned, then, as a thought occurred to her. "Perhaps it is that I am no Eve."

She looked so perfectly discomforted by the idea that this

could be true that West was moved to leave his chair and place a very thorough kiss upon her mouth. "There is nothing lacking in you or your apple."

Ria set her glass down and pressed two fingers to her slightly swollen lips. His kiss had tasted of red wine and currants. It required a certain amount of determination on her part not to follow him back to his chair. "Oh my," she said softly.

West stretched his legs, crossing them at the ankles. He folded his arms casually against his chest. His easy posture belied the grave set of his features. "We have said nothing about Miss Petty."

"I know." It was something of a relief—albeit a small one—to know this is what he meant to discuss. When he turned such a sober expression in her direction, she thought he meant to tell her he was leaving straightaway. It did not bear refining on how far her spirits had plummeted. "But that is because I have had good news—of a sort."

"Oh?" West did not indicate by so much as a flicker of an eyelash that he was in receipt of the same information.

"Mr. Lytton has written to me that he queried every dressmaker on Firth Street, and there were some positive responses. Jane was remembered by several of the dressmakers as being in the company of a young gentleman. It seems he was purchasing her a new wardrobe, just as Jane told Amy he meant to. Mr. Lytton lists the items, if you would like to see his letter. He was very thorough with the details."

"I should like to see it, yes."

Ria went immediately to the adjoining room and took the letter from her desk. She gave it to West. Her discomfiture was evident in that she would have remained standing at his side while he read it if he had not directed her back to her chair. "He writes that Jane was reported to have been in fine humor. Do you see that? And the gentleman was ardently desirous of pleasing her."

West lifted a brow and gave Ria a significant look. "He

also writes that the gentleman introduced himself as Jane's brother and guardian. What do you make of that?"

"I imagined it was because he is young himself and did not mean for anyone to know he was setting up a mistress." She regarded West frankly. "You did not think I supposed that he meant to marry her. Jane may have still been thinking that was to be the outcome, but I assure you, I did not."

"Mr. Lytton does not identify the man. Did you not wonder about that?"

Ria thought West had come very quickly to the matter that troubled her most. "Of course I did. I have already penned my reply and asked for precisely that information. I realize there is little I can do about Jane's situation, even though I wish it were otherwise, but I can write to her and let her know she is missed and may apply to me for what help she needs at any time. Jane was naive to place so much trust in this man, but she is not unintelligent. She must realize by now that he has deceived her and means only to be her protector, not her husband. If she does not wish to continue that arrangement, then I want her to know she can still seek me out. It seems—"

"Ria," West said gently. "Stop." He could not allow her to go on. She was trying very hard to make it right in her own mind. The things she said were in aid of convincing herself—not him—that Jane had come to no harm. "There is not much more than a grain of truth in Mr. Lytton's letter."

Ria's hands fell to her sides. Her slender fingers curled around the seat of her chair, gripping it hard enough to make her knuckles white.

"I wanted to arrive before you received his report but knew there was little chance of it. What I have to tell you will not be easy to hear. I wish I could have spared you the false hope Mr. Lytton has given, though after listening to you, I think you are more desirous of wanting to believe, than of truly believing."

She nodded slowly, reluctant even now to admit the truth of it.

West went on, telling her about his meeting with Lord Herndon and his invitation to join the board of governors. He explained how he came to know she would be receiving Mr. Lytton's letter as well as what particulars it would contain.

"I would have been suspicious of the report regardless of any information I had to the contrary," he said. "Lord Herndon wanted me to know this business with Miss Petty had been concluded satisfactorily, yet he told me after he had offered me a seat on the board. I think his purpose was to disarm me, to lull me into thinking the invitation to join them was genuinely meant, not offered in the hope of preventing me from asking more questions about Jane."

"They are afraid of you," Ria said.

"I doubt that. They are not so easily frightened, nor do I think they are given to acting precipitously. There has been time enough since I spoke to Beckwith for them to discuss what they wanted to do. I believe they are more curious about me than concerned."

Ria picked up her wineglass and brought it to her lips, surprised when it did not tremble in her hand. She was made of sterner stuff than even she realized. Still, she drained her glass. "The things you are saying about Lord Herndon, Mr. Beckwith . . . indeed, all of the governors . . . it is still difficult to credit."

"For you," West said. "It is difficult for *you* to credit."

"Perhaps you are giving credence only to that information which supports your view of them."

"It is always a possibility."

Ria set her empty glass down. She absently ran her fingers along the edge of the table. "But you don't think that is the case here."

"No," he said. "I don't. Do you want to hear what my informant told me about her visit to the dressmakers?"

"Yes. Yes, of course I want to hear."

"Miss Petty was indeed remembered by two of the dressmakers on the street, but only two. She was quiet, they said, willing to allow the gentleman to make all the decisions regarding the purchases. She did not offer a single word to gainsay him, even though she seemed uncomfortable with his choices. It was clear to them, at least, that it was no trousseau he was preparing. Only one of the dressmakers supposed the girl was already aware of that. The other was not so certain of it. The articles of clothing that were arranged to be made for her were all fine silk or the sheerest batiste. There were corselets and stockings and silk garters; slippers with ribbons long enough to lace them to the knee. The items included not a single piece of outerwear. No cloaks. No walking gowns. Nothing for the theater, the races, or for carriage rides in the park. There were no bonnets or shawls. No boots. No scarves. No gloves."

West could see the effect his words were having on Ria. What color washed her complexion was compliments of the candlelight, not the warm infusion of her own blood. He pressed on, giving her exactly what Elizabeth had reported to him. "I will allow that not all of those articles would have been purchased at a dressmaker's, but they all could have been purchased on Firth Street. One would think he would have done the whole of it then and there."

"Perhaps he began to find the fittings tiresome. Men do, you know. Or mayhap Jane found it so and pressed him to leave." Ria had only to hear herself say these excuses aloud to know she believed neither of them. She pressed two fingers to her temple and massaged lightly, closing her eyes for a moment. "I'm sorry. I promised myself I would not do this."

"Is there something I can get you?" he asked. "A headache powder? Another glass of wine?"

Ria declined both offers. "You can finish it," she said. "Just finish it."

He hesitated only a moment. "Very well. There appear to be no more purchases made for Jane in any of the other

shops. My informant tells me that by way of some rather ribald humor, one of the dressmakers remarked that it seemed
the gent was not going to let his young ladybird out of the
cage once he taught her how to sing."

Shoulders sagging, Ria bent her head and stared at her
hands. They were shaking now, though she felt so numb that
the reason for it eluded her. "She is but fifteen," she whispered. "I know you think she is not yet a child, but she is,
and she has lived a mostly protected life here."

It was Lady Northam's opinion also, West could have told
her. Elizabeth had been thoroughly disheartened to learn
Miss Petty was so young and that she knew so little of the
world. Now he had two women urging him to make a certain
whoreson account for his transgressions. "I understand," he
said. "She has already been ill-used, whether or not he has yet
put her in a cage." The shiver that went through Ria cut him.
He reached for the teapot and poured her a cup. It was still
hot enough to chase the worst part of her chill. "Drink this."

Ria accepted the offering but did not raise it to her lips.
She held the china cup in her palms and allowed the curling
ribbons of heat to bathe her face. "There is a name?" she
asked. "Was your informant able to discover a name?"

"Mr. Swinbourne. Mr. Wallace Swinbourne. It is the name
both dressmakers used to credit the purchases."

Ria's short laugh held no humor. "I am surprised that he
gave it. That he could be so coldly confident that his behavior is above reproach is truly proof that he is as loathsome
as—" She stopped suddenly. "Swinbourne? That is something, at least. There is no one by that name with a seat on
the board."

"It is not his name, Ria. The Wallace Swinbourne I found
is a solicitor in a rather shabby firm near Covent Garden. He
no more matches the description the dressmakers supplied
of the gentleman than I do. What is more likely is that he has
an arrangement with this gentleman to pay for bills that are
directed to his attention."

"You didn't ask him?"

"I didn't need to. I simply needed to be certain he was not the man my informant described. Still, I went to his office later that night and looked for documents that confirm his arrangement with Jane's fellow. It is hardly surprising that there were none. It is always better for both parties that there be no documents when something improper is going on."

Ria's eyes narrowed a fraction. "Then you can't be certain of a connection between them."

"I know what I saw when I spoke to him. I am accounted to be a fair judge of when people are circumnavigating the truth. Mr. Swinbourne was."

For a moment Ria did not think she could draw air. Her chest was tight with pressure inside and out. "You know, don't you? You know who Jane's abductor is."

Nodding, West put the last of it before her. "The man both dressmakers described is very likely Sir Alex Cotton."

The cup almost fell through Ria's nerveless fingers. She caught it just before it spilled and placed it on the edge of the table quickly. "Oh, but—"

"Piercing blue eyes," he said. "Do you know they each used the identical phrase you did? To confirm it beyond any doubt, I shall require a sketch of Sir Alex. Miss Taylor has already proved her talent. Perhaps you can persuade her to do another portrait. A copy of the one in the hall will be sufficient."

"What will I say to her? She will want to know why I want such a thing."

"I trust you to be inventive. Something will occur."

Ria sucked in her lower lip to keep it from trembling.

West stood, took Ria's hand, and applied only that pressure necessary to bring her to her feet. She stepped willingly into the circle of his arms, and his hands clasped together at the small of her back. He nudged her until she allowed herself to fall forward and come to rest against his frame, her forehead pressed to his shoulder.

Ria wanted to sob, but her eyes remained curiously dry.

"What manner of men are they?" she asked plaintively. "Sir Alex. Mr. Beckwith. Lord Herndon. All of them are involved in some way. Who have my employers been these past six years?"

West's chin rubbed the pale crown of Ria's hair. "You know," he said quietly. "I told you at the outset."

"You told me about schoolboys playing cruel games. Sir Alex is a man, West. What is he doing with one of my girls?"

He didn't respond, but simply held her more tightly.

"You will find her," she said. "Promise me that you will find her."

"Yes." He felt her shoulders heave once, then she was weeping softly. "I promise." He held her in just that way until she quieted, then he led her back to her bed. This time it was he who helped her out of her clothes and into a nightdress, and he who neatly turned back the covers once she was in bed. He laid a cool compress across her swollen eyelids and sat beside her until she fell asleep; then he left a note that she would be certain to see when she woke.

It was not long past eight o'clock when he finally took his leave of Miss Weaver's Academy, and he was careful to seek out Mrs. Jellicoe before he did so, paying her the compliment of remarking that her plum pudding was the finest he had tasted. On his way to the kitchen, he warmly greeted Miss Webster and Mrs. Abergast. He then happened upon young Amy and three of her friends in the entrance hall, and they fairly danced around him as he was escorted to the front door by Miss Taylor. Everyone inquired as to his health, and he replied that he had been very well taken care of.

Draco had been brought forward from the stables and was waiting for him in the drive. West fixed his bag to the saddle and accepted the leg up Mr. Dobson supplied. He tipped his hat in the direction of Amy, her friends, and Miss Taylor, then gave Draco a sharp kick with his heels and left the school behind.

* * *

Ria woke, found West's hastily scrawled note, and knew a keen sense of disappointment. Of course he had to leave. He could not very well spend the night in her apartments, not with the entire school knowing he was there. And there were the paintings that must be returned to Mr. Beckwith, if West did not determine that it was already too late.

She took a headache powder, then went to her sitting room. The table had been cleared, the leaves dropped back in place. The candelabra was set once again at the center of the polished mahogany surface. She lighted three of the candles, then lifted it by its pewter stem and carried it into the hall.

Except for the intermittent creaking that was commonplace in a structure as old as Miss Weaver's, the school was quiet. Ria checked the front door and found it securely barred. Perhaps Miss Emma Blakely meant to remain in her room this evening, she thought. It was a bitterly cold night for a tryst by the firs.

Smiling a little crookedly, Ria turned away and mounted the steps back to the hall. She walked slowly along the corridor, holding her light up to each portrait, studying the men who had governed the academy since its inception.

Perhaps the most evil thing, she decided, was the benevolence she saw in their eyes. They were posed rather stiffly; invariably their form was correct, solemn and dignified, most of them unsmiling, but it had always seemed to her that with few exceptions there was kindness in the eyes.

The portraits of the founders gave way to the governors of the middle of the last century, and she discovered it was more of the same right up until the present day. The style of posing changed only a little with the passing years, the manner of dress a little more. The somber black of the founders was replaced in due time by fine satins in brilliant hues and heavily embroidered waistcoats. Those were abandoned for the ruffled, foppish fashions that remained the vogue until Brummell dictated that simplicity would be the common mode. Over the course of more than a century, wigs became increasingly elaborate, then less so, and finally, among the most recent governors, they disappeared entirely.

Mr. Beckwith's founding forebear was at least more candidly cruel in his expression than the others. There was a sharpness to his eyes and mouth that made Ria think he had not the patience for sitting under the artist's scrutiny. Perhaps the artist had been moved to paint his subject more honestly than the others had painted theirs. Perhaps they were all as cruelly featured as this first Beckwith, but had demanded that their portraits reveal a kindness to their nature that did not, in fact, exist.

She studied Sir Alex's portrait last. His eyes were deeply blue, nearly the color of cobalt. They were also direct in their gaze, frank and forthright. It was his manner of regarding people straightforwardly that made his eyes seem piercing. There had been occasion for Ria to come under Sir Alex's scrutiny when he visited the school, but she had lived with the Duke of Westphal for too many years to be cowed by someone merely taking measure of her resolve. Sir Alex had only been mildly inconvenienced by her insistence that he wait until the girls were done with their lessons before taking them on a carriage ride.

The light from the candelabra flickered wildly as Ria lowered it suddenly. Fat droplets of wax beaded on the floor. She brought it up quickly but could not hold it as steadily as she had before. It was her knees that were shaking, threatening to give way under her. Turning, she leaned against the wall and struggled for composure. She was glad for the lateness of the hour. If someone had witnessed her distress, she would have been hard-pressed to offer an explanation.

Ria's breathing calmed slowly. Why had she not remembered Sir Alex's offer to the girls before? He'd come in the middle of the week so many long months ago. Tuesday? Wednesday? In the earliest days of autumn, she thought, at the end of September. She had put it out of her mind as soon as he left. An unannounced visit from one of the governors was not without precedent. She always accepted it as a good thing, an indication that the governors were interested that a certain standard of care was observed.

The girls had been thrilled to be invited to ride in his carriage. Plump leather squabs. Well-sprung. Brass fittings. He had ordered his driver to ferry them back and forth to Gillhollow, where he purchased ribbons and trifles for them. Ria hadn't had the heart to deny them such a pleasure, nor deny Sir Alex the pleasure of providing it.

That was how she had delivered Jane Petty to the very devil.

Ria jammed her fist to her mouth to keep from crying out. "God," she whispered against her knuckles. "Oh, dear God."

She stayed in that position, back to the wall, one hand pressed hard to her lips, the other with a death grip on the candelabra, until she knew her legs would support an independent step. The first was tentative, the second stronger, then she was running for her own apartments, careless that the candle flames winked out one by one by one.

She let herself in and closed the door quickly, leaning against it while she caught her breath. Her fingers loosened around the candelabra and it thudded dully to the floor. She let it lie.

"Ria?" West stepped away from the apron of the fireplace and made himself visible. "Ria? What has happened?"

She stared at him, wide-eyed and openmouthed, but had the presence of mind not to scream.

West's long stride erased the distance between them. He took her by the elbows and gave her a little shake. "Tell me what has happened."

Raising her face to his, she said with steely calm, "Release me."

His hands dropped away immediately, and he took a step back.

Ria slipped through the opening West created between

himself and the door. Her restlessness could not be contained, and she paced off ten steps to the window, then half again as many back. Her fingers gripped the top rail of a Windsor chair. "I have realized that I might have prevented it, that is what has happened. Jane went with Sir Alex because I permitted it. She rode in his carriage like every other girl, but he used that opportunity to single her out. He culled her like a lamb from a flock of sheep, and I had a hand in allowing it."

West wasn't certain he understood all that she was saying, but he had a clear enough sense that she was blaming herself. "You didn't know. You couldn't have known. Ria, listen to me; if you take this upon yourself, then you mitigate the responsibility that should be Sir Alex's. Do not do it. Do not make yourself sick over what you had no cause to do differently."

Her head came up. "What if you cannot find her, West? What if we cannot prove what he has done? How will I protect the girls when he comes again to pluck another?" She saw that he did not have an answer at the ready, and the lack of one frayed her last nerve. Her vision darkened at the periphery first, then she could not draw a deep enough breath. Light-headed and off balance, the room tilted as suddenly as she did.

The last thing she knew was that West could not possibly catch her before she fell.

Ria's eyelids fluttered open. She was lying on her side in bed, and West occupied the chair she had previously used to watch over him. His head was tipped back, and his eyes were closed. Her guardian angel had fallen asleep. She smiled, stretched, then winced as pain shot through her shoulder. Feeling for the tender spot, she found it just below her collarbone. She peeled away the nightdress and looked at her skin more closely. Candlelight at her bedside was sufficient for her to see the slight discoloration that would certainly become a livid bruise in a day's time.

She squinted at the clock on the mantelpiece, trying to remember when she had wound it last and whether it could possibly be accurate within even half an hour. According to it, it was a quarter past one o'clock. She had never fainted before, but she did not think it was natural to have remained unconscious for so long. It had not yet been eleven when she left her apartments to have a look at the portraits.

"Feeling more the thing?" asked West, drawing himself up in the chair.

She nodded. "I think I took leave of my senses," she said. "I am sorry you were witness to it."

"I'm not, and there is no apology needed. Your nerves were overwrought."

Her mouth curled disapprovingly. "Margaret's nerves are overwrought. I went a little mad."

West chuckled. "As you wish." He pointed to the decanter of sherry on the table and the glass beside it. "I tried to get you to take a little bit of this earlier when you came around, but you would have none of it."

"I came around?"

"You don't remember? No, I suppose you don't. You cursed me, you know, then you promptly fell asleep. I decided the wiser course was to let you remain that way. You can curse me anytime."

Ria blushed a little. "Have I said or done anything else I must atone for?"

West pretended to consider this. "Atone? No, I don't think so . . . but perhaps you will explain the other remark you made . . . the one immediately before you cursed me."

"I made a remark?" Her voice fractured the words a little as her throat tightened uncomfortably. "What did I say?"

"Let me think on it. It was deuced peculiar." When Ria looked as if she might sling a pillow at him, he decided to be done teasing her. Resting his forearms on his knees, he regarded her frankly. "You said, 'I am very sorry to report it, Your Grace, but I have developed a tendre for you. Damn you to bloody hell.'"

Ria was silent for several moments, then she nodded faintly. "A Banbury tale if ever there was one."

Chapter Eleven

"I take it that means you don't intend to explain yourself," West said, grinning.

"It means I don't believe you—therefore I have nothing to explain."

One of his brows kicked up. "Are you quite certain you didn't say it?"

Ria wasn't, but she knew she could ill afford to waver here. "I am not some great, gaping trout to be reeled in with that sort of bait," she said tartly. "Though it was a good effort and very well timed."

"Thank you."

Sitting up, Ria tugged on the fallen shoulder of her night-dress so that it covered her properly again. "What did I strike when I fainted?"

"Aaah, yes. That's going to be a nasty bruise, I'm afraid. You tipped the chair on yourself when you went down."

"Then I didn't really manage it gracefully." She lightly massaged the site of her injury. "That is unfortunate."

West chuckled. "Perhaps you will improve with practice. It is the sort of thing better done in my arms."

"I fainted," Ria said. "I did not swoon." She gave him a

meaningful look. "What *are* you doing here, and *how* did you get in this time?"

"I hope you will appreciate my efforts to be discreet. I deliberately made a public farewell when I left some five hours ago so I could return without notice."

"Oh." She wondered if he knew she was suddenly a little breathless. "That was very clever. Then you never meant to go to the manor."

"So you did find my note. I left it in the event someone came looking for you. It was simply meant to support the story you gave that I had taken ill."

"You manage details very well."

He nodded. The colonel had always depended on him for that. "It is part and parcel of being a good clerk."

Ria did not take issue with that assertion. It was true enough on the face of it, she supposed, but if West had ever been a clerk in the foreign office, then she was a bolt of Brussels lace. "And the other?" she asked. "How did you make your entry?"

"That couldn't have been simpler. I left a window in your sitting room unlatched."

"Of course." Affecting what she hoped was credible sangfroid, she said, "You have not yet come to the purpose of your visit."

"No, I have not." West rose and began unbuttoning his frock coat. "I am coming to that directly."

What small amount of imperturbability she had remaining vanished when confronted with the vaguely wicked glint in his eyes.

"You have no objection?" he asked, pausing as he was shrugging out of his coat.

"I . . . no . . . that is, no, I have no objection."

"Good."

He seemed perfectly at his ease, she thought, while she was nowhere near so. The only reason she could find for this turn in the road was that he was plainly initiating this encounter, and although she was more experienced now, she was less certain of what he might expect. "Will we be engaging in illustration number one?" she asked. "Or the other?"

West's head broke clear of his shirt, but his arms were still overhead as he peeled it off. She was a complete original, and if he should forget it for even a moment, she was likely to remind him—saucy little baggage. He served up the answer that was certain to give her pause. "Neither."

Ria swallowed. "Neither?"

"I find myself in need of a good night's sleep. It seems I do that considerably better when you're near." He hung his neckcloth, shirt, and coat inside her armoire and allowed her a few minutes to decide if she was complimented or insulted. By the time he sat to remove his boots, it seemed to him that she had made up her mind. She was lying down again, stretched out on her side with her head supported by only one pillow. The other was plumped invitingly beside hers. Her outer arm extended at an angle along the edge of the blankets that were folded down, and her hand was curled in readiness to lift them and welcome him inside.

It proved, he supposed, that he was a more accomplished liar than she.

Wearing only his drawers, he slipped under the covers she raised for him. He turned on his side and faced her. Her hand brushed his arm as she drew the blankets up. She let them go, but her hand continued its climb, sliding along the slope of his shoulder, his neck, then stopped when it cupped his jaw. Her thumb brushed the corner of his mouth.

"Good night," she said. She leaned forward and kissed him on the lips. It was not a gesture of passion but of sweetness.

"Ria." Saying no more than her name, West changed the nature of her intentions to make them fit his.

Her mouth moved over his, softly at first, dreamily, nudging his lips apart with her own, tasting him on the tip of her tongue. She edged closer, bumping his knees. He made room for one of her legs between his. The intimate tangle brought the hem of her nightdress to her thighs. His hand slid under the fabric and palmed her naked hip. She pressed forward and felt the hard and hot outline of his arousal against her.

Ria's fingers threaded in his thick, coppery hair and toyed with the curls at the nape of his neck. She felt him shiver at the lightness of her touch and left the stamp of her satisfied smile on his shoulder.

He cupped her bottom and brought her hard against him where she had only teased him before. Her hips moved without the press of his fingers, rocking and sliding so that the barrier of material separating them became something better than insignificant; it became part of the abrading tension, resistance meant to be overcome—slowly.

She caught his face in her hands again, planting kisses at the corners of his mouth, along his jaw, at the hollow behind his ear. She remembered how he had caught her lobe between his teeth, and she nipped him in just the same way, then flicked the spot with the damp edge of her tongue. The dimple that was always in evidence when he smiled held her attention for a time. Just as intriguing, though, was its less showy twin. She traced it with her nail tip and watched the curve become more pronounced as the corners of his mouth lifted.

"It is a good thing they are not identical," she whispered. "It is all that stands between you and perfection."

West gave a shout of laughter that was cut short by Ria clamping her hand over his mouth.

"Have a care," she said earnestly. "Else the entire school will know you have returned. Your earlier ruse will have been in vain."

He nodded and felt the pressure of her hand lifting. Catching her wrist, he held her close a moment longer and placed a kiss on her fingertips. "You're beautiful, you know."

"It is a pretty compliment, but unnecessary."

"Compliments are never necessary. They are simply . . . compliments." West folded her fingers so that his hand enclosed hers. "Did you think I meant to flatter you? To what purpose? I am already in your bed, and you know now that my purpose was never to sleep here, so if I say something to you, it is because I mean it." He squeezed her hand. "You are beautiful, and I should have said I thought so from the first."

Ria was properly skeptical. "You did *not* think so from the first, so it would have been a lie—and highly improper to say so, even if it weren't."

That made him pull her close; his arms wrapped tightly around her. He nuzzled her neck and growled low against her ear, "And you know all about what is proper."

He kissed her then. Deeply. Hard. Wonderfully hard. Ria felt herself respond in kind, offering herself up to his greedy mouth, because in giving, she was also given.

He turned onto his back, and she came with him, lying full length along his solid frame. Working in tandem, they raised the hem of her nightgown to her hips, then her waist, past the level of her breasts, and finally pulled it over her head. It twisted and tangled in their hands before they were free of it, making them both laugh softly at the clumsiness born of haste.

West stroked her back, the heels of his hands running along the outside of her ribs. He tickled her nape with his fingertips, pushing aside the heavy curtain of hair. "What's this?" he asked. His fingers traced a thin ridge of flesh that rose from her shoulder, across the back of her neck, and disappeared into her hair. "Did this happen when you fell?"

"No." Ria drew his hand away from it. "It's nothing," she whispered. "A very old scar." She kissed him. "Nothing."

Sitting up, she straddled him and urged him to help remove his drawers. They managed it with considerably less difficulty than her nightshirt, then West lifted her and helped her find a new seat, this one joining them ballocks to buttocks. He watched her face as she eased herself onto him, the way she looked at him with something akin to wonder, her eyes darkening with pleasure, her lower lip caught in her teeth to make her cry a whimper. Her nostrils were drawn in as she took a measured draught of air. Her head fell back and exposed the slim length of her neck to his hands. He raised them there, brushing the hollow of her throat with his thumbs, then letting his hands drift lower.

Her slender form gave way to the fullness of her breasts. He stroked them lightly. The nipples puckered and became erect. His thumbnail grazed one, and Ria's entire body shuddered. She found his wrists and held him there so his hands were open across her breasts, then she moved against them, thrusting herself into his palms as part of the same slow, undulating movement of her hips.

She held him that way even as he urged her forward. He used his strength to move his hands at the last moment and take the tip of one breast lightly between his lips. It didn't seem to matter that she held him captive when she was the one surrendering to the hot suck of his mouth.

Ria heard a soft, mewling sound and realized it was coming from the back of her throat. Her skin was hot and too tight for her now. She felt stretched taut by the rising curve of pleasure she was riding. Her hands uncurled around his wrists and slipped into his open palms, the fingers splayed wide so they could thread with his. Their clasped hands tightened into fists. Her breath caught as he bucked hard under her. She rolled with him when he drove her onto her back. Urgency stripped away any pretense of gentleness as they were enjoined in a battle.

She wrapped her legs around him tightly as her hips rose and fell. The tip of her tongue wet her parted lips. She saw his eyes drop to her mouth and darken. He strained against her, grinding between her open thighs. She tried to lift her head and catch his mouth with hers, but he avoided that touch and placed his lips against the curve of her shoulder instead, nuzzling her hair aside, kissing her just where the faint ridge of scar tissue followed the line of her neck.

She wanted to wrestle him onto his back, but he was too strong. He only gave up to her what he wanted to, but what he wanted to do was please her. Ria felt herself being lifted just as she began to contract around him, and then they were both sitting up, her legs across his thighs and curved around his back, his folded under him to make a throne of his lap. She stared at him, startled by this new position, face-to-face with him and as secure in the nest as a fledgling bird.

"Do it again," he whispered against her ear.

She did not know what he meant; then the muscles of her vagina contracted involuntarily, and she heard him give her throaty encouragement. Her brows lifted slightly as she realized that she was like a fist around him. When her muscles contracted again, it was done of a purpose. She laughed in delight, heady with this new power, fully aware that he had given it to her.

"You are a good man," she said. Lifting her pelvis the narrowest fraction, she tightened herself around him as she rose. Her hands slid to his shoulders and her breasts scraped his chest. "A very good man."

West did let her catch his mouth this time. He supported her hips as she continued to squeeze him rhythmically, her outward movements so slight as to be as invisible as her inner ones. He slipped his hand between their bodies and made a trail to her open thighs. She shivered lightly as he began to stroke her. Touching her here was like dipping his fingers into honey. Warm. Viscous. Sweetly scented. He caressed her more intimately than before, sliding back the slick hood of her clitoris just once and letting her experience a pleasure so intense that it was like sparks being struck when a steel blade was forged.

Ria came in a violent shudder, sparks spinning like pinwheels trapped under her skin, brilliant white heat and light rising from the center of her. She was lifted, arching away from West's body, crying out softly at the loss of him. Even then, in the moment of her sharpest pleasure, she knew what he was about. For the span of a heartbeat, she thought of denying him the right to let her go. Caution, good sense, fear—these things asserted themselves, and she knew she would not betray him or herself with such a selfish act.

He came as she fell back on the bed. He followed her

down, taking his weight on his forearms as he leaned over her. Their breath mingled—hot, ragged, no longer synchronous. They stared at each other for a long time, candlelight chasing shadows across their faces. Fine beads of perspiration made their skin glisten. In the cold room, heat rose from their bodies.

West lowered his head slowly and kissed her once. Then again. Infinitely gentle now. He rolled to the edge of the bed. Ria reached for him, but he was already standing, light and lithe on his feet, and her hand merely hovered in the air before she withdrew it. He disappeared into her dressing room and reappeared a few minutes later with a basin in his hands and towels folded over his arm. He washed the evidence of their lovemaking from her body, just as he had from his own; then he set the basin on the floor and the towels beside it.

"Do you want your shift?" he asked.

She nodded. "Please."

He handed it to her, then put on his drawers. For the second time this night, she held the covers up for him, and he climbed in beside her. He offered the shelter of his shoulder, and she accepted it. One of her arms lay across his chest, and her head fit neatly into a hollow that seemed carved for it.

"What do you make of us?" he asked her when she had settled at his side.

The question was not asked lightly. Ria did not have to lift her head to know that his eyes were grave, and there was no humor shaping his mouth in that singular curve. "I don't allow myself to think on it," she said. "I think it might make me very sad."

He nodded slowly. "You would not consider being my wife, then?"

"No."

"My mistress?"

"In London, do you mean? With a house and servants and a phaeton to take me to the park? Your Grace has already taught me how to sing—there is no need to cage me as well." She regretted her words as soon as they were out. Not only did they seem flippant and vaguely cruel, but they were in her mind because of what the dressmakers had said about Jane Petty. "I'm sorry," she said quickly, rising up to see his face and know that he could see hers. "It was a horrible thing to say. You have done nothing that I have not asked you to do. Even tonight, I hoped you would come back. I wanted to lie with you again. This will have to last me the whole of my life, you know." Tears welling at the lower rim of her lashes spilled over and fell on his cheeks. "I don't expect there will ever be anyone else, not because you say there shouldn't be, but because I am not a woman who will ever go from one man's bed to another, seeking naught but my own pleasure. What you have taught me, I shall cherish." Her tears fell in earnest now, and her body began to shake with the force of her sobs.

She had cried before in his arms, but this was different. The last time it had been for fear of what she had done to Jane. This time she feared what she had done to herself.

West let her cry. A woman's tears did not frustrate or frighten him. He had known them at an early age at his mother's knee. She had laughed through them sometimes, tousling his head so that he would not be alarmed. At other times she would excuse herself and hide away in her bedroom for an afternoon, an evening, sometimes an entire day, emerging when the melancholia had passed, or when the duke came to take her away.

He did not know why he began to tell Ria these things, but once the first words came, it was a little like weeping, and he discovered there was good reason to see it through to the end. Life had been an ache in his chest for a very long time; humor had never served to deflect it, only to keep it contained.

"My mother's name was Meg," he said. "Did you know that?"

Ria shook her head, knuckling the last of her tears away. She used a corner of the sheet to erase the trail they had left on his cheeks as well, then slipped beside him again.

"Not Megan or Margaret or Meggie. Just Meg Marchman."
He felt Ria's arm slide across his chest, and he laid his fingers over her elbow and stroked the soft inner curve. "She was the daughter of the widowed tutor employed by the seventh Duke of Westphal for his son, the future eighth duke. She grew up with my father as her boon companion until he was sent away to school. The duke arranged a good living for her father as schoolmaster for the village's children. You might not credit, but both of my grandfathers were progressive in their ideas about education."

Ria had not known this, either. She wondered if it did not perhaps explain why West's own father had finally indulged her decision to teach. It seemed that his tutor, as well as his own father, had had some measure of good influence on him.

She closed her eyes and let the images form in her mind's eye as West unfolded his tale. She saw the young Meg, winsome and quite lovely at seventeen, become more than a companion to William Fairchild as he came into manhood. Straight, broad of shoulder, he cut a handsome figure and could have had his pick of any of the young ladies presented to him during the Season. He vowed he would have no other than Meg, but he spoke the vow only to her. They were not so naive that they believed either of their fathers would bless a union between them, but neither were they willing to be parted. They married in secret, by special license, and William promised that it would not remain secret forever, that he would wear his father down eventually. Their love was true, his father would come to understand that, and they would prevail. Once again, he spoke the vow only to her.

Ria tried to imagine William broaching the subject of his feelings for Meg with his father. It would have been difficult for him. He would have wanted to appeal to his father's reason and found the going treacherous. Perhaps he had not even tried so very hard. West was of the opinion that he had not.

"My mother told her father about the marriage as soon as she realized she was going to have a child. She begged him not to go to the duke, but to allow her husband more time to influence his own father. He agreed, most likely against his better judgment, but he honored his promise and spoke to no one, even when he saw his daughter's belly begin to swell and knew the truth of her pregnancy would become apparent to all."

West threaded his fingers through Ria's and tapped his thumb lightly against hers. "The fact that my mother was going to give birth put pressure on William to do something quickly. What he did was confess to his father that he was my mother's lover and that he had got her with child. If he hoped to add that he had already married her and that the child had been conceived in wedlock, he never had the chance to speak of it. His father vented his spleen by striking him across the face, then offered his reluctant congratulations on the impending bastard birth."

Ria winced. It was less a reaction to West's description of events than it was to the edge of ice in his tone. It was not overtly chilly; rather, it spoke to a hard-frozen center that had never known a thaw.

"I don't know what my father thought—I can only judge him by what he did," West said. "And what he did was agree to marry his father's choice for him, Lady Jane Caldwell, the proper daughter of an earl with an inheritance in her own right. My father demonstrated neither courage nor charity by not telling my mother himself. She heard of the marriage when the first banns were read."

Lifting her head, Ria glanced at West again. His features remained stoic, almost without expression, and she had a sense now of the cost to him. She laid her cheek back against his shoulder and quietly wept the tears he could not.

"She went to the duke," he said, squeezing her fingers so they folded around his. "And she told him about the marriage. He demanded proof, and she could offer none. Those papers were left in her husband's care, and when he was confronted, he not only did not produce the proof, he denied every part of her story. Official record of the marriage also disappeared. My mother was made to be desperate—which she was—and scheming—which she was not. Her lawful husband married Lady Jane the following year, shortly after I was born. That is how I escaped the name William for my own. As the first son, it surely would have been mine, just as it was for every duke before me."

West's chest rose and fell on a deep sigh. "Lady Jane and her bigamist husband conceived one son who lived and five others who did not. The miscarriages took a considerable toll on her health, and she was confined to her bed through many of the pregnancies and then afterward as well. My mother's father died when I was yet an infant, and without his income, my mother had to find employment. She was a good seamstress, so she began to take in mending, then fashion dresses. She accepted money from the duke—not my father, but the man who was rightly her father-in-law—and opened a shop in the village. Do not think my mother was not a proud woman. She was, but circumstances compelled her to also be practical."

Ria dashed surreptitiously at the tears still welling in her eyes. "Do you think the duke believed her story, and that is why he offered her money?"

West shrugged. "He may have, but he was also of a pragmatic nature. He had ambitions for his own son, and he wanted to assure that my mother would not raise the subject of the alleged marriage again. The money was foremost a bribe, though it may also be as you said. Even if the duke came to realize his son had lied, what could he do? There had been a very public wedding with Lady Jane. He could not expose his son as having two wives."

Easing his fingers free of hers, West gave Ria a corner of the sheet to wipe her eyes. In return, she gave him a watery, slightly embarrassed smile. He shook his head. "No one has ever cried for me before."

Ria glanced at him, frowning. "But your mother . . . you said she cried a great deal."

"She did, but not for me." He bent his head and kissed the

crown of hers. When he spoke, his breath brushed silky tendrils of her hair aside. "For all intents and purposes, I was a bastard, but she was a bastard's mother. In a village so small as Ambermede, it did not make her an outcast, but it always set her apart. The duke died when I was three, not long after Tenley was born, and my father was made Duke of Westphal. That is when he began to come around again."

"She took him back?" asked Ria.

"On occasion. She loved him and hated herself, or hated him and hated herself."

"But she loved you," said Ria. "She always loved you."

His smile was a trifle crooked, a little weary. "Is it so important that she did?"

Ria simply stared at him, her heart in her throat.

"Ease your mind, Ria," he told her gently. "I was not unloved."

Her mind was not eased, not when he said it in such a fashion as he had. "What was she like, West?"

He was a long time in answering. "I think you will not believe me in light of what I have told you, but she was cheerful. Determinedly so, perhaps. She held her head up and made no apology for what others believed about her. What she knew to be the truth was her shield. She was my champion, after a fashion. No one called me a bastard in her presence."

"But when she was not around?"

"A different kettle of fish."

"You did not know the truth then?"

"No. Never. I understand now that she did not trust me with it. My father was becoming considerably influential in politics, and his continued success depended upon her silence—and mine. I was always recognized to be the duke's son. No one questioned it. That he had a bastard was never more than a nine days' wonder except in Ambermede. My mother also pitied Lady Jane, though this feeling was hardly mutual. The duchess hated my mother, but she probably feared her more."

"She knew about her husband's other marriage?"

West gave a short bark of laughter at the thought. "No. Most definitely not." He sobered gradually. "What she eventually learned was that the duke was still visiting my mother and had deeded her the cottage I told you about. She discovered that he was paying for my education at Hambrick and had every intention of supporting me at university should I decide to go. She thought such attention to his bastard was excessive."

Ria ventured her opinion softly. "It does seem he was rather more generous than most."

"Does it? It was the price my mother exacted. That the duke was willing to pay it says something about how very much he wanted her."

"Perhaps it says something about his guilt."

West shook his head. "The duke was not disposed toward the same base emotions that plague other mortals."

Now Ria sat up in bed, unwilling to let his comment pass with no rejoinder. She looked down at him, her attention frank, even a little challenging. "How do you explain, then, the duke making a confession of his first marriage before his death? I do not think you could have become the ninth Duke of Westphal if not for your father's guilt."

"Do you think I wanted this inheritance under those circumstances? To give the selfish bastard peace of mind? That's what his deathbed confession was in aid of. He could have set things right at any time, yet chose what caused him the least inconvenience. He despised me, Ria. If I stirred an emotion in him, it was loathing."

"Self-loathing," she said quietly. "I do not think he despised you at all. I think he despised himself for not being a better man, one who could bear the stain upon his reputation if the truth were known. He wished he were a man who could suffer what others might say about him and remain standing tall and straight and proud. It is probably truer that he cared too much about how he was thought of, not too little. It seems to me that he should have liked to have been a man who could do what was honorable, not merely what was convenient."

Ria placed her hand lightly on West's chest. "I believe he wished he were more the man you are."

West felt a pressure in his chest that was out of all proportion to the weight of Ria's small hand. The tightness of his throat made his voice sandpaper-rough. "Being a bastard helped shape the man I am. Do I thank him for that, Ria?" He put his hand over hers. "Should I dismiss the years of torment he visited upon my mother because he was unable to do what was right? My father did not know enough about the child I was to understand the manner of man I became."

"He was weak," she said. "A weak man, not an evil one."

West was uncertain if he believed that. "Weakness begets evil."

"Yes." She did not think he realized how tightly he was squeezing her hand. She let him do it because she sensed she was his lifeline now, and she could not set him adrift. "Weakness can do exactly that."

He glanced at her, and a faint smile crossed his face. "You are not going to argue with me?"

"No. I am learning it is not always necessary, nor even wise, to do so." She felt his grip ease, still without conscious thought. She bent her head, placed a lingering kiss upon his lips, then straightened before he could tempt her with something more than she intended. Weakness did not always beget evil, she thought. Sometimes it begat another bite of the apple. "When did you learn the truth?" she asked. "I think you did not hear it for the first time from the duke's solicitor. Mr. Ridgeway would not have had the courage to deliver the whole of it to you. He must have been profoundly discomforted to inform you that you were to inherit."

"Profoundly," West said. "I believe he thought I meant to kill the messenger. I am certain the duke warned him that I would not take kindly to learning of it." He rubbed the stubble of beard with his knuckles. "My mother told me about her marriage while I was still at Cambridge. She judged I was sufficiently mature to receive the news."

"Were you?"

"I spent an entire fortnight drinking and whoring."

"I see."

"Then I rode to London and confronted my father."

Ria's eyes widened. Very much afraid she knew the answer, she forced herself to ask, "Confronted him? How?"

"I called him out." West saw that Ria had no words to properly express her horror, but that emotion was clearly stamped on her features. "He refused the challenge, said I was too drunk to be held answerable for it."

"Then he did you a favor."

"I don't know. I have often wondered why he said it. I was completely sober at the time."

"Can you not conceive that he didn't want to burden you with the sin of patricide?"

"Have a care, Ria," West said. "Else you will next be making an argument for his sainthood."

Ria had no patience for his gently mocking tones. "The man who cut your back to ribbons with his stick will never be a saint," she said sharply. "But neither will I make him a devil. Did you go to your mother and demand an accounting for the choices she made?" For a moment she wondered whether he might actually strike her, and she remained poised for the blow, believing it was not deserved but willing to take it because her words were truly meant.

West did not raise his hand. Instead, he curled it into a fist at his side while he collected his thoughts. "You are fearless," he said finally. "I cannot say otherwise." His hand rose slowly, the fingers unfolding with equal deliberation. He touched the curve of her neck, brushing aside the fall of her pale hair. She remained very still, and he gave her full marks for not flinching when he found the narrow ridge of scar tissue at her neck. Here was evidence that she was familiar with the sharp snap of the duke's walking stick. "Tell me about this."

"You know."

He suspected, but he didn't know. "He struck you." Ria nodded, but West saw that she was regarding him curiously. "He was angry with you?"

"No. Not at all. He was angry with—" She stopped, collecting her thoughts. "You don't remember? I have always thought you remembered."

His index finger traced the long line of the scar. "I don't understand. What is it that I should remember?"

"You told me at the outset that you had not forgotten the occasion of our very first meeting."

"I haven't. I bear the scars of it."

"As do I."

Deep creases appeared between West's brows. "I don't understand," he said cautiously. "How did you—" He stopped because suddenly he *did* understand. A single moment in time came back to him with crystalline clarity. He was once again lying sprawled in the sweet and prickly grass, his shirt only slightly more tattered than the flesh it covered. He could hear the shrill whistle of the ebony walking stick slicing the air and feel the searing pain of the blow as if it were being freshly dealt. Bewilderment and betrayal cut him a second time. Then, surprisingly, there was the weight of something unfamiliar on his back, and when his father's stick whistled again, there was no more pain, only blessed darkness.

West could not quite believe the conclusion he had drawn, yet it made sense to him also. Four, or twenty-four, it was the sort of mad, brave, heroic thing Miss Ria Ashby would do.

"You climbed on my back," he said, more certain of it now. "You took a blow for me."

Ria found she could not hold his eyes. Vaguely embarrassed by his regard, she looked away quickly and tried to shrug his fingers from her neck. He held her fast, not hurtfully, but firmly. "You took many for me," she said.

"They weren't for you. The duke . . . the others . . . they thought I pushed you in the lake. Those blows were meant for me." He gathered a heavy handful of her hair, twisted it, then exerted just enough pressure to bring her leaning toward him again. Just as he intended, she had to stretch herself along his length to find relief from this gentle coercion. "You were very young," he said, suspicious of her memory. "What do you really know about that afternoon that has not been told to you?"

"It is just the opposite of what you think. It is my earliest memory, and it is surprisingly clear. What happened that day was rarely discussed, even when I inquired. I heard few accounts from others to cloud it." She laid her hand against his cheek so that its curve softened the taut angles of his face. "I remember running and falling and running again. I remember the cast of the sunlight on the lake and thinking I could walk on that mirror. Imagine how surprised I was to find nothing solid beneath my reckless feet. Sometimes I think I can still taste the lake water in my mouth and the sting of it in my nose. You found me, dragged me out, and while I was passed into the arms of my mother, you were hauled from the water and beaten. Do you think that even then I did not know it was because of me?"

"They thought I pushed you," West said again. "And perhaps I did. I could not catch you, and so I lunged. It could be that—" He stopped because Ria was shaking her head.

"You didn't," she said. "I know you didn't. I would have told them so if I could have done other than cry. Do you know what is my most vivid recollection of that day? It is the duke's enraged countenance. His complexion was a deep shade of red, and his features were changed in a way that made him almost unrecognizable—and frightening—to me."

"Yet you did what no one else watching him would do. I think he might have killed me if you had not taken a blow yourself. Striking you may have been the thing that brought him to his senses."

"That is what I've heard," she said. "I do not remember

leaving the protection of my mother's arms or anything that followed until I woke much later in the day. The gash on my scalp and shoulder was already stitched. My mother was sitting at my bedside, but I remember that the duke was also there, and that he remained until I fell asleep again."

West was not impressed by his father's show of concern. "Who explained what happened to you?"

"For a very long time, no one did. Not the truth of it. I was told it happened during my spill into the lake. Rocks, or some such nonsense, is what I was asked to believe. It was Tenley who finally told me the truth—not because he wanted to, but because I had annoyed him in some way and he couldn't seem to help himself." Ria responded to the question West raised only with the slight uplift of one brow. "It was shortly after my parents died, and I was sent to live with the duke at Ambermede. Tenley needed to get some of his own back for whatever I had done to him, so he made certain I knew I was in his home on sufferance, that it was because his father needed to make amends that I had come to live at the manor."

"Did you go to the duke immediately for confirmation," West asked, "or did you simply threaten to?"

Ria tempered her smile so it was not unseemly in its smugness. "The latter. Tenley was infinitely more amenable after that." Her smile faded. "And you?" she asked, her features grave now. Tenley had told her how quickly everyone had departed the lake. The duke himself had lifted her from West's back and taken her to his carriage. If there was anyone who did not favor leaving a young boy bleeding and unconscious at the lakeside, it was not mentioned in the duke's presence. "What happened to you after we left the lake?"

West shrugged. "I woke at dusk and made my way home. My mother nursed me, upbraided me for intruding on the duke's picnic, but also swore that she would not permit him to visit the cottage. He came three days later while I was still abed and took my mother to hers. I pretended I didn't know that he had been there, and she pretended to believe me."

"I'm sorry," Ria whispered. "I wish I—"

He shook his head, silencing her. "You are not to blame. It is not so easy to admit that my father was punishing me for being his son, not for what he imagined I did to you. He would have done it whether you were there or not." He touched her lips with his. "You were his excuse, perhaps, but you were my angel."

Ria's mouth parted and she kissed him long and sweetly, responding to the craving she had for the taste of him, the pressure of his lips, the damp, slightly rough edge of his tongue against hers.

The need was mutual and this touch, a prelude. She knew his body more intimately now, knew what response he would make when she kissed him on the mouth, at the neck, behind his ear. She tested this knowledge by doing the things that gave him pleasure: her fingernails lightly scoring his chest; the caress of her hand along his inner thigh; her mouth gliding over his taut abdomen. These things pleasured her also, and in giving, she denied herself nothing.

She stroked his back, felt the narrow pinching of his flesh where his wounds had healed badly. She laid her mouth over his heart where the wound was only now beginning to close.

He stared at the ceiling, dry-eyed, and felt something inside him cave at the gentleness of Ria's touch. His heart. His will. His stubborn pride. The name for what he was surrendering to her eluded him. He did not know if it mattered. For a moment he simply *was,* and in the next moment, he was simply hers.

He sifted through the silky threads of her hair with his fingertips and stroked the back of her neck. When she looked up, he beckoned her with his eyes. Smiling, she came to him and laid her mouth tenderly across his.

He took over the kiss, removing all tentativeness from its touch. He felt her respond immediately to what he wanted, following his lead so that it became what she wanted as well. Tenderness gave way to teasing, playfulness to purpose.

The pillow from under Ria's head was pushed aside as

she was turned on her stomach. She rested her cheek on the back of her hands and closed her eyes. She was made more aware of him, not less. Anticipating his touch was so arousing that it made little difference where he touched her, only that he did.

He would not be hurried. The placement of his hands and mouth was careful. Deliberate. He judged her readiness by the subtle changes in the cadence of her breathing and the small, throaty cries she could not restrain.

Ria's fingers curled into fists as her hips were lifted. The discarded pillows were pushed under her. She felt him move behind her. His hands palmed the rounds of her bottom, slid over her thighs. She caught her lip. The anticipation of this touch was almost too much bear, yet it was exactly what she did until he entered her. His slow, fierce control was her undoing. She thrust back sharply and took all of him into her, then held him in exactly the way he had once encouraged her to do. He bent over her, kissed the back of her neck, and whispered something against her ear that she could not quite make out. It didn't matter. She hummed with pleasure anyway.

He reared back, then caught the rhythm she had begun. His hand fell on the small of her back. He felt her shiver as his thumb brushed the base of her spine. His fingers trailed across her hip, then slid under her and between her parted thighs.

Ria sucked in a lungful of air and held it. The delicious heat that he made with that gentling hand held her perfectly still. She heard him admonish her softly to breathe. She did, though it was through a small, strangled cry that she drew air.

The shudder that began in her ended in him, and what vestige of gentleness remained was there for them to use to hold each other as their breathing calmed. They fell asleep in a tangle of limbs and blankets, her head tucked into his shoulder, his hand covering her breast. His mouth lay softly against her hair, her knee was slipped between his.

Sometime later, they came to a drowsy state of awareness that he was deeply inside her again and that she wanted him to be there. They made love without ever quite waking up, dreaming as much of what they did as doing it.

When Ria woke a second time, she was alone in bed. West was standing at the window. He had drawn back the drapes and was looking out. There was a hint of sunlight on the horizon, and this is what Ria supposed held his rapt attention. He would be taking his leave soon, she knew. He had only to put on his greatcoat to be ready to go, and it lay over the chair beside the fireplace waiting for him.

"West?"

He let the drapes fall and turned from the window. "You don't say my name often enough," he told her.

"I don't?"

He shook his head and approached the bed. "Not nearly often enough."

The husky quality of his voice made her feel warm of a sudden. In spite of that heat, she drew the blankets up around her as she sat up. "I shall endeavor to do better, Your Grace."

West sat down, his faint, appreciative smile fading the longer he regarded her. "I have to return to London," he said. He pressed a finger to her lips when she would have spoken. "I'll go to Ambermede first so my presence can be accounted for, then tonight I visit Beckwith's home, though not Mr. Beckwith. I cannot make the return trip to London as quickly as I came. Draco will not stand for it, and in truth, neither will I."

Ria was relieved he was not going to ride hell for leather over the countryside. She waited for him to withdraw his finger. "You will write regarding news of Jane?"

He nodded. "I will."

"I wish I might go with you."

West didn't doubt it. He also suspected that Ria knew all the reasons she must stay, chief among them her responsibility to the girls of Miss Weaver's. "There are things I must do in London apart from finding Miss Petty," he told her. "But they will not engage me overlong."

"I understand," she said. "You will have a great many invitations to choose from. You cannot avoid the *ton* forever."

"You do *not* understand. It is not the *ton's* affairs I must attend to, but the colonel's."

"Oh." She searched his face, but found that his expression yielded nothing in the way of his thoughts. "Colonel Blackwood is rather more to you than you would have me believe." Ria was not deterred by his shrug, finding that it communicated something other than the indifference he intended. "And your friends, I think, are not at all what they seem."

"They are friends," West said slowly. He gave her full marks for trying to draw him out with a lengthy silence. It was a good effort, but she gave in before he did.

"They are friends," she repeated. "And something more besides."

"If you wish to think so."

The singular look that Ria gave him indicated she was not fooled by his mild protests. She did not pursue the subject, but chose another. "Thank you for the book of verse," she said. "I should not have left it to so late to tell you how much I treasure it."

"It was my mother's."

She nodded. "I thought it might have been."

West found her hand and squeezed it. "Do not forget that I will need a copy of Sir Alex's portrait."

"Yes. I remember. You shall have it as soon as Miss Taylor can accomplish the thing."

"Good."

They fell silent again, not to draw the other out, but because each was reluctant to say the thing that was uppermost in their mind. It was West who finally spoke.

"Last night . . . the last time we . . . you are aware that I did not . . ."

"It was this morning," she said, taking pity on him. "And I am perfectly aware."

"Just so."

"If there are consequences, I will write." Ria reconsidered what the waiting would be like for him. "I will also write in the event there are none."

He nodded once. "Thank you." Releasing her hand, he stood. "You will tread carefully if any of the governors visits the school."

"Yes. Of course." She glanced toward the window. Sunlight was beginning to filter through a part in the drapes. "You must leave now, else you will be seen."

West nodded again and turned to go. Almost immediately he paused, spun on his heel, and roughly pulled Ria from the bed. He brought her flush to his body and kissed her hard and long and deeply.

Just as he meant her to, she felt the stamp of his mouth on hers long after he was gone.

From what West could determine, the French Ambassador's ball was a glittering affair, inside and out. A light snow covered the ground outside the grand residence. Carriages lined the street in front of the gate and filled the drive leading to the main entrance. Drivers, footmen, and young tigers, all splendidly turned out in their best livery, waited stoically in the cold January night to be of service again. Strains of music could be heard from the opposite side of the street where West stood, taking up his post against a stone pillar. He wore neither the livery of the servants, nor a fine satin waistcoat or frock coat that was the uniform of choice for the ambassador's gentlemen guests.

It was not West's ambition to be noticed this evening. He had accomplished what was to be done in the ambassador's very private study and was now awaiting the results of his efforts. He remained huddled inside his black greatcoat, leaning back against the pillar, the brim of his beaver hat tipped forward over his brow. If he drew someone's attention, it would be because he was perceived to be sleeping. No one who did not know him well would comprehend that he was alert to everything.

His task had been made simple enough by the colonel's preparation and the ambassador's cooperation. He had only to make certain the ambassador had not changed his mind. West discovered upon making his undetected entry into the man's study, that he had kept his word. The documents and jewelry that were meant to trap the Gentleman Thief were still there as promised. He stayed in the small room that adjoined the library only long enough to glance at a few of the books that had been secreted away. It said something about the breadth of Beckwith's collection that the ambassador's own could not hold a candle to it.

Now, standing at his post, his thoughts strayed back to Ria even as he watched the entrance. He wondered if she would have liked to have attended such an affair as this one and if she would have been made happy or less so to have attended it on his arm.

It did not seem likely that there would ever be cause to escort her. His own invitation lay on a silver tray in his town house, left there because his work did not require him to join North and East inside. He did not have to mingle with the ambassador's guests to accomplish his task. That is what he told himself, but in this quieter moment he knew it was not the entire truth.

Beneath this greatcoat, he fingered the letter he had received only that afternoon. Ria was not going to have his child.

He should have been relieved, he told himself.

What he was, was alone.

Chapter Twelve

Ria examined the drawings Miss Taylor had completed of three of the governors. She had engaged the teacher's cooperation by suggesting she had an idea for a special present of thanks to the board. The girls would write letters that described their experiences at Miss Weaver's and make their own drawings, but to assure that there was one to serve as a centerpiece, Miss Taylor's talent was required.

"I am not certain that any of these quite captures the look of them," she said, glancing up from behind her desk. It was difficult to keep the disappointment from her voice, but she struggled to do so because she did not want to hurt Jenny Taylor's feelings.

"You think they are not good enough," Jenny said. From the opposite side of Ria's desk, she was studying them critically as well. "They are not what I hoped for, either. I am afraid none of them is an inspiring subject, though please do not repeat that I have said so. I should not want anyone to think I meant to be insulting."

Ria forced a small smile. "No one would think that of you," she said, collecting the drawings into a pile. The one on top was Sir Alex's. "Allow me to keep these so I may begin to think of how to arrange them with the girls' letters and their own watercolors. If you should like to begin on the others, or even to make a second attempt at these, I would consider it a great favor. You did that very lovely drawing of Jane Petty." Ria was careful to offer her next suggestion tentatively. "Perhaps if you tried watercolors instead of ink, you would find you like the result better."

"Perhaps."

Ria did not think Miss Taylor sounded at all certain, but did not press her. She held up the three sketches. "May I keep these?"

"Of course." She started to go, then hesitated. Her plump arms crossed in front of her, lifting the shelf of her bosom. The posture was not challenging, but uncertain. "Is there news from London?"

Ria regretted that she had not conveyed more satisfaction with Mr. Lytton's report at the outset. She did not know if the teachers had sensed her uncertainty or if she had sensed theirs, but in the end it had not mattered, because she had informed them she would not let the matter rest. A few days after West had gone, Mrs. Abergast had stepped forward and asked somewhat diffidently if the duke might not exert some influence in the matter of finding Jane. Ria admitted that she had asked him and that he had agreed to help. She was aware of the excitement this engendered among the staff, for the news did not remain long with Mrs. Abergast. Miss Webster and Miss Taylor came to her in turn, followed by the housekeeper, Mrs. Jellicoe, and Mr. Dobson. What news she had for one went swiftly to the others.

A full sennight passed and a letter arrived from Lord Herndon announcing the Duke of Westphal's appointment to the board of governors. Ria dutifully passed this along to the teachers, staff, and students, as she would have for any new member, but she understood the adults, at least, believed it had special significance.

"There is nothing from London," she said. Because Miss Taylor's disappointment was a palpable thing, Ria added, "I will tell you as soon as I know something of import."

Miss Taylor caught her lower lip in her teeth to keep it from quivering. When she could trust herself, she released it. "Jane was one of my best pupils. I miss her."

Ria nodded. "I understand." She watched Miss Taylor turn sharply and hurry away, then sat back in her chair and closed her eyes. She rubbed them for a moment, thinking that West's continued silence made the passing of every day a little harder to bear. She knew she had his promise that he would write with news of Jane, but she could admit to herself now that she'd hoped he would write regardless.

Penning the letter to him in which she revealed there would be no child had been difficult. She had begun the thing on three separate occasions and stopped because weeping had caused the ink to smear. Her tears surprised her. She had been truthful about not wanting to present him with a bastard, but perhaps less than honest about wanting a child. When her courses came, she could not reconcile the sense of loss she felt with the reality of her situation. Loss of what? she wondered. She'd had nothing but hope for a time. There was never any child to mourn, only the knowledge there would be none.

Ria turned over all of her thoughts as though she were looking for the right and wrong side of a bolt of cloth. Right and wrong was not so easily established, however, and she came gradually to the realization that had the outcome been different, she would be crying as well. He would have insisted that they marry, and her choices then would have been narrowed to two, neither of which was likely to bring her happiness.

She touched her fingers to her lips and imagined she could feel the impression of his mouth on hers. Since he'd gone, there were times she shuddered awake in the middle of the night, just as though she'd been pleasured. Afterward, she would lie awake for a time and wonder if the same ever happened to him, or if he had found release in a very real way in the bed of another woman.

Those thoughts made her impatient with herself. It was

never welcome to discover that after years of thinking she knew her own mind, she was merely out of it. Dark, self-deprecating humor was something else she'd learned from West, and she found a certain comfort in it.

Sighing, she wondered how her circumstances might be changed if she'd told him that she loved him. What would he have done with that confession? Teased that he'd known for some time? Made his own confession? Kissed her quite breathless? Perhaps all of those things, but she would still be here in Gillhollow and he would be in London, and having said the words aloud, she would not just be alone, but lonely.

There had been news from London, though not from West. Margaret and Tenley had come down from Ambermede to bring it to her. They had learned that the notorious Gentleman Thief had been caught and that Lord Northam—if one could depend upon the *Gazette* to have gotten the story right—had been shot. Whether the shooting had occurred during the apprehension was much less clear, but Margaret gave an account that touched on the threads of each tidbit of gossip she'd heard and repeated the whole of it as if it were fact.

Margaret found a moment outside of Tenley's hearing to inquire discreetly after West, and Ria had admitted she'd heard nothing at all from him. She could tell that Margaret found this odd, though why that should be so was not discussed, as Tenley came upon them.

The visit was a pleasant surprise, and Ria welcomed the diversion. Margaret was reasonably at ease; Tenley behaved himself. It seemed to Ria that something had been changed between them, and it made her wonder what West might have said on the occasion of his last visit to Ambermede, or whether he'd said anything at all. They must have been surprised by him again, arriving at the manor a second time without notice or invitation. What excuse had he given for taking his leave so soon after his arrival?

The thought of it made Ria smile. She would have liked to have been listening at that door as West made his explanations to a curious Tenley and an even more curious Margaret.

Ria leaned forward in her chair and fanned the drawings across her desk again. There was no disputing that they were not Jenny Taylor's best work, nor even her second best. Each of them bore a passing resemblance to the men who were their subjects, but none was quite right. Jenny had not been able to capture their features as well as she had done for Jane Petty. What had inspiration to do with this task? Ria wondered. Sir Alex, at least, was a handsome enough man, his piercing eyes and taste for young women notwithstanding. It seemed to Ria that Jenny might have been inspired by the look of him, if not by the others.

There were five more drawings to be done to complete the current board, and Ria did not think she could press Jenny any harder to sketch these three a second time. Telling Jenny the real reason she needed the drawings was not possible. No one must know the suspicions that West, and now she, harbored. Not yet, not without proof.

There was nothing for it but to send Miss Taylor's rendering of Sir Alex to West.

"The post has arrived," Mr. Blaine said. He raised the neatly tied bundle for West to see, then entered the library at his employer's indication he should do so. He set them on the table at West's side. "Will there be anything else?"

West stopped sharpening his knife long enough to examine the blade. "Inform Mrs. Corbell I will be gone from home this evening, Blaine. Dinner at Northam's tonight."

"Very good."

Out of the corner of his eye, West watched Blaine make a slight bow and exit the room. He waited until the butler was gone before he set aside the whetstone and picked up the post. The knife was so sharp that it met virtually no resistance as it cut through the string. West placed it beside the stone, then sorted the mail. The letters he identified as invitations were tossed immediately back on the table for attention at another time.

He riffled through the others, looking specifically for Ria's distinctively bold scrawl. It was there, the third from the bottom. He broke the seal on the small packet and unfolded the wrapping. A letter bearing his name lay on top of a lightly creased piece of parchment paper. He opened the letter first and began to read.

Ria's missive was three pages. It described her visit from Tenley and Margaret, the girls' latest venture into Gillhollow to be measured for new shoes, and Mrs. Abergast's tumble from a step stool which left her with a badly sprained ankle. It seemed that someone named Julianne Chester—a student, West surmised—had been moved to free the hens from the henhouse, and they were still searching for their best egg layer. Amy Nash had contracted chicken pox and was confined to the infirmary. The students were working on a special gift for the board of governors, one that included copies of the portraits in the entrance hall. What arrangements had His Grace made to add his own portrait to those at the school?

West grinned as he read this last. His portrait in the hall at Miss Weaver's Academy? Not bloody likely.

He finished the letter, then read it two more times. Ria had painted vivid images of what was going on all around her, but gave no attention to herself at the center of it. He was left to wonder how she fared, and it troubled him that she was not forthcoming. Did she truly think he did not want to know?

She closed by inquiring politely after his health and the health of his friends, most particularly Lord Northam. West supposed it was encouraging that she had not simply asked after his friends.

"Well," Elizabeth said, looking up from the letter. "She does inquire about your health. That is something, at least."

West sighed. "It is hardly an overwhelming statement of affection." He held out his hand for the letter. "She evinces more concern for your husband."

"He was shot," Elizabeth said crisply. "Whereas you were not."

"A detail."

"Which you are inordinately good at managing." She took the folded parchment he held out for her and opened it. "This is Sir Alex Cotton?"

West nodded. "I do not believe it is a good likeness."

"He could be anyone."

"That is what I thought. The pen sketch does not give due attention to the color of his eyes." He watched Elizabeth as she studied it. "Will you take it to the dressmakers?"

"Of course." She glanced at him. "Perhaps it will be enough."

West hesitated, choosing his words carefully. "You will be discreet in this? Much depends upon it."

"Do you mean, will I keep this from my husband?" she asked, her dark amber-colored eyes narrowing a fraction. "Or will I refrain from waving the thing about on Firth Street."

"I would not ask you to have secrets from North."

"Good, because I cannot do it." She paused a beat and offered up a slightly guilty smile. "Or at least I can do it no longer."

A consequence of the shooting, West thought, but probably not only that. "It will be enough if you refrain from waving the sketch about," he said. "I shouldn't like North's mother to get wind of it, though. I know you are often about with her. If the dressmakers can confirm this is the man who was in their shop with Miss Petty, it will help a great deal."

Elizabeth nodded. A tendril of silky brown hair fell across her forehead, and she pursed her lips and blew upward, lifting it back into place on a puff of air. "I'm happy to do this small thing for you. Northam will not object, or at least he will not object overmuch. He cannot, can he? Not after he has made plans to ride with you and Eastlyn to Marlhaven."

West chuckled. "Have you already forgotten that you were the one who pressed us to go after South? By my reckoning, it was only an hour ago that you were insisting we rush to his aid."

"A small price for an excellent dinner, I think," she said. "And I believe it was East who suggested that following South was rushing to his aid. I am always for a plan."

"There will be one. I'm certain of it." He stood. "You will have the information I need upon my return from Marlhaven?"

"Yes. And you will deliver my husband safely to me."

It was not a question, West noted. "Of course."

"Miss Parr also."

There was a slight inflection at the end of this, indicating that Elizabeth was not as certain this would be possible. West answered with more assurance than he felt. "If she is with South, then, yes."

Elizabeth stood as well. "Will you say farewell to Northam and East, or shall I bid them good night for you?"

"Make my excuses for me. If I am to leave for Marlhaven on the morrow, then there are things I must attend to tonight."

"You will write to Miss Ashby?"

He gave Elizabeth full marks for her perceptiveness. "Yes," he said. "It is one of the things I must attend to."

Elizabeth crossed the distance to West and touched him lightly on the forearm. "Will you write that I am desirous of making her acquaintance? After reading her missive, it seems to me that she is precisely the sort of person I should know better." Her pause lasted no longer than a heartbeat. "And I do not think it would come amiss if you told her that you love her."

"You will excuse me, girls," Ria told her class. She glanced toward the hallway where Mr. Jonathan Beckwith stood out of sight of her students. "Emma. Please review the map again. Trace the Roman campaigns across Europe from the reign of Julius Caesar to the assassination of Emperor Commodus." She gave Emma the pointer and slipped out of the classroom, pretending she did not see all the necks that were craning to have a look at what had captured her attention.

"Mr. Beckwith," Ria said, dipping her head slightly in greeting. This small gesture of respect gave her opportunity to compose herself. "How good it is to see you. May I inform my class that you have come to pay us a visit?"

"Pray, do not disturb their studies. I wish I did not have to interrupt you."

She drew him down the hallway, away from the open door of her classroom. "Allow me to tell Mrs. Abergast that my students are alone. She will look in on them until I can return."

"Of course. I will wait for you in your apartments."

Ria could find no reason to protest this arrangement other than her own discomfort. It was not so long ago that she would have welcomed Mr. Beckwith without any misgivings. Now she had to keep those feelings strictly suppressed so she would not give herself away. "As you wish." Knowing that he never liked to dine with the students, she asked, "Shall I arrange for luncheon?"

"Please."

Nodding, Ria excused herself and went in search of Mrs. Abergast. The teacher was immediately aflutter with the news that they were being visited by one of the governors, and Ria had to calm her before she could make her exit.

Mr. Beckwith had already made himself comfortable behind her desk by the time Ria arrived in her apartments. "I thought we would eat in the sitting room," she said.

"Yes. That will be fine." He smiled. "But we will talk in here."

Ria was struck first by the coolness of Beckwith's smile, then by his words. She was suddenly given to the suspicion that he had used her absence to search her desk. "Very well," she said, relieved there was no tremor in her voice. She accepted his direction to seat herself and chose the Queen Anne chair situated on the other side of the desk. "I gather there is something particular that brings you here. How may I help you?"

He leaned back in the chair and laid his hands firmly on the arms. "First, permit me to say how pleased I was to read Mr. Lytton's account regarding Miss Petty. While it is not the best we might have hoped for, there is at least the assurance that she found a protector, if not a husband."

Ria nodded faintly. "As you say, it is not the best we might have hoped for. I am still waiting to hear that he has put a name to the gentleman who invited Jane to leave the school."

"You will not take any action, I hope, without approval by the governors. I must insist on that."

"I have no wish to blacken the gentleman's name. It is only my desire to inform Jane that she is welcome here if she requires help."

Beckwith looked at Ria sharply. "Help? What sort of help? You must allow that she will be the poorest sort of influence on the other young ladies if she were to return here."

"I disagree," Ria said calmly. "She may provide the very best example by way of demonstration of the consequences."

"I'm afraid no one will approve of her return."

Ria did not press her point. If West was right about everything regarding the governors, their approval would not matter a whit. "I understand," she said. "I will not compromise the reputation of the school or the education of the students by acting rashly." Ria saw immediately that instead of placating Beckwith, she had inadvertently pointed him to precisely what he wanted to say. He was looking eager of a sudden, like a dog who had the scent of a meaty bone.

"Will you not?" he asked bluntly. "Do you not think you acted precipitously in speaking to Westphal about Miss Petty's elopement?"

"In hindsight, perhaps I did. I was frustrated by Mr. Lytton's lack of progress. It has been brought to my attention that I should have sought permission from the governors before broaching the matter with him."

"Oh? Who said so?"

"The duke. After he met with you. I thought he was conveying your concerns. He was, wasn't he? You will not be surprised to learn that he had no liking for being thrust into the middle of things."

"Gave you a proper dressing-down, did he?"

Ria nodded. She did not affect a contrite mien, believing it would be overplaying her role. With the governors, she was invariably respectful but not spineless, and she remembered it was Beckwith who had suggested that West tether her. "I realize that as headmistress of Miss Weaver's, I have no voice in determining the membership of the board of governors . . ."

"But? Speak freely, Miss Ashby. It is clear to me that you wish you had been consulted on this occasion. You have some objection to your guardian joining the board?"

"It is not an objection, precisely—rather more of a caution."

"Really? A caution. You mean to tell me, don't you?"

The chilly undercurrent of mockery in Beckwith's tone was so unlike him that Ria was alarmed. There was no mistaking the prickle at the back of her neck, and she could hardly credit how difficult it was not to shiver in response. She forced herself to answer evenly. "It is only that I do not think the duke is entirely dedicated to the cause of our school. He means to be controlling of me, or that is my interpretation of his desire to be a governor."

"Then you did not encourage him."

"Oh, no. Not at all." Ria found it was far simpler to keep up her side of the conversation with Mr. Beckwith when she was speaking the truth. "I was adamantly opposed."

Beckwith studied her for a long moment. "He said as much."

"Did he?"

"I think your opposition to his plan confirmed the need for it." He waved aside the objection Ria was preparing to make. "You will have to learn to live with his interference, I expect. Whatever his motivation, Westphal will be an asset."

Ria pulled a frown, looking properly doubtful.

"Your suspicion is understandable, yet it is as you said—as headmistress, you have no voice in certain affairs of the board. It is unfortunate for you, perhaps, that Westphal feels the need to exercise some control over your affairs, but it has been a boon for us, and the school will benefit."

It was no simple thing to take measure of Beckwith's sincerity. The fine hairs at the back of Ria's neck were still raised, but it seemed that he meant what he said. It left her with the disconcerting thought that there was another significance to his words that she did not understand.

"Westphal is in London?" Beckwith asked.

"I suppose he is. I have not heard otherwise."

"So he is not as controlling as you feared."

Ria answered carefully, "I think he is biding his time."

"You do not trust him?"

"On the contrary. He is an honorable man. I would trust him with my life."

"But not your future, is that it?"

Ria was saved the necessity of making a reply by the arrival of their luncheon. She helped arrange the drop-leaf table with two place settings and uncovered the platters. Mr. Beckwith waited for her to be seated before he took his chair. She was reluctant to dismiss the maid, but the choice was removed from her. Her guest assumed the right to send Sarah away.

Beckwith filled his plate and did not hesitate to tuck into his meal. Around a mouthful of food, he said, "What news have you had from London?"

Ria assumed that Beckwith meant this in the most general sense. "Precious little. We have heard there will be a British settlement in Singapore very soon. A coup for the Prince Regent, I think. He has been in support of such a measure for some time. Oh, and of course, that the Gentleman Thief was apprehended, but that is weeks old now."

"Then you have not heard that Miss India Parr is returned to the Drury Lane Theatre."

Knowing that she was being watched very closely, Ria

was careful to keep her features schooled. "Had she been away? I'm afraid I don't know much about it. We have a great deal to occupy us here. Drury Lane receives very little of our attention except when the girls are choosing a play to perform. They are likely to know more about Miss Parr than I do."

Beckwith considered this as he buttered his bread. "I thought that Westphal might have written of it to you."

"I can't imagine why he would." Had Beckwith missed his paintings? she wondered. She knew that West intended to return them, but perhaps it had not been possible before Beckwith realized they were gone. What other reason could he have for mentioning India Parr? Sharing the latest *on dit* from London was nothing Ria had ever done with any of the governors. It seemed wholly inappropriate now. "I had not realized the absence of a single actress from the stage would cause a stir. It must have, if you remark on it. Have you seen her perform?"

"Several times. She is a favorite."

Knowing she would blanch, Ria tried not to think of the paintings. She could not even show her relief that Miss Parr was safe without giving too much away. "Then you must be pleased that she will be trodding the boards again. I wonder if some of the older girls would like to attend a London play, or do you think the trade at the Drury Lane is unsuitable?"

"It is not as rough as it used to be. I think something of that nature might be arranged."

Not anytime soon, Ria hoped. She regretted putting forth the idea.

"Westphal does not have a box, but his friend the Marquess of Eastlyn does. You might apply to your guardian for consideration."

"I would not presume upon him."

"As you did when you went to him with your concerns for Miss Petty."

Ria flushed. She had stepped into that and had only herself to blame. There was nothing she could do but acknowledge his point. "You are right, of course. I should have said I do not want to take advantage again."

Beckwith shrugged. "If the gossips can be believed, Miss Parr's name has been linked to Viscount Southerton. I believe he is also one of Westphal's closest friends."

"I don't know," Ria said with considerably more calm than she actually felt. "His Grace and I are only recently acquainted. You will understand that he does not apprise me of his society. You are infinitely more familiar than I am."

She was relieved when Beckwith accepted this and asked her instead about the school. Ria reported on the most recent accomplishments of the students and the need for something more to be done to the roof than simply patching it. She invited him to tour the school before he left, but he proclaimed himself satisfied with her report and refused the offer.

Ria thought the interview was ended when Mr. Beckwith pushed his chair away from the table. Only later did she realize how she had been lulled into thinking he'd already made his most important revelations.

"The governors will meet in March," he told her. "In London. In light of some changes we are considering, it will be necessary for you to be there."

Ria was a moment catching her breath. "What sort of changes?"

"A second school, perhaps. One closer to London. Westphal has the sort of friends who might be prevailed upon to support such an endeavor."

The same could have been said for West's father, yet Mr. Beckwith and the rest of the board had refused to allow him to join. Ria did not comment on this fact, preferring that Beckwith believe she found nothing odd about it. "This is the first I've heard of a second school. It's an exciting and ambitious proposal."

"As you have often pointed out, there are more deserving young ladies than we have room for. It is an idea whose time has come." He raised an eyebrow in question. "You have some objection?"

"No," she said quickly. "None at all. There are things to attend to here, of course. I would not want to see Miss Weaver's suffer because funds are diverted to a new school."

"I understand. That is precisely why you must meet with us." He named a date, time, and place. "Does it present a problem?"

Ria shook her head. "I will be happy to be there."

"Good. You see, you do have more voice with the board than you thought." He tossed his napkin onto the table and came to his feet. "As always, Miss Ashby, it is a pleasure. I will meet with some of the girls and teachers on my next visit, when I am not so anxious to arrive at the inn at Weybourne before nightfall."

"Then you are going straightaway to London?"

"Yes."

Ria stood as well and offered what she hoped was a genial, gracious smile. "The Drury Lane Theatre, perhaps?"

"They are performing Morton's *Speed the Plough*. It will mark Miss Parr's return to the stage."

"Then I wish you every enjoyment of it." She vowed she would write West immediately. India had a right to know that Beckwith would be in the audience at the Drury Lane. If the actress still wanted to perform, then she should do it with the full knowledge that this man would be there, fixing her with a stare that was as dark as his intentions.

Ria escorted Mr. Beckwith directly to his carriage, stayed in the drive until it was under way, then returned to her apartments where she hovered over the washbasin until she was rid of the contents of her stomach.

West lay in bed on his back, his head cradled in his hands. He stared at the ceiling, but his attention was focused on something he couldn't see. The creaking that had wakened him came again; this time, the noise was sustained. A door opening? A window? He couldn't be certain from so great a distance.

He rose from the bed, then quickly removed his knife

from the sheath in his boot. He crossed the room, his tread much lighter than that of the intruder below stairs. His door swung soundlessly, and he knew where to step to avoid the bowed floorboard. At the top of the stairs, he paused. It was silent again below, but he waited patiently, certain that what he'd heard hadn't been caused by any natural phenomenon.

His patience was rewarded when he heard the pad of footsteps in the hallway, lighter than before. He hunkered down, perched on the lip of the landing like a great bird of prey, and waited for his quarry to turn the corner at the newel post before he swooped.

The lamp on the table in the foyer did not provide West with enough light to make out the cloaked figure clearly, but it was sufficient for him to take full measure of the size and stealth of his opponent. In this case, size and stealth were not going to present a problem.

"You have a great deal to learn about—"

Ria gave a sharp cry and clutched the newel post with one hand for support.

Unperturbed, West continued. "About entering a domicile undetected." He stood slowly. "Do you have your feet under you?"

Since her heart was in her throat, Ria merely nodded.

"Good. Then come up here." When she pushed back her hood to get a better look at him, then appeared to hesitate, he could not fault her for finally showing some good sense. "Do I look as if I mean to turn you over my knee? I assure you, it is what I'm thinking."

Placing the matter so boldly before her seemed to give Ria courage. West saw her figure stiffen as she braced herself, then begin the climb. When she reached the step two below his, he held out his hand and waited for her to take it. It appeared that she was not eager to do so, but he would not be moved aside. Once he had her in hand, he stepped aside so she could join him on the landing.

"I wonder if you can fully comprehend the risk you took by coming here in just this manner?"

"Obviously not," she said tartly. "Else I would have knocked harder."

"Why didn't—" He stopped, frowning. "Harder? You mean you did knock?"

"Is there some other way I should have said so? Yes, I knocked. Several times, in fact. When no one stirred, I decided on this other course. I cannot help but wonder if your colonel knows how deeply you sleep. I should have thought a spy would—"

Kissing Ria was more expedient—and more effective in quieting her—than putting her over his knee. He backed her up against the wall and placed his mouth within a hairsbreadth of hers. "I am not a spy." He did not give her an opportunity to challenge this statement, but touched her lips with just enough pressure to ease them apart.

West did not mean for the kiss to linger, but once begun, it was not so easily ended. She would probably find it amusing that he had not been sleeping at all when, as she claimed, she'd knocked, but sitting up in bed, reading. If he had not closed the book and stretched out, he might not have heard her entry through the window.

The taste of her mouth was something he had missed, but the feel of her tucked against his body was something he had craved. He held her so tightly that he doubted she could breathe properly, yet rather than protesting, she seemed to want to insinuate herself under his skin.

He broke the kiss reluctantly and laid his forehead against hers, collecting himself. "Bloody hell, Miss Ashby," he whispered. "What are you doing here?"

Even as deliciously off balance as she was, the absurdity of West addressing her so formally was not lost on Ria. "I am kissing Your Grace." She angled her head back the few degrees necessary to make that statement a fact. Cupping his face in her gloved hands, she began precisely where he had ended.

West caught Ria's wrists and drew her hands gently away from his face; then he lifted his head, breaking the kiss. He

shook his head slightly when she would have raised herself
on tiptoe.

It was too dark in the hallway to make out his features
clearly, but Ria heard the uneven cadence of his breathing
and understood that he was in want of self-possession, not
reckless passion. She withdrew a little into herself then, embarrassed by her impulsive desire to continue kissing him
when he was clearly not of the same mind. Easing her wrists
free of his light grip, she apologized in carefully neutral
tones that conveyed neither her hurt, nor her impatience with
herself.

"Ria?"

Too late, she realized it was the rigidity of her posture
that gave her away. "May I speak to you?"

"Ria." This time he said her name as one cajoling a recalcitrant child. It was the wrong tack to take with a woman so
fiercely independent-minded, and West actually took a step
back when she upbraided him for being patronizing. He threw
up his hands in surrender. "The library," he said. "There will
still be a fire there. I will not be long joining you." Without
waiting to see if she would go, West turned and headed back
to his room.

Finch arrived minutes later, bleary-eyed and confused
that West was dressing. "I heard voices," he said. "Is there
something I might do for you?" He had already picked up
West's discarded nightshirt and was hanging it up.

West gave Finch his neckcloth. "A simple fold, if you will."
Then he stood with ill-disguised impatience as the valet tied
it for him.

"Someone is here?" asked Finch, smoothing the cloth before pronouncing it satisfactory.

"Yes, just arrived."

"Shall I summon Mr. Blaine? Mrs. Corbell? I do not think
they know you have a guest."

"Do not trouble them. I am uncertain if she will be staying."

"She?" Finch shook his head, his expression vaguely disapproving. "It is not my place, but—"

"You are exactly right, Finch. It is not your place."

The sharpness of West's tone gave the valet pause. He was accustomed to being permitted certain liberties, chief among them being able to speak his mind whether it was his place or not. He clamped his jaw, then decided against such caution. "I had hopes for Miss Ashby," he said quickly. "It would be a terrible shame if you permitted a lightskirt to come between you and—"

"Damnation, Finch, who do you think is waiting for me below stairs?"

Finch's eyes actually protruded from their sockets as he gaped at his employer.

"Exactly my thoughts," West said. "Now, close your mouth, Finch, before I put a hook in it."

Finch's jaw slammed shut again. He held out West's frock coat and brushed it off once he approved of its fit.

West turned around and fastened the coat's three buttons. "Do not stray far. I may have need of you. Better yet, sleep with one eye open."

"As you wish."

"That does not give you license to listen at the door." West was not fooled by his valet's affronted expression. "If Northam offered you enough coin, you would do it."

"You insult me."

West paused, considering the gravity of Finch's tone. "The countess, then," he said, suddenly suspicious. "You would do it for Lady Northam."

"Well, there you have me."

Ria was sitting on the upholstered bench, staring at the fire, when West strode into the room. The glass of sherry in her hands bobbled a bit as she was brought abruptly back to the present. She had removed her cloak and gloves, and although she was not as bedraggled as she was the first time she had visited his home, the wearing nature of her journey was evident in the creases pressed into her muslin gown and the way the collar lay limply against her throat. There was also a slight downward turn in the line of her mouth that matched the slope of her shoulders, and her eyelids were heavy, the lashes fluttering occasionally to a half-mast position and remaining there for what seemed an inordinately long time.

In the hallway, a clock chimed the two o'clock hour. One of West's brows raised pointedly at this reminder of the lateness of the evening. His significant look did not go unnoticed. Ria's flush climbed from beneath her drooping collar until it washed her face in pink color.

"I am aware that you are out of sorts with me," she said with quiet dignity. "There is no need to underscore your feelings with irony."

"I disagree." He crossed the room to the drinks cabinet and splashed a crystal tumbler with whiskey. *"Out of sorts* hardly describes it. Could you not have written that you intended to come here?" He glanced out the window toward the street and saw no carriage or driver. "Did you take the public coach again?"

"Yes, of course. The school cannot spare a carriage for me to journey to London, and Mr. Dobson has more responsibilities than serving as my driver." Her chin came up. "And I did write. I sent word better than a fortnight ago."

"Just as you knocked."

"You do not believe me?" Ria's hand trembled with the strength of her disappointment. "I did both, but I will not insist that you accept my word. I have lied to you so often, it is a wonder you allow me to make any explanation at all."

West saluted her by raising his glass. She had neatly given back as good as she got, underscoring her feelings with heavy ironic inflection. "I received no correspondence from you," he said. "Not in the last fortnight. Not any since you sent Miss Taylor's drawing of Sir Alex."

Ria frowned. "But that was more than a month ago. I have written at least once each week since then."

That gave West pause. His brow creased as he considered

the implication of what Ria was telling him. "Didn't you find it odd that I repeatedly asked the same question in all of my letters? That is a good indication I was not receiving a reply from you."

"Your letters? I received none."

"None?"

She shook her head, her expression deeply puzzled. Her eyes followed him as he crossed the room and sat, hitching his hip on the upholstered arm of a chair rather than using the cushion. He stretched one arm across the back and one leg out to the side for balance. He looked supremely at his ease—and in every way vigilantly attentive.

"Since you left Gillhollow, I have had correspondence from the board of governors," Ria told him. "Also letters from Margaret and the children. My great-grandfather, who resides in Greenwich, wrote to me as well. I suppose we can conclude that there is nothing wrong with the post. It is peculiar I would have none of your letters."

"My thoughts are the same." He sipped his drink. The matter of Ria's ill-conceived journey to London could wait, he decided, until this bit of business was sorted out. "How is the post collected at the school for sending?"

"All letters are placed in a basket expressly used to collect them. You may have noticed it. It is located on a table in the entrance hall, close to my apartments. There is usually at least one trip each day to Gillhollow, and whatever correspondence there is in the basket is taken at that time."

"Then anyone might remove a letter."

"I don't think that is very—" She stopped, realizing that West was making no accusation. It was merely an observation on his part, and one she should be willing to consider, rather than defend. "Yes," she said after a moment. "Anyone might do so."

"And letters that come to the students and teachers at the school? How is the post managed then?"

"It is brought directly to me for sorting. When I have removed what is meant for my attention, I give it to one of the teachers to make the appropriate deliveries."

"Brought to you by whom?"

"By whomever picked it up in Gillhollow."

"And that is rarely you."

It was not a question, but Ria confirmed his supposition. "Rarely."

"Then you do not really see it first."

"No, but—" Ria bit her lip, gathering her composure. She did not want to go where he was leading her. "No. I am not the person who generally sees the post first."

West was not unfeeling of Ria's dilemma, but at the root of this lay what trust they had been able to nurture. If they believed that each of them had written to the other, then some explanation for the disappearance of the letters was necessary. For Ria to place her full trust in him meant accepting that she had been betrayed by someone else.

"Tell me about the letter I did receive," he said. "Miss Taylor's drawing of Sir Alex . . . how was it posted?"

Ria stared at her glass of sherry, thinking back. "I put it in the basket . . . No, I gave it to Mr. Dobson, who was collecting the letters from the basket."

"Then it did not have opportunity to be seen by anyone else."

"No. He took the post immediately to Gillhollow."

"And it arrived here."

"Yes."

"And none of your other post did. Nor any of mine to you. Can we agree the failure does not lie with my staff or the post delivery?"

Ria took a large swallow of sherry and relished the warmth of it all the way to her stomach. "We're agreed," she said. "Someone at the school is responsible."

"Do you wish to suggest a name?"

"No. I cannot."

"I think we can eliminate Mr. Dobson as the culprit," said West. "Everyone else, I'm afraid, remains."

"I doubt it is Mrs. Abergast. I cannot recall the last time she elected to go to Gillhollow, and she almost never is the one to deliver the post to me. It must be someone else."

West finished his drink and put his glass down. "It is probably less important to know who than it is to know why."

Nodding faintly, Ria's fingers tightened around the stem of her glass. "Before I sent the drawing, there was another letter I wrote. Did you receive it?"

He tried to catch her eye but failed. "Yes, you sent it by express post."

Her slim smile was apologetic; she wished she had not asked the question. "Of course. I had forgotten." She glanced up at him. "Then you know I'm not here because of a child."

"I know," he said gently.

Ria's eyes swiveled away quickly as she wondered at the hint of regret in his voice. Had she imagined it, or were his thoughts about a child as confused as her own? "My other letters to you . . . and yours to me . . . should we assume they were not only taken but read?"

"I think it is a safe assumption."

"I see." She hesitated, then plunged ahead in spite of her reservations. "You will probably want to know what sort of things I wrote to you."

"That would be helpful."

"I doubt it. You will not find it particularly edifying. It is more of what I wrote in the missive I sent with Sir Alex's portrait. I described the routine of the school and what manner of mischief the girls were devising. I believe I reported in some detail on the health of the teachers, the inclement weather, the success Amy Nash had at learning and reciting the 'quality of mercy' speech from *The Merchant of Venice*."

"Impressive."

"Yes, it was." She had not missed the mocking gravity of his tone but went on as if she had. "Amy is the youngest student ever to have learned the speech."

"There was a reward, I hope, for such an accomplishment." He caught Ria's small, negative shake and came upon the truth in a flash of insight. "Aaah, she was made to learn it in penance for some bit of mischief."

"How did you know?"

West grinned with devilish charm. "How do you think I learned it?" He dropped to the cushion of the chair and stretched his legs before him, a posture that declared himself entertained. "What else did you write?"

As weary as she was, Ria was also not proof against this encouragement. "I informed you of Margaret and Tenley's visit. In fact, they visited several times, and I wrote in great detail of each one. I believe I lamented that our time together was so short."

"A great change, indeed. You were comfortable in Tenley's presence?"

"His attentions to Margaret were just as she would desire them, and he was in every way like an older brother to me."

"You put that to paper?"

"No." She pressed herself to be certain of that answer, aware again that her most private thoughts had been read by at least one other person. "No, I don't believe I did."

West nodded. "Did you inquire about my progress with Jane Petty?"

"Yes. In every letter."

"And you probably asked why I wasn't keeping you informed."

"Yes. Most of my questions had to do with Jane, but I also wondered why you did not tell me about the Gentleman Thief. I learned about his apprehension from Margaret and Tenley. There was also no news about Miss Parr. I thought I had given you offense in some way, or that you had reconsidered helping me, or perhaps you thought I had no interest in your friends. I did not know how to—"

West shook his head, interrupting her. "I wrote to you of the Gentleman and Miss Parr and more besides. Do you believe me?"

Ria believed it absolutely. "I do." She set her sherry aside and smoothed the folds of her dress over her knees. "I cannot like it that someone else has been privy to what was meant for me. Will you tell me what you wrote?"

"There was precious little regarding Jane, though Lady Northam confirmed for me that Sir Alex was indeed the gentleman who was with her at the dressmaker's. Jane is not, however, staying at his residence in town. Sir Alex also maintains a home that he uses to set up a mistress. There is no one living there now. It is disappointing, I know. You had hoped for there to be more."

She nodded. "And what of the rest that you wrote?"

"The rest?" he asked. "I'm afraid I did not stray far from expounding on a single theme."

"Oh? That is unlike you. What theme?"

"Marriage."

Chapter Thirteen

"Marriage?" Ria had to swallow hard to dislodge the word from her throat. "Were you advocating or opposing?"

"I was proposing."

This time Ria did not try to force a response. She came perilously close to gaping at him.

"I see that you are not prepared to answer the question I put to you in every one of my letters." Before she could give any indication that this was true, West stood and turned his back on her. He drew a short, steadying breath. "It is just as well," he said, striding toward the bell pull. He gave it two sharp tugs. "I have gone about the thing badly. It deserves a prettier speech, even if I am to be rejected." Glancing over his shoulder, he saw that Ria was hardly yet recovered. She looked paler now than at any time since she entered the room. "When did you last eat?" he asked. "Did you make the journey from Gillhollow in two or three days?"

"Three," she said, shaking off her torpor. "And it does not matter when I ate last. I am not hungry. But I should like to know if you have a pretty speech at the ready."

"No."

"Will you not say it plainly, then?"

"Will you marry me?"

"That *is* plain."

"I believe I mentioned that." He regarded her closely, but for once Ria's thoughts were shuttered from him. "Well?"

"No," she said quietly.

"That is also plain."

She nodded, her smile slightly rueful. "I think I should like to hear the prettier speech."

"Of course." West opened the door to his valet's knock. "Rouse Mr. Blaine. I want a light repast for my guest. I will also need a cab that can take Miss Ashby to the residence on Oxford Street. Make certain the driver is not deep in his cups and gives a good accounting of himself. Mrs. Corbell should accompany her and see that everything is made ready there."

Ria started to protest, but West stepped into the hallway and gave the last of his instructions to Finch there. When he reentered the room, Ria was visibly resigned to him having his way.

"I did not think you would send me away," she said. "I suppose that was foolish of me."

"I am not sending you away. I am sending you away for what remains of the night. You cannot stay here. There is no suitable chaperone, and you are familiar with the house where the duke lived when he was in town. I have not cared to make it my own home, but there is no reason you cannot stay there. In the morning I will send a letter around to Lady Northam. I think she will be willing to accompany you as necessary so that we may meet without rumor attaching itself to us."

"You are my guardian. There is no reason I cannot be alone in your company."

"Rumor knows no reason. I have heard so much idle talk taken as fact among the *ton* that it would fill all the betting books in London if it were recorded. It is necessary to look no further than Eastlyn's coil to be certain of the truth of it. The gossips had it for months that he was engaged, and where did that set him but squarely before the altar?"

Ria raised one eyebrow. Her tone was wry. "I hope he was happier about the turn of events than you seem to be."

West gathered the threads of his patience. "I am not unhappy about it, but as you are the one set so intractably against marriage, I am honor bound to put the consequences of rumor before you."

"That is very good of you, but I sincerely doubt my presence in town will be noted."

"I think it will. There is a reception in Colonel Blackwood's honor tomorrow evening. The East India Company and certain very happy members of parliament are thanking him for his assistance in raising support for the Singapore settlement. It is East's tinkering, of course, that made it possible, but the colonel is ultimately responsible and will accept the accolades that East cannot. I should like it if you would plan to attend."

Ria blinked. "Has finding Jane Petty interfered with your receptions and galas and musicales?" She saw a muscle jump in West's jaw but went on without pause. "I suppose that you must honor your obligations to go to such events, but I cannot see that I will have a free moment to do the same. I must prepare for the governor's meeting three days from now and do whatever I can in the meantime to locate Jane. I thought that you—" She broke off when his glance became so sharp she thought it might cut her.

"Go on," he said. "Say it all."

"I thought that we would search together. I came here with that uppermost in my mind. Even without knowing about the missing letters, it was clear to me that we were found out. Mr. Beckwith did not say as much, yet I cannot ignore the odd nature of his visit to the school. I thought you should know before we are in the meeting together. It could be awkward at best, calamitous at worst."

Ria took a deep breath. It shuddered through her upon release. "I apologize for intruding upon you. You may well comprehend now that I didn't know I was unexpected. I *wrote. I knocked.* And I can find my own way out. The hack has probably already been summoned." She was halfway to her feet when he ordered her to sit. "I am your ward, Your Grace, not your subject." She straightened, her chin coming up in the same motion, and started off in the direction of her cloak and gloves. "In the event you decide to offer marriage again—and in the event I decide to accept—know that I am unlikely ever to be a biddable wife."

West felt as if all the air had been driven from his lungs and the last vestige of reason pounded from his brain. He stepped in front of the door when she approached and blocked her exit. "Until I recover my wits," he said, "a show of force is all that is left to me."

"Have the courtesy or good sense to step aside."

He didn't move.

Ria laid her cloak across her shoulders and began to put on her gloves. "You are being ridiculous."

"Quite possibly. You will perhaps not credit it, but it does not disturb me in the least. I will also have my say, Ria, and you will listen."

In her agitated state, Ria was finding it difficult to manage her kid gloves. She pulled on them with clumsy fingers, stretching the leather, cursing softly under her breath when they would not settle smoothly over her hands but twisted uncomfortably instead.

West enclosed Ria's hands in his, stilling them in a sure clasp. When she looked up at him, bewildered and uncertain, he gave her benefit of his most steady reassurance. He meant to have his way, and he meant her to know it.

"Will you detain me at the point of your knife?" she asked.

"If it comes to that, yes." He squeezed her hands gently. "Sit with me, Ria. Please."

She nodded once. Her sense of loss was quite real as he released her hands and guided her to the bench. He removed her cloak and waited patiently for her gloves, then he placed them on the chair he had occupied so he could take his seat beside her.

"You have said a great deal that I must answer," West said. "It is difficult to know how to begin."

Ria waited, offering no encouragement for him to begin at all. She wanted nothing so much as to leave.

"I see," he said softly. "You feel I have betrayed you, then. It is understandable. I am also finding it difficult to reconcile that we are not to blame for the lack of letters between us. I find myself thinking that if you had written more often, another letter would have slipped through. I think I should have written daily, hourly, then perhaps you would have received one and known something of my thoughts.

"Do you know I grieved because we had not made a child between us? No, don't say anything. Let me say it all. I grieved, true, and at the same time I was glad of it. I could not brook the thought of you bearing my bastard child, nor did I have the stomach to force a marriage upon you that you did not want. You know it is not my way to try to convince others that I am in the right of any matter, yet I broke with my own beliefs and began a campaign to convince you that marriage would suit. I described all the benefits of marriage, the reason it exists, the purpose of sustaining it, how it brings a certain order to society and security to a family. I wrote that you would not find me intolerable as a husband, that I would settle your inheritance on you so that you might always have control of it. I knew it would be important to you not to abandon the school, and I offered my assurances that you could involve yourself in its operation, even as my duchess. It occurred to me that your influence might be more widely felt in that position than as the headmistress, so I set out to persuade you of the same.

"I put forth every conceivable argument to prevail upon you to accept marriage, or at least I thought I had. Lady Elizabeth—Lady Northam now—she said something that made me realize I had neglected to mention one thing of import."

West caught Ria's chin when she would have turned away and brought her around to look at him. Her beautiful blue-gray eyes were luminous with unshed tears, but their expression was still shuttered. He thought she wanted to hope but was afraid to.

"Shall I put it before you plainly, Ria?"

She nodded.

West watched as Ria's small movement caused a tear to slip free of her lower lashes and slide down her cheek. She seemed to be unaware of it, neither raising her hand to brush it aside, nor blinking back the others that threatened to follow in its wake.

"I love you," he said. "That is what I had not written in support of a marriage between us. It is what I did not say when I asked you to marry me earlier. It is because I love you that I could not let you leave without hearing me out, and it is because I love you that I will still ask you to leave when I am done. I wanted to believe it was understood between us, that I did not have to say the words aloud, but that does not acquit me of being a coward for failing to do so."

West let his hand fall back to his lap and watched her follow the movement. "I do love you, Ria."

She closed her eyes a moment, pressing her hand to her throat. Emotion made it difficult for her to speak. Whispering in a reed-thin voice, she said, "Ask me again."

He knew what she meant. "Will you marry me?"

"Yes." She launched herself into his arms. "Oh, yes."

"It was not a pretty proposal."

"It was perfect." Ria said this against his neck as she buried her face there. "Perfect."

He pressed his smile against her silky hair. "Does this mean you have developed a tendre for me?"

Ria drew back, her features set solemnly, even gravely. "A tendre? That is inadequate to describe what I have felt for so long. There is tenderness and passion in my heart. There is affection and wanting and sometimes a sort of helplessness that I cannot feel differently toward you. There is such a surfeit of love that it has made me afraid. I have been afraid of what price I would be asked to pay for it, afraid it was unwanted, afraid to embrace it, enjoy it, or even exploit it. With so much to fear, what was left to me but to guard it closely, hide it occasionally even from myself, and hope you would not tease the truth from me and immediately regret that you had done so? A *tendre* is what I felt when I was yet a young girl, and I would steal into the duke's gallery to look upon your portrait and imagine you were looking back at me."

Ria's solemn expression faltered, and her slight smile was shaped by guilt. "I do not think I could become so angry with you if it were still a mere *tendre* that attached you to my heart. I am quite certain it is love that provokes that other response."

"Is that so?" he asked wryly. "I shall endeavor to remember it."

Ria began to speak, but the arrival of the repast West had ordered interrupted her. She did not know what effect confession had had on her soul, but it had most definitely whet her appetite. It was all she could do not to fall ravenously on the tray of vegetable broth and warm bread that was carried in. West did not share in the generous portions they were given, and Ria could not induce him to do so. She was aware that he watched her instead and derived some amusement from her carefully measured bites. It was a certainty he knew how hungry she was.

Out of the corner of her eye, she gave him a significant look. "If this is what you mean to do at every meal, I will be moved to murder. *Your* murder, you understand. No one else's. You must not attend me so closely."

Grinning, he poured himself a cup of tea. He carried the cup to the fireplace and poked at the logs. "Is it acceptable for me to speak?" he asked, glancing back at her.

"As long as you are not in expectation of a reply. I mean to continue eating." She tore off a chunk of bread and dipped one corner into the broth. "Go on. I am listening."

West didn't doubt that she could listen to him. What he

remained skeptical of was her ability not to insert a comment or question. "It is about tomorrow's reception. Sir Alex Cotton will be there. As will Herndon." He replaced the poker and turned around. The piece of bread Ria had torn off from the loaf and sopped in the broth simply hovered in front of her open mouth. Droplets of broth fell back in the bowl. She seemed to be unaware of holding it in her hand.

"They are both heavily invested in the East India Company and had a great deal to lose if the settlement did not proceed. They will be present to extend their thanks to the colonel for making it possible, and I will be there to mark their trail afterward. Still, I do not mean to misrepresent my interest in going there. I would have attended this reception regardless of their presence. It is merely fortuitous that we will cross paths. Eastlyn is my friend and deserves my loyalty, my support, even my admiration. Colonel Blackwood has been my mentor, my confessor, my fiercest advocate and critic, and when he cannot help himself, more father to me than my own. So, yes, I will pause in searching for Jane Petty long enough to stand by the people who have stood by me. If you believe I have failed you in some way because I cannot fail them, then you should know that I will fail you again . . . and again."

For a moment Ria could not breathe as it was borne home to her how deeply she had cut him. She slowly lowered her hand and replaced the corner of bread on her plate. "I do not deserve to be forgiven for speaking rashly when I understand so little, therefore I will not ask for it. What I know, though, is that you could not have come to love me so well if you had not learned how to love them first. It is far more likely that I shall fail you, not the reverse."

West shook his head. "You do yourself a grave injustice to think so. It is not a failing to speak with passion, though perhaps you might refrain from honing your tongue to such a fine sharpness."

Ria's eyes dropped to the edge of the table where her hands rested, and she did not look up until she heard West's throaty chuckle. "I am most sincerely contrite," she said. "What is it that amuses you?"

"Only that you manage that particular mien so beautifully."

"It is because I often have had occasion to use it."

That raised West's knowing smile. "I thought you might have had considerable practice."

Ria decided she was done with being contrite. Her mouth flattened in a faint line of disapproval, which predictably deepened West's amusement. There was nothing for it but to distract him. "If you still mean for me to attend the reception tomorrow, then you will have to find me something to wear. I brought nothing suitable with me."

"I have seen the contents of your armoire," he said. "You *own* nothing suitable."

"Perhaps if you were to increase my allowance."

"So that you can turn your students out better than yourself? Not likely. If the Lady Northam cannot manage a suitable gown for you in a day's time, it will be the first thing she has not been able to manage. I am confident that placing you in her hands will bring the thing about."

Ria was not as certain the countess would appreciate having this charge thrust upon her, but she deferred to West's judgment. "And after the reception? What then?"

"That can wait until tomorrow. I want to hear about Mr. Beckwith's visit to your school." When Ria opened her mouth to speak, West held up his hand. "Also tomorrow. There is also the matter of this meeting of the governors that brought you to London. I was informed about the meeting, but not that you had been invited. It seems likely they intend to confront us there, if not close ranks around us. As you mentioned, we have been found out."

Ria pushed her chair back and came to her feet. "Can I not persuade you to allow me to remain here?"

"No."

"But there is a pledge of marriage between us."

"You and I will share a bed again when there has been an exchange of vows."

"You are fixed on this."

"I am."

Ria crossed the room to the fireplace and set her mouth within a moment of his. "I love that you honor me, that you honor marriage." She kissed him, not as a temptation, but as one sealing a promise. Drawing back, she studied his face. "You still have a rogue's smile," she said at last, and she was not at all displeased by it.

Ria was not permitted the luxury of lying in bed the following morning. The Countess of Northam arrived at the Oxford Street residence before Ria was properly awake, and by way of introduction, put Ria through the morning rituals of bathing, dressing, and breaking her fast in just under two hours. Lady Northam repeatedly apologized for the haste with which Ria had to be made ready, but it was a matter of getting to Firth Street before the modistes were so busy that not one of them would accept the challenge of dressing Ria for that very evening.

"It will be a narrow thing," Elizabeth confided as the carriage pulled away from the town house, "but West has been very generous with his coin. That is always helpful."

There was little for Ria to do except allow herself to be managed. It happened so infrequently that she found she could enjoy the experience. Lady Northam made it comfortable for her to be led about from one shop to the next. Although they were of an age, the countess was vastly more knowledgeable about fabrics and fashion. She had a superior eye for color and seemed to know instinctively what not only suited Ria, but what Ria would suit. She never made a choice without asking Ria's opinion, and she never seemed to make a wrong choice.

Madame Poncelet did not respond to Lady Northam's cajolery, but she was sufficiently flattered by the sum Elizabeth promised that she agreed to make a gown for Ria. Every seamstress in the shop was summoned from the workroom for the fitting. While Elizabeth and Madame Poncelet discussed particulars, Ria stood on a stool, stripped to her thin cotton chemise, and suffered the indignities peculiar to having a dress fashioned: being measured, poked, prodded, and pinned, then having every aspect of her form critically discussed by other women as if she were not present.

They agreed on a mint-green bombazine gown trimmed with bands of satin ribbon under the bosom. Puffed sleeves, edged with the same fine satin bands, would be visible under the slashed, capped sleeves that provided an accent for her exquisite shoulders. A top hat trimmed in ostrich feathers, satin gloves, and kid slippers were all to be fashioned in the same fabric and color, and for some extra coin in her purse, Madame Poncelet agreed to find the milliner, glover, and shoemaker who would have it all ready at seven.

"It will never be done," Ria said, taking her seat in the carriage again. "They are seamstresses, not magicians."

"Don't you believe it," Elizabeth told her. "For what West has paid, Madame and her girls will do nothing today but work on your gown and still find themselves able to turn a profit."

Ria accepted the fact that Elizabeth was confident, even if she wasn't. "Is Madame Poncelet one of the dressmakers you spoke to about Jane Petty?" She could see immediately that she had surprised the countess with her knowledge. "West told me that you made the inquiries on Firth Street for him. It was kind of you to lend assistance. After seeing you with Madame, I understand why he asked you to help. I do not think he would have been so successful with any of the modistes as you were."

"Then you underestimate his smile." Elizabeth's almond-shaped eyes shone with a teasing light. "Do not worry. My husband has such a smile, although without those parenthetical dimples that bracket West's mouth. I should not be able to live with him if he had those dimples."

"I know," Ria said softly. "They make him entirely too . . ."

"Perfect?"

"Well, very nearly. One is deeper than the other."

Elizabeth laughed delightedly. "I hope you have told him so."

"Yes."

"Good. He enjoyed hearing it, I am certain." Elizabeth smoothed her fur-trimmed pelisse over her knees. "It was the colonel who first asked me to speak to the dressmakers. I would have done it for West, but it would not have occurred to him to ask me."

"He did later, though."

"Yes. It was no easy thing for him to do. I think he felt he had little choice. It was no trouble for me and small enough repayment for all the assistance he lent to me and to my husband."

"They are as close as brothers, are they not? The Compass Club, I mean."

"As close as we like to think brothers can be and rarely are. The rhyme is their creed. *North. South. East. West. Friends for life, we have confessed. All other truths, we'll deny. For we are soldier, sailor, tinker, spy.* Southerton wrote their charter when they were still at Hambrick Hall. You know it, don't you? West recited it for you?"

Ria shook her head, mouthing the last words more than saying them aloud. "Soldier. Sailor. Tinker." She looked at Elizabeth, the line of her mouth vaguely wry. "Spy." Ria pressed two fingers to her temple and massaged it lightly. "He always denied it. I knew, or at least I thought I knew, but he never admitted as much."

"Do not take it literally," Elizabeth said quickly. "South would be the first one to tell you that too much should not be made of the last line. Deny. Spy. It is all about the rhyme and has no greater significance than that."

Ria realized she could accept Elizabeth's explanation without swallowing the whole of it and graciously did so. As the carriage wended its way back to Oxford Street, Ria listened, entranced, to Elizabeth's version of the Compass Club lore from their days at Hambrick Hall.

West was waiting for them at the town house. Elizabeth greeted him warmly and reported on the most important aspects of the morning excursion; then she accepted West's offer of refreshment but insisted on having it alone in the library.

"You do not truly expect me to chaperone, do you?" Elizabeth asked, her amber eyes darting between West and Ria. "I thought not."

When she had disappeared, West turned to Ria. "It seems we are expected to conduct ourselves above reproach."

"Really? I did not have that same sense."

Before Ria could elaborate on her view in front of the servants, West escorted her into the drawing room and closed the door. He kissed her soundly, then separated himself before he could not. He had almost left it to too late as it was, and the generous pouting line of Ria's mouth did not help in the least.

"Pull in that lower lip," he said. "Bite it if you must, else I will summon one of the maids to dust it off."

Ria laughed. "As you wish." She pushed away from the door and followed him into the room. He ignored the damask-covered couch in favor of a pair of wing chairs and bid her choose one. Ria did not tease him about the selection of the chairs over the couch. There was nothing about his demeanor now that suggested lightheartedness would be welcome.

West waited until Ria was sitting before he lowered himself into the chair opposite her. "Tell me about Beckwith's visit to the school," he said without preamble, just as if there had been no interruption of last night's discourse.

Ria picked up the threads of their earlier conversation and told him everything she could remember. He listened carefully, interrupting from time to time to ask her to repeat a detail or describe the nuance of Beckwith's tone and manner.

When she finished, he merely sat back in his chair and remained thoughtfully aloof.

Ria was grateful for the diversion that the arrival of tea brought. She dismissed the maid and poured for both of them. "There is one other thing," she said, handing West his cup. "I wrote to Miss Parr about Mr. Beckwith's desire to attend her performance of *Speed the Plough*. Do you think she received my letter?"

"I know she did not."

"How can you be certain?"

He used his fingers to tick off the reasons. "The Drury Lane Theatre is still standing. Mr. Beckwith continues to draw breath. Miss Parr performed to widespread acclaim. You must believe me when I say that South would have influenced one or all of these things."

"Perhaps Miss Parr did not tell him." She saw that this clearly had not occurred to West. "If she was as certain as you that Lord Southerton would act so recklessly, she might have been moved to protect him from himself."

"I assure you, there would have been nothing reckless about South's actions. There would have been a plan. South always has a plan." He regarded Ria steadily over the rim of his teacup. "I think Miss Parr is done keeping secrets from South. There is every possibility they will marry."

"Truly?"

"There is a wager among us to that effect. I have pledged twenty shillings." He chuckled at Ria's surprise. "You may as well know now that there is always a wager. Unless North's mother has involved herself in it, however, it is never for more than a few sovereigns."

"This is something you did at Hambrick Hall, is it not?"

He nodded. "Our pockets were invariably light in those days, and in truth, until very recently I could not have held my own with the rest of the club if they had chosen to place substantial bets."

"They made certain you could be included, then."

"Always." The curve of West's mouth softened. "Are you

concerned about this evening, Ria? I believe you will find they are in every way decent, honorable men."

"I don't doubt it. You chose them as your friends."

"Perhaps," he said. "Then, again, perhaps they chose me." He finished his tea, then leaned forward in his chair and rested his forearms on his knees. "They will like you enormously."

She flushed a little that he had divined her uncertainty. In truth, she had been less anxious on the occasion of her first presentation to society. *"Friends for life, we have confessed,"* she recited quietly. *"All other truths, we'll deny. For we are soldier, sailor, tinker, spy.* You must see that your compass is a formidable circle. It can be no easy thing to be part of it."

"You have already been taken in—it is only that you've been unaware."

Ria considered this. "There is a wager concerning us?"

"Most certainly. I do not know the particulars, but I suspect that Elizabeth set it in motion and that Finch, traitor that he is, has become her primary source of information."

"Your valet? Why, that is—"

"Underhanded? Appalling? Deuced clever?" West laughed. "She is only turning the tables. She and North were subject to such a wager and it all has ended well enough. Better than that, for they are most certainly in love." He saw Ria's light flush deepen even as she held his gaze. "Is Elizabeth the one who told you our club charter?"

"Yes."

"You cannot make too much of it. South was ten, I believe, when he wrote it."

"That may be, but Lady Northam says that North became a soldier, South, a sailor, Eastlyn, a most extraordinary tinker, and you . . . well, it is clear you were not merely a clerk in the foreign office."

West shrugged. "In regard to South and Miss Parr, they must be told about Beckwith's interest in her performance."

Ria offered no reaction when West brought their conversation back to the matter at hand. Perhaps it was only that he was not accustomed to discussing the manner in which he'd been employed by the colonel, but she thought it just as likely that he did not regard his contribution—whatever the exact nature of it had been—as unexceptional. She decided she could let it pass unremarked for now, but that he would learn she would not always accommodate him in such a fashion.

"Will you tell them this evening?" asked Ria.

"No. This afternoon. There is every possibility that Herndon and Sir Alex have seen Beckwith's paintings, or own others like them. South and Miss Parr will want to know what you learned before they attend."

"Then you think they'll come regardless?"

"I am certain of it." His green gaze was keen on hers. "When Sir Alex leaves the reception, Northam and Elizabeth will follow in their carriage. South and Miss Parr have agreed to follow Herndon. East and Sophie were quite willing to do their part, but we are all agreed that their part is to enjoy themselves at the reception and to keep Herndon and Cotton from departing too early."

"Why should the time of their departure matter?"

"Because I should not like to be caught out in one of their homes."

"I see." She pressed her lips together as she considered what it was that West had not said. "And my part? What am I to do? It seems that everything has been set in motion because of me, yet I am given nothing to do."

"Recall for a moment that I did not anticipate your arrival. Our plans were made more than a sennight ago. It occurs to me that you will be safe enough with North and Elizabeth, unless you wish to remain at the reception with Eastlyn and Sophie."

Ria did not particularly like either choice, and it showed in the set of her shoulders and lift of her chin. "I should prefer to go with you."

West was not even mildly astonished. "That is not one of your choices."

"Of course it is. It is merely one you don't intend to give me. Do you think I can't do it?"

"Not at all. I think I can't do it. Not if you're with me."

Ria's disappointment was not lessened, but she did understand. "Very well, then I will go with Lord and Lady Northam." To her thinking it would be the lesser of two evils. At least she could embrace the illusion she was *doing* something. "You will have to overcome your reluctance to allow me to participate at your side. We will both be at the meeting of the board of governors. If it is to be the trap you think it is, then I must be as prepared for it as you."

West did not reply immediately. There was no good way to say it to her, he realized. There would be an argument regardless. "You cannot attend the meeting, Ria. I hope you can—"

"I beg your pardon?"

He knew perfectly well she had heard him correctly; it was only that she did not want to believe she had. "You must not be present at the meeting."

"That is absurd."

"I don't doubt that you think it is, but you still do not appreciate the breadth and depth of the bishops and their cruelties. Whatever is afoot here is not the work of a few men. By nature of being a member of the Society, every one of the governors is involved in Miss Petty's disappearance. Sir Alex may have acted alone to lure Miss Petty away from the school, but it is not possible that he acted without the sanction of the rest of them. They do not have secrets from one another. They have secrets from everyone else."

"It is still difficult for me to credit all of them with such cunning and deceit," she said quietly, "but that is only because I have come so late to understanding the base character of these men. I am convinced you are right in every way about them."

"It is not enough. You cannot be convinced and still find it difficult to believe. There will be very few people at tonight's reception who know the Society of Bishops exists outside the corridors and classrooms of Hambrick Hall, yet the reason they will be able to celebrate a British settlement in Singapore at year's end is because Eastlyn challenged five of their number and defeated them."

Ria's brows lifted slightly. Her lips parted on a silent "O."

"The paintings of Miss Parr were done by an artist who was a member of the Society at Hambrick."

"You said nothing of that when we spoke of the paintings."

"Miss Parr had been abducted earlier by the very same person, and Southerton had asked for my silence. It was not for me to say then."

Ria could not completely shutter her hurt. "You thought I would tell someone?"

"It was not a matter of whether I trusted you with a particular piece of information," he said. "It was simply not for me to say. If that does not satisfy you as an explanation, I cannot make any apology for it." He could not even offer a smile to take the sting from his words, but waited patiently for her to understand that given the same circumstances again, he would act in just the same manner.

Ria's chin dropped a notch and her blue-gray eyes softened from accusing to reluctant acceptance. "I don't suppose I can take you to task for being discreet when I have depended on the very same from you." She mocked herself with a faintly derisive smile, then sobered again. "Are the governors also responsible for what happened to Miss Parr?"

West shook his head. It would have been better if he could have answered otherwise. "Miss Parr's abductor acted alone." He added quickly, "Do not take hope from that. The circumstances are most unlike what happened to Jane Petty. I do not know how Beckwith purchased his paintings from the artist. It is quite possible there was an intermediary. It is also unclear if any of the other governors own such paintings. For Miss Parr's sake, it is one of the things I hope to discover this evening. However, even if I should find similar works in the homes of Cotton or Herndon, it is proof only that they share an interest in certain erotic subjects—and I think we know already that is true."

Ria carefully poured herself a second cup of tea as she considered this. "How is the fact that Miss Parr's artist was also a bishop of import?"

"To further illustrate how the bishops are known to one another, even when they are not actively part of the same smaller circles. This artist did not belong to any organized enclave of the Society as an adult, but it is not unreasonable to assume there was knowledge that Jonathan Beckwith was a bishop when arrangements were made for the paintings to be sold to him."

"The bishops only place their trust in other bishops."

"I am not certain they trust at all, but they only confide their secrets to each other. It is perhaps a fine distinction, but I believe it is an important one."

"The Compass Club is different?" asked Ria.

"There *is* trust."

She nodded slowly, still troubled. "You are only four making a stand against a Society of hundreds."

"I know. We have often remarked that it is hardly fair to them."

"More evidence of your impoverished wit."

West grinned, unrepentant. "You are kind to characterize it as merely impoverished. Some people have been moved to point out that the four of us do not have gray matter enough to make a half-wit."

Ria sighed. "There is no insulting you, is there?"

"South might take umbrage," he said cheerfully, "for he is, by all accounts, brilliant. The rest of us are too thick-witted to be so thin-skinned."

There was nothing for it but to laugh, and the release was precisely what she needed to clear most of her anxieties. What she could do, she decided, was extend her trust to him and his friends. Soldier. Sailor. Tinker. Spy. She regarded him thoughtfully, her mien perfectly grave now. "Am I permitted to know what you will do at the governors' meeting?"

"Of course." He reached for his teacup and held it out for Ria to pour him another. "Assuming that none of the governors knows yet that you have arrived in London, they will learn of it soon after Herndon and Sir Alex see you this evening. I am not certain why they did not inform me of your invitation to the meeting, except that they meant to surprise me with your presence there. It intrigues me that they thought such a thing was possible, and I can only imagine that they believed you and I would have no opportunity to communicate prior to the meeting."

"We almost didn't," she said. "Only two of my letters reached you, and none of yours came to me."

"But you are still my ward. They had to have suspected you would visit me upon reaching London."

"I suppose so, but perhaps they learned it was originally my intention not to arrive in London until the day of the meeting."

"You told Beckwith this?"

She shook her head. "Not Mr. Beckwith. My teachers."

"All of them?"

"Yes. We meet regularly to discuss our students and what is required of us as their instructors. There is always something regarding the building. Naturally, I mentioned that I had been invited to London to a meeting of the board."

"What was their reaction?"

"Hardly any. It is not without precedent. I have had occasion to come here for meetings before. I am certain I told them that in light of how busy we all were, I would plan to leave so that I would be gone only the shortest time necessary."

"And when you decided to leave earlier?" he asked. "Was there anyone who tried to influence you to change your plans again?"

"Miss Webster was concerned that she would not be able to manage the discipline of the older girls, but she always frets about that when I am to be away. Mrs. Abergast took my early departure in stride."

"Miss Taylor?"

Ria said nothing for a long moment. She had always liked Jenny Taylor, even admired her work. What she had to tell West was not easy to admit, most especially to herself. "Miss Taylor's influence was of an unconventional nature. She became ill."

"Do you suspect it was a ruse?"

"I had no reason to suspect it then. I do now."

"Why?"

Ria sipped her tea, then replaced the cup in its saucer. "Several reasons, I suppose. It is unlike her to make any complaints of illness, even when the rest of us can see that she is not at all well. When I suggested summoning the physician, she opposed it. That is not unexpected, but she was more persuasive this time, and I did not send for him. I would have agreed to stay longer if Mrs. Abergast had not offered to accept some of Miss Taylor's duties. I had a fleeting thought that Miss Taylor did not appear as pleased as she should have been, but I let it pass unremarked and didn't think of it again until now.

"Since last night I have done considerable thinking about the post. You will not be surprised to learn that Miss Taylor was the person most often delivering and collecting it. She is also the one who suggested Mr. Oliver Lytton as the person to investigate Jane's elopement, and most damning, I think, is that she is considerably more talented than her drawings of the governors would suggest. You know it yourself from her portrait of Jane."

"How long has she been at Miss Weaver's?"

"I'm not certain. I've been there six years, and she was there at least five years before me."

"Why wasn't she made headmistress when the position became available?"

"I don't think she wanted it."

West considered that. "Perhaps it is by mutual agreement that she does not serve in that capacity. If there is a serious problem at the school, it is most likely the headmistress will be the one dismissed. The governors would not want Miss Taylor gone, not if she serves as their eyes."

"A spy, you mean."

West's teacup and saucer rattled as he set both down. "More than that," he said, coming to his feet. Without a word to explain his intention, he left the room, only to appear minutes later, carrying a book under his arm. He held it up for Ria to see the dark-green leather binding and the gilt embellishment on the spine. "I do not think North would forgive me if Elizabeth had found this in the library. I brought it with me today and put it where I thought you and I would be having this conversation. You recognize it?"

"I should be a perfect dolt if I did not."

He was glad to see that despite the sharp edge of her tone, Ria still had the capacity to blush at the sight of it. "I learned some interesting bits about the book when I took it to Sir James Winslow. He is my source for all things related to publishing. In short order he was able to tell me the book was most likely made between 1750 and 1790, based on the style of binding and quality of paper. He knew of two printing-and-engraving houses that were still engaged in the same work. Either might have done the work or have some knowledge of it, and he graciously offered to inquire at both."

Ria slid forward to the edge of the chair as if she meant to rocket to her feet at any moment. "And?"

"And he reported to me a short time ago that this book was printed by a small press no longer operating. They primarily distributed religious pamphlets and sermon collections, if you can credit it, but it seems they were known by some to have also published books of this nature. It was a profitable enterprise until the French Revolution. The owner journeyed to Paris sometime after the fall of the monarchy, and he was arrested and summarily executed for publishing seditious materials." West set the book down and offered a shrug with an unmistakable Gallic flair. "I don't suppose he had an opportunity to show some of his prurient works, else he might have been allowed to live."

Ria's mouth flattened, disapproving of the tenor of his humor. "It is still a man's life, and not to be spoken of with so little regard."

"The man's name was Neville, Ria. George Andrew Neville." West did not flinch as Ria leapt to her feet. He had been expecting just this reaction. "You are familiar with the name, then."

How could she not be? she wondered. It was engraved on a gold plate beneath another of the portraits that she passed regularly in the academy's hall. Ria knew that West required no confirmation of his statement, but she could not remain silent. "His son sits on the board. His father was a founder. One of his grandsons has already left Hambrick. The other is there now. I suppose you will tell me that both boys are bishops."

"Yes. The colonel verified it for me."

Ria's look was one of helpless confusion. "What is the exact nature of this legacy they have wrought?"

"Wealth. Position. Influence. The ability to compel others to do their bidding is central to the Society. Power, Ria—in any form. It was political power that motivated the bishops that Eastlyn confronted. The founding governors of Miss Weaver's Academy had a slightly different bent." West opened the book and showed Ria an illustration of the young man with his back pressed to the Ionic column and the woman on her knees in front of him. He pointed to the man's face, drawing her eyes there. "Do you know who this is, Ria?"

She studied the features, then shook her head.

"I would not have seen the resemblance myself," he told her, closing the book. "It is Jonathan Beckwith's uncle. Anthony Beckwith. This drawing was done years before his portrait, years before he became a governor. Because of the background that is common to some of the portraits, it suggests that certain privileges are afforded those who will inherit a position on the board."

Ria shivered. "How can you be certain it is Sir Anthony?"

"Someone James Winslow spoke to—an old man now—remembered him."

"Surely not. Not from so long ago."

"Apparently Beckwith was a frequent visitor to Neville's printing shop when the engravings were being done. This gentlemen was an apprentice in that same shop all those years ago. You will admit that the illustrations are not easily dismissed from one's mind."

"I will not admit it," Ria said.

West tempered his smile. "You will like this last information even less. The woman in the other illustration—"

Ria interrupted. "You cannot possibly have a name to put to her face."

"No. Unfortunately, no. But this same gentleman remembered something that Neville and Beckwith said while they were examining the engravings. They said Sheridan did not know the half of it when he wrote *The School for Scandal,* that Miss Weaver would have opened his eyes to what was of import in education." West held up his hand, staying Ria's questions. "I also wondered why he would recall such an exchange of words. He was only a printer's apprentice then. A mere boy. But perhaps his age explains his keen interest, and the reason Neville and Beckwith spoke freely, though rather cryptically, in his presence.

"He had seen a performance of *The School for Scandal* only a few days earlier, so he understood the reference to the play. He thought Miss Weaver must be the name of the woman in the illustration. He linked the two immediately in his mind and has never forgotten. I think we can trust his memory on this, Ria, even though he did not comprehend the import of what he heard."

West approached her and took her hands in his. "You and I both know Neville and Beckwith were referring to Miss Weaver's Academy."

Ria nodded jerkily.

"Shall I say the rest for you?" he asked gently. "Or would you rather not hear it aloud."

"Say it," she said. "Say it all."

"It is most likely that both the young women in the illustrations were students at the school, chosen for their fine looks and manners to be of service in precisely the way you saw them on the page. It is equally likely that Miss Jenny Taylor is the Society's whoremistress."

Chapter Fourteen

The reception was a squeeze. Ria inched her way through the gathering clogging the ballroom's entrance until she found an unoccupied niche beside a potted fern every bit as tall as she was. The delicate, feathery fronds swayed, sometimes brushing her cheek as currents of air were stirred by the sweeping circles of the dancers. Ria snapped open her sandalwood fan and used it to politely hide her unseemly yawn.

Lack of sleep was taking its toll, she realized, no matter that she was a single nerve stretched taut as a bowstring. She'd had little enough rest on her journey to London, then only a few hours since arriving. Elizabeth had insisted she nap before the reception, but after West's revelations, she found it impossible to do so. Lying on the bed in her room, she had merely stared at the overhead canopy and wondered why she did not feel something more than numb.

And Miss Jenny Taylor is the Society's whoremistress. The words were no faint echo in her head. She could make them out more clearly than anything that was being said around her. While the voices in the ballroom hummed indistinctly, she still heard West's exact intonation in her head.

She wished she might have fainted or even been sick. West had hovered momentarily as if he expected either of these reactions might occur, but the initial shock passed so quickly that Ria came to understand it was not precisely shock that she'd experienced at all, just benumbing resignation. That she did not feel his words as a physical blow made her realize how long she had been harboring similar suspicions. Not that she could have spoken them aloud, she understood now. Some thoughts were so appalling that they resisted even the most private of examinations.

Emily Barret. Amanda Kent. Mary Murdoch. Sylvia Jenner.

Ria turned over the names in her mind as if she were taking attendance. They had all been students at the school during her six-year tenure, and all of them had departed before their graduation. Unlike Jane Petty, none of them left unexpectedly, and no one worried what would become of them. The future of these young women had seemed remarkably brighter when they exited Miss Weaver's than when they entered it.

"You are as colorless as curds and whey," West said.

Startled from her unpleasant reverie by what was certainly an accurate observation, Ria's nerveless fingers lost their grip on the fan. It fell, still open, and dangled awkwardly from her wrist by its silk cord. She fumbled with it for a moment before managing to snap it closed and secure it in her palm.

Seeing that her composure was badly strained, West offered his elbow. "Come, the portico is empty. Not many guests are willing to brace the cooler temperatures to enjoy the fresh air."

Ria placed her arm on his and allowed herself to be drawn outside. While she had only been able to move through the crowd in fits and starts before, on the Duke of Westphal's arm, guests made way for them. At the edge of the wide portico, Ria disengaged herself from West's arm and braced herself on the marble balustrade. The night was clear and crisp and stars glittered in the deep indigo sky with as much luster as the diamonds in the ballroom.

"Shall I send you back to Oxford Street?" asked West. "I

can have my driver take you. You do not have to leave with North and Elizabeth." Her hesitation was telling, he thought, but she finally shook her head, and West doubted he could change her mind. "I cannot stop you from blaming yourself, Ria, only say that you are wrong for doing so. You couldn't have known about the others."

It did not strike Ria as at all odd that West should have divined the tenor of her thoughts. "But I did know," she said softly. "Or at least it seems that I did. I should have told you about them at the outset. I should not have waited until you confronted me with the whole of it."

West turned and sat on the edge of the railing. He laid one hand over Ria's. "What should you have told me? That four students left Miss Weaver's because families came forward to take them in? It must have seemed like reason to celebrate, rather than the opposite. It is only hindsight that allows you to see similarities to Miss Petty's situation."

Ria knew he was right, yet it was no easy thing to absolve herself. "All of them had benefactors on the board of governors. They came to the school at an early age, every one of them from workhouses. They were easily among the prettiest girls. Mary and Emily showed talent on the pianoforte. Amanda Kent was lively and cheerful, very popular with the other girls. Sylvia was the best student, quieter than the others, scrupulously polite and always charitable." Ria glanced sideways at West. "Like Jane, Miss Taylor took a special interest in them. I thought it was because they had no one." Her smile faltered, at once rueful and self-mocking. "I suppose I was not wrong. Not really. What do you imagine has become of them?"

West had no answer to that. In fact, he tried not to imagine. By Ria's account, it had been a little more than a year since Sylvia left the school. Her departure occurred just before Ria had been assigned the position of headmistress. The other three had gone earlier. Months, sometimes years, separated the exits. Emily was fifteen when she went with the childless couple from Nottingham. Amanda and Sylvia had each just passed their sixteenth year when they left the school for homes in London. At fourteen, Mary had been the youngest to go.

"You cannot be certain they were *not* taken into homes and families that welcomed them," West said.

"I'm certain," Ria said dully. "So are you. I would rather you did not try to raise my spirits with false hope."

West conceded that she was right. It seemed to West that it was Ria's turn as headmistress that had made the governors reluctant to remove girls from the academy in the usual manner. There would have been some trepidation among them about appointing her to the position, but he suspected those misgivings were quieted by her connection to the duke. Still, they must have worried that she would be more thorough than her predecessor in looking after the girls once they were gone from the school. She was, perhaps, not so likely to be lulled into complacency by an occasional letter penned by one of them. Ria Ashby would take it upon herself to visit the young women who were expressly in her care and make certain they were doing well and fulfilling their promise.

When Jane Petty had sufficiently matured to catch the eye of Sir Alex Cotton, he conceived a different approach. This time there would be no family. Jane's sudden departure would point to an impulsive elopement and result in nothing more than a nine days' wonder. What Sir Alex couldn't have known was that Jane would keep her gentleman admirer a secret from everyone but Amy Nash, and that Amy Nash would take so long to come forward with that information. In the meantime, it simply seemed that Jane had disappeared, raising more alarms than it quieted. Hiring Mr. Lytton to find Jane provided temporary respite, but Sir Alex and the governors were confounded again by the death of the duke. They must have realized the enormity of their mistake in naming Ria headmistress when she went straightaway to London to ask the new Duke of Westphal to involve himself in the school's affairs.

"I do not like leaving you here," said West. "I am not certain you are at all well. You ate very little at the supper."

Ria straightened. They were beyond the circle of candlelight coming from the ballroom, but she could make out his features sufficiently to mark his concern. "You mustn't worry about me. I have promised a set to Eastlyn when Sophie sits with Colonel Blackwood, and I am certain North and South will be obliged to take a turn with me when their wives are similarly occupied. The colonel has promised to entertain me as well, and I have so many questions for him that he is sure to regret the offer."

West did not miss the note of forced well-being in her voice, and he smiled because she meant him to. He did not point out that he had found her hiding in the shadow of a potted fern. "I suppose if you mean to interrogate Blackwood, I cannot be gone overlong, else I will have no secrets left."

Ria nodded, searching his face. "You will be careful, won't you?"

"Yes." He bent his head and kissed her lightly on the mouth. Her lips were dry and cool and passionless. "I will make it right, Ria," he whispered, taking her into his arms. "I promise you I will make it right."

She made no reply, but held him tightly until he gently drew back. Without a word passing between them, they returned to the ballroom, and he slipped away in the crush of guests.

Ria did not want for companions. The marquess approached her first and reminded her of their promised set. Ria accompanied him onto the dance floor and took her place in line. Eastlyn proved himself to be an easy partner, engaging her in just enough conversation to keep her from dwelling on West's activities.

"He knows what he is about," East assured her.

Ria noticed that the streak of fire in his chestnut-colored hair flashed as they passed under the crystal chandelier. "Would he admit it if he did not?"

"He would." His half-smile appeared. "But I wouldn't."

She frowned slightly, uncertain of his meaning. "Are you saying that—" She fell silent, stumbling when she caught sight of Sir Alex Cotton standing at the edge of the crowd. He appeared to be attentive to the animated conversation of a woman who was batting him playfully on the forearm with her fan.

"Chin up, Miss Ashby," East said, helping Ria recover gracefully. "Eyes on me. My wife says I am a handsome enough fellow and that I improve upon acquaintance, but you will easily convince me otherwise if I cannot hold your attention for the length of a single reel."

The pink in Ria's cheeks might have been from the heat of the room or the exertions of the dance, but they both knew it was not. "You will not let me faint, will you? I have only ever done so once, but I did not manage the thing with any grace."

"I will hold you upright if I must stand you upon my toes." He saw that his solemnly made promise raised her faint smile. "Is it Cotton that you spied?" he asked. "Or Herndon?"

"Sir Alex. Who is he with?"

"She is Lady Powell. Several years a widow and an inveterate flirt. She has independent means and no designs on marriage. It makes her a much desired companion."

Ria wondered at Sir Alex's interest. Was it feigned? Lady Powell was certainly attractive enough to capture a gentleman's notice, but Ria knew something about this gentleman's tastes that made her think the lady might be too long in the tooth for him. Then again, perhaps the girls at the school were merely a diversion, an entertainment enjoyed once, then easily dismissed. It might be that he was genuinely intrigued by the trifling attentions of a woman who was his social equal.

Eastlyn drew Ria's attention back to him. "This summer past I thought she would set her cap for Southerton, but he managed to elude her."

The viscount stood taller than many of the men at the periphery of the dance floor. Still, Ria heard his laughter before she caught sight of his shock of thick black hair. His head was slightly thrown back, his long neck exposed, and his enjoyment of the moment was evident. Although she could not see Miss Parr, nor either of South's parents, she suspected they were nearby and being vastly entertained by him.

"Do not think he is distracted from his task," East told her. "I am certain he knows the precise location of his quarry."

"I didn't think it for a moment. He is watching Herndon, then?"

East nodded. "And North is responsible for Cotton, at least as long as I am with you."

Ria thought the marquess had pulled the short straw. She said nothing, because he was sure to gallantly deny it. Instead, she concentrated on matching his steps and allowed the music to fill the silence between them.

North invited her for a turn on the floor next, then South appeared to do the same. Made easy by their confidence and diverted by their good humor, Ria occasionally was able to forget that she felt so abominably guilty and found pleasure in their company.

It was no different once she was seated beside the guest of honor. Between interruptions by those in attendance who had not yet offered their congratulations, Colonel Blackwood spoke knowledgeably of art, literature, music, and, finally, of West. Ria was attentive to every part of their conversation, but especially to the last. It was not necessary to interrogate the colonel. He spoke freely, and with evident affection, of West as a younger man. She was quite certain there was a lot that of necessity was left unsaid, but Blackwood filled in a great many of the gaps that West had not.

The colonel finished off his drink and rolled the empty tumbler between his palms. "I am boring you," he said. "Is that it? I have regaled you with one too many of his harrowing exploits, and they no longer have the power to astonish."

Ria quickly lowered her fan. "What? No! That could never be the case."

"My dear," the colonel said gently. "Although you are yawning with considerable delicacy behind your fan, you are yawning nonetheless, and I do not think I am mistaken that your occasional darting glances are in aid of finding West or discovering the time. I can say with complete assurance that West has not returned, else he would put himself immediately at your side. As to the other . . ." Blackwood consulted the timepiece inside his frock coat. "I make it to be half past the ten o'clock hour."

"So late." Ria had nerves enough left to modulate her distress but not hide it entirely. "Why hasn't he returned?"

"Because he is not finished," the colonel said simply. "You think I am making light of his absence, but I am not. Trust me to know my men, Miss Ashby. West is nothing if not thorough."

"You are not afraid for him?"

Blackwood stopped rolling the tumbler and regarded Ria gravely. She seemed young to him of a sudden, or perhaps it was only that he felt so old. "I will not insult you by saying that I've never been afraid for him, but it has rarely been about the things you think." He smiled softly and let her make of that what she would. Holding out his glass, he asked, "Dare I impose upon you to—"

Ria stood immediately and took the tumbler from his hand. "I should have offered before," she said. "I will only be a moment." She was grateful for the opportunity to do something, even something so small as refilling the colonel's glass. Since arriving at the reception, she had been watched over and coddled. She was all but suffocated by the cotton wool of good intentions.

Clutching Blackwood's empty glass, Ria seized this chance to escape. Refreshments were served in the adjoining room, and Ria set off determinedly in that direction. It was not distance that posed the problem but the veritable clot of people at the entrance. Sidling and occasionally ducking, begging the pardon of two matrons and one elderly gentleman for trodding on their toes, pausing occasionally for a polite exchange of inconsequential pleasantries, and finally wielding her closed fan like a poker, Ria was able to move through the crush with no injury to herself and only minor inconvenience to others.

As was so often the way of these things, once she broke through the tight pack of guests in the doorway, the people milling about the refreshments room numbered exactly eleven. A footman, who had evidently been deterred by the crowd, stepped forward quickly and relieved Ria of her glass. She followed him to the large crystal punch bowl, but when he lifted the ladle, she stopped him.

"I don't think it is ratafia that was in there," she said. As she was negotiating the entrance, she'd had the colonel's tumbler pressed close to her chest. It was not the scent of fruit juice and brandy, nor the sweet flavoring of almonds that she detected rising from the glass. Leaning forward in the manner of sharing a confidence, Ria told the footman, "Whiskey, I think. The best that you have. It is for Colonel Blackwood."

"Of course." The footman turned to the sideboard behind him and in short order produced the tumbler with two generous fingers of whiskey. He handed it to her and waited in expectation of a request for herself.

"I am not certain I can manage two glasses," Ria said, glancing back the way she came.

"There is another route." The footman let his eyes slide sideways, pointing Ria to his left.

She followed his gesture and saw that the walnut wainscoting was not a single, solid piece and that the mural on the wall above it cleverly concealed most of the outline of the door. The small brass ring set into the wall was what had drawn her eye and revealed the rest. Smiling gratefully, Ria said, "If you can produce a glass of sherry, I shall gladly accept it."

"Certainly." He turned again, poured, and gave her the delicately stemmed glass. "It will take you to the gallery," he said. "From there you will find the hall or pass into the library. Will you not allow me to take your drinks and escort you?"

"No. That is unnecessary. I'm certain I am not the first to leave by that exit this evening, and no one has been lost yet."

"No, indeed."

Holding up both hands, Ria reminded the footman of the glass in each. He saw her dilemma and went straightaway to the door panel and opened it just enough for her to slip through. Ria paused on the other side as the panel clicked into place behind her.

The gallery was not deserted. There were always those in attendance at any gathering of the *ton* who preferred the company of their intimates to the company of the crowd. If circumstances had not compelled West to be elsewhere and his friends to be in the ballroom, Ria suspected this is where she would have found the Compass Club. She could easily imagine them taking up position in one corner of the long room—perhaps beneath the large portrait of their host's ancestor on horseback—and making wagers as to the identity of the next person to walk through the wall. Moreover, they would wager on whether or not a refreshment would be carried and what it might be.

Smiling faintly at her own musings, Ria started across the gallery to the door that would lead her into the hall. She was aware of heads turning as she passed, though whether there was some objection to her intrusion, she couldn't fathom. Caught up in each other, the couple on the settee paid her scant attention. The trio of matrons deliberately paused in their conversation. One gentleman turned from his study of a painting to apply the same scrutiny to her, another standing close by merely took a pinch of snuff. At the table where cards were being played, the game continued without interruption, though one gentleman found it was possible to raise his quizzing glass and make his trick simultaneously.

Ria would have liked to linger, but the softly lilting sounds of the stringed orchestra beckoned her back to the ballroom. She was also aware that her absence would not go unnoticed for long. The colonel would certainly be in want of his drink, even if he did not desire her company.

One of the ubiquitous footmen hastily stepped forward from his sentinel position at the door and opened it as Ria approached. Ria declined his offer to assist her with the drinks as she passed into the hallway. The music was louder here, as was the conversational drone of the guests. She glanced down the hall to the group of people milling at the entrance to the ballroom, and she knew she could not bear to go back there just yet. The door behind her was already closed and did not offer an easy retreat.

She remembered the footman in the refreshments room had mentioned a library. It seemed like an offer of sanctuary now. Ria could not imagine that in a home as large as this one that there was but one way to arrive at the room. Pivoting soundlessly on her slippered heels, Ria set off—and walked directly into the path of Lady Powell.

In spite of her astonishment and the awkwardness of the encounter, Ria managed to avoid spilling the sherry. The generous pour of whiskey that she had been holding protectively at the level of her bosom was another matter. It sloshed over the rim of the tumbler and splashed the bodice and skirt of her gown.

Throwing up both hands as if to ward off another determined advance, Lady Powell jumped backward. At the same time, she issued a soft *"Ooh"* from her perfectly shaped bow mouth. When she saw how much of the drink was staining the front of Ria's gown, she gathered courage enough to examine the condition of her own attire. Except for a few droplets of whiskey collecting in her cleavage, she was perfectly dry. The satin bands that crisscrossed her bosom and held her ice-blue tunic in place were unmarked, as was every fold of her draped silk gown.

Assured that she was all of a piece, Lady Powell turned her attention to the real casualty in this unfortunate collision. "Oh, my poor dear. You have taken the brunt of it, I'm afraid, though it was very good of you to do so."

"I had no notion that you were just behind me," Ria said.

"And I had no notion that you meant to spin like a dervish and reverse your course." She gazed significantly at the glasses Ria still held. "Nor any idea that you were armed. Here, allow me to take this one." Without waiting for an invitation, she relieved Ria of the nearly empty tumbler. "Come, we will find somewhere for you to make repairs and I will fetch a servant. They are everywhere, are they not, except when we have need of them." Looping her arm in Ria's just as if they were fast friends preparing to engage in a *tête à tête,* she led Ria down the hall away from the ballroom. "I am Lady Powell," she said. "My late husband was the Honorable Edmund Powell."

"I am Maria Ashby."

"Yes, I know. My husband knew the Duke of Westphal quite well. Similar political interests, I think, and business schemes. All of it beyond my ken, I assure you. Dull stuff. I rarely had occasion to cross paths with Westphal. I know his son considerably better."

Ria concentrated on not spilling the sherry, though seizing the carrot Lady Powell dangled in front of her was tempting. She suspected her ladyship was acquainted with Tenley every bit as well as West, but had little doubt it was West to whom she was referring.

"Aaah, here we are." Lady Powell stopped in front of a polished, paneled door and set her palm around the brass handle. "I believe this is the music salon." She opened the door a crack. "Yes, there is the pianoforte and the harp. There can be nothing wrong with you using the room until I am advised of more suitable accommodations. Go on. It will only be a minute before I return. No longer." She threw open the door wider so Ria could enter. "A sip or two of the sherry would not be amiss," she advised. "You are unaccountably pale."

The door closed behind her before Ria could react. Lady

Powell was wrong. There was most certainly an explanation for the ashen state of her complexion: she was not alone in the salon. Sitting on the bench at the pianoforte, facing her, was Mr. Jonathan Beckwith.

Reaching behind her, Ria groped for the handle. Her fingers curled around it, and she pulled. The door rattled but did not open.

"Do not blame Lady Powell," Beckwith said. "She thinks her effort is in aid of supporting a lovers' reconciliation." He stood, smiling narrowly at Ria's patent expression of disbelief. "What? Never say you would not choose me over Westphal."

"I would not choose you over a toad."

He sighed, not at all offended. "My, that is lowering and uncommonly ill-mannered of you. As it happens, Lady Powell was not asked to credit it, either. She has a charmingly diabolical turn of mind, but there are limits to what she can be made to believe. She thinks only that I am acting on Westphal's behalf and that my function is to keep you here until the duke arrives."

"Why does she think Westphal and I are lovers?"

"I suppose because Sir Alex told her you were. Herndon also dropped that interesting bit of salacious gossip. You must acquit me of stirring the pot, as I did not mingle with the guests. You will perhaps find it shocking that I was not invited to this affair." He motioned to Ria to join him at the piano. "Come, we must go now."

Ria didn't move. What she did was open her mouth to scream. The loud, discordant crashing of the keys on the pianoforte cut her off and left Ria feeling outmaneuvered. Only someone passing in the hall would have noted the noise and probably not made much of it. She slowly closed her mouth until her lips were just slightly parted, then she raised the glass of sherry and sipped. "I will not be going anywhere with you, Mr. Beckwith, so you are welcome to play another tune."

A dark brow arched dramatically. The effect was one of icy amusement, and Beckwith saw that he had hit his mark with it. Ria's hand was not quite as steady on the stem of the sherry glass as it had been the moment before. "Insolent baggage." He smiled suddenly. "It is not entirely without appeal, though it can become wearing."

Ria tried the door again, but the handle remained jammed. On the far side of the piano were a pair of French doors. She supposed that Beckwith meant to escort her out through one of them and into the garden. There was a possibility that she could reach the portico and slip back inside, or at least call attention to herself. It was a certainty that someone would be looking for her. She had but to delay their departure.

Beckwith pointed to a spot on the floor directly in front of him. "You will come here." He paused a beat, then added in a tone that was like the snap of a whip, "Now."

Ria's stomach turned over. The effects of eating too little at supper and having had so few hours of sleep combined to make her feel unsettled and light-headed. At least it was what she told herself. She would not let herself believe it was Beckwith's sharp command. Her knees wobbled, and she took a second swallow of sherry. It struck her suddenly that fainting might just be the delaying tactic she required. Eyes darting around, she quickly assessed what pieces of furniture she must avoid.

"Don't do it," Beckwith said, divining her thoughts. "Are you not eager to see Miss Petty?"

Without conscious thought, Ria took a step forward.

"Very good." Beckwith encouraged her action with a condescending smile. "Another, please. Then another. Truly, Miss Ashby, I cannot be held responsible for what befalls Jane if we are not gone from here soon. Her welfare depends greatly on your cooperation. Do you understand?"

Ria did. She set her glass down and crossed the room, stopping at the precise spot that Beckwith had indicated earlier. "You will take me to see Jane?"

"That is my intention exactly." He did not press when she would not accept his frock coat to thwart the cold, nor when she refused to take his arm. "This way, Miss Ashby. There is a hack waiting for us." He paused just before he opened the doors to leave the salon. "You will not want to call attention to your departure. There is so much more at stake here than the well-being of one of your students. You will want to consider the well-being of all of them."

The threat was so large and so bold that Ria did not want to believe it had any teeth. Too late, she realized that her features were imperfectly schooled and that some measure of her doubt was displayed.

"Would you care to wager on it?" Beckwith asked calmly. "I have already explained the stakes."

Ria shook her head quickly. It was not possible to stave off the shiver that was climbing her spine. Instead of crossing her arms in front of her, she kept them quietly at her sides and did not try to resist the shudder.

"Good." Beckwith's expression did not change, but his tone was approving. "We should make haste." He opened the door and ushered Ria outside.

It seemed to her that the evening air was infinitely colder than it had been earlier. She glanced at the portico and saw that not one of the guests had ventured outside. Beckwith hurried through the small enclosed garden, and Ria followed. He pushed aside the servants' gate, waited for Ria to precede him, then caught up and took the lead once more. The hack that Beckwith had hired was near the end of a long line of carriages waiting for the conclusion of the reception. The driver recognized Beckwith and hopped down from his perch to assist in the boarding.

Ria seated herself in the corner. When the driver realized she had no coat, he offered her his own rug. She did not want to take it, but her teeth would not stop chattering. Refusal was absurdly inappropriate. She saw, but could not hear, Beckwith give the driver an address before he climbed inside. Ria thought he would choose the bench opposite her, so when he sat beside her she almost recoiled.

Striving for a measure of dignity, Ria told him, "I have no plans to leap from the cab. There is no need to block the door."

"Is that what you think? I meant only to flatter you with my attentions." He chuckled when Ria pressed herself more deeply into the corner. "I am certain you do not mean to be insulting, Miss Ashby, but it is difficult to think of your actions in any other way."

"You must not strain yourself, Mr. Beckwith. I mean to be insulting."

"You smell like a whore come up from the docks. What did you spill on yourself?"

Ria had steeled herself not to flinch, and this time she was successful. "Whiskey. The drink was for Colonel Blackwood."

"So you were the cripple's serving wench."

She did not respond. There was an edge of coarseness in the way Beckwith spoke the words. The odor of whiskey was so strong that she could not tell if he had been drinking.

"A tavern maid," Beckwith said. "Would you enjoy that, do you suppose? Serving drinks to the rough trade. Taking orders from the regiment."

"Where are we going?" Ria struggled not to sound desperate. She was coming to understand that Beckwith liked the idea that she could be made to fear him. Neither did challenging him have the desired effect. He did not respond as West did. Beckwith's amusement was somehow detached, not engaged. There was no applauding her effort, no appreciation. When Beckwith regarded her, there was pity in his dark glance, but even it was contemptuous. It was the kind of pathos reserved for one who didn't comprehend that struggling was hopeless. The fly in a spider's web. The moth in warm candle wax. The bee in a schoolboy's inverted glass jar.

That was how Beckwith saw her, Ria thought: deserving of his study, his fascination, and finally his cold compassion because there was no more hope for her than the fly, the moth, or the bee.

Beckwith was silent so long that Ria believed he did not mean to answer her. When he finally spoke, his response was a riddle.

"We are going to a place that will be at once familiar and alien. You have seen it many times, yet do not know it."

Even in the deep shadows of the carriage, Ria observed that he seemed inordinately pleased with his answer. She did not reveal her impatience and managed to keep her voice carefully neutral. "Jane will be there?"

"Yes. Oh, yes. You must not believe that I will lie to you, Miss Ashby. Everything that will happen depends upon you knowing that I speak only the truth. If I say I will do it, I will do it."

Ria held herself very still as Beckwith grasped her chin between his thumb and forefinger. He had put on his gloves, and the leather was cold and faintly rough against her skin. There was no hint of gentleness in his grip.

"If I say it will be done, it will be done. Do you understand what I am telling you?"

"Yes."

"I wonder." He released her chin. "Show me your hands, Miss Ashby."

Bewildered, Ria turned back the rug. Her elbow-length gloves shone pale as the hack passed a street lantern. She raised her hands in front of her, despising the gesture for its implication of surrender. Now she knew what Beckwith would do before he did it and made no attempt to shake him off when his fingers circled her wrists.

"I will have your mouth now." Lowering his head, he placed his mouth hard on hers and ground his teeth against her closed lips.

Ria tasted blood, though whether it was hers or his was not possible to know. Its presence did not ease the pressure that Beckwith applied. Ria's stomach clenched, then roiled. She wondered what satisfaction Beckwith would find from the taste of the bile rising in her throat. Her last thought before she was sick was that she should have eaten more at supper.

* * *

Upon returning to the reception, West was not surprised to find that the colonel was still holding court. He approached the circle around Blackwood but stopped short of becoming part of it. He listened with half an ear to what the colonel was saying to the appreciative audience, while allowing his eyes to wander about the ballroom. On two occasions he thought he glimpsed Ria on the floor, but each time the women were turned in his direction, his mistake was immediately apparent. It seemed to him that Elizabeth could have approved a color other than the mint-green that Ria was wearing. To his way of thinking, there was far too much of it present this evening. He spotted that cool hue sweeping by once more, but this time on a woman almost half again as wide as Ria. The woman noticed his attention as she passed in front of him and gave him a coquettish smile over the shoulder of her unsuspecting partner.

West winked boldly at her and was gratified to hear her laugh delightedly. Eastlyn's mother did not even pretend to be scandalized. He watched her lightly tap her husband on the cheek to keep him from glancing around to find the cause of her amusement. As Sir James and Lady Winslow moved on in perfect time to the waltz, West realized he had yet to see East or Sophie on the floor.

His eyes wandered over the guests again, this time searching for East's thick shock of chestnut hair. When he didn't find him, he looked for North. That worthy's bright helmet was the color of sunshine and easily spotted in a crowd—but not this time. Frowning now, West's sharp green glance sought out Southerton and India Parr.

Gone as well. Even the niche beside the potted fern was unoccupied. West stepped back into the entrance hall and eyed the cupboard under the stairs. It had been the subject of some amusement earlier when East's parents had been seen slipping inside. West knew they were no longer using it, but it begged the question of whom might be. He opened it.

"I beg your pardon," he said, mentally cursing his lamentably poor timing. The gentleman did not reveal himself from under the spread of the lady's gown, so West could not be certain of his identity, but Grace Powell's exquisite features were perfectly visible—as were her naked breasts, a good expanse of silken calf and thigh, and one polished gold-and-ivory earbob.

Given the circumstances, West thought her ladyship regarded him with considerable aplomb. Although she blushed prettily enough, she made no attempt to cover herself and, for a moment, looked as if she might invite him to join her, or at least watch.

West pointed to the man kneeling on the floor in front of her, his head buried between her thighs. "Not Sir Alex Cotton, is it?" he whispered.

Lady Powell gave a small, negative shake and waved him off.

Uncertain if he could believe her, West gave the gentleman a second glance, and this time noted that he was wearing the livery of their host's servants. *A footman?* Lady Powell was perhaps fortunate that he was the one to stumble upon them, for she would know she could depend upon his discretion.

"You will want to secure the door," West said by way of taking his leave. He ducked out of the cupboard, closed it, then leaned his shoulder casually against it. Several guests milling at the entrance to the ballroom had taken note of his peculiar behavior. He smiled wanly at them and offered no explanation. When he heard the door being drawn tightly into place, he straightened and left his post. If Lady Powell kept as firm a grip on the door as she had on the hapless footman's head, she would experience no more interruptions.

West returned to the ballroom and discovered the gathering around the colonel had thinned but not moved on entirely. Two directors from the East India Company were present in the group, along with their wives and several of the Prince Regent's representatives. Prinny himself had come and gone, but had permitted many in his entourage to remain behind to continue expressing the Crown's admiration for the colonel's success. Had Prinny been standing at the colonel's side, West would have had to make a more circumspect approach. Since the regent was absent, West forged ahead with all the subtlety of a fishmonger plying his wares.

"The colonel has been expressly forbidden to exhaust himself," West said. "And I am the unfortunate fellow who must enforce his physician's edict. You will excuse us, won't you?" Without giving Blackwood opportunity to mount an argument or permitting his well-wishers to have another word, West grasped the back of the wheeled chair and pushed it resolutely into the hall.

"You have some destination in mind, I collect," the colonel said dryly. "If not, there is a library one can find by this route. The third door, I believe, then through the gallery."

The library was not deserted, as West had hoped. Several guests were idly chatting near the fireplace, another had climbed on a footstool and was examining titles from the room's uppermost shelves. A young man and his pretty companion shared the settee, their fingertips touching. They broke this light contact a shade guiltily when West wheeled the colonel in.

West expected that he would be the one to order them out, but it was Blackwood who explained that he required a few moments of privacy. They were immediately amenable to vacating the room.

"I had no idea what you would tell them," the colonel said when he was alone with West. "But I suspect you would have them believe I am hammering on death's door." He paused, waiting for West to come around to the other side of his chair. The tumbler of whiskey in his hand prevented him from smooth navigation. "You have seen the others have all gone, then. That accounts for your precipitous actions. It is not well done of you, West. I depend upon your caution and good sense not to call attention to yourself in the manner you just did."

In other circumstances, West would have acknowledged the colonel's dressing-down with a respectful nod, whether or not he thought the rebuke was deserved. It was a sign of the considerable agitation he was still suppressing that he did not do so now. "None of them was supposed to leave until I returned. That was the plan we agreed upon."

"And like a decent frock coat, it required some alteration," Blackwood said calmly. "East was unable to delay the departure of either of the gentlemen. Lest you think he made a poor attempt, I will tell you that Lady Sophia also tried to occupy their interest. It was clear to us that they were most determined to leave. Since you had not yet arrived, precautions had to be taken. Eastlyn and Lady Sophia left at the same time to divert suspicion. North took up Sir Alex's trail, and South followed Herndon."

West felt the pressure in his chest ease slightly. It was a small enough change in their plans. "What do you make of Herndon and Cotton leaving before the guest of honor? They spoke to you this evening, didn't they?"

"Paid their respects. Thanked me." He shrugged. "The Singapore settlement will add substantially to their coffers. They were, naturally, grateful."

"No mention of the bishops?"

"None."

West knew it was unlikely that they would do so. It presented Herndon and Cotton with a conundrum. The settlement was achieved because five of their fellow bishops were bested, yet they were made even more wealthy by that defeat. "They do not suspect you know they are members of the Society?"

The colonel shook his head. "There is no reason that they should." He sipped his drink and enjoyed the liquid heat rolling down his throat. "I think it's probable they noted your absence from the reception."

West nodded. His thinking had been turning in that same direction. "It would explain their desire to leave." He permitted himself a slight, mocking grin. "I don't think they trust me."

"I imagine you're right. Tell me, what did your foray yield? You learned something that will be useful, I hope."

"Only proof that they share Beckwith's interest in the erotic arts. Nothing that hints at Miss Petty's whereabouts. Herndon's collection is more varied than the others, but he has been assembling his works over a long period of time. If there is a theme, it is not sexual, or rather it is not only sexual. These men desire to subjugate women. They have made it a ritual, I think, a sadistic rite of passage that they play out again and again as the whim strikes them."

"With Miss Weaver's Academy as their secret garden," the colonel said. He did indeed feel far older than his years. "Forgive me. I should not admit it, perhaps, but I would rather you and I were plotting Napoleon's demise again. There was honor there, at least. These bishops have none. Taking little girls from the workhouses, seeing that they're nurtured, educated, then removing them for their own pleasures . . ." Blackwood knocked back what remained of his drink. "I take it you will not want to settle this in a public manner."

"No. Too many innocents would be hurt. Any public accounting will have grave consequences for the young women."

"You cannot call all the governors out."

"No, although it is tempting." West raked his hair with his fingertips. "I must find Jane Petty first," he reminded Blackwood. "Then I can demand their resignations. It is an imperfect solution, I know, and not nearly as satisfying as relieving them of their ballocks, but it is what is left to me if Ria and the school are not to be touched by scandal."

"You will wait to hear from Northam and South?" the colonel asked.

West nodded faintly. "I am not as hopeful that either Herndon or Cotton will lead them to Jane. If they left because they were aware I was gone, then it is likely they merely returned to their homes."

"You left everything in order?"

"I did." They would never know with certainty that he was there—until he told them.

"The meeting in two days' time . . ." The colonel paused, adjusting his spectacles. "They mean to spring a trap, you know."

"I know."

"I don't like it."

West grinned. "I am gratified to hear it."

"Daniel into the lion's den," the colonel muttered. He regarded West with a keen eye. "And do not flatter yourself that the lion will not make a meal of you. God is not necessarily on your side."

"Then it is a good thing that you are."

Blackwood grunted softly. "Push me back to the ballroom. I can assure you that my absence has been duly noted, and there are upwards of half a dozen men planning what they will say over my grave."

West chuckled. "Perhaps I *did* exaggerate the state of your health."

Setting his empty tumbler between his knees, the colonel began to turn his chair for West to take it up. "You will have to collect Miss Ashby before you leave," he said, "unless you want me to deliver her to Oxford Street."

"Pardon?" West grasped the colonel's chair and pulled it sharply around. "What do you mean, that I should collect Miss Ashby? Isn't she with North and Elizabeth?"

"Steady, West. She is all of a piece, or at least she is making herself so." Blackwood saw he was making things worse with his explanation, not improving them. West's jaw was rigid with the control he was exerting; a muscle ticked in his cheek. "She went for refreshment." He held up his tumbler. "You know yourself that it was a squeeze to get there. She bumped into Lady Powell in the hall and spilled my whiskey on her dress. Lady Powell says it was a generous pour and that Miss Ashby retired to the salon to repair the damage as best she could. She is waiting for you there. Under the circumstances, I did not think she would want to accompany North and Elizabeth, but would rather return directly to your residence."

"You have this from Lady Powell?"

"Yes. When she delivered my drink."

"Where is the salon?"

"I couldn't say."

West kept his frustration in check, but only just. He pushed the colonel back to the ballroom, made certain he was comfortable, then found a footman to show him the salon. Not wanting to create a stir, West knocked softly, then called Ria's name. When there was no response, he tried the door. He stepped aside to allow the footman to try.

"It appears to be locked, Your Grace. I will find the first butler. He will have the key."

West hunkered down and peered at the lock. "Do not trouble yourself. Stand here so I am not disturbed. Something has been jammed inside."

Contrary to what the rest of the Compass Club thought, West did not always carry a knife in his boot. On occasion, he carried it in the sleeve of his frock coat. To the footman who was watching over his shoulder, the blade appeared as if snatched from the air. West ignored the man's startled murmur and applied himself to picking the lock. Only a few seconds passed before he had the offending piece dangling from the tip of his knife.

"Why, it's an earbob," the footman said. "What do you make of that?"

West knew precisely what to make of it. He'd glimpsed one just like it earlier—and only one. He glanced down the hallway to the cupboard under the stairs. Pocketing the gold-and-ivory earring, but not his blade, West dismissed the footman. As soon as the servant had turned his back, he slipped inside the salon.

His heart slammed hard against his chest. Preparing himself to discover that it was empty was not the same as finding it so. He looked around quickly and saw there was no exit from the room except the door he had come through and those leading to the outside. If Ria had truly been here—and the glass of sherry that he found made him suspect she had been—then she could have only left by the French doors.

He tried to imagine what cause she would have to do that. Nothing occurred to him except that he was perhaps squandering valuable time. There was little to be gained by puzzling it out when he possessed such scant information.

West fingered the earring in his pocket, then went in search of the owner. Lady Powell had a great deal to answer for.

Ria awoke in bed. Her first thought was that it was not her own. She wondered if it was everyone's natural inclination to orient themselves to their surroundings first, then wonder how they had come to be there second. It was far easier for her to answer the latter question. She had a clear memory of being sick all over Mr. Jonathan Beckwith, as well as being thrown to the floor of the carriage afterward. The governor had made certain she knew he was fastidious about his person. There was nowhere for her to go that she could avoid the sharp jabs of his satin pumps. The defense of a hedgehog was all that was left to her.

She stretched gingerly, feeling the ache in her shoulder, hip, and back, and knowing it could be much worse. The taste in her mouth made her want to wretch again. Drawing her legs up to her chest and rolling onto her side, Ria fought the urge.

The first she knew she was not alone in the room was when a cool glass of water was pressed at a somewhat awkward angle to her lips.

"Drink this, Miss Ashby."

Ria did not grasp the glass; rather, she reached for the hands that held it. The tears that blurred her vision were of no importance because the voice was precisely as she remembered it. "Jane," she whispered. "Dear, sweet Jane."

Chapter Fifteen

At Jane's insistence, Ria drank. When the glass was removed, she pushed herself upright and caught Jane's arm as the girl started to rise. "No, don't go. I've been so worried. I need to—"

Jane gently pulled away from Ria's light grasp and stood. "It's all right, Miss Ashby. I'm only going to light a candle so you can see for yourself that I'm all of a piece." She set the glass on the washstand, picked up a candlestick, and used the embers in the fireplace to light the wick. When she returned to the bed, she carried the candle so its light bathed her face, but once she was at Ria's side, she held it out to make her own inspection.

"Did he hit you, miss?" she asked. "Your lip's swollen."

Ria touched her fingers to her mouth. Her lower lip was indeed tender. "I don't remember being hit." She used the tip of her tongue to trace the line and tasted a hint of blood. The memory of Beckwith's mouth on hers was suddenly clear enough to make her blanch. "He kissed me."

Jane merely nodded, then pointed to Ria's shoulder. "He didn't put his mouth on you there."

Glancing down, Ria examined the curve of her bare shoulder. The skin was already faintly discolored in preparation of what would be a livid bruise. What bothered her more than this evidence of injury was the realization that she was no longer wearing her gown, or even her own chemise. The shift she had on was of so fine a batiste as to be virtually transparent.

"Where are my clothes?" Ria asked.

"Gone."

"Gone? I don't understand. Did you take them?"

Jane shook her head. She placed the candlestick on the edge of the washstand, then soaked a flannel in the porcelain basin. Droplets of water splashed the front of her own batiste shift, making it cling to her skin until she plucked it away. "You won't need your clothes. We all wear shifts here."

Ria let her head drop back as Jane pressed the cool, damp cloth to her brow. The girl's self-possession was disconcerting. There were no tears. No hysterics. No sense of relief of any kind. Indeed, Jane showed little in the way of emotion. Ria took up holding the cloth in place as Jane's fingers slipped away. "Are you well, Jane?" she asked softly.

"Yes."

It did not escape Ria that Jane did not meet her eyes. "Who is *we?*" she asked. "You said that we all wear these here. Who is *we?*"

Jane shrugged.

"Are you not permitted to say? Is that it, Jane? Mr. Beckwith has perhaps instructed you not to talk to me." When no reply was forthcoming, Ria tried another tack. "Is this Sir Alex's house?"

"No, miss. Or rather it is not just his house."

Ria had to strain to hear Jane's answer. "Will you not speak up?" When Jane said nothing, Ria understood it was all the response she would receive. Her own voice dropped to a mere whisper. "Are we in London?"

"Yes."

Ria removed the flannel from her forehead and pressed it briefly to her bottom lip. Her eyes darted about the sparsely furnished room. There was nothing that was not serviceable

present in the chamber. No figurines rested on the mantelpiece. There was no gilt-edged clock. No paintings adorned
the darkly paneled walls. A cheval glass stood in the corner
near the door, and a washstand was situated close to the bed.
There were no dressers or trunks. No cupboard for linens.
The floor was also bare. On the same wall as the fireplace
was a panel door. Ria lifted her chin in the direction of it and
asked the question with only her eyes.

"For taking visitors," Jane said.

This answer initially surprised Ria, then frightened her as
she considered the fuller meaning Jane meant to convey. "I
do not know this place," she whispered. "Mr. Beckwith said
it would be familiar to me."

Jane took the flannel from Ria's hands. "I don't know
about that. Shall I dampen this again for you?"

"No." She watched Jane carefully fold the flannel in quarters and place it on the edge of the basin. The girl's fingers
trembled slightly, the only outward sign that her composure
was on a very tight leash. The movement riveted Ria's attention to the slender, golden bracelets that circled each of
Jane's wrists. Her eyes immediately went to her own wrists
to see if the same bands had been placed around her. When
she saw they remained unadorned, she also knew it would
not always be so. "Can you remove them?"

Jane retracted her outstretched hands quickly. She
brought them to her lap and tried to cover her wrists. Her fingers were inadequate to the task and when Ria laid a hand
over hers, she stopped fidgeting and let them lie still. She
bent her head, eyes downcast, unable to look anywhere but at
her lap. "They were made for me, Miss Ashby."

Ria leaned away from the bedhead and raised one of
Jane's hands to examine the bracelet. The girl's wrists were
small and delicate and the gold circlet was a close fit. Ria
tentatively tried to move it up to the fleshy ball of Jane's
hand. It would go that far and no farther. Looking for a
clasp, Ria turned the bracelet and found only a small, raised

nub on the surface to show where it had been forged closed. The bracelets had been indeed made for Jane.

"Has there been occasion to use them?" she asked carefully. The small shiver that went through Jane's hunched figure was answer enough. Ria let the blankets fall away and scrambled to her knees. She put her arms around Jane's narrow shoulders and hugged the girl to her breast. There were still no tears; Ria expected none now. Jane seemed too wounded to cry, or perhaps too afraid. She shuddered in the embrace but made no sound, and Ria noticed she never allowed herself the luxury of collapse. She remained stiff and unyielding in the arms that were meant to comfort her.

Ria eased her arms away and permitted Jane to straighten. She touched the girl's cap of silky blond hair with her fingertips, separating some tangled strands at her nape. "Can you say nothing at all to me, Jane?" She felt the small, negative shake of Jane's head and did not press.

Ignoring the ache in her shoulders and back, Ria left the bed. She bathed her face at the basin, then rinsed her mouth a second time. The floor was wretchedly cold beneath her feet, but she took it as a good sign that she was not numb to it and resolutely finished her ablutions. Aware that Jane was watching her, Ria began to explore the small room. Save for a skylight, there were no windows. The skylight did not lend itself to escape, but seemed put there of a purpose to tease one with the possibility. Ria saw immediately that it could not be reached. Standing on the bed would not raise her sufficiently to grasp its latch, and there were no chairs she might stack. There were no tools on the fireplace apron to extend her reach, and nothing to be gained by breaking the glass.

Walking the perimeter of the room did not prove particularly useful. She found the panel door was tightly closed, and her attempts to open it failed. Out of the corner of her eye, she saw that Jane did not stir from the bed. It was a certainty that she knew the door could not be opened, Ria thought.

Had it been otherwise she might have tried to prevent it. On either side of the fireplace, an iron hook was set into the wall. Ria assumed they were there in aid of supporting a lantern and gave them no more thought. When she turned and saw still more set into the other walls at different heights, she understood they had a far less benign purpose. Glancing at Jane again, she saw the girl was turning one of the bracelets in something that might have been agitation, but might also have been a communication.

Ria moved on quickly and made a cursory attempt to open the room's other door, knowing full well it would offer no exit. She returned again to the fireplace and stood in front of it, trying to warm herself. "Is there no wood?" she asked. "If I could poke at it, perhaps I could make this log give up more heat."

"You must come back to bed," Jane said. "I will fetch wood, but you must sit here first."

Ria complied because she was curious. Shivering now, she sat down and tucked the blankets all around her. Jane, she noticed, seemed almost immune to the room's pervasive chill. The girl rose and crossed the room to the panel door. She made two sharp raps with her knuckles. A moment later, the door opened and she disappeared through it. Ria could not get out of bed fast enough to follow. Her attempt left her with one foot on the floor and the other still tangled in the sheets. Frustrated, she dropped back onto the bed.

Several minutes passed before the door swung open again. Jane entered, carrying several logs on her extended forearms. She was followed into the room by Jonathan Beckwith. Jane dropped to her knees in front of the fireplace and angled her arms so the logs rolled out and onto the apron. Beckwith closed the door but stayed there until she had added the logs. Ria did not see the iron poker he carried until he lifted it away from his thigh. He pressed the tip of it against Jane's shoulder, moving her aside, then he stirred the embers until one of the logs crackled and caught. Beckoning to Jane with the crook of his finger, he bid her rise, then indicated the hook on the left side of the mantelpiece.

Ria's mouth went dry as Jane walked calmly to the place Beckwith pointed out, raised both arms above her head, and affixed herself to the wall anchor by her gold bracelets. This required that she stand slightly on tiptoe, a position that most certainly caused her discomfort, yet Ria could not see that Jane was bothered in the least by it. Features that Ria recalled as animated and lively were virtually without expression now.

"It is a good position for her," Beckwith said, leaning the poker against the fireplace. "Do you not think so, Miss Ashby?"

Ria had no idea how she was meant to respond to his outrageous statement, even if she'd had the wherewithal to do so.

Beckwith turned over his palm to indicate Jane's slender form. His eyes, however, never wandered from Ria's. "You can observe how it extends the length of her so beautifully? She has lovely breasts. This position causes them to be lifted at just the right angle of offering. The chill has a purpose, do you see?" He sighed. "I suppose that the warmth we have just added to the room will make those particular puckering charms disappear. More's the pity." At Ria's continued silence, Beckwith was moved to approach the bed. He stopped within a few feet of it and regarded her closely. "Will you take a drink? Something more suitable to the palate, perhaps, than water. There is wine. Sherry. Brandy. Indeed, I am certain there is nothing you could request that is not available." He paused, considering that promise. "Except ratafia. That we do not serve."

"Wine."

"Of course." He picked up the poker on his way out, smiling with certain significance as he did so. "I should not like to feel this laid sharply across my skull, and I suspect you would like nothing more than an opportunity to do so. Is that right, Miss Ashby?"

Ria did not deny it.

"Just so." Beckwith left the room.

Disengaging herself from the blankets, Ria hurried to where Jane stood. "Will you not come away from there? Oh, please, do not avert your eyes. Look at me, and tell me what power he has to make you do this to yourself." When Jane said nothing, Ria stood on tiptoe herself and tried to lift the bracelets from the hook. Without Jane's cooperation, it was impossible. The girl's own weight held her in place until she could be lifted free. Jane pointedly refused to offer assistance and Ria's strength was not enough to manage the thing on her own, not when she comprehended that Jane would struggle against her efforts.

Ria's voice dropped to a whisper. "We must help each other if we are to leave this place, Jane. You cannot be resolved to do nothing. I will—" She broke off and stepped away quickly when she heard movement at the door. There was too little time to return to the bed and perhaps even less sense in doing so. Ria was almost certain that she and Jane were being observed.

Ria stood in the middle of the room, her hands at her sides, as the door opened. She did not look away as Beckwith made a complete study of her person in the near-transparent gown. He could only shame her, she thought, if she allowed him to do so. She was careful not to appear insolent or challenging, knowing full well how these attitudes raised Beckwith's immoderate temper.

"Your wine," he said, nudging the door closed with the tip of his shoe. When it clicked in place, he carried the drink to her. "I believe you will find this to your liking."

Ria accepted the glass and moved closer to the fire. She sipped the wine carefully, gauging the taste of it for anything unfamiliar.

"It is only wine," Beckwith told her.

She thought he seemed amused by her suspicions. "Where am I?" she asked. "You said I would know this place."

Beckwith pointed to the fireplace. "Have a care you did not stray too close, Miss Ashby. A single popping ember will ignite the fabric of your gown. Jane can tell you the truth of that. Like a candlewick, it goes."

Ria glanced at Jane, but she stared fixedly at a point on the far side of the room. Had it happened to Jane? she wondered. Or had she witnessed that event? Ria drank more deeply of her wine.

"Will you not sit down, Miss Ashby?"

It occurred to Ria that this invitation was really more in way of an order. She decided not to test it. She sat on the edge of the bed, hooked her heels on the frame, and drew a blanket across her lap.

Beckwith shook his head. "You may not use the blanket in my presence. Indeed, you must not cover yourself in any manner save for the gown you've been given. Do you understand?"

"But it is still so very cold in—"

Ignoring her, Beckwith turned on his heel and closed the distance to Jane. He took the puckered tip of her right breast between the knuckles of his index and middle finger and twisted hard. Jane cried out, but Ria's cry was louder.

Throwing off the blanket, Ria jumped to her feet. "Release her!" The demand was unnecessary, for Beckwith let his hand fall away as soon as she discarded the blanket.

"Sit down, Miss Ashby." There was a biting emphasis given to each word. He turned away from Jane. "Cause and effect," he said simply. "Mayhap it is clearer to you now."

Ria nodded slowly. She made no attempt to reach for the blanket. It would not have prevented the shiver that coursed her spine and raised the hair at the back of her neck.

"Good," Beckwith said. "You are a quick study, though I expected nothing less. The girls generally do not have benefit of your age and experience to guide them in such matters, and it can take longer for the connection to be made clearly in their minds. Jane is just such a case." He glanced back at

Jane. "You may speak, dear. Tell Miss Ashby how many stripes I raised on Sylvia's back and bottom before you learned proper obedience."

"Four stripes, Miss Ashby."

Beckwith patted the girl's cheek lightly. "And now you are very well disciplined." He let his hand fall back, but his fingertips grazed her throat and passed lightly over the tip of the breast he'd pinched so viciously minutes earlier. Turning away, he regarded Ria again. "We are in London," he said. "That was your question, was it not?"

"Where in London?"

"Number 48 Whittington. Does knowing so much relieve your mind? I am never certain why anyone wants such useless information, but everyone demands to have it. Do you find that peculiar, Miss Ashby?"

Ria didn't answer. Before she understood what was happening, Beckwith had turned back to Jane and slapped her smartly across the cheek. "Why did you do that? I didn't—"

"You didn't answer my question."

For a moment Ria could not think what he had asked. Her stomach clenched as she thought he might strike Jane again because she was too slow with her response. "No," she said as it came to her. "No, I don't find it peculiar. I suppose each of us wants to place ourselves somewhere. And, yes, it relieves my mind."

He smiled. "But you don't know Whittington Street, do you?"

"No."

"And you have no idea what part of London we're in."

"No."

Beckwith just shook his head, still mystified by the importance each new visitor to this house placed on knowing where they were. It was not as if they could leave of their own accord. "You will want to know why you are here, of course."

"I think I understand that."

He chuckled. "Yes, I suppose you do. At least some measure of it." He reached into the pocket of his frock coat and removed a length of ribbon. "Hold out your hands, Miss Ashby."

Ria did as he instructed. The struggle was to keep them steady as he used the ribbon to measure each of her wrists. He made a sharp crease in the satin to mark the circumference. Ria wanted to look away and could not; the image of herself wearing the bracelets was too powerfully real.

"Come with me," Beckwith said.

It did not matter that she was no longer certain her legs would support her. She stood quickly and waited to see if she would remain so.

"This way."

She knew better than to hesitate as he turned toward the door, but she was still compelled to ask, "What about Jane?"

"Jane is exactly as she must be." He paused a beat in anticipation of Ria making some response. When she didn't, he merely smiled approvingly, perfectly satisfied with her silence. "This way." He rapped sharply on the door and it opened for him. He stepped through, held it open for her, then gestured for her to follow.

Ria stood on the edge of the threshold but could not cross it. She knew this place, just as Mr. Beckwith had told her she would. At once familiar, yet alien. It was exactly so.

The chaise longue was sapphire blue. The heavy velvet drapes were the color of rubies. Lighted sconces caused the jewel tones of the fabrics to be reflected darkly in the polished walnut walls. It was the room she had seen in the painting of India Parr. It was the same chaise that Sir Alex had been sitting on for his portrait.

It was, in fact, Sir Alex who was sitting upon the chaise now, his cobalt-blue eyes sharply assessing her. Surrounding him was the entire board of governors of Miss Weaver's Academy, save for the newest of their number.

Ria did not know if it was better or worse for her that the Duke of Westphal was not among those gathered for this hellish welcome.

* * *

West was the last to arrive. It was immediately obvious to the others that he had not slept. He no longer wore the formal attire from the previous evening's affair, but he appeared to have been a reluctant and impatient recipient of his valet's attentions. Proof that Finch had drawn him a bath was there in the damp copper locks at his collar, but there was no evidence that he had found his soak in any way a useful respite. To all of those present in the colonel's home, West looked as if he might simply come out of his skin.

It was his very stillness that was alarming. They knew him too well to suppose that his calm was anything but affected. He took up the seat they had left for him in the colonel's favorite wing chair, stretching out in the most casual manner. He closed his eyes for a moment, his head back, his hands clasped in his lap. The posture might easily have been mistaken for one of prayer—and no one among them could say that it was not—but they understood it better as West's means of composing his soul.

So that he might not be moved to act precipitously, they gave him all the time he needed.

West opened his eyes, edged himself upward a few degrees, and fished for the card in his pocket. "This was waiting for me when I returned home. It is the reason I sent word around for you to meet me here. The colonel has told you what happened last evening?"

North nodded. "I wish you had called upon us earlier, West. With nothing to report, Elizabeth and I went home after observing Sir Alex go straightaway to his own residence."

Southerton's smile was wry. "I know I have been remiss in not asking for help when it was most certainly needed, so I can't very well upbraid you for it, but—"

"But you mean to do it anyway," West said. "Let us consider that it has been accomplished."

"Good of you to spare us that speech," East said, helping himself to a cup of tea. "What is to be done, then? The colonel says that Miss Ashby most likely left with Beckwith. Can that be right? He was not even among those who received an invitation."

Blackwood adjusted his spectacles to read the card West had passed to him. "From the description Lady Powell supplied, we are as certain as we can be that it was Beckwith."

"The lady has a great deal to answer for," South said.

West shook his head. "She was simply a convenience for them. If not she, then someone else would have been found."

The colonel looked up from examining the card. He handed it to East. "You say that the card came this morning?"

"No. Mr. Blaine told me it was delivered shortly after midnight. I only received it when I returned home."

Eastlyn flicked the card with his fingernail before passing it to South. "They meant for you to see it much earlier, then."

"Yes. I suppose they couldn't know I would start searching for Miss Ashby immediately."

South gave the card a little toss and it sailed directly into Northam's waiting hands. "You will admit it was a more reckless decision than you are usually wont to make. With so many hours passing in the interim, they may well believe you do not intend to come for her at all."

"That's possible," West said. "But they have been privy to the exchange of letters between us. I think they know I will not avoid a confrontation."

North slipped the card between two fingers of West's outstretched hand. "Love letters, were they?"

"I was rather late in declaring my feelings," West said. "I proposed marriage first." The regard of his friends was uniformly chastising and mildly amused. "Yes, well, she's forgiven me. I should like to think she did not extend her trust unwisely." His gaze wandered to each of the others in turn. "You are with me, then?"

South set his cup down in its saucer. "Now, there is a fool's question. We are certainly not assembled at this hour to take the bishops' part." This assertion was supported by others. "You have but to tell us your plan."

"Yes," West said. "My plan. I will come to that directly." He tapped the card with his forefinger. "I am unfamiliar with this address. Number 48 Whittington. Do you know where it is?"

Eastlyn offered the information. "The West End. It is a private gentleman's club. Webb's. My wife's cousins had occasion to go there, and things being what they were, I had occasion to see them being admitted. The Earl of Tremont was a bishop, of course, but it never occurred to me that the club might be exclusively for the Society. You may well know the place by another name. I have heard it sometimes called The Flower House."

West stopped tapping the card. His complexion, already pale from lack of sleep, became paler yet. "The Flower House is a brothel."

East considered how he might put it to his friend. "I shall depend upon you not to kill the messenger."

"Go on."

Quite aware West had made no promise, Eastlyn went on in spite of it. "The Flower House is indeed a brothel, one that caters to certain . . . umm, peculiarities. It is my understanding that entree is only given to club members. If it is true that membership is only for bishops, then it follows that those in the house serve at the will and pleasure of the Society."

West looked to the others to see if they had anything of import to add. They remained silent, as much struck by East's information as he was. "The name of the club again?" he asked.

"Webb's."

"Spell it."

East did so.

"Mightn't it just as easily be Webs?" South asked, picking up the thread of West's thinking. "The kind one associates with arachnids?"

"Of course," East said. "I have never seen it written."

"Spiders," North said quietly. "The bishops are that."

"It certainly fits, doesn't it?" The colonel rubbed his chin with his knuckles as he mused on this. "Nature's extraordinary weavers. Wouldn't you say so, West?"

Pushing himself completely upright in his chair, West nodded. "Miss Weaver's Academy. The pieces fit rather more neatly than one could have first supposed." He glanced at Eastlyn. "What else do you know about The Flower House?"

"Only what I have told you. Rumors. I have never been closer than the gated entrance."

"Footmen?"

"No. One can easily go as far as the front door without being stopped. Admittance would be a trifle more difficult after that. One would require identification . . . a password, perhaps. Something that—"

West held up the card. "This?"

"That is certainly how *you* are meant to gain entrance, but whether it will work for the rest of us . . ." His voice trailed off as he considered the problem. "Is there time for me to have more printed? I will take it to Sir James. It can be accomplished in a few hours."

"I cannot wait so long, but knowing you will follow in due time will be considerable comfort."

North held up one hand. "We should all go together, West. Not you first, with us trailing behind. What if the cards don't give us entree?"

"Then you will be resourceful, I expect, and find some other means." He glanced at East again. "Tell us about the house."

"It sits squarely in the middle of a row of others exactly like it. The trade entrance is below the ground floor at the front. I imagine servants use the rear. I cannot tell you any more than that."

"There you have it, North," West said. "It is sufficient for our needs. I am confident you will find me. The governors are expecting me to come alone."

"To close their trap," the colonel said.

"Without a doubt, yet if we arrive together they may do

nothing at all. I need them to reveal where Ria is, not hide her away. Going there alone is a risk worth taking."

"That is your plan?" asked South. "You will advance as the spy and we will follow?"

"Essentially, yes."

"You don't think it requires some refining?"

"Wellington made it work." West regarded his friends. "Do you mean a soldier, sailor, and tinker cannot do the same?" He glanced at Blackwood. "Even when a colonel commands it?"

Ria stared at the tray of food that had been brought to her room. It was a light repast only: shirred eggs, two fingers of toast, half an orange, and a cup of tea. She'd been told to eat but had no appetite to do so. The consequences of refusing the order, even one so small as this, were at the forefront of her mind.

They had explained to her what she might expect while she was their guest. *Guest.* It was the word they had actually used to describe her presence in the house, and she still felt slightly ill when she considered how easily the explanations came to them. They took turns telling her how she would pass the time.

Sir Alex discussed her primary responsibility would be to tutor the young women in their subjects. They were all agreed that intelligence enhanced the desirability of their students, and though they regretted that she could no longer be headmistress of Miss Weaver's, her arrival here was perhaps more fortunate than not.

Lord Herndon explained there would be menial tasks as well, though none that she should consider beneath her, and all of them essential for the smooth management of the establishment. The conservatory was his special interest, and he took considerable pride in the flower house. It should be the very equal of the one in his own home. If not, he would know the reason why.

Ria heard from all of them. She would sweep the floors on Tuesdays. Change the linens on Wednesdays. Her turn in the kitchen would come every ten days, and she would be expected to assist the cook in whatever manner was required.

It was Mr. Beckwith who explained there would be no chores in the evening. Nothing would be required after that except that she make herself available to any one of them who wanted her. "Do you understand?" he had asked politely.

And Ria had nodded.

"There will be no formal ceremony to serve as your initiation," he went on to say. "That sacred rite is performed when virginity is to be offered. You cannot offer us that, can you?"

Ria had no difficulty bringing to mind the slender Ionic column and altar that were so perfectly realized in the illustrated book and the painting of Miss Parr. The purpose of the altar was borne home to her again. "I am not a virgin," she told them.

"That is a certainty. You are a whore."

"No."

"You lifted your skirts for Westphal."

Ria said nothing.

"You spread your thighs for him."

Ria could feel their eyes on her, their narrowed gazes boring into her. She could have been wearing a suit of armor and still felt as vulnerable as she did in the thin batiste gown.

"You invited him into your bed," Beckwith said without inflection. "And you let him mount you."

Ria had brought her hands to her ears then, only to have them pulled away and held. She was forced to hear the intimacy of her lovemaking with West described in the most vile terms imaginable. And when the words finally provoked tears, Beckwith smiled.

The memory of weeping in front of them heated Ria's cheeks now. She picked up her fork and stabbed at the egg. Nothing she had done shamed her as those tears had. They had waited until she could hardly breathe for the shudders that wracked her, until her head was bowed and her spirit crushed, and then Sir Alex led her back into her bedchamber and locked her inside.

Jane was no longer in the room, and Ria was able to find a small measure of relief in her absence. She had checked the door through which Jane had been removed and found it locked. It was too much to hope, she thought, that someone would make the sort of mistake that might lead to her leaving this place.

Ria raised the forkful of egg to her mouth, then set it down without taking a bite. The smell of the food made her stomach roil. She could not imagine that she would be able to swallow it without being sick. Placing the tray on the floor, she wondered if she was being observed even now. Would someone come in and insist that she eat what was prepared, or were there allowances made when no demand was expressly made by one of the bishops? She had not been ordered to eat, she recalled. The tray had merely been presented to her.

No one came. Ria knew this did not necessarily mean she was unobserved, and she kept this in her mind as she pulled a blanket around her shoulders and rose from the bed. The house was quiet, eerily so. Except for the occasional creak of a floorboard under her feet and the rush of wind across the skylight overhead, she heard no other sounds. As much as she abhorred the idea of being watched, the uncertainty of it, coupled with the silence, was almost as unnerving.

Ria blew out the candle on the washstand so the room's only light came from the fireplace. She walked the perimeter of the room as she had done before, this time examining the paneled walls more closely, looking for a sliver of light that might indicate an opening to another room. She found it beside the fireplace, just to the left of where Jane had raised her hands and hooked her gold bracelets to the wall. Ria pushed very lightly at the panel but would have been astonished if she could have moved it. When it didn't budge, she turned around and surveyed the room from this angle. She was able to gain some idea of what was visible when the slotted panel was opened. Most of the bed could be seen, but Ria thought if she stayed close to the head, she was not entirely within an observer's line of sight. The area just below the panel and along the fireplace wall was also not visible. Stepping as little as a foot away, however, would put her back in view.

Ria continued her exploration but found no other means by which she could be watched. She wished she knew what use she might make of this understanding and settled for the small comfort the discovery brought her.

When the room's chill drove her back to stand in front of the fireplace, Ria reflected on what Beckwith and the others intended for her. She did not know precisely when she had ceased thinking of them as the governors of Miss Weaver's, only that they were firmly in her mind now as the Society of Bishops, and that everything West had told her about them, she had come to experience herself.

Their cruelty still had the capacity to take her breath away, but she supposed that in time she would become inured to it. How could one survive otherwise? Jane seemed well on her way to finding a place within herself where she could escape the vicious attentions of the bishops, and Ria suspected the same would be true for her.

By making one girl subject to the painful consequences of disobedience by another girl, the bishops had found an effective method for quickly gaining cooperation. Ria knew that she might inadvertently cause Beckwith or one of the other bishops to punish Jane, but that she would never deliberately provide them with an excuse to do so. It seemed likely the other girls would act no differently. Rebellion held little appeal when someone else must always be made to pay for it.

Ria returned to the bed and huddled at the head of it. When a wave of shivering passed, she slipped between the sheets, drew the blankets around her, and turned on her side toward the fireplace. She craved sleep, but more than that, she craved escape. To that end, she closed her eyes and waited for the weariness that anchored her limbs to the bed to have the same influence on her mind.

That peace was denied her as her thoughts merely tripped and tumbled over each other. West. Miss Weaver's. Jenny Taylor. The bishops. West again. Jane. Amy Nash. The altar. West in her bed. The Society watching. Whispering. The *ton* observing. The *Gazette* reporting.

Soldier. Sailor. Tinker. *Spy.*

Ria could not suppress a shudder, nor turn her head into her pillow fast enough to stifle her small cry. It was no longer a simple thing to distinguish what part of her reaction was hope and what was despair.

She had always known West would come for her, but she had avoided considering what it would mean when he did so. The bishops would use her to punish him, to force his surrender just as they had used Jane to make her compliant. She thought she could bear anything for herself, but to see West being made to do the bishops' bidding, that was pain of another kind, and she had no sense of her tolerance for it, nor his.

She slept at last, fitfully at first, then more deeply. If there were dreams, she did not recall them upon waking. The room was already being cast in shadow when she opened her eyes; the skylight revealed that dusk was upon London. She was surprised she had been allowed to sleep so long, but she did not mistake it as a courtesy extended. It was far more likely the bishops had some other business to occupy them.

She had barely begun to stir when a movement in the hallway caught her attention. Cocking her head, she heard a key turn. Almost immediately, the door swung into the room. Jane was there, this time with Sir Alex a step behind her. Ria watched Sir Alex lock the door and palm the key, then indicate to Jane that she could proceed to the bed.

Ria did not miss the look of concern on Jane's face when she saw that the tray of food had been ignored. Jane did not speak to her but directed her comments to Sir Alex.

"She hasn't eaten. There is nothing on her tray that has been touched."

Sir Alex's dark-blue glance dropped to that food at Jane's feet. "Perhaps she thinks it is tainted. Show her it is not."

Jane bent and picked up one cold finger of toast and bit it. Swallowing, she held it out to Ria. With her head turned away from Sir Alex, she was able to mouth the word *please*.

Sitting up, Ria took the offering. It had the grit of sandpaper on her tongue, but she managed to swallow one bite, then another. Sir Alex came to stand at the foot of the bed and watched silently until Ria ate some part of everything she'd been given.

"Place the tray on the mantel, Jane," he said, "then yourself at the wall."

Ria did not look in Sir Alex's direction, but she sensed he was closely observing her reaction rather than watching Jane. She did not make the mistake of asking him why Jane must attach herself to the wall. She understood now that it was in aid of proving Jane's obedience, and the purpose was simply that he wished it so. Ria's eyes were drawn away from Jane and back to Sir Alex as he reached into the pocket of his frock coat. She thought he was simply putting the key away; then she realized he was exchanging it for something else.

She blanched when she saw the bracelets he held out in his open palm. They were not identical to the ones Jane wore, but their purpose was precisely the same.

"Until yours are ready," he said. "Give me your wrists."

Ria thought she could not do it, yet she watched her hands extend themselves toward him, her palms turned upward, just as if they were possessed of a will separate from her own. What Sir Alex placed around her wrists and locked individually into place were iron cuffs. They were not connected by a chain, but the cuffs could be fixed together as desired with an iron pin. Sir Alex showed her how it worked by crossing her wrists so the hooks on each cuff fit together to make a tunnel for the pin. Once the pin was in place, she could not grasp it with her own fingers to pull it free. Someone else would have to do that, and Ria understood immediately that it would not be Jane or one of the other girls. She would be freed just as she would be bound—at the whim of the bishops.

Sir Alex laid his slender hand over the cuffs. "They are heavier than those you will come to know later, but that is all to the better, I think. You will not mind the bracelets so much once you have worn these for a time."

Ria thought he would remove the pin from between the cuffs, but he did not. He touched her face instead, brushing her cheek lightly with his knuckles, and spoke to her in a pleasant, matter-of-fact tone, just as he might use if they were conversing over tea.

"You cried very prettily earlier," he said. "I have often wondered if you could be made to cry. Jane does, you know, though not as easily now as she did in the beginning. She imagined herself in love with me. Did you know that? Go on, you may speak."

"Yes," Ria said, keenly aware of Jane's presence. "I came to realize that. I don't think she would have left the school otherwise."

"Love makes fools of us, is that it, Miss Ashby?" He did not wait for a response. "It must certainly be true in your case. You took the bastard duke to your bed. I readily admit I could not credit it at first, but Miss Taylor was most convincing in her missive. She came upon you, it seems, in your own apartments at the school. It was careless of you to entertain Westphal there, but perhaps more careless that you did not make certain you could not be disturbed. As headmistress, you must see that your conduct has to be above reproach. We thought we could count on that." He shrugged. "It seems we could not."

Sir Alex's thumb made a pass across Ria's lower lip. "Do you think Westphal will have you after you have been with us?" he asked. "There is a wager on the outcome of it. We are going to arrange a tasting. What do you think of that?"

His words meant nothing to her, but the barely audible moan from Jane did. Ria's blood ran cold. If this *tasting* could elicit that response from Jane, then it must truly be something to be feared.

Sir Alex stood and walked over to Jane. "Do you have something you wish to say?"

"No, my lord."

"Then mayhap you are weary of standing."

"No, my lord."

"Look at Miss Ashby, Jane, and tell her what a tasting is."

Jane's head swiveled in Ria's direction. Her lips parted but her voice failed her.

"Tell her, Jane, or I swear I will not wait to have Sylvia punished for your disobedience. Miss Ashby is handy enough for those purposes." As if to make good on his threat, Sir Alex started to turn back to Ria.

"A tasting is when they all have a turn at you," Jane said in a rush. "They . . . they watch each other and . . . and count their strokes and place wagers on who will stay between your thighs the longest."

Ria had not yet recovered any color to her face, so there was no more to be lost. What she could not do for a moment was breathe.

Sir Alex's blue eyes darted between Ria and Jane. The smile that edged the corners of his mouth upward was a satisfied one. "Well done, Jane. I think you explained it very well indeed. Miss Ashby certainly seems to have gotten the gist of it." He helped Jane down from the hook and escorted her to the door. He inserted the key and turned the handle with a small flourish. "Go on," he told her. "You may leave. I'm quite sure you have neglected your chores."

"Yes, m'lord." Jane ducked her head and hurried from the room. She was not quick enough to escape the flat of Sir Alex's hand as she passed. His palm landed smartly on her bottom and the sound of it covered her sharp intake of air.

Sir Alex shut the door and twisted the key, pocketing it again. "She's a good girl," he said as he turned back to Ria. "I doubt that I will tire of her soon."

"What is to become of her?"

"A better question is what is to become of you. Jane is no longer your concern." He smiled suddenly. "But I will indulge your curiosity. This place is not vastly different from the school in Gillhollow. You might say it is Miss Weaver's *other* academy. We also tutor the girls, first so that they may serve our own needs, then so they may serve the needs of others. The best among them become courtesans, the less talented are sold to brothels. Damaged goods become the property of the street."

Damaged goods. He spoke blithely of girls he had used as *damaged goods*. Ria felt as if there was a great weight pressing against her chest; drawing a full breath was not possible. "It is a slaver's trade."

"You are bold of a sudden, Miss Ashby. You must learn to guard your tongue. My patience is not infinite. Jane is not far, and it is a simple enough thing to call her to attend us again." He beckoned Ria to stand, then called her forward. "You did not think you could do it, did you?"

"No."

"We test your mettle here. I am of the opinion that you will prove your worth to us in many ways. Come, I wish to see if I am right." Grasping Ria by her pinned wrists, he led her to the wall opposite the fireplace and pointed to the hook above her head. "The cuffs are more difficult to secure, but I believe you can manage the thing."

Ria felt her knees weaken, but she remained standing. She understood very well why he had chosen this wall, this hook. Her placement here was so she would be in full view of anyone looking through the panel. She could not tell if it had been opened—the play of light and shadow on the wall hid it from her—but she suspected the adjoining room was no longer lighted, so that someone could observe without being seen.

She raised her arms over her head as she had seen Jane do, then lifted herself on her toes to catch the hook. The posture strained her arms. It required two attempts before she was able to slide the cuffs over the hook, but her effort was rewarded by a slight easing of the tension in her shoulders. She resisted the instinct to try to free herself. It was what Sir Alex expected, she thought, and in this small way she could refuse to comply.

"Beautiful." Sir Alex stepped slightly to one side and made a study of her form. "It is unfortunate that you crossed Beckwith in the carriage. The bruises will not be easily masked. Lord Herndon does not like the petals of his flowers crushed and I am inclined to take his side. Beckwith, though, is not so particular. He finds pleasure inflicting a certain amount of pain, and almost as much again in seeing the evidence of it. We are not all of that bent, Miss Ashby." He placed his fingers in her pale hair and drew some of it forward, then followed the curling tip of it until his hand was covering her breast. "Have you been thinking about the tasting? Who do you think will outlast all the others?"

Ria knew he expected an answer. "I collect it will be you."

Sir Alex Cotton gave a bark of laughter. "Very good. Yes, I shall certainly wager on myself." His hand dropped away from her breast and rested on her hip a moment. "But what of Westphal? Could he do us all one stroke better?"

Ria's mouth was dry as dust. Her tongue cleaved to the roof of her mouth.

"Will you take some wine?" Sir Alex asked. At her nod, he went to the adjoining door, knocked twice, and waited for it to open. He was gone less than a minute and returned with a glass of claret. "I will hold it for you." He placed the rim of the glass against her lips and tilted it carefully. He did not remove it until she had drunk deeply. The wine stained Ria's perfectly shaped mouth the color of rubies. "Lovely."

Ria closed her eyes as he bent his head and laid his lips across hers. She tried not to give him the satisfaction of her resistance, but it was impossible not to hold herself still when he pressed himself hard against her and forced his tongue past her teeth. The hand that was on her hip slipped between her thighs, and she jerked wildly when the batiste gown proved itself no barrier to his probing fingers.

Sir Alex lifted his head, but he did not remove his hand. "Well?" he asked. "What of Westphal?"

Beckwith slid the panel closed and opened the shutters on the lantern he held. Light bathed the small chamber and illuminated the hard features of the man at his side. "How do you think she answered?" he asked. "Will she flatter Sir Alex, or will she tell him that you will win the wager?"

West's fingers uncurled slowly. They were stiff and very nearly bloodless from being held for so long in tightly clenched fists. "What do you want, Beckwith?"

"It is not just for me, you understand. It is for the Society."

"Yes. Name it."

"You must prove yourself first, I think." He regarded West for a long moment, as though still considering his offer. "Then you will give us the colonel in exchange for your whore."

Chapter Sixteen

Ria bit her lip to keep from calling after Sir Alex as he left the room. Her arms and shoulders ached from the unnatural position she was forced to maintain. To support her weight, she had to stand on pointed toes; the muscles in her calves and thighs burned with the effort. He did not say how long he would be gone, only that he had other matters to attend. She thought he would release her. He had toyed with her cuffs as if he meant to, but then he'd merely run his palm down the length of her arm, smiled with disarming appeal, and left her alone to contemplate what, exactly, was to be her fate.

She wondered if she was being watched even now. Were the bishops wagering on whether she would try to free herself? It was tempting to glare in the direction of the panel, just as it was tempting to struggle against the iron bands, but Ria resisted both temptations because of Jane. No matter that Sir Alex tried to distinguish himself from Beckwith when it came to inflicting pain—Ria knew very well they were cut from the same cloth.

She closed her eyes. There were other kinds of escape, she thought, ones the bishops could not so easily prevent. In her mind's eye, Ria saw the lake at Ambermede. The summer grass was high, and it tickled her knees as she ran for the water's edge. She plucked one of the blades and raised it to her lips. Her cheeks puffed as she tried to make a whistle of it. The note she hit was shrill to her own ears and perfectly annoying to those around her. Her mother called, "Ria. Ria, come here."

She did not go, of course. She did not even consider going. The sun was warm on her face and a light breeze ruffled her hair. The water beckoned her more powerfully than her mother. She abandoned the blade of grass in favor of spinning like a top, arms extended wide as if she could embrace the entire world in them. "Ria," her father called to her. She paid him as little heed as she had her mother. "Maria." Aaah, she must be behaving badly if someone was moved to intone her Christian name. "Reee-a!"

She giggled. Why should she go to them? she wondered. It seemed infinitely more important that they should join her. She would take another blade of grass and play the pied piper for them. Her mother, her father, the duke . . . all of them would leave their blankets and step lively to her tune. She spun away, showing them as splendid a form as a Paris opera dancer, her arms gracefully curved above her, her long legs elegantly lifted *en pointe*. "Ria." A chorus of voices called to her, and she blithely ignored the accolades of her audience. Let them come to her, she thought again. Let them come.

"Ria." West yanked on the pin that coupled Ria's cuffs. She moaned softly as her arms fell limply to her sides. He pulled her roughly against him and held her there, letting her use all of him for support. Her head rested heavily against his shoulder. His hard embrace was all that kept her standing.

"You came," she whispered. "I knew you would. The others, too. I said let them come to me and they did. I knew if I played for them, they would come." It was almost too great an effort to smile, but somehow her lips managed to press that sweet curve against his coat. "How simple it all is, really."

"Shh."

Was it a secret? she wondered. Or did he only mean that she shouldn't talk? It didn't matter. There was nothing else she wanted to say just now. He was lifting her in his arms and everything was just as it should be.

West set Ria on the bed. She tried to hold onto him as he straightened, but he could see her arms had no strength left in them. She was able to keep them raised for only a few moments before they fell heavily back to the mattress. It was an agony for West to step outside of her reach. To reassure her, he said, "I'm not going anywhere."

Ria regarded him with alarm. "Why not?"

He placed one restraining hand on her shoulder before she could try to struggle up to her elbows. "Allow me to give you my coat."

It was no answer to her question, and Ria was beginning to think clearly enough to realize it. "I want to leave this place."

"No more than I want you gone." He removed his frock coat, then helped her sit up long enough to place it around her shoulders. "You should put it on properly."

"This is better," she told him softly. "As if your arms are still around me." Ria had not meant to cause him pain, yet that was the precise nature of what she saw cross his face, then come to reside in his eyes. "It's all right. You have nothing to answer for." She was able to lay one hand over his just before he withdrew from her side. Turning her head so she could follow his movements, Ria watched him use the toe of his boot to nudge the logs in the fireplace. One of them turned over and blazed to life. She smiled as he jumped back to avoid the licking, leaping flames.

West turned and gestured to the fire. "Would you like to sit here and warm yourself?"

Ria shook her head. "Mr. Beckwith warned me that this

garment flashes like a candlewick." She did not miss the grim twist of West's lips, even though it came and went in the space of a single blink. "It doesn't matter now," she said. "You have banished all of the bishops."

"There are always bishops."

"Then you have banished these bishops. It is a good beginning in some respects. A better ending in others."

West approached the bed. One of the blankets lay in a mound at the foot, the other had fallen to the floor. He picked up both, spread them open between his arms, then covered Ria and tucked them around her. He saw that she expected something more from him—his arms under her, perhaps, lifting her, taking her first toward the door, then beyond it. Sitting at the edge of the bed, West took one of Ria's hands in his. He brushed the iron wristcuff. She was watching him closely now, and he managed not to wince at the feel of this cold, alien hardware under his fingertips.

"I would remove this if I could," he said. "You know that, don't you?"

Ria's eyes darted to her wrist. She saw his thumb run across the edge of the cuff. Odd, she thought, that he had been touching her there and she had not known it. She looked back at him. "Sir Alex has the key."

"Yes. I know."

Her brow puckered slightly as she considered what this meant. "You were watching when he was here?"

He nodded.

Ria's fingers tightened in his. "For how long?"

"You were lying here when I first saw you. I thought you were asleep, but I came to realize you were not. Miss Petty and Cotton came in shortly afterward, and you seemed to know it immediately."

"But if you were there . . ." Ria realized she still did not understand. "Why didn't you—" She stopped because he was shaking his head.

"I couldn't go to you," he said. "I didn't dare make the attempt." He could still hear Beckwith graphically describing what would happen to Ria if there was the slightest misstep on his part. Even now, if he was not careful, the end might be the same. Perhaps he had already said more than he should have. It was hard to know. Beckwith had not been clear as to how much leeway he would be allowed in negotiating this end for the bishops. The fact that the doors remained closed was a good sign that he was still within the limits they had in mind. West did not believe there would have been any hesitation to come in and drag him from the room.

"We are not leaving, are we?" There was so little inflection in Ria's voice that it was hardly a question.

"No. Not yet."

Ria nodded. Her eyes darted toward the panel, then she looked at West for confirmation of the thing she dared not ask.

He squeezed her hand and saw, more than heard, her soft intake of breath. In that small way, she communicated her understanding.

"They call it a tasting," Ria whispered.

The words had barely any sound and West had to bend his head to hear her. "Yes," he said. "I heard Sir Alex tell you."

"Of course. I forgot—you were there."

West tugged at the blanket until it rested just below her breasts. He laid open one half of his coat and stretched the wide neckline of her shift over her shoulder so the bruise he had glimpsed before was laid bare. "Beckwith?"

Her nod was almost imperceptible. She knew he saw it because he looked as if he might be moved to murder. Perhaps he would be, she thought. But not now. Now he was treading carefully, even with her, especially with her. Ria understood they were being observed, but that did not account for every aspect of caution that she sensed in West. He was uncertain of her, she realized. It hurt a little that he could not trust her responses entirely, but she also acknowledged his good sense. She did not think she would give the game away in the event he told her what it was, but she was not sure.

Sir Alex told her this was the place where the bishops

tested one's mettle. He had meant that in a very particular way, but Ria thought it might be true in many others. She removed her hand from West's and raised it to touch his cheek. Her fingers trembled a little, and she felt the weight of the iron cuff, but neither of those things held her back.

"Go on," she whispered. "Whatever you must do, do it before I lose my resolve."

He grasped her hand and brought her knuckles to his mouth. He pressed a kiss there, holding her in just that manner for a long moment before he released her. "Will you sit up?"

She did. Whatever she had expected, it was not that he would throw off the blankets and remove his coat from her shoulders, nor that what he would take from the coat's pocket would be the iron pin that had coupled her cuffs. "What do you mean to do with that?" But even as she asked it, she knew the answer.

West stood and carried the coat to the hook that had so recently secured Ria. It was not often, he supposed, that one of them was used in support of an article of clothing. He stared at it, steadying his breathing, before he returned to the bed.

When he pivoted, he saw that Ria had already pushed herself flush to the headboard. She sat with her hands behind her back, her knees drawn toward her chest, and she was staring warily at his closed fists, trying to determine which one held the pin.

"I won't fight you," she said.

"I know." He felt as if his heart was in a vise. "Can you stand on your own?"

Ria didn't know, and she didn't want to find out. How fast her resolve had crumpled, she thought. He had only to show her the pin. She pushed back the sheet tangled around her ankles and slid her feet over the side of the bed. When she stood, her knees held. Her chin came up a little as she pivoted in West's direction, then fell again when she saw he was no longer standing where she expected him to be.

"Here," he said simply. "I want you here."

Ria blinked. He was beside the cheval glass. It was angled differently now, and when she turned, her full reflection came immediately into view. It was as if she were already standing at his side. She decided she would rather be there in fact than in fiction and closed the distance between them on surprisingly steady legs.

"Here," he said again. "In front of the glass."

Sipping a shallow breath, Ria took a single step sideways.

"Look at yourself, not at me."

With some difficulty, Ria dragged her gaze away from West and looked in the mirror, though not at herself. Her eyes fell on a point past her own shoulder. She could see most of the bed behind her. Her heartbeat tripped over itself, and when she drew her next breath it was too slight to fill her lungs.

West came to stand at her back and placed his hands on her shoulders. When Ria's eyes flew to his, he shook his head and directed her back to her reflection. "Look at my hand." He raised his right one and watched her eyes follow it. She was wondering what he had done with the pin, but he was not prepared to reveal the sleight of hand that had hidden it from her.

Ria fixed her blue-gray glance on West's fingers as they trailed along her collarbone. She felt his touch, but it was as if it were happening to someone else. His hand grazed her skin so lightly it could not properly be called a caress. If touch were sound, then his fingers were whispering.

His index finger trailed along the edge of her neckline, sometimes slipping under the material, scoring her skin lightly with the tip of his nail. He bent his head once and kissed the bruise on her shoulder, then straightened and used both hands to begin removing her shift.

Ria's hands came up. She flinched when she saw the iron cuffs so plainly held in front of her. For a few minutes she had forgotten them, yet here they were, hard and heavy and black, a stark and frightening contrast to the soft, nearly transparent shift.

"Put your hands down," he said.

She lowered them slowly. "It's not because you told me to," she said with quiet dignity. "I'm testing my mettle."

He smiled then. It was faint, briefly held, but it touched his eyes. "I know your mettle." He placed his lips against the pale, silky hair next to her ear and told her that he loved her.

Ria's eyes flew to his, but when he raised his head, he was no longer smiling. Neither was he catching her glance in the mirror. His eyes were on the lowered neckline of her shift. She looked down at herself, then at her reflection. He eased the material over her breasts, first the high, full curve, then the puckered aureoles. The shift fell to her waist, but his hands stayed where they were, cupping her breasts. His thumbs passed over the tender nipples, teasing them to full arousal. She sagged a little in his arms, moaning softly as a measure of heat began to uncurl inside her. Her eyes fluttered closed.

"No," he said. His hands quieted. "Watch."

It was with no small effort that she lifted her lashes and stared at the images in the mirror. Her breasts felt heavy; they fairly filled his palms. She wondered what it would be like to see his mouth there, to watch him suckle her, to feel the draw of his tongue and teeth at the same moment she was seeing his lips on her flesh. Her breath hitched.

His hands slid from her breasts to her waist and rested on the curve of her hips. His fingers were long and slender, the nails buffed and squared off. Her skin pinkened where his fingertips pressed. He made no comment about the bruises that were just becoming visible on her thigh and below her rib cage, but Ria did not miss the way his hand paused as it passed over this evidence of abuse. Afraid of what she might see in his eyes, she did not glance in that direction.

Instead, she watched him lift his hands so that her shift could complete its descent to the floor. She stepped out of the cloud of fabric at her feet when he ordered her to, though she was hardly aware of doing so. She didn't notice that he pushed it away with the toe of his boot.

West's hands dropped to his sides, but he supported Ria

solidly when she leaned into him. The curve of her bottom rested snugly against his thighs; the crown of her head fit under his chin. Judging by the darkening centers of her eyes and the vaguely disquieted gaze, West doubted she had ever studied herself in so frank a fashion before.

"Lift your hands."

Ria blinked. She watched threads of her hair ripple as her body fairly vibrated in response to West's uninflected command. She raised her hands slowly to the level of her breasts and crossed them at the wrists in the manner she knew he would ask her to. She saw him rake back his hair with his fingers, then the pin was there in his hand again, and he was slipping it between the cuffs, coupling them just as Sir Alex had.

"Come," he said.

She hesitated, uncertain where he meant for her to go. He had stepped away from her but not indicated a direction.

"The bed."

Ria glanced back at the bed, quite certain she could not retrace her steps to it. She gasped softly as the choice was taken from her. West lifted her off her feet and carried her the short distance. He laid her down, then pulled the pillow from under her head.

"Lift your hips."

Biting her lower lip hard enough to draw blood, Ria concentrated on that pain instead of what she was doing. She did not know the pillow was under her until she felt the gentle, insistent pressure of West's hand on her hip, pushing her down. Her skin retracted as his palm ran up the flat of her abdomen and came to rest between her breasts. He slipped his fingers under her linked wrists and raised them.

"What are you—" Ria cut off her question, craning her head around to see the truth herself. Embedded in the headboard was a hook like all the others in the room. It would be like the illustration in Beckwith's book, she realized. That was how he had known the hook was there. He meant to fix her wrists to the headboard, spread her thighs, and climb between them. Even the pillow was positioned exactly as it had been in the drawing.

Ria understood then that it was Beckwith's specific commands that were guiding West. This performance was for him, perhaps for him alone.

Looking back at West, seeing the small muscle jump in his cheek, Ria offered no resistance as he attached the cuffs. She thought of his purpose again in disrobing her in front of the cheval glass and drawing her attention to his hands at her throat, on her breasts, and caressing the curve of her hip and inner thigh. He had made her the observer, taught her how to watch what he was doing to her almost as if it were happening to someone else. That is how she would survive this, she thought. That was what West had given her, a means to survive.

Seen through the lens of her mind's eye, there would only ever be two of them in this room.

Ria closed her eyes as West ran his fingers along her arm, grazing the soft, sensitive underside of her elbow. A small shiver slipped under her skin. She felt a wave of tension come and go and a certain heaviness, not entirely unpleasant, settle over her limbs. It was as if she was bound by nothing more than his touch now, the weight of his palm on her shoulder, cupping her breast, her heartbeat, laying a trail across her skin that ended with his fingers slipping between her thighs.

"Open for me."

Lifting one knee, Ria did exactly that. She did not try to avoid this caress, but gave herself up to it instead. If it was inevitable that he would be forced to take her, then this was in aid of not hurting her, and she felt herself respond to the steady, insistent pressure of his stroking fingers.

Surrendering, she became aware of the first stirrings of wanting. Her hips lifted a fraction. Between her thighs, she was wet. There were times when the heat of his fingertips was almost too much to bear, then his touch would ease and give her a moment's respite.

She opened heavy-lidded eyes and watched him from beneath the fan of her lashes. His features were set, remote, and in startling contrast to the warmth he provoked in her, they were cold. Ria would have reached for him if she'd been allowed the freedom to do so. She would have laid her hand across his cheek and erased the lines at the corners of his grim mouth and the terrible chill from his eyes. What she did was show him her own naked need; in submitting to him now, lay her strength.

She felt her breath catch as he slipped one finger inside her. She held it for a moment, contracting around him, then did the same a moment later when the first was joined by another. Her heels made small crescents in the sheets as she found purchase there and rocked her hips. It was not always easy to know what she invited and what she could not help, but in the end, Ria supposed it did not matter.

She no longer felt unprotected; West had made her feel desired beyond all reason. It was all she could do not to cry out when he removed his hand and got to his feet.

Standing at the bedside, West began to loosen his stock. He glanced upward as a smattering of raindrops tapped the roof. Through the skylight, starshine caught his eye, and he glimpsed the cluster that was Cassiopeia. More rain pinged lightly off the glass. He glanced back at Ria and saw that her darkening eyes were still vaguely focused on him. She seemed wholly unaware of the approaching storm.

West tossed his neckcloth to the foot of the bed and unbuttoned his waistcoat. He shrugged out of it and let it drop beside the neckcloth. Tugging on his linen shirt, he pulled it free of his trousers, then yanked it over his head. Instead of pitching it aside, he snapped it once, spreading it open, then let it fall so that it draped Ria from her breasts to her thighs.

As his shirt drifted over her, Ria caught the faint change in the tilt of West's mouth. The line of it was still grim, to be sure, but there was something else there as well—a certain dark humor that was finally asserting itself. Like the flicker of candlelight across his face, what she thought she saw there passed very quickly. She wondered at it for all the time it took to come and go, then did not think on it again. She lay under the fine linen fabric of his shirt, wrapped in his fragrance, the very breath of him, and waited for him to come to her in just such a way, so that it was not the linen against her skin, but him.

West unfastened the buttons at his fly, then sat on the edge of the bed. He paused, considering the problem of his boots, and decided against removing them. Stretching out beside Ria, he used his body to shield her from the view of the hidden panel—then, a moment later, from the shattering, splintering, shower of glass.

Shards of the broken skylight scattered across his scarred back, but West had barely any feeling for the pain. He held Ria protectively in his arms, covering her with his broad shoulders and torso until the rain of glass and pebbles ended. In quick succession he heard the panel being slammed shut, the sough of the wind overhead, profanity and pounding in the adjoining room, then a friendly, familiar voice calling from above.

"I say, West, the decent thing to do would be to avert my eyes, but I'll break my neck in the fall if I do."

"South." West identified the voice for Ria in the event she couldn't. To his friend, he called, "Miss Parr will break your neck if you don't."

"Right," South said. "Looking away now."

West sat up and quickly released Ria's wrist cuffs, first from the hook, then from each other. He helped her sit up and briskly massaged her stiff arms before he pulled his shirt over her head. She was shivering now, partly in response to the eddy of cold air that whipped into the room from the opening in the roof, but perhaps more so from the shattering skylight and the astonishing fact that South was standing above them.

Dazed, but game, Ria allowed herself to be dressed first in West's shirt, then his frock coat. Holding onto his arm, she got her legs under her and rose to her knees as he swept aside pieces of glass. When he stood, she followed, even though he would have had her stay where she was.

"I'm not letting you go," she said. She wobbled a bit on her bare feet, her long legs as uncertain in their first steps as a foal's.

West lifted her so she would not be cut on the glass and set her down only when he reached the fireplace. "Clear!" he shouted up to South.

Almost immediately, the viscount was tumbling through the opening. He hung from the lip of the skylight's wooden frame for a moment, then released his grip and landed rather lightly on his feet. Except for broken glass crunching beneath his boots, he had swooped as quietly as a bird of prey. He brushed his hands off and regarded West with satisfaction at having accomplished the thing so neatly. Making a small bow to Ria while keeping his eyes politely on her face, he asked, "You are all of a piece, Miss Ashby?"

She blinked widely, but found she had pluck enough left to nod.

"Good." He glanced at West. "You can get us out?"

"Now I can." He reached inside his boot and recovered his knife. Handing Ria over to South, West hunkered in front of the door to the adjoining room and slid his blade along the crack in the panel until it caught the latch bolt. He wriggled the slim steel blade back and forth a few times before it smoothly depressed the latch.

The paneled door gave way, opening a few narrow inches. West threw it open the rest of the way. "Beckwith fled as soon as the skylight shattered," he told South. "Where are North and East?"

"Waiting for us to stir these bishops from their nest."

"You have a weapon?"

South unbuttoned his coat and pointed to the butt of a whip handle poking above the waistband of his trousers. He took it out with something of a flourish, snapping it once to show the long, supple lash. "It seemed fitting somehow."

"Indeed." West looked to Ria. "Give me your wrists."

She held out her hands and marveled at their steadiness as West used his blade to try to remove the cuffs. She concluded before he did that his knife would not do the trick. "It's of no import," she told him, letting one hand fall and waiting for him to release the other. "They present no deterrent to leaving this place."

West looked to South for guidance, but his friend merely shrugged. "Very well," he said reluctantly, knowing they could ill afford to take more time in the task. "You will stay close behind us."

"Of course." Before either of the men could stop her, Ria ducked back into the room where she had been a prisoner and began twisting the nearest hook from the wall. South saw immediately what she was about and began to help her turn the screw.

"Bloody hell," West said. "What are you doing?"

"Weapon," Ria told him succinctly. She regarded him pointedly, daring him to tell her she couldn't have it, all the while twisting the hook with South's assistance.

Expecting no sympathy from Southerton, West did not even look for it. Instead, he used his knife to loosen the paneling around the hook so they could turn it more quickly. Once Ria had it in hand, he led them into the adjoining chamber. To be safe, he checked the dark cubicle where he had been forced to watch Sir Alex restrain and fondle Ria. It was empty. Beckwith had indeed not chosen to cower there, running instead.

They moved out of the room with the sapphire chaise and blood-red drapes and into a narrow hallway at the top of the stairwell. There were no other rooms on this attic floor, and the three of them hurried down the steep stairs. In the hall below, West ordered Ria to stay by the landing while he and South went room to room along the corridor looking for Herndon, Cotton, Beckwith, or any other of the bishops who were still about.

They found one girl kneeling at the apron of a fireplace,

tethered there by a slim leather collar and chain attached to an iron ring in the bricks. She had been left unattended for so long that her forearms and the back of her hands sported tiny burns and blisters where popping embers had caught her skin. Her chemise was speckled with ash and a host of small holes where flames had licked the fabric. West sawed through the leather collar with his knife, and South escorted the girl to Ria for shelter.

"Sylvia," Ria said gently. She took the dazed young woman into her fiercely protective embrace, and they stood in just that manner until they were joined by Mary Murdoch, then Amanda Kent. "What of Jane?" she asked them.

But none of them knew, or if they did, they were too afraid to say. They huddled around Ria, but she sensed it was a fragile bond. She caught their fearful, darting looks toward the stairs as if they anticipated a sudden surge of bishops from the floor below. Ria realized she could not depend upon them to help themselves. Obedience and fear had been too well ingrained.

When West and Southerton returned, she regarded them more determinedly than before. "What of the bishops?"

West and South exchanged looks. "Two are in hand," West said carefully. South had trussed a corpulent baron over a padded bench so the man's pink arse was raised like the tender hindquarters of a roasted pig. Another bishop caught with pants below his nether regions was now hoisted upon the same hook that had held his much younger victim. "You will not want to see."

Ria was not so certain. "Jane?" she asked.

West shook his head.

"And Sir Alex?"

"Not yet. Nor Beckwith, either. If they fled by the front or rear of the house, North and East will have already reeled them in."

Ria nodded, but she was not as certain of it as West. She took her cue from the young women around her, who still plainly feared some reprisal. She communicated this to West with a single sweeping glance, first at the girls, then in the direction of the stairs.

Using his knife to indicate what he wanted South to do, West led the way downstairs, and this time South brought up the rear behind Ria and the girls. It did not take them long to determine that the ground floor had already been abandoned. Ria ushered her charges into the relative sanctuary of the humid conservatory while South and West opened the doors for Eastlyn at the front of the house and Northam at the rear.

Eastlyn had two liveried footmen in tow, but he let them go before he came inside. North had chased all the fleeing servants away once he was certain there were no bishops hiding among them.

"Where is Miss Ashby?" East asked.

"Caring for the girls we found. She is with them in the conservatory."

"Of course," Northam said. "The Flower House."

"Herndon's idea," West told them. "I've learned more than I want to know about this place since I left you. The academy's board of governors made a point of educating me, but you will have to wait to hear it. South and I only came upon two. They're secured above stairs, but every one of them was here earlier. Beckwith was in the garret when South made his theatrical entrance."

South shrugged. "Miss Parr's influence." He pointed to North. "And when we realized it was the best way to gain admittance, he dared me."

West held up his hand, enough said. "The girls are frightened. One of them has burns that require attention—all of them have been hurt in ways that defy explanation and reason. I don't know if they can be persuaded to give up the bishops, but it is probably true that they know where they've gone. Jane Petty is still missing." He regarded the others frankly. "Beckwith wanted to negotiate for the colonel. That was the price the Society was asking for Miss Ashby's release." His voice grew a shade rougher. "That, and something else besides." West said nothing else regarding the other demand and knew that South would never repeat any part of what he had witnessed through the skylight. "Give me a moment to speak to Miss Ashby. Then we will plan a strategy to search the house a second time."

When West was out of hearing, Northam said, "He looks as if he's seen hell."

"He has," South said quietly. "And leaving here won't put the demons behind him."

Ria met West just as he entered the conservatory. He looked past her shoulder to where Mary and Amanda shared a stone bench, surrounded by pots of orchids and tall grasses. They were also sharing his frock coat. He frowned at that, but knew better than to suppose Ria could have done differently. Sylvia Jenner sat on a cushion at the feet of the other two, her legs drawn up to her chest. She had the back of one burned hand pressed to her lips and the other deep inside a watering can. There was a ragged bandage around one forearm, and the uneven tail of West's shirt flapping just above Ria's knees told the rest of the story.

She held out her hands to him, and he took them in his, squeezing lightly, rubbing the backs with his thumbs. Reassurance, though, was not one-sided, but mutual.

"What have they told you?" he asked.

"Precious little. They think the governors will return for them."

"Return? Do you mean there was a way out we didn't know existed?"

"I'm not certain. I have the sense the girls think they're still here. There are more girls missing than Jane. Sylvia told me there are six others. I know she is just as afraid of what will become of them."

"Ria." West said her name firmly, brooking no argument. "You must discover where they think the bishops have gone. If you can't, I will."

"No," she said quickly. "No, I'll do it. They're afraid of you."

"Me?"

Ria's faint smile was gentle. "You're half naked," she reminded him, "and you're carrying a knife. It gives one pause."

He hauled her against him hard and buried his face in her hair. He whispered at her ear, his voice low and urgent, and the words that tumbled from his lips were barely intelligible, even to him. It didn't matter if she understood what he said—the embrace communicated all of that and more.

Across the conservatory, Mary and Amanda exchanged glances, then shared the same with Sylvia. If Miss Ashby trusted the bedlamite so completely that she would risk being crushed in his arms, could they do any less?

West disengaged himself from the embrace reluctantly. He could feel the pressure of time passing in the quickening of his heartbeat. Here was urgency that could not be dismissed. "Talk to them," he said. "I will be outside with the others."

She nodded and waited for him to go.

The rest of the Compass Club had come to stand in the hall on the other side of the door. South held out a shirt to West. "Courtesy of the baron. It will be too big, of course—the man is a swine in so many ways—but it will serve."

West thanked him and handed over his blade until he put the shirt on and tucked it in. It billowed around his waist anyway. "Ria says the young ladies are afraid of me."

"I shouldn't wonder," Eastlyn told him. "I'm afraid of you."

With some effort, West managed a wry smile. He glanced at the pistol East held in his hand. "Primed?"

"It doesn't do much good if it isn't."

Nodding, West's attention swiveled to North. "You won't get shot, will you?"

Northam merely grinned and revealed his own pistol. "Where do we begin our search?"

"A moment yet," West told him. "Ria is questioning the girls again. If they do not tell . . ." He let his voice trail off. They knew well enough what he would be forced to do if that was the case.

It seemed that a long time passed before the door to the conservatory opened, but the true reckoning was that it was less than two minutes. Ria felt the expectant eyes of every one of them as she stepped into the hallway.

South saw she had given up West's frock coat, and he quickly stripped off his and offered it to her. "Where are they?"

"Below stairs," she said, pulling the coat around her shoulders like a cape.

"The kitchen?" West asked.

"No. Below that. The girls say there is a large room deeper underground."

"Another way out?"

"They don't think so. They have never seen anyone leave by any means except the way they entered." Her flint-colored eyes darted between West and Southerton because she knew they would understand her reference. "It is the altar chamber."

West nodded gravely. "I wondered why we did not come upon it before." He explained to Northam and Eastlyn what they could expect to find there, but it was Ria who described the purpose of the chamber.

Northam shook his head slowly when she concluded. Candlelight glanced off his bright yellow hair. "It is yet another circle of hell."

"One Dante neglected to mention," East said.

Agreeing with these observations, South added, "How do we find it?"

"I will show you." It was not quite true that soldier, sailor, tinker, and spy gaped at her, but it was a narrow thing. "You will not find it without me."

West took a steadying breath. "Time is of import here," he told her. "Give us the directions the girls shared."

"Come," she said, starting to walk away from them. "I swear to you it will be quicker this way."

West looked as if he might argue. It was North who put a light restraining hand on his shoulder and cautioned him against it. With little choice left to them, they followed her. She led them toward the rear of the house and down a poorly lighted staircase to the large kitchen. The oven had been fired earlier and left to die when the servants abandoned their posts. The aroma of rising bread filled the room. A clutter of utensils lay on the cutting block beside a basket of eggs. A kettle of soup bubbled in the open hearth.

"Mary told me the kitchen is always in use," Ria explained. "It is because of the hours the bishops keep. Everything must be in readiness for them at all times."

West knew the girls were subject to the same demands. He suspected his friends required no further explanation to arrive at the same conclusion. When he glanced around and saw their grim faces, he took it as confirmation that they had.

Ria lifted a lamp from the scarred oak table and lighted it. She held it up as she led the others out of the kitchen and through the pantry, scullery, and ironing room. She stopped when they came upon a door heavily embellished with carvings of clusters of grapes along the frame. The center panel was a deep relief of the Greek god Dionysus overseeing a harvest celebration in his honor. The revelers around him danced and drank and, in some exquisitely lewd examples of artistic liberty, debauched.

Ria turned her back on the door quickly and groped behind her for the handle. "The wine storage," she said unnecessarily, unable to quite meet anyone's eye. "We must go through here."

West reached around her for the handle before she could twist it. "Let me go first."

She surrendered the lead without argument and stepped inside the cool, slightly damp interior of the room only after West indicated that she could. At East's request, she raised the lamp higher so they could see the interior more clearly.

There were long racks of wine, four deep at the center of the room. From floor to ceiling, the walls were lined with still more racks, most of them holding the full complement of bottles.

"Dionysus, indeed," Eastlyn said under his breath. "I do not think even Prinny has such a collection." He gave the room a second cursory glance. "But where now? There is no other exit."

"There is," Ria said. "This way." She brushed past West and went to the wall of wine opposite the door. The floor was cold on her bare feet and the lamp shook slightly in her hand. She was grateful when North relieved her of it. "Forty-three and thirteen," she told them. "We must count, starting from the left, then down that row from the ceiling."

West came upon the bottle first. He put his hand on the neck and waited for the others to confirm it was the correct one. "Do I pull it out? Or twist?"

Ria shrugged uncertainly. "I don't know."

Examining the clearance in the room, trying to determine if the rack would swing in or out, or perhaps slide sideways, West made his decision quickly. He pushed the bottle in. They all heard the telltale click. It was the last sound they clearly caught. Once the secret panel opened a mere fraction of an inch, the cries and shouts from the other side deafened them to even the sound of their own thoughts.

West glanced back at the others and saw they were prepared to advance. North pressed the lamp into Ria's hand again, and she had to give ground as he and the others stepped in front of her. Satisfied that she was protected in that way, West gave the nod that they would move ahead.

"I should rather like to flatten one of these bishops," he said over the din, harkening them all back to their Hambrick Hall days.

South grinned. "Brilliant."

"Excellent," East agreed.

"Top drawer," North said. "Really, top drawer."

West pushed the panel harder. It swung another foot into the adjoining room, then began to slide sideways. The activity in The Flower House's deepest chamber subsided slowly as North, South, East, and West filled the threshold shoulder to shoulder.

Nothing they had seen, heard, or knew from their own experience prepared them for the tableau they were facing now. Behind them, they heard Ria's sharp intake of breath and realized at once they had neglected to fully protect her from the view.

Jane Petty was at the center of the marble temple, positioned on the altar as a sacrifice, her arms and legs secured by short gold-plated chains. A wide collar of beaten gold was attached to a ring in the altar so that she could not lift her head, nor easily turn it to the side. The thin pink lines crisscrossing her pale skin and the delicate batiste fabric lying in shreds around her were proof that a lash had been used repeatedly to strip her of her gown.

At each corner of the altar were Jane's handmaidens. Their gold bracelets were fastened to iron rings in the marble base. They knelt in attitudes of prayer on the smooth, cold floor, their drawn features tearstained but stoic. The fluted marble column, with its Ionic influence at the capital and base, supported another young woman, who was stretched so tautly by her bonds that her toes barely scraped the floor. The chamber's final female occupant was seated on a bench, untethered by any chains or rings or straps, but positioned in a way that she was forced to detach herself from the drama and watch it as one of the audience.

The bishops were almost unrecognizable in their dark-ruby cassocks and full-head masks, every one of them a likeness of a beast. They stood in various postures of astonishment, some with their arms thrown up, others trying to shield their shriveling erections, all of them breathing hard enough to mimic the great snorting beasts they had imagined themselves to be.

Lord Herndon stood beside the column, his right hand still on the tender, pink-tipped breast of his captive. West recognized that long-fingered, rather fragile-looking appendage as the same one he'd seen stroking the delicate orchid petals in his conservatory.

Sir Alex Cotton stood at the head of the altar. He continued to absently stroke Jane's fine silky hair, his fingers curved like talons against her scalp, while his distinguishing blue eyes stared fixedly from behind a falcon's mask.

It was Beckwith who had wielded the whip. He stood at the back of the altar, his cassock open from collar to cock, his hand hovering at the level of his ram's head, the wrist poised to snap and strike. The lash dangled darkly from the end of the handle, twisting like a serpent until it lay still.

So this is where they'd fled to, West thought. At South's entrance, Beckwith had raised the alarm, and those who could move swiftly to this hellish sanctuary had done so. It was not entirely clear if this theatre of venal indulgence was the desperate final act of men in expectation of being cornered, or if the bishops were celebrating their narrow escape. West believed it was probably the latter. It was not like the Society to anticipate defeat. If further proof was required, it lay in the fact that there was no avenue of escape from the room.

Ria wanted to hold West where he stood. Her hand hovered near the small of his back, and she could feel the faint tremor in her fingers as she fought the urge to grab a fistful of his shirt. She would not do it, though. She understood his need to go forward and take them on. It was no different for the others. All four of them were fairly vibrating on the threshold, their rage all the more terrible because it was restrained with such consummate confidence.

At Hambrick, she remembered, West and his friends had

gone looking for a fight when one found them. This time they would strike first, spreading out like the points of the compass they had always meant to be. Ria held her breath as she watched them go.

The bishops were six strong. Not one of the young women could be depended upon to assist in their defeat.

It hardly seemed fair, she thought, then she realized she should have known better. To level the playing field, the Compass Club paused in their tracks and divested themselves of their weapons, handing them over to her.

Soldier. Sailor. Tinker. They waited as one until the spy among them planted the first facer. When Beckwith's ram's head crumpled under the force of West's blow, they threw themselves into the fray.

Epilogue

It was still in the earliest hour of the morning when Ria and West arrived at his residence. The sun had not yet appeared above the horizon, but a thin carpet of light was already spreading across London rooftops in advance of it.

West waved off his friends as he and Ria mounted the steps to his home. He wasn't surprised when they remained hovering on the walk until he had Ria safely on the other side of the door.

The foyer was crowded with servants in varying states of wakefulness. Some had positioned themselves in an awkward recline on the stairs. Two were sitting on the floor with their legs drawn up, their heads lolling uncomfortably to the side. Finch was sharing a small bench with the rather large housekeeper. They remained upright by supporting each other shoulder to shoulder.

It was the butler who responded to the summons at the door. He clapped his hands smartly, rousing all of the employees in his charge to alertness, and offered West a rather stiff, though not embarrassed, explanation of the vigil.

"They needed to know Your Grace was safely returned," Mr. Blaine said. "And there was particular concern about Miss Ashby."

West and Ria were not so bone-weary that they were not touched by this welcome, though giving voice to their appreciation was considerably more difficult. They managed to smile through the haze of their exhaustion, but for those who had spent a restless, uncertain night in waiting, it was as if twin suns had broken the horizon.

With morning clearly upon them, the servants quickly dispersed and took up their tasks as the butler and housekeeper assigned them. A maid ran ahead of West and Ria to turn down their beds, while Finch closely followed their slow ascent up the stairs as though he anticipated having to catch one or both of them.

West escorted Ria to the chamber that was made ready for her, then stood in the doorway until she simply dropped onto the bed. He was quite certain she was asleep before her eyes were properly closed. Satisfied that she would rest soundly for a few hours at least, West left her under the care of one of the maids and accepted Finch's directive to retire to his own room.

Almost as boneless as Ria, West found it hard not to collapse in a heap on the bed as she had. He managed to keep himself upright while Finch removed his boots, though in the end he was propped on his elbows in a half recline. "Do you think the servants noticed Miss Ashby's unconventional attire?"

Finch set the second boot down and straightened. "I'm uncertain what you mean, Your Grace. In what way was she not the first stare of fashion?"

West found he still had the wherewithal to chuckle. He took it as an encouraging sign that his world was slowly righting itself on its axis. There had been some attempt to find Ria's clothing before leaving The Flower House, but the search had given them nothing. She had arrived on his arm, still wearing his shirt and South's coat, bare legged and barefoot. He had wanted to carry her up the walk, then later up the stairs, but she had refused those offers of assistance and demonstrated she could not only carry herself, but could do so with the bearing of one of the royal family. Given so much regal confidence, perhaps it was true that none of the servants had noticed the state of her clothing, or perhaps it was truer that it was of no consequence.

"You're a good man, Finch," West said.

"Your Grace is kind to say so." Finch plumped two pillows and helped West stretch lengthwise along the bed. "How long will you wish to sleep?" When there was no reply forthcoming, Finch simply drew the comforter over his employer, closed the drapes, then quietly backed out of the room.

The faint scent of lavender made his nose twitch. Silky threads of the fragrance touched his cheek and lips. When he opened his mouth, he could taste it on his tongue.

Smiling sleepily, he nuzzled the crown of Ria's head with his chin. His day's growth of beard rasped pleasantly against her hair. Untested by hours of sleep, his voice was edged by its own soft rasp. "You shouldn't be here."

Ria burrowed more deeply into him, finding the perfect fit for her bottom against the curve of his groin and thighs. "Throw me out."

West slipped an arm around her waist instead. She was no longer wearing the frock coat, but it was still his fine linen shirt that was next to her skin. He could tell she had recently bathed. Her hair was lightly damp and the warm fragrance of the salts clung to her. "Was no one sent to Oxford Street to retrieve your clothes?"

"Yes."

When she offered nothing else, West merely pressed his smile against her hair. He heard her soft sigh, felt the last traces of tension slip away, then the even rise and fall of her gentle breathing. In moments he was deeply asleep beside her.

* * *

It was the steady tattoo of dripping water that woke Ria. West was no longer beside her, nor was he in the room. The heavy damask drapes were still drawn, but by the slender beam of pale light slipping through a part in the panels, she saw that dusk was already upon them. Except for a single, brief bout of wakefulness, Ria realized she had slept almost the entire day.

She stretched and felt the ache of inactivity in every one of her muscles. Reaching behind her, Ria found West's pillow. She lifted it over her shoulder so she could hug it to her chest. It did not seem possible that he could have left the bed without her sensing it immediately, but the coolness of the pillow sham attested to the fact that he had been gone for more than a few minutes.

The dripping water that had disturbed her dreams and drawn her slowly out of sleep, caught her attention again. Over the top of the crumpled pillow, Ria's blue-gray eyes darted to the source of the sound. The adjoining dressing room door was slightly ajar. She lifted her head, cocked it to one side, and when the next droplet of water splattered the floor, she knew where it had come from.

West had lowered himself so deeply in the water that it lapped at his Adam's apple. His head rested against the lip of the copper tub; his eyes were closed. One arm rested along the edge, and a wet flannel dangled from his fingertips. Another bead of water was collecting at the tip of the cloth and in mere seconds would become part of the small puddle forming below.

Ria snatched the flannel from West's hand and wrung it out directly over his face. Water splashed his forehead and cheeks. A fat droplet landed squarely on his bottom lip.

"Do you mean to be annoying?" he asked calmly enough. "Or is it simply that you cannot help yourself?"

Snapping the flannel open, Ria let it fall on his upturned face. By the time he had removed it and opened his eyes, she had his shirt over her head and was preparing to join him in the tub.

"It will be a squeeze," he said.

"I hope so."

Grinning, West sat up and made room for her. Water sloshed over the sides as she lowered herself between his thighs. She rested her hands on his knees and her head against his shoulder. A thin film of warm water was all that separated them.

Ria welcomed being held in the intimate shelter of his body. When the water stilled, there was only the gentle sound of his breathing and the steady beat of his heart at her back. In this warm and liquid cocoon, she finally felt safe enough to ask what she could not earlier. "Last night was not the end of the bishops, was it?"

"No. Hambrick Hall is a spawning ground for the Society. There will always be bishops."

"And perhaps others like you and your friends?"

"Sworn enemies? Yes, I hope so."

"When will you release them from the altar chamber?" she asked.

"When Miss Petty and the other young ladies decide that I should."

"Oh, but they might never—"

West nodded gravely. "Precisely."

She tried to gauge how seriously he meant his words but could not. "When did you decide this?"

"When you were tending to Miss Petty and the other girls, and my friends and I were cleaning up the mess we made. Beckwith spilled a lot of blood when I smashed his nose. I didn't think it sporting to let him drown in it. Herndon had a nasty scalp wound where North cracked him against the marble column. Those bleed like the very devil, you know. And, courtesy of South, Sir Alex lost two teeth. I am not certain what injuries Eastlyn produced in the others, but he seemed to be enjoying using his fists for a change."

Ria had been witness to all of it. She knew she could not have turned away if it had been demanded of her. East *had* been enjoying himself, and it was equally true of the others.

There was no denying that she had found a certain satisfaction in the crushing blows that forced the bishops to their knees. When any one of them tried to get to the entrance she guarded, she smartly snapped South's whip until she drove them back into the fray. Had they attempted to rush her, she was quite confident she could have used East's pistol.

Still, she was not certain about the punishment that was being meted out now. "North and the others agreed with you . . . about imprisoning the bishops there, I mean?"

"Yes. It's not unjust, Ria. I am not convinced it is even cruel. They will be watered and fed. That is more compassion than I think they ever demonstrated for the young women they held captive." He laid his hands on her shoulders and lightly massaged the taut cords in her back. "You know better than any of us what manner of things passed for entertainment inside The Flower House."

"I do," she said quietly. "But I think you mistake my concern. It is not for the bishops, but for their keepers. They will be in danger each time they enter the altar room to pass food and water to their prisoners."

"The bishops are not free to make any advances."

"What do you mean?"

"Hoist with their own petard." At her questioning look, West explained, "They are chained, Ria, and I am quite sure that is a fitting end. I do not expect that Jane or any of the others will suggest granting the bishops their freedom before a sennight passes."

"What if they lose their nerve? Beckwith is clever. So are the others. Poor Jane believed Sir Alex was in love with her. It is not beyond her reasoning to think that she is still in love with him. The bishops are prisoners for the time being, but you must entertain the notion that one of the girls can be induced to release them, even if she does not believe it of herself now."

West's hands paused in their gentle massage of Ria's back. "We have considered that. That is why the colonel will be sending reinforcements to The Flower House. Northam was to make the arrangements after he and the others escorted us to this residence. I am certain everything has been made ready. The young ladies you calmed and cared for so splendidly last evening will have nothing at all to do with their former tormentors. The bishops will be looked after by others whose hearts will not be softened so easily."

Ria raised one shoulder under West's hand, reminding him his fingers were no longer offering their comforting pressure along her back. She sighed softly as he began kneading again. "I think it will not be easy for the girls to have other men in the house. The ones who witnessed the melee you created in the altar chamber will be especially suspicious."

"That is why North will ask the colonel to send women."

Ria was so startled by this intelligence that the water rippled around her. "Women? Do you mean it?"

"Pray, do not embrace the idea too closely. I am not yet recovered from the intrigues of the past two days, and frankly, I should like to be the one member of my club who does not have to concern himself that his wife and the colonel have formed some unholy alliance."

"I do not think it would be unholy," she said mildly. "Colonel Blackwood is quite charming and everything considerate. He has a superior intellect and an acerbic wit that I find vastly entertaining."

West was certain that the nature of her reply would bode ill for him at some future date. His sigh was perfectly audible and quite telling. "I don't suppose I should like you half so well if you weren't so provoking."

"Provoking? Do you think so? I don't mean to be."

"You are also a consummate liar, but it is one of your chief appeals."

She chuckled and brought his arms around her. They fit nicely under her breasts. "I have been thinking that some arrangements will have to be made for Jane, Sylvia, Amanda—indeed, for all the girls. Their lives are extraordinarily changed. I would like to offer them opportunities different from the ones the Society gave them."

"Some will still become courtesans and prostitutes."

Ria nodded. "I know." She idly ran one hand back and forth along West's forearm. "It will require a goodly sum to provide for the ones who will want to do something else. Decent homes in respectable areas of town will not come cheaply."

"That is why the former governors of Miss Weaver's Academy will lend their considerable fortunes to the enterprise."

"Truly? Can they be made to do it?"

"Of course. I suspect after a few days of confinement, they will contribute generously to the rehabilitation of your young ladies."

"And after they are released?" she asked. "Can we depend on them to honor their promises?"

"No. What you can depend upon is that certain pressure will be brought to bear to encourage that they act honorably."

Ria was sure there was a great deal he was not saying. She might ask for the details later, she thought, but not now. Some things she was not prepared to know just yet. "None of this can touch the school, West. They must not be allowed to ruin Miss Weaver's or the reputations of its students."

"Before I left Gillhollow the last time, I arranged with Tenley that he should look after you and the school. Margaret was also apprised of my concerns. Their visits to Gillhollow had more than a single purpose."

"You were watching me so closely even then?"

"Especially then," he said. "Ria, the first thing I did when I realized Miss Jenny Taylor was in the employ of the bishops was to inform my brother. I am confident that he has received the missive by now and has acted accordingly. You can be assured that Miss Taylor has been removed from the school and that Mrs. Abergast and Miss Webster are providing direction in your absence."

"You have considered the whole of it, then."

"I wish I were so omniscient, but we have made a good beginning."

Ria hugged him to her. It seemed that they had. She appreciated the comfortable silence that settled over them. The water was still warm, though perhaps a few degrees cooler than the heat they shared between them. After a time, she said quietly, "This is my second bath today."

"I know. You came to my bed smelling of lavender."

"Did I? Perhaps I was too liberal in using the salts. I wanted to wash away the stench of that wretched place."

Though Ria said these words matter-of-factly, without rancor or particular distaste, West found himself tightening his arms ever so slightly around her. "You cannot know how I wish it might have been different."

"I think I do know that," she told him. "Will you be surprised to learn that my only regret will be if you hold yourself responsible?" She felt, rather than heard, his sharp intake of breath. "Did you imagine I would not know? When they made you come to me and would have watched while you lay with me, I knew which of us would suffer more. You were so gentle, even when you coupled the cuffs, even more when you fastened them to the bed." She found his hand and took it in hers, drawing it beneath the water toward her heart. "I was never afraid of you, West, only afraid for you . . . for us. It would not have been rape, not between you and me. If that act was done, then it was done by the bishops to both of us, but I do not think they succeeded in any measure. They had a great deal of understanding about mastery and submission and none at all about how love bridges the distance between them."

She twisted her head a little, raising it so she could see if the grim line of his mouth had softened. "I wanted you, you know. Perhaps I reveal too much by admitting it, but I did. When you called me to stand in front of the mirror and put your hands on me, you showed me then how I might survive what they wanted. You made it seem as if it were happening to someone else, that I was more observer than participant, and yet it *was* me . . . and you . . . and the desire was as real as anything I have ever felt. Should I punish myself for that?"

"No." West closed his eyes briefly. "God, no."

"What about you?"

This time West hesitated.

Ria's fingers threaded in his. "See? You do not yet forgive yourself. You saved me, West, just as surely as you did that long-ago afternoon at the lake. You did not deserve to be punished for what you did then, nor do you deserve it now." She kissed his cheek, then whispered against his ear, "Mayhap it is something that can be washed away. What have you done with the soap?"

West stayed her hand. He stared at her darkening blue-gray eyes for a long moment, took in the sweet offering of her parted lips, the frank and unashamed desire that defined her exquisite features, and thought how utterly uncomplicated she made it all seem.

Perhaps it truly was.

He released her wrist and reached over the side of the tub for the soap. Smiling a trifle crookedly, he placed it in her open palm and watched her fingers curl around it. At the very first touch of its slippery warmth, he thought he would be undone.

They were heedless of the water that splashed over the side or that when there was laughter, it could be heard well beyond the bedchamber. Their bodies were made slick by the soap, and they moved easily against each other with no regard for friction or the restrictions of their setting, tangling arms and legs in ways that made them catch their breath with the sheer pleasure of it.

Dripping water in their wake, they abandoned the tub for the bed. Under the covers, Ria lay fully on top of West, pinning him down with her slight weight and the circle of her fingers around his wrists. She drew his hands upward to the level of his shoulders and lifted her head so she could look clearly into his eyes.

"Do you know," she said, "that your friend South has the most lamentable timing?"

"You are speaking of when he broke the skylight."

She nodded, absently rubbing the raised tendons in his wrists with her thumbs. "But I think you knew he was there, didn't you?"

"Yes."

"How? I looked up when I heard the first raindrops, yet I didn't see him."

"But you saw the clear night sky, didn't you? And the stars?"

"Yes."

"So you should have known it wasn't rain that you heard. No clouds, no rain. I realized then it was a shower of pebbles against the glass, a sure warning of what was to come. I didn't know, though, that it would be South coming through the skylight. He was reckoned to be a good enough monkey in the rigging of His Majesty's ships, but one never knows how he will do on a rooftop."

Ria gave West's wrists a little shake. Her breasts rubbed his chest as she drew herself up. "You might have warned me."

"I couldn't."

She was silent, considering this. "No," she said at last, "I don't suppose you could."

Sensing something of her hurt, West told her, "It was not because I thought you would betray us, but because I didn't think there was enough time to prepare you."

She kissed him fully on the mouth. "You prepared me well enough. You covered me with your body."

"Mmm."

"The glass must have cut you."

"It's nothing."

"Let me see." Ria slipped to one side and waited for him to turn on his stomach before drawing back the covers. Her eyes fell first on the tiny scratches that sprinkled his back, then on the faintly ridged scars that were evidence of the caning he'd received at his father's hand. It was humbling to know that he had taken both for her. She laid her palm gently on his back and moved closer. She kissed his shoulder. "I love you."

Because she said it in the manner of one confessing it for the first time, he smiled. "It is gratifying to know you haven't changed your mind, because I am still determined that you should be my wife."

Ria's sumptuously curved mouth took the shape of a beatific smile. When he covered it with his own, her arms came around his shoulders, and she opened her mouth, then all of herself to him. He came into her deeply at the very first thrust and held himself there, just as she wanted. She was tight and warm and needy and did not mind at all that he knew it. Her willingness to make herself so vulnerable to him and give so generously of herself still had the power to confound and please him, most often in equal parts.

Ria raised her arms toward the headboard and stretched, arching under him, lifting herself on the wave of pleasure he created. He held her and was held in turn, and they shared all that was splendid about coupling when they were greedy and hurried and pitched with a fever of wanting.

And later, when they could afford patience and tenderness, when their hearts beat less fiercely at the outset, they shared what was fine and right about this expression of love.

Ria stirred sleepily against West. Burrowed deeply under the covers, with her body once again fit neatly to his, she knew profound contentment. The sound that rumbled lightly at the back of her throat was very nearly a purr.

"She-cat or kitten?" West asked.

She pressed her nail tips into the back of his hand. "You decide."

He merely chuckled, and realized the sound of it was not so different from hers. That raised his grin. He pushed aside the thick fall of her pale hair and kissed the sweet curve of her neck. "I do not think I can wait for the banns to be read, not when you are so wickedly persuasive as you were today. If a gentleman's dressing room is no longer his sanctuary, and he can be assaulted in his bath, then a special license is all that is left to him."

"Do I tempt you?"

One of his eyebrows kicked up. "Can you doubt it?"

She laid her hand along his. "No, I suppose not, but it is surprisingly gratifying to hear it."

West let her nestle against him more deeply, not at all averse to having her under his skin just now. In time her breathing slowed, the cadence changed, and he knew she was sleeping.

He marveled that she could be so completely a whirling dervish in one moment, contemplative in another, and then find the perfect stillness of sleep. If he were fortunate, he reflected, she would always draw his attention in ways both subtle and bold, giving back as good as she got, and most often giving better.

West watched her because he could not help himself, not because he was by nature a spy. She bested him, embraced him. She laughed with him, occasionally at him. There was nothing about Ria that had not been good for his soul.

At Hambrick Hall, he had been given his direction by his friends, but it was in loving Ria that he had found his compass.

ABOUT THE AUTHOR

JO GOODMAN lives with her family in Colliers, West Virginia. She is currently working on her newest Zebra historical romance, once again set in the Regency period. Look for it in August 2005! Jo loves hearing from readers, and you may write to her c/o Zebra Books. Please include a self-addressed stamped envelope if you would like a response. Or you can visit her website at www.jogoodman.com

Put a Little Romance in Your Life With
Betina Krahn

__**Hidden Fire**
    0-8217-5793-8 $5.99US/$7.50CAN

__**Passion's Ransom**
    0-8217-5130-1 $5.99US/$6.99CAN

__**Luck Be a Lady**
    0-8217-7313-5 $6.50US/$8.99CAN

__**Just Say Yes**
    0-8217-7314-3 $6.50US/$8.99CAN

__**The Paradise Bargain**
    0-8217-7540-5 $6.50US/$8.99CAN

Available Wherever Books Are Sold!

Visit our website at **www.kensingtonbooks.com**.